Stephen L. Carter
BACK CHANNEL

Stephen L. Carter is the William Nelson Cromwell
Professor of Law at Yale University, where he has
taught since 1982. He is also the author of six novels and seven books of nonfiction.

ALSO BY STEPHEN L. CARTER

Fiction

The Impeachment of Abraham Lincoln

Jericho's Fall

Palace Council

New England White

The Emperor of Ocean Park

Nonfiction

The Violence of Peace:
America's Wars in the Age of Obama

God's Name in Vain:
The Wrongs and Rights of Religion in Politics

The Dissent of the Governed:
A Meditation on Law, Religion, and Loyalty

Civility: Manners, Morals, and the
Etiquette of Democracy

Integrity

The Confirmation Mess:
Cleaning Up the Federal Appointments Process

The Culture of Disbelief:
How American Law and Politics
Trivialize Religious Devotion

Reflections of an Affirmative Action Baby

BACK
CHANNEL

Stephen L. Carter

WITHDRAWN

VINTAGE BOOKS
A Division of Penguin Random House LLC
New York

FIRST VINTAGE BOOKS EDITION, MAY 2015

The Library of Congress has cataloged the Knopf edition as follows
Carter, Stephen L., [date]
Back channel : a novel / Stephen L. Carter.—First edition.
pages   cm
I. Cuban Missile Crisis, 1962—Fiction.   2. African American women—Fiction.
3. Suspense fiction.   4. Spy stories.   I. Title.
PS3603.A78B33   2014 813.'6—dc23   2014019240

Vintage Books Trade Paperback ISBN 978-0-345-80487-7
eBook ISBN 978-0-385-34961-1

Book design by Cassandra J. Pappas

www.vintagebooks.com

Printed in the United States of America
10 9 8 7 6 5 4 3 2 1

For Lynn Nesbit
with gratitude, admiration, and affection

"You may not be interested in war, but war is interested in you."

—*Attributed, incorrectly, to Leon Trotsky*

The Sacrifice

The President was in one of his moods. He stood at the bedroom window, tugging the lace curtain aside with a finger, peering down onto East Capitol Street. Outside, Washington was dark. He picked up his bourbon, took a long pull, and rubbed at his lower back. Margo sensed that he would rather be pacing, except that he was in too much pain just now; he never complained, but she had spent enough time around him these last few days to tell. All the same, she marveled at the man's aplomb, given that he was quite possibly presiding over the end of the world.

"Long day, Miss Jensen," he said finally.

"Yes, Mr. President."

"I've got people telling me I have to invade." His suit jacket was slung over the back of a chair. His tie was loose. The thick brown hair was mussy, and before he departed would be a good deal mussier. Margo wondered who owned this townhouse. The bedroom was plush to the point of decadence. Her grandmother, her beloved Nana, would have been appalled at the thought that Margo was in such a place with a man, even if he was the President of the United States.

"Invade Cuba," Kennedy clarified. He reached for his glass but didn't drink. "My people keep telling me it's my only choice. They seem to forget we tried already, just last year. And I don't mean Keating and all those armchair generals on the Hill. I mean my own people. I've moved the troops to Georgia and Florida, just in case we decide to go in." He let the curtain fall, turned half toward her, in profile tired but still dashingly young: the first President born in the twentieth century, as his supporters endlessly trumpeted.

Margo sat on the chaise longue, knees primly together in the evening dress. She had told her roommates that she was going to a party in Silver Spring, careful to sound nervous enough that they would guess she was lying. It was important that they suspect she was off on some other journey than the one she disclosed: important to the fiction that she was required to maintain.

As was tonight's meeting: what historians in later years would suppose, wrongly, to have been an assignation.

The fiction. The vital fiction.

Margo Jensen was nineteen years old, as bright as morning, quick and curious and perhaps a bit fussy, more handsome than pretty, displaying a fleshiness that belonged to a more mature woman. From an oval face a shade or two shy of mahogany, curious eyes strove to find order in a world rushing toward chaos.

Kennedy moved to the gigantic bed, gave a small laugh; sat. "I say to them, 'If we invade Cuba, take out those missiles, what does Khrushchev do?' They can't make up their minds." Kennedy groaned. It occurred to her that in the midst of a crisis that could lead to nuclear war, the President had advisers galore, but nobody to whom he could simply vent without back talk; and so, given that the plan required him to see Margo daily in any case, he had chosen her as his foil.

It wasn't as though she could tell anybody.

"LeMay says the Sovs are so scared of us, they won't do a thing," Kennedy continued. He was massaging the small of his back again, grimacing. Maybe he was hoping she would volunteer to help. "McNamara tells me they'll have to respond, just to save face, but their response will be limited, probably in Berlin. Two or three others think they'll press the button."

Margo shut her eyes. She still could not quite grasp that any of this was happening. It was October 1962, and a month ago she had been nobody, a sophomore government major at Cornell University, chasing no larger goals than finishing college, going on to graduate school, and getting married. Now she was skulking around Washington, D.C., worried about being caught by someone who knew her—or, worse, by the people who would very much like her dead.

At odd moments, she asked God why she had been chosen for this role. She was no soldier and no spy; two years ago, she had been in high school. She was not equal to the tasks demanded of her. They should have picked someone else. She wanted more than anything not to be here. Her boyfriend, Tom, a physics major, liked to say that the universe was unpredictable but never absurd. Just now, however, "absurd" was the only word to describe the bizarre concatenation of circumstances that had led her to tonight's secret meeting in this grand-luxe bedroom. But there was no escape. She was the only candidate: that was what they kept telling her. It was Margo or nobody.

"Those are my choices," the President was saying. "Either live with nuclear missiles ninety miles off our shore—missiles that are capable of reaching two-thirds of the country—or risk thermonuclear war. Come over here."

She tensed. "No, thank you."

"It's okay. Sit with me a minute."

"I'm comfortable where I am, Mr. President."

Kennedy seemed to understand. "We would spare you all of this if we could, Miss Jensen, believe me. We're not the ones who chose you." He drank. Drank again. "You do realize, don't you, that there's a good chance I'm going to be the last President of the United States?"

Margo swallowed. "I'm sure that's not true, sir."

Actually, she was lying. She believed exactly that. The likelihood that this was the end plagued her dreams.

Kennedy pinched the bridge of his nose. His exhaustion was palpable, a live creature in the room, and yet he tamed it and kept moving forward. "Some of my advisers have already sent their families out of the city. They want to know what provisions I'm making for Jackie and the kids. I tell them not to worry. There isn't going to be a war. By keeping my family in Washington, I show them I mean what I say. Maybe that's terrible of me. I don't know." He shook off the contemplative mood, stood up straight. "It's time, Miss Jensen."

Margo's eyes snapped open. Now came the part of the evening she hated most. "Yes, sir," she said, rising.

He was on his feet, turning back the comforter on the bed. She went around to the other side and helped. They tossed the extra pillows into the corner. Kennedy went to the bucket and poured her a glass of champagne. Margo drank it right off, knowing she would get tipsy, which was the point: otherwise, her courage would fail.

Besides, it was important that the Secret Service agent who would drive her home later smell the alcohol on her breath: again, the fiction.

The President poured her another glass. The room swam. She sat on the bed, trembling. She kicked off her shoes, let one of the shoulder straps slide down her upper arm. Kennedy undid his tie, dropped it on the floor, and walked toward her, smiling that crooked smile.

"Now," he said, "let's get some of that beautiful lipstick on my collar."

More fiction. He took her hand, lifted her to her feet. Margo stepped into his arms and, once more, shut her eyes. *You're helping to save the country,* a voice in her head reminded her. *And the world.* But as she turned her face upward toward his, Margo found herself wondering again what Nana would think, and all at once none of it mattered—not Kennedy, not Khrushchev, not her role in trying to stop the nuclear war that was about to start—none of it mattered, and none of it would have happened, if only she could turn back the clock to the day they came up from Washington to tell Margo that it was her patriotic duty to go to Bulgaria to babysit a madman.

She should have said no.

PART I

Standoff Position

September 1962–October 1962

Ithaca, New York | Varna, Bulgaria | Washington, D.C.

ONE

Deductive Reasoning

I

"Suppose you're a teller in a bank," said the great Lorenz Niemeyer, his small round body rolling merrily across the stage at the front of the lecture hall. "A man walks in and hands over a note. The note says he has a grenade and will blow up himself and you and the other customers unless you give him five hundred dollars. How many of you would comply?"

A nervous moment, students sneaking glances at each other, trying to figure out whether Niemeyer was testing their fortitude. Finally, a few hands went up, then more, until nearly all two hundred and fifty were in the air. Margo's was among the very early risers, for she possessed little capacity for self-delusion.

"Of course," said Niemeyer, happily. The students stirred in relief. The vast room was stifling in the September heat, but the doors and windows were tightly shuttered, the hallways patrolled by the great man's teaching assistants. His course on Conflict Theory was among the most popular on the Cornell campus, and he wanted nobody not enrolled to hear a word he said. "We'd all agree. We have seen before that threats have to be credible, but doubting the fool with the note does not seem a reasonable course of action. Blowing oneself up for five hundred dollars might seem incomprehensible. Still, you don't want to take chances. So you hand over the cash. But now look what happens next." Juddering to a halt. His belly jiggled in the vested suit. "The robber notices that there's a lot more money in your cage than he suspected. You have a good five thousand within easy reach. So he leans over and says to give him the rest, or he blows you both to bits. Now do you comply?"

Not as many hands went up. Margo hesitated, then kept hers on her desk. Niemeyer looked around. He asked why those who would now refuse to turn over the money had changed their minds. He called on somebody—not Margo, but one of his most fawning acolytes, a silly rich boy named Littlejohn—who announced confidently that he would have to consider the loss to the bank.

Niemeyer put his small hands on those ample hips. He had been advising the Pentagon on nuclear strategy for a decade, and he rarely bothered to hide his contempt for the rising generation, a group he considered soft on Communism, and stupid into the bargain.

"That answer is so bad it's not even wrong," said the great man. "And rather exculpatorial, I might add. A fellow like you would hand over the money without a second thought, Mr. Littlejohn, and we both know it. Whereas the rest of them"—pudgy hands made an arc—"well, the rest of them wouldn't. Know why? Because, now that the amount of money involved is so large, they're not sure they believe the robber's note any longer. Remember. The more the blackmailer wants, the more time we spend analyzing whether he's really serious. Every second-grader turns over his Twinkies to the playground bully. But even a schoolboy would hesitate if the bully demanded his clothes instead. We're past the hour. Go. Dismissed." Nodding toward the center aisle, where Margo always sat four rows back: "Miss Jensen. A word."

She stood, surprised to be addressed by name. It had never occurred to her that the great Lorenz Niemeyer might know who she was. A couple of students sitting nearby had their heads together, whispering speculations.

The professor beckoned, and Margo hurried forward, wondering whether she was in trouble. Last week, Niemeyer had booted another girl from the class after she turned out not to have done the assigned reading. Close up, the tubby little man looked slightly ridiculous in his wire-framed glasses and expensive suit. One of his hands was bent and twisted; the fingernails were misshapen. He was packing the ancient leather briefcase that had traveled with him to Nuremberg, to Tokyo, to Moscow, depending on which President he had been serving, and in what capacity.

"Walk with me," he said.

"Yes, sir."

The professor led the way, a trio of teaching assistants falling into line behind as they left the lecture hall together. Margo sensed the envious glances of her fellow students and, determined to project serenity, clutched her books tightly.

"What are you doing in my class, Miss Jensen?" said Niemeyer as they burst into the dappling Ithaca sunshine. "Planning to negotiate with the Soviets one day? Or just hoping my name on your transcript will impress the law-school admission committee?"

"I find the subject matter fascinating," she began.

He waved her silent. "You won't do better than a B. You do realize that no woman has ever received an A in my class?"

Margo swallowed. "I intend to be the first, sir."

"Don't be ridiculous. And stop trying to impress me. My ego is far too large to be flattered." They crossed between the somber statues of the university's founders, the teaching assistants still trailing their master like obedient pets. "You're second-generation Cornell, aren't you? Didn't I read somewhere that your father was an alumnus?"

Again he had managed to surprise her. "Yes. Yes, he was. Class of 1941." Margo chose not to mention that her father had died without ever laying eyes on her—or that her mother had died when she was seven—for she craved not pity but admiration. "He was an engineer."

"Yes. That's right." Niemeyer had conjured a cigar from somewhere. He shoved it unlit between his teeth. "Following events surrounding Cuba at all?"

The abrupt change of subject took her aback. "If you mean the Bay of Pigs, I naturally—"

"Pfah. A year and a half ago. Ancient history, Miss Jensen. I mean now. Current events. Following them or not?"

"I read about Senator Keating's speech in the *Times*," she said carefully. On an adjoining walkway, a fortyish man wearing one of those silly alumni hats was heading in the same direction, his cadaverous wife holding his arm. They were gawking and taking pictures of everything.

"Indeed. And your evaluation?"

"Keating thinks the Soviet Union is sneaking nuclear missiles into Cuba. Kennedy says it isn't true."

Niemeyer frowned. "Incorrect, Miss Jensen. Kennedy's people say only that they have no evidence to suggest that it's true. So—let's be precise, shall we?" Margo colored. He shifted his bag from his good hand to his bad, then waggled a finger in her face. "I understand Professor Bacon had you in Intro last spring. His views are rather antediluvian, to be sure, but he says you're rather sharp. Are you?"

Antediluvian, Margo registered. She collected, recreationally, six-syllable words with a stress on the fourth syllable, and Niemeyer used a lot of them. Just this morning, she had noted *incomprehensible* and *exculpatorial,* which she was not even sure was a word.

"I do my best, sir," she said.

"Well, let's see, shall we? Whom did he have you children reading? Dahl? Lipset? Lazarsfeld?"

"And the classics. Machiavelli and Tocqueville"—pointedly, and correctly, omitting the "de"—"and a few others."

"Bernard Crick?"

"No, sir. I know a little of his theories on American ideology—"

"If you haven't read him, you don't know a thing about his theories. Never mind. Let's think, shall we, Miss Jensen?" In the classroom, a favorite phrase. "Let's think hard. Based on what you've studied so far, both this year and last year, if you were the Soviets, would you put strategic nuclear missiles in Cuba?"

Margo met his gaze. This was her moment. This was what she lived for: blowing her professors away. Nana had taught her not only to study harder than the white kids, but to show off to those in authority as much as possible. *If you don't toot your own horn,* Nana liked to say, *they'll never hear you in the front.* Nana had gone to college more than forty years ago, when maybe two dozen Negroes in the country attended the best white schools, and knew what she was talking about. Nana was always extolling the genius of her son—Margo's father—and although Margo had never met him, she was determined to prove herself every bit as brilliant.

"No," Margo said. "No, I wouldn't."

"Why not? We have missiles in Turkey. We have missiles in Italy. We have missiles in England. Our Polaris submarines prowl their waters. Our B-52 bombers circle right off the Aleutians, very near Soviet territory. We have them surrounded, Miss Jensen. If we ever pull the trigger, they might not have time to react. We must have them scared half to death. Cuba's their only ally in this hemisphere. So why not match our strategy? Surround us, too? Didn't Bacon teach you the virtues of tit-for-tat?"

"The first rule of conflict theory is to keep the other side guessing," Margo said. She knew she might be blundering into a trap, but a wrong answer, Nana always said, is better than none. "They can't know for sure what's in your mind, and they have to worry that you might overreact to small provocations. Like the playground bully you mentioned in class. Somebody to stay away from. That's in Schelling's book."

A flicker in the clever eyes. "You've been reading ahead, I see."

"Yes, sir. My point is, the Soviets couldn't be sure how we'd respond. They might think putting missiles in Cuba just equalizes the situation. But we might not see it that way. We might see a threat. We might even go to war to keep missiles out of Cuba. That's why they wouldn't do it. Because the stakes are too high. They'd be crazy," she said, and wondered whether, in her enthusiasm, she'd gone too far: a thing that tended to happen when her mouth ran ahead of her brain in the excitement of the intellectual moment. But this was argument, and argument was what she loved best.

"That all sounds rather methodological of you, Miss Jensen. Trying to fit people to formulas rather than the other way around. But the Sabbath was made for man, not man for the Sabbath. There is such a thing as a mad ideology. I seem to recall that we just recently fought a war against one, although I suspect you were busy being born at the time." Despite the rebuke, Niemeyer's tone was placid. It was a compliment, everyone said, that he would even bother to correct you. "Tell me something, Miss Jensen. Do you love your country?"

She looked for a trap, found none. On the adjoining walkway, the alumnus and his wife kept pace. "Of course I do," she said.

"Despite how we treat your people?" Niemeyer made a clucking sound: the question was rhetorical. "Tell me, then, Miss Jensen. When you say you love your country, do you love it, say, as much as an immigrant who becomes a citizen does?"

"I think so. I hope so."

They had reached the government department. Niemeyer stood close to her on the granite steps, forcing her to lean against the balustrade as his assistants filed past. "Are you aware, Miss Jensen, that the citizenship oath required of naturalized citizens includes the promise to fight for the country if called upon?"

"Yes, sir."

"And does that apply to the ordinary citizen as well? To you, say, Miss Jensen? Would you fight? Would you risk your life? If, say, the country's survival were at stake?"

"I would." She did not understand why he was pressing the point. "It would be my duty."

"Oh, that's a fine answer, I must say. You'll do excellently well." He actually patted her shoulder. "See you tomorrow, then," said the great man, and scurried inside.

Margo stood alone on the step, unaccountably worried. Niemeyer had been all bonhomie, but she had the peculiar sense that he had just signed her up for something. At last she shrugged, and turned away, just in time to notice the alumnus in the funny hat snapping her picture.

II

That was Wednesday. On Saturday afternoon, everybody went to the stadium to watch Cornell play football against Colgate. Clouds scudded across a gray sky. In the frigid wind whipping up from the lake, the ball fluttered all over the field. Margo sat high in the student section with a brace of friends. She wasn't much of a fan, but went because Tom loved sports. They even shared a blanket, but she kept her hands in position to defend herself against Tom's occasional efforts to engage in what Nana called taking liberties. Midway through the second quarter, with Cornell already trailing badly, she decided she'd had enough of the game, or maybe of those liberties. She excused herself, citing the need to do research for her paper for Niemeyer's class.

"It's not due for two months," Tom protested.

"I don't like to wait for the last minute," she answered.

His eyes were already back on the field. "Pizza later? Usual place?"

"Usual time," she promised.

The stadium was a cavernous structure of cut stone, with wooden benches and shadowed tunnels leading to walkways through the underbelly of reinforced steel struts. Margo never failed to marvel at the complexity of the edifice. She was on the ground floor now, her attention mostly focused on the architectural detail far above her head. As she waded through the crowd thronging the refreshment stand and the restrooms, a prickle on the back of her neck told her she was being watched, but when she turned she saw only a sea of faces, none of them staring. She sidled around a massive cinder-block structure enclosing a fire stair, and noticed, not for the first time, the green gunmetal door on the far side, bearing the black-and-yellow poster signifying a fallout shelter.

She had been noticing fallout shelters more often since enrolling in Niemeyer's class, probably because he enjoyed taunting his students with the likelihood that, were the balloon ever to go up, as he put it, there wouldn't be enough room for all of them, and in any case the first group to arrive at the shelter would bar the doors and refuse to admit the stragglers.

"Have you ever seen the inside of a fallout shelter?" Niemeyer had asked them. "Believe me, if it's a choice between taking your chances in the open and spending a month or two in some airless basement, eating foul crackers and smelling the latrine, you'd rather be caught in the open."

About to head back toward the crowd, she hesitated. She glanced around, but nobody was looking. In truth, the answer to Niemeyer's question was no: Margo had never seen the inside of a shelter. It had long been her habit to explore secret and forbidden places. According to Nana, who had often been called upon to punish Margo for various trespasses, the curiosity was inherited from her late father.

She tried the door.

It was locked, of course, a protection against looters and squatters and vandals: an illustration of what Niemeyer called the *Petits Paradoxes,* dilemmas that arose from overlooking the casual details of everyday life. The lock, sensible though it might seem, would make the shelter useless in an actual crisis, unless by some happy chance the man with the key could be found in time. In a perfect world, Niemeyer had pointed out just the other day, you'd be able to run for shelter, as the British had run into the tunnels of the underground during the Blitz. At that point, some bold, foolish soul raised his hand to suggest that in a perfect world there would be no war.

Niemeyer had snickered.

"And are we intelligent in your perfect world? We are? Then your answer is not even wrong. As long as there's intelligence, there will be invention. As long as there is invention, there will be acquisition. As long as there is acquisition, there will be war."

Remembering now, she wondered whether Niemeyer was right, and war was a necessary consequence of human nature. Unless he was wrong, the nuclear age might be the last age mankind would ever—

"Hello, Margie."

She startled, and spun, but it was only Philip Littlejohn, whom Niemeyer had so badly embarrassed the other day in class. He was a junior, red-haired and swaggering, the creepiest and wealthiest member of her study group.

"Hello, Phil."

"Tired of the game?"

"I have work to do."

"That's my Margie. Hey, know what's down there?" Inclining his head. "I saw you looking over at the sign."

"It's a fallout shelter." She always felt a little stupid in his presence, even though she knew she could run intellectual rings around him, and had the grades to prove it: her grades were the reason she had been invited to join the study group in the first place.

"Door locked?"

"Yes."

He tried it anyway. He had broad shoulders and powerful hands, was a star of the school's lacrosse and hockey teams.

"Mmmm. Too bad, Margie." He knew she hated that name. "Tell you what. If you really want to see the inside of a shelter, my frat has one in the basement. Did you know that?"

"No, Phil."

He leaned close, towering over her, one strong arm braced against the cinder blocks as if to prevent her escape. He breathed beer into her face.

"Why don't we walk over now? I'll give you the tour."

"No, thank you."

"Come on, Margie. It's interesting. It's got barrels of water, crackers, that cheese crap, you name it. Also blankets and mattresses. Lots of mattresses. You know, to propagate the race after the next war? I was thinking you and I could inspect the mattresses together. See how comfortable they are."

She colored. "I don't find that amusing."

"You think I'm joking?"

"I hope you are. Now, if you'll excuse me, I have work to do."

Still smiling, he dropped his arm. She headed back toward the crowd. Then she stopped. The same alumnus who had snapped her photograph three days ago was standing on the stairs, camera pointed her way, still wearing his funny hat. He took a couple of quick shots, then backed into the crowd and disappeared.

TWO

First Contact

I

The freighter *Poltava* plowed through the squall. Dark, angry waves broke over the bow. As usual, the weather forecasts were wrong. On an ordinary voyage, the crew would have ignored the reports on the official Soviet channel and used the engineer's clandestine radio to listen to the capitalist frequency.

But this was no ordinary voyage.

In addition to cargo and crew, the ship carried a political officer and a contingent of military police. To be caught using an illegal receiver would likely mean prison. And so the *Poltava* risked the unpredicted mid-Atlantic storms, rarely varying course or speed, because the mission had been assigned the strictest of time lines. They were required to make port in Mariel, Cuba, by September 15, and be unloaded and ready for the return trip by the second day following.

No excuses permitted.

In the high pilothouse, set just past midships, the helmsman struggled to hold course. The storm lashed the windows. Visibility was nil. In every direction was the same grim rain. Gray water sloshed over the decks, where, between the folded heavy cranes, trucks and farm equipment were tightly lashed, along with ranks of containers and crates stenciled REFACCIONES clearly enough for the American spy satellites to read at a distance.

The helmsman cursed as the freighter rolled. He fought the wheel. He fought the instinct of a lifetime that screamed at him to change heading before they foundered. This was no squall; this was a full-blown tropical storm.

They rolled back the other way, and a cup of foul coffee slid off the navigation table to the floor.

He cursed again, and felt a reassuring hand on his shoulder. The officer of the deck sat beside him, watching the instrument panel. Even in the stormy darkness, the bridge gleamed. The *Poltava* was a new ship, first of a planned series of heavier cargo vessels laid down at the Black Sea Shipyard in Nikolayev. The freighter had been designed to ferry lumber. But earlier this year, it had been returned to drydock and fitted with more powerful cranes and longer deck hatches. The crew had been vetted afresh, and several sent packing. All in preparation for this mission: their small part in the operation known as Anadyr.

The captain had been banished to his cabin after quarreling with the political officer, who had refused to let them circle around the storm. The deck officer shared the captain's view, but had prudently kept silent.

"*Chto eto?*" said the helmsman, pointing to a long black shape that had appeared without warning off the port bow. It looked like a whale, except that it was flying.

"It's a plane," said the first mate, also in Russian. "Hold course, Comrade. He will make way."

The two men on the bridge watched in fascination as the large aircraft bounced along beside them in the storm, not two hundred feet above the roiling sea. The plane had to be American. Nobody else would be so crazy. The craft had twin propellers and a transparent nose cone. They hadn't seen it swooping in because, except for the nose, the entire fuselage was painted black.

On the deck below, the soldiers were scurrying for cover, and for a moment the first mate was worried. Then he realized that their fear was not of being attacked but of being seen. The political officer, wearing an unmarked greatcoat, had moved to the gunwale, where he used an ungainly East German camera to snap photographs of the intruder.

"Who are they?" said the helmsman.

"They are brave men," said the mate, a good-humored Ukrainian named Evanishyn. "They are risking their lives to follow us."

The ship rolled again, this time to port, and the plane climbed away. When they settled again, it was overhead.

"We're risking our lives, too," the helmsman grumbled. "For what?"

"For the Motherland. For what we carry below."

"Which is what?"

"I am sure you have guessed, Comrade." Evanishyn nodded toward the political officer, still snapping his pictures. "My mother always said you can tell a bird by its droppings."

II

Another man came in. He wore a threadbare sweater, but the four white stars on each epaulet told them that he held the rank of lieutenant commander in the Red Navy. Ordinarily, an officer of such rank would not be caught dead on a freighter, even the shining new *Poltava*. His presence signaled the importance of the mission, and his orders, they had been told, were to be followed without hesitation.

"Give me the field glasses," he said.

A fresh wave rolled the ship hard to starboard, but the men were braced. Down on the deck, the chain securing one of the trucks was slipping, and a pair of crewmen fought their way toward it. The plane was still directly above, seeming almost to hover in the storm. Much lower and it would have struck the crane assembly, which extruded well above the wheelhouse in the center of the ship.

The naval officer lifted the glasses. "It is an American reconnaissance plane," he said after a moment's study. "They designate it the P-2H, or Neptune. The dark paint makes it difficult to make out. They call themselves the Flying Phantoms."

"What is it doing?" asked Evanishyn.

"Taking photographs of your ship, Comrade." He pointed to the trucks ranked on the deck. "He hopes to discover your cargo."

"The cargo is mostly below."

The plane had dipped lower again and was now just twenty yards off the port bow. The naval officer continued his study. "He will photograph the cranes and the hatches. From this the American analysts will try to calculate the size and weight of the cargo." He lowered the glasses. "Our destroyer escort is less than half an hour behind. Were our orders not otherwise, we could shoot him down."

Evanishyn was alarmed. "We are not at war, Comrade."

The lieutenant commander gave a tired smile. "We shall be soon."

"How is that possible?"

"Come, Comrade. You yourself have reached the same conclusion. Sooner or later, the Americans will find out what we are ferrying to Cuba."

"And then?"

"And then they will destroy us."

THREE

Uncle Sam Wants You

I

On Monday morning, Niemeyer called on Margo in class for the first time. He was once more rolling along the stage, this time telling the class of an evacuation exercise the government had performed nine years ago ("Maybe some of you remember? No? Children. Pah!") and how, although there had been some small logistical glitches, such as the dispersal site in Ohio that nobody had thought to tell the Ohioans about, for the most part things went as planned. Thousands of essential federal employees reached their designated resettlement areas, far from likely Soviet targets. The exercise lasted three days.

"After the drill was over," said Niemeyer, twisting his good hand in an air like a conjurer, "they held the usual meetings, slapping each other on the back, handing around congratulatory letters and medals, and no doubt trying to figure out how to handle certain unexpected pregnancies among employees of the fairer sex"—from the students, more gasps than laughter, although Littlejohn brayed like a donkey—"but then, when everyone was through shaking hands and slapping backs, one fellow spoke up. An unpredicted and unfortunate burst of pure honesty. Do you know what he said? He said, 'Of course, if this had been the real thing, I'd have skipped the evacuation. I'd have gone to find my wife and kids instead. I'd rather die with my family than live doing my duty.' And at that point the whole thing fell apart. Everybody was suddenly demanding to know what provisions were being made to evacuate their families to places of safety, and so on. The final Civil Defense report on the exercise is classified, but I'm sure you can imagine what it said. Let's play guess-the-conclusion, shall we?"

He selected, as first victim, a boy she didn't know, a clever junior named Chance.

"The report," said Chance, without hesitation, "would have said that evacuation was impossible because of the problem of families. Further—"

"Not even wrong." Niemeyer picked someone else, whose answer was not even wronger.

Then he spun toward the middle aisle. "Miss Jensen. Explain to them."

Margo opened her mouth at once, but for two full seconds not a sound emerged. A part of her head was still down under the stands at the stadium. Then she heard the titters and remembered whose granddaughter she was. "If we're assuming that the report told the truth"—and here she found herself inserting a Niemeyer-like aside—"not often the case with official government documents"—this won her a few appreciative chuckles—"then there's only one possible con-clusion. Nobody knows how people will respond under the pressure of the real thing." Her voice gathered strength. "We can speculate in the classroom, and the Civil Defense planners can speculate around a table. They can take surveys, study data, calculate numbers with their slide rules and their computers. But in the end they're talking about people. Trying to predict what people will do. Family versus duty. Obligation versus fear. All the dynamics that make everyday life so rich and complex and unpredictable. We can't predict how people will behave with a nuclear warhead on the way until there's a nuclear warhead on the way. We have no data. We can't run a realistic test. So the only right answer is that there is no right answer."

Niemeyer gave her a long look while the class waited. "Not entirely wrong," he grunted: high praise. "The human factor is indeed the most dangerous part of any equation. Capricious, mercurial, given to spasms of emotionalism. Fear and anger are the big ones to worry about, but there are others, too. Ordinary covetousness and lust, of course. And also the regrettable tendency to overestimate one's own capabilities—what Joe Stalin called 'dizziness due to success'—and the odd unexpected moment of bravery or integrity or whatever this week's admirable character trait might be. Enough. Hour's up. Go forth and err." But the great man's appraising eye was on Margo, and she understood at once that she was not included in the general dismissal.

"I told you, you're his favorite," muttered Littlejohn as he filed past.

"He likes you," whispered Annalise Seaver, her best friend, not specifying whether she meant Niemeyer or Littlejohn. "Be careful."

Margo ignored them. By the time she reached the front, Niemeyer was gone. In the back hall behind the stage, she found him waiting, as she knew she would. A pair of acolytes stood in the doorway, like bodyguards.

"Miss Jensen. A word," said Niemeyer, just like last week. "Walk with me."

II

"Ever met Kennedy?" he asked as they followed the same path as last time across the quad. She half expected to see the alumnus with the camera.

"Once," she said, very surprised.

"Tell me."

"He was campaigning in New York, and he was talking to teenagers. They wanted the cameras to catch a few Negroes in the group. My grandmother is well connected in politics, so I wound up in the pictures." For some reason, she was blushing. "I didn't talk to him or anything. He told us how important it was to get a good education, and about how his own father started with nothing and built a fortune. How America's the best country in the world. Probably fifteen minutes."

"This was two years ago?"

"Yes. Summer of 1960."

"So you were, what? In high school?"

"I was seventeen. About to start my senior year."

"Any reason he'd remember you?"

Again the question surprised her. "I don't see why."

"Well, they do say our President has an eye for the ladies. Ah. Here we are." At the government department once more. His acolytes marched past, just like last time, but Niemeyer remained on the step, holding the door. He lifted a hand, palm upward, and gestured toward the entrance. "In you go."

"I have Professor Hadley's political anthropology seminar in five minutes. It's the other way."

"Tris Hadley is a fool, and political anthropology is humbug."

"Yes, well, I still—"

"My office, Miss Jensen. Now."

Margo hesitated. She hated to be late for class, or, worse, to miss, and the term was only three weeks old; but this was Niemeyer.

"Of course," she said, and stepped nervously inside.

Their footsteps echoed in the tiled hall. Learned men dead half a century glared down as they passed. "What you said to me the other day, Miss Jensen. About doing your duty if called upon. Were you serious, or was it just so much pap?"

"I was serious."

"You're very sure?"

"Yes."

"Well, then," he said, as if matters were out of his hands. She remembered the photographer, and wondered again if she had signed up for something.

Niemeyer's first-floor suite would have done duty for four senior professors. The teaching assistants had desks in the foyer. A prim, disapproving woman named Mrs. Khorozian guarded the inner sanctum. Her husband sold antiques out in the countryside somewhere, and campus rumor had it that the two of them were resettled spies.

"They're here," said Mrs. Khorozian.

"Excellent," said the professor. He opened the door of his grand office, and great clouds of pipe smoke rolled out. He stood aside and allowed Margo to precede him, and that was when she noticed the two men in dark suits and narrow ties who had risen silently to their feet. One was tall and very pale, the other dark-haired and broad-shouldered.

"These gentlemen have come from Washington, Miss Jensen. I have placed my office at their disposal. They would like to ask you a few questions."

"Me?" said Margo, addressing Niemeyer. "Questions about what?"

"They will explain. Please cooperate. The safety of your country is at risk." He saw her expression, and his own grew severe. "I am not joking, Miss Jensen, and I never exaggerate in matters of national security. Is that clear?"

"Yes, sir."

"You are to answer all of their questions, fully and without hesitation."

"Yes, sir," she said again, now more frightened than confused.

The professor hesitated, and she saw, for the first time, the kindliness beneath the cynical mask. "I'll be in the next room if you need me."

He left.

III

The taller man turned out to be from the Federal Bureau of Investigation, and had the laminated credentials to prove it. His name was Stilwell, and the pugnacious set of his slim jaw told her that he was prepared to disbelieve every word out of her mouth. The broader of the two was Borkland. He represented the State Department, and his role in the drama seemed to be to smile conciliation every time his counterpart was rude.

"You're from New York, aren't you?" Stilwell began, without preamble. "Born in New Rochelle, isn't that right?"

"Yes, sir," said Margo to the space between the two men. The office was dark wood and books, and large enough for this six-person conference table along with Niemeyer's desk. Photographs along the far wall expressed the gratitude of the world's leaders. A grandfather clock in the corner ticked far too loudly, or perhaps it was just that her senses were on high alert.

"What year?"

"I'm sorry?"

Stilwell had long pianist's fingers, but when he laid his hands on the table, the fingers pointed like twin guns. "What year were you born, Miss Jensen?"

"Um, 1943."

"You hesitated."

"I—"

"Mother's name?"

"Dorothea Jensen."

"I meant her maiden name."

Borkland was smoking a short-stemmed pipe. His puffing made the air thick and heavy. Margo stifled a cough, instinct telling her to display no weakness. "My mother's maiden name was Massey. May I ask—"

"Father was a doctor?"

She looked at him very straight. "He wanted to be. He died in the war."

Stilwell made a sound. "I meant your mother's father, not yours."

"We're just doing a job, you see," murmured Borkland, a rare interjection. He adjusted his glasses, gave a helpless shrug. "Sorry, Miss Jensen, that's the way it is."

Underneath the table, Margo had taken hold of the skin on the inside of her wrist, and was pinching it, hard, a trick she used in the classroom to keep a tremor out of her voice.

"My mother's father wasn't a doctor. He was a doorman at a Manhattan hotel. He and his wife also had a store in New Rochelle." She fought the urge to lick her lips. "My father's father was the doctor."

"So your father married beneath his station, did he?" said Stilwell. "You say he wanted to be a doctor, too?"

"Yes."

"Because it says here he drove a truck in the war."

Margo squeezed tighter, but this time refused to drop her eyes. She spoke the words with her grandmother's bitterness, for Nana told the story often, and with anger. "My father was a brilliant man. He had a degree in chemical engineering. From here. He made Phi Beta Kappa. He planned to go to medical school. And because he was a Negro, the United States Army made him drive a truck." Although she realized that she sounded snappish, retreat was not her style. "Anyway, I don't see why this is any of your business. What's this about?"

Borkland, the diplomat, trampled on Stilwell's annoyed response. "I'm afraid we're not allowed to say, Miss Jensen. Not just yet. In a bit, after this part of the interview is over." The smile seemed waterproof. "As Professor Niemeyer said, the nation's security is at stake. I know that's hard for you to accept. For the moment, I only ask you to bear with us." With that, he put the pipe back in his mouth.

Margo's gaze slipped from one man to the other, before settling in the middle distance, where a younger Niemeyer, in black and white, leaned over President Truman's shoulder, pointing to a line in a document.

"A man followed me on campus the other day," she said, instinct screaming not to let these cold bureaucrats master the conversation. "He pretended to be an alumnus, but he was taking pictures of me. Why?"

The two men exchanged a questioning glance: *One of yours?* Each shook his head slightly.

"We wouldn't know anything about that," said Borkland.

Stilwell put the point another way: "If he'd been working for us, you'd never have seen him. Probably just likes photos of pretty girls."

"He followed me again on Saturday—"

"Well, he couldn't have been much good at it if you spotted him. And now, if you're done with the trivialities, let's get back to the questions."

She continued to focus on Truman's thoughtful mien. She supposed that there was nothing they could do if she stood up and marched out of the office, but her curiosity was aroused, as no doubt they intended. And of course there was also the matter of her not wanting to disappoint Professor Niemeyer, who had evidently singled her out for—well, for something. And if Niemeyer decided to push her career . . .

"By all means," she said.

Stilwell wrote a couple of lines in his notebook. "Good. Back to your parents, then. Your father died in action, did he?"

"An accident in the war. His truck crashed." She kept her voice even. "I was ten months old. I never met him."

"And your mother ten years ago?"

Squeezing harder still. "Closer to twelve. Cancer."

Stilwell tapped his pencil on the table, the sound very loud in her state of tautened attention. "Siblings?"

"An older brother. Corbin. He's married and lives in Ohio."

"The two of you raised by your father's mother, is that right? Charlotte Jensen?"

"Claudia."

"Quite the battle-axe, I'm told." He turned a page. "She graduated Smith, I see. Why didn't you follow in her footsteps, Miss Jensen? Wait. Let me guess. You're following the footsteps of the father you never met. How dutiful." He chuckled at her blush. "Or maybe it's just that Smith doesn't have boys. You're seeing a young man now, aren't you? This Tom Jellinek? He's physics, you're government. So how did you meet, if I might ask?"

He had lost all capacity to surprise her. "Freshman English was seated alphabetically," she explained. "We were next to each other."

"So you're blaming coincidence. Well, why not? You gals have to blame something, I'd imagine." Evidently satisfied, he sat back and glanced at Borkland: *Your witness.*

Borkland was the diplomat, his smile well practiced and smooth. "Please forgive Agent Stilwell. His job in this thing is to make sure you're who you say you are."

The smoke, she decided: the clouds of pipe smoke were making her punchy. Surely she hadn't heard him right. "I beg your pardon."

"You'd be surprised what the Soviets get up to. No, you wouldn't. Professor Niemeyer seems to think you're rather bright. Congratulations. He praises men rarely, and women not at all. Like traveling?"

"I haven't done much."

"Ever been to Varna?"

Margo was taken aback. Varna was a dying country town due east of the campus. A couple of bars served everybody without checking driver's licenses, and although Nana would have had a heart attack on the spot, Margo had visited each a time or two.

"Yes," she said.

"Recently?"

This time she did drop her eyes. It seemed absurdly unlikely that these two had come from Washington to give her a citation for under-age drinking, but one never knew. "Two weeks ago," she said.

Borkland had a wide, mellow face, and comically thick glasses, but Stilwell's countenance, like his voice, was ugly and twisted and disapproving. "Did you get down to the docks? Notice any of the ships? That sort of information is always helpful to your government."

Margo's confusion grew. Perhaps they were testing her. "I don't think any shipping goes through Varna."

The men looked at each other. "The Soviet Black Sea fleet is head-quartered there," said Stilwell. "I thought you were supposed to be smart."

Borkland touched his colleague's arm. "I believe Miss Jensen is referring to Varna, New York." To Margo: "The Varna we are asking about is in Bulgaria."

She colored. "Oh. No. I've never been anywhere in Europe."

Stilwell: "Well, you're going now."

Borkland greedily snatched back the narrative. "There's a State Department program that provides grants for student journalists to report from abroad, especially behind the Iron Curtain. You applied for a fellowship."

"I didn't."

"Well, no, not exactly." A shy smile. "But you were approved anyway." He slid the form from his briefcase, handed it over. "Take a look."

She did. There were the various questions answered in her own block capitals, and there was the essay, in her own handwriting, complete with the little dagger-strikes for the lowercase "g" and "j," and the many cross-outs that characterized her writing in haste. Reading the lines, she could almost imagine penning them. Her boyfriend was teaching her to play chess, the essay explained, and she wanted to go to Varna, the Bulgarian one, to watch the Chess Olympiad, where several dozen countries would send squads of four players each to battle over the course of a month for gold and silver medals. Thus would she combine her interests in chess and study of the Cold War.

The essay looked and sounded exactly like her work.

The trouble was, she had never seen it before.

"I don't understand," said Margo, managing to keep the tremor out of her voice. "Who wrote this?"

Borkland tapped the signature line. "You did."

FOUR

The Social Contract

I

"This is a forgery," she said after a moment.

"It's as genuine as it needs to be." Stilwell's chilly voice brooked no argument. "Maybe we were a little naughty. Let's get past that, shall we?"

"So—you want me to go to Bulgaria?" She looked at the paper. "To the Chess Olympiad? This is how you want me to—to protect my country? Why?"

Borkland slipped the application from her hand and slid it back into his briefcase. He pointed the pipestem her way. "Well, this is where we have a problem," he said, with a confiding frown. "We don't actually want you to go. If we could spare you the trip, we would. Unfortunately, Miss Jensen, the matter is out of our hands. There is someone else we need rather urgently to do something for us there—well, for America, really—and he adamantly refuses to help us unless we send you, too. So here we are."

Mystification, fear, fury: all were swirling now. At least she understood what Stilwell was so angry about. "Who is he?" When they said nothing, she asked a different way: "Why won't he go without me?"

The diplomat gave a doleful shrug. "Alas, the identity of the gentleman in question cannot be disclosed until you have agreed to make the trip. And the information in any case is not ours to vouchsafe. You'll have to come to Washington to get your explanation. All I am allowed to tell you this afternoon is that your country needs you."

"You expect me to agree to fly to Europe, with a man you refuse to name, and you won't tell me why?" She finally exploded. "What kind of woman do you think I am?"

At this Stilwell smirked and made a note. Borkland's tone became if anything meeker. The pipe appeared to have burned out. "My apologies, Miss Jensen. Certainly it isn't that sort of trip. We'll send a chaperone. An older woman. What we call a minder." She was about to reply, but he lifted a finger. "All I can tell you at this moment is that the task we need the gentleman in question to perform is vital to the nation's security. Nobody else can do it, and, as I said, he will not do it unless you go. Unfortunate, but there it is. He rather has us over the proverbial barrel, Miss Jensen. Thus this visit."

Margo's fear was growing, but so was a peculiar thrill of excitement. The national security apparatus of the United States was going to all this trouble—fake documents, a minder, goodness knows what else—because they wanted her. Her. Margo Jensen. A man was going off on a vital mission, and wouldn't go without her. Ambition began to trump caution. This morning she had been nobody, and now, suddenly, she was nearly as indispensable as the man they refused to name. Yet she would not yield so easily. After all, as Niemeyer liked to remind them, only a fool shows his hole cards before the final bet. And so she took refuge in practicalities.

"I can't go to Varna. I have classes. I have a boyfriend. What will he think of me running off to Europe?"

Stilwell's turn. "The dean has been spoken to. You're excused from classes. As for your boyfriend—well, you gals have ways of dealing with your menfolk's anger, don't you?"

Trying to get a rise from her; and so she damped down her slowly uncoiling ire. "At least tell me what I'll be doing." She selected a sassy tone. "Will I be helping this man you won't name do the task you won't tell me?"

Borkland again: "In Bulgaria, Miss Jensen, you'll be watching the chess and sunning on some of the most beautiful beaches in Europe. Maybe you'll be called upon to attend a couple of meals. That's all." He smiled at her bewilderment. "You'll be away two weeks at the most, and then you'll be back, with the thanks of a grateful nation."

Margo took this in stride. Anger had cleansed her mind, and she could read the genuine desperation in his round face. Whatever they needed, they had to have. The trick, she reminded herself, was to get the opponent to show his cards first. "Suppose I say no."

"You live in a free country, Miss Jensen. If you would rather take its benefits for granted when you could have helped protect it, that choice is yours to make." The men were suddenly on their feet. "Take a little time to think it over, Miss Jensen—bearing in mind that we need your answer before we leave for Washington."

"When are you leaving?"

The diplomat glanced at his watch. "In about an hour." He nodded toward the door. "Take a moment. Speak to Dr. Niemeyer. Ask his advice."

"And *only* to Niemeyer." Stilwell lifted a warning finger. "Breathe a word of this to anyone else, Miss Jensen, and you'll be leaving this building in handcuffs."

But the silky threat was unnecessary, and the satisfied looks on both their watchful faces said they knew they had her.

II

"What's this really about?"

Lorenz Niemeyer shook his head. The government department backed on a private garden shared by several buildings, and they sat together on a stone bench. She supposed the men from Washington were watching from one of the many windows; maybe somehow listening, too.

"I know less than they told you, I'm sure," said Niemeyer. He brushed at a low branch, whipped by the wind against his pudgy face. "All I can tell you is that the people behind this are people I've known a long while."

She caught something in his tone. "Is that an endorsement or a warning?"

"It's neither." He fixed her with those brilliant eyes. "I want to be very clear, Miss Jensen. Whatever they're asking you to do, you can say no. That is absolutely an option. It won't come back to bite you. You won't be marked down in some file as un-American. Is that clear?"

"It's clear," she said, but wasn't sure she believed him.

"You still sound uncertain, Miss Jensen. Let me tell you a story you won't read in the papers. Last March, two Soviet military aircraft overflew Kuskokwim Bay and entered American airspace over Alaska. They were on a reconnaissance mission, and they flew unheeded for almost half an hour before we were able to intercept them. An intrusion of that magnitude and duration couldn't have been accidental. They were taking a titanic risk. Suppose we'd shot them down? Do you realize that, merely by sending military aircraft across our borders intentionally, the Soviets committed an act of war?" He had plucked a dying blossom from the branch, and now began to pull the petals, one by one. "And this isn't the first time this sort of thing has happened, Miss Jensen. It's getting more frequent. It doesn't make the papers, because we tend to keep it quiet."

"Like Gary Powers."

Niemeyer's plump face dipped in a nod of grudging respect. "Gary Powers was shot down in his U-2 in May of 1960, and Eisenhower's summit was canceled. That was very public. Let me tell you what isn't. Prior to Powers, the Soviets had shot down a good eight to ten of our surveillance aircraft—possibly more—with significant loss of life. A couple of years before, eleven of our airmen survived the downing of a C-130 over Soviet territory and were never heard of again. Presumably, they've spent all the time since under interrogation. That's top secret, you understand. You're not cleared for it, but you have the right to know." He stood up and brushed off his shapeless tweeds. "Things are very bad, Miss Jensen. Much worse than I can tell you in the classroom. Much worse than the Administration can admit. We are dangerously close to a shooting war with a regime possessing several hundred nuclear warheads."

She felt a chill of excitement and fear, mixed. "You're telling me I should do it."

"The decision is yours, Miss Jensen, just as I said. All I'm telling you is that, whatever you may decide, childhood has reached its end." Somehow they were on their feet. Niemeyer was holding the door. "And whatever you may decide, I know your father would be proud." He saw her expression. "I knew him well, Miss Jensen. I don't believe I've mentioned that."

Margo swayed on her feet. "My father died in the war."

"Which is where we met."

"Excuse me, Professor. I don't see how that's possible. You said in class you were in the OSS. Behind enemy lines in Europe."

"Indeed."

"My father was in a transport battalion in North Africa."

"Quite."

"Then how could you have known him?"

He tapped the face of his watch. "I believe your deadline is upon you, Miss Jensen."

III

She had not anticipated how difficult her departure would be. Tom Jellinek, the only boyfriend she had ever had, was wounded: How could she have applied for the fellowship and not told him? How could she say yes and not ask him? For they had promised to keep no secrets from each other, not least because they were busily keeping each other secret from their families, neither of which would have approved dating outside the race. But he was a kind young man, and made her promise to write twice a week, even, given that she would be behind the Iron Curtain, though her letters would be read, as he put it, by both sides' secret police—a comment he intended as a joke, although as it turned out he was right. Her roommate, Jerri, took the news more in stride. Jerri was a professor's daughter and a professor's niece, and her grandfather had been provost at Princeton. She fancied herself a great radical and talked incessantly of the coming revolution, but, given that she rarely attended classes and was usually high, she could not have expected to play a significant part in the struggle. Jerri made Margo promise to bring back oodles of revolutionary literature— that was what she said, *oodles*—and then she went back to her dope, which she called mezzroll. Margo's only other real friend in Ithaca was Annalise Seaver, a blue-eyed South Carolinian. They were outsiders together on an Ivy League campus, the black girl from Westchester County and the Southern belle. Both were government majors, and both were enrolled in Niemeyer's course. It was Annalise who raised the question Margo had not considered:

"Is Niemeyer going? Is that why he wanted to talk to you after class?"

"Why would Niemeyer be going?"

"Another girl told me the story. A couple of years ago, he had an absolute *thing* for one of his graduate assistants. Well, Niemeyer didn't want to try his chances on campus, so he got his buddies at State to arrange for the two of them to go to New Zealand together for a month. Supposedly, she came back pregnant."

This caused Margo an uneasy moment: was it possible that Lorenz Niemeyer was the one who was being sent to Bulgaria, and refused to go without her? If so, she decided, she would never set foot on the plane. But she doubted it. The concern in his eyes just before he threw her to the wolves had seemed genuine.

Hardest of all was explaining to Nana. Margo called her, collect, from one of the booths across from the front desk in her dormitory foyer, and apologized that there would be no time to come home before she left for Bulgaria. But Nana, who spoke very loud because she assumed others were as deaf as she, was enthusiastic. She believed in traveling the world, and had been to Europe herself a number of times, always by ship, because those fancy airplanes were death traps—didn't Margo read the papers?

"Get them to send you by ocean liner," shouted Nana. "And make sure they give you a decent cabin. Oh, and tell them you want dinner at the captain's table."

Late that night, as her roommate slumbered noisily, Margo sat up in bed, clutching the snapshot of the father she had never met, clad in his Army uniform. She kept it in her desk drawer, along with the telegram that began, "Dear Mrs. Jesson." They couldn't even get the name right. It was impossible, of course, that Niemeyer would have known him. She supposed that he had mentioned her father as a kind of goad. Whatever his protestations, Niemeyer obviously wanted her to say yes.

Or else her imagination was running away with her. She thought again of the alumnus in the funny hat, and wondered whether she had really seen him twice; or even once.

"Go to sleep," she whispered in her grandmother's stern voice, but instead continued to study the photograph. It was wrinkled and smudged, because she had spent so many hours over the years holding it, wondering what he was like. His smile was bright and confident and, she liked to pretend, noble. Or maybe it was just that she wished he had died more nobly. The family seemed to consider the manner of Donald Jensen's death an embarrassment. He had tried to volunteer for the war, said Nana, but they rejected him because he was colored, only to draft him six months later. She was volunteering, too: still following in her father's footsteps. She wasn't sure why she felt like a fool.

IV

In the morning, Tom drove her to the tiny Tompkins County Airport for the flight to Washington. Niemeyer was waiting in the lobby, and for a bad moment Margo was prepared to credit Annalise's doleful speculations. But all the great man wanted was a private word before she left. They spoke in a corner, near the battered vending machines. She wanted to ask about her father, but he gave her no chance.

"I've been thinking things over since yesterday," said Niemeyer. "Now, listen carefully. There's only time to say this once. What you're doing for them isn't supposed to be dangerous. On the other hand, they've sort of thrown this thing together on the fly. A lot can go wrong even in the best-planned intelligence operation, and this one isn't the best planned. You do understand that, don't you?"

"Yes," said Margo, voice suddenly faint.

"I don't know what private instructions they're going to give you, but, if the ploy goes to pieces? You don't go back to your hotel. You don't go to your minder. You march straight into the American consulate, nowhere else. Ask for a counselor named Ainsley. Mr. Ainsley is an associate of mine, and he'll take care of you." He put his good hand on her arm. "Borkland might make it all sound like sun and fun, Miss Jensen, but you'll be behind the Iron Curtain. Remember that, and be careful."

On the plane, she almost threw up. *Intelligence operation,* Niemeyer had said.

FIVE

Counterintelligence

I

"There's some kind of jurisdictional fight going on," said the American. "Both State and the CIA want to run the operation."

The Russian frowned. The two men were sitting in a car outside a small restaurant in Warrenton, Virginia, an hour or so from Washington. "I have never understood the chaotic nature of your bureaucracy. Surely there exist clear rules to determine the matter."

"Rules are made to be broken, Viktor."

"So your people are always saying. I find it a miracle that your country has survived this long."

"Me, too." The American laughed, but only for a second. "The point is, they're going to put in an agent. It doesn't matter whether Langley or Foggy Bottom winds up with the charter. Either way, we'll be doing your work for you. You want to know who Smyslov was working for. They'll find out, and I'll let you know."

The man called Viktor was uneasy. He adjusted his gold-rimmed glasses. He didn't much care for this rich country and its soft, pampered people. Certainly he didn't like the man seated beside him. But the struggle to protect the Motherland often required compromise. Even Comrade Stalin had made temporary strategic alliances, first with the German fascists, then with the American capitalists.

"What do you know about the operation?" Viktor asked.

"Not much. Not yet. I understand that Langley is calling it QKPARCHMENT."

"QK?"

"That's the digraph for Bulgaria. I'm sure you know this stuff by heart. If it's AE, it's against the Soviets. You. If it's JM, it's Cuba."

Viktor did indeed know the Agency's digraphs by heart. Most Soviet intelligence officers did. Viktor had not been aware that the Americans officially conceded this. But, then, the man with whom he was negotiating was anything but official. His name, if anything at all, was Ziegler, and he represented that uniquely American species, the consultant, a man with connections everywhere and responsibilities nowhere.

"You do understand," the Russian said, "that we will do all that we can to stop this operation."

Ziegler's laugh was humorless. "That's what I'm counting on."

A strange man, Viktor reflected. Betraying his country with such enthusiasm, when the only reward would be an intensification of the crisis. Presumably he had his reasons for cooperation, just as Viktor did.

"Tell me about the agent," he said.

"I don't have his identity yet, but I'm working on it."

"And once the agent is identified?"

Again that strangely cruel laugh. "Bulgaria is on your side of the Curtain, Viktor. Your territory, your rules."

II

The American left the meeting ground first. This was in accordance with their practice. Viktor returned to his borrowed vehicle and headed back toward the city, relying on his pickets to ensure that he was not being followed. He assumed that Ziegler had his own methods of detecting and avoiding surveillance, and he had no interest in them. They shared a temporary goal, to be sure, but they were enemies.

Viktor did not know precisely how contact had been established between his people in Moscow and the faction represented by the strange American. There were moments when he suspected that the approach must be a provocation, intended to create a diplomatic incident. But his superiors had ruled the task worth the risk. If matters went according to plan, the Motherland would enjoy a great success, and the cause of worldwide socialism would be immeasurably advanced. A defeat would mean a catastrophe—not only for the Motherland but for Viktor personally, and perhaps for his family as well. He understood full well how his employers dealt with failure.

His full name was Viktor Borisovich Vaganian, and he was a captain in the counterintelligence unit of the First Chief Directorate of the Committee for State Security, commonly known in the West as the KGB. The Americans had a poor understanding of the workings of the Soviet intelligence service. The formal rank of captain meant nothing, reflecting only years of service. What mattered was the particular appointment one held in the hierarchy. Thus it was not unusual, for example, to be part of an operation in which a junior case officer who was a full colonel would take orders from a senior case officer who was a major. Vitkor was still a captain because he had been with the KGB only three years. But in those years he had developed both a particular specialty and a particular reputation. And as a member of Counterintelligence, he could, in the proper circumstances, give orders even to a general.

This authority mattered just now, and explained his presence in Washington. The Motherland was in the midst of the most important intelligence operation it had undertaken since the end of the Great Patriotic War, an operation that, if successful, would end once and for all the American strategic superiority—and there was a leak.

More than a leak.

Someone on the Soviet side intended to tell the Americans what the Soviets were doing in Cuba, and, presumably, to help them stop it. This was intolerable, and had to be prevented. Viktor and his team had been sent to Washington to trace the source, because efforts to find out the answer in Moscow were being frustrated. Whoever was betraying the country had powerful friends.

But their influence would not extend past Soviet borders. In America, Viktor could take whatever measures he deemed necessary to discover the source.

As for the agent heading to Bulgaria, well, that problem was for Viktor's colleagues to deal with. It was just as Ziegler had said: Our territory, our rules.

SIX

Anadyr

I

"Have you ever heard of Vasily Smyslov?" asked the woman wearing the agate brooch on her jacket. She was prim and withdrawn and fifty, and dropped just enough "r"s to let you know how lucky Radcliffe was to have had her. She wore a schoolmarm bob and her father's gold watch, and Margo had the sense that she kept the family heirlooms at home in the safe, but wore the cheap pin to work at the State Department because only new money showed off. Her name, she had announced as if in surprise, was Harrington, and her role, she said, was prep. Actually, Harrington was the fifth or sixth functionary Margo had met on her two-day trek through official Washington. Borkland had conducted her from one interview to the next, sneaking in the side entrance of some massive but anonymous government edifice, taking the freight elevator in a fancy Georgetown apartment building, and, once, crossing the back yard of a stately home just north of Washington's unfinished cathedral. "We have to get you ready," Borkland said. "On the other hand, you can't actually meet the people you're meeting." And he smiled the warmly apologetic smile that, as Margo had learned ruefully, represented less an offer of compromise than a polite acceptance of your surrender. And so she answered questions and filled out forms and received travel documents and posed for mug shots and now, somewhere in the bowels of the Department of State, was to be briefed at last on what Harrington insisted on calling her "mission parameters." Margo sat across from the older woman at a conference table that would have done duty for twenty, although the two of them were alone. Unlike her other meetings, this one was conducted with a uniformed Marine outside the door, a change in routine that Margo found anything but reassuring.

"Smyslov," Harrington repeated. "Vasily Vasiliyevich, born Moscow, R.S.F.S.R., 1921. Is that a name to you at all, my dear?"

"I'm afraid not," said Margo.

"I read somewhere that your delightful young man is teaching you chess."

"Yes, ma'am."

"Your Tom was quite a chess player himself a couple of years ago. Went to the World Youth Championships when he was in high school. Did he mention that? Poor lamb, he finished eighteenth out of thirty. But it's an honor to be invited, don't you think?" Her trilling laugh was beginning to grate. Perhaps that was its purpose. "Yet your Tom has never mentioned any of the top Soviet players to you? Botvinnik? Tal? Petrosian?"

Margo hesitated. "I think Botvinnik is the world champion."

"Why, so he is, my dear. So he is. Very well done." She even applauded, to Margo's secret fury. "So you have heard of one or two, it seems. But Smyslov you don't know. Oh dear. Well, let's get your information topped up, shall we?"

"Please."

"Vasily Smyslov is also a Soviet chess grandmaster, my dear. One of the strongest players in the world. Won the world championship four or five years back, although he lost the rematch." Harrington recited this history with a delighted smile, to make sure you knew she had only recently studied it up. "He's going to be at Varna, so we're told. On their team for the Chess Olympiad."

"Is he the reason I'm going?"

But women of Harrington's class did not allow themselves to be rushed. "This past summer, there was a grand tournament down on Curaçao. Such a lovely island. Eight of the strongest chess players in the world battled for a month, twenty-eight games apiece, the winner to play a match with the world champion, you see. Smyslov wasn't invited this time, poor lamb, but he dropped in for a few days to watch the others. Four Soviets out of the eight players in the tournament, so I imagine he would have been cheering them on and so forth. On a free day, they all took the boat from Curaçao and went to the beach. Now, the thing you have to understand, my dear, is that the Soviet chess grandmasters are followed everywhere they go by special security agents, known as the gorillas. When the Soviet masters travel abroad, the only foreigners with whom they are allowed to socialize are their fellow chess players. There was one American in the Curaçao tournament, my dear, and that day at the beach, the American and Smyslov stayed in the boat while the others waded or swam or whatever one does. Even the security gorillas were enjoying the sun, so Smyslov and our source had a bit of time together. Smyslov evidently had flown to Curaçao by way of Havana, where he had been on a goodwill tour, playing an exhibition. He had talked to some friends there, people who we believe, from his description, must be part of the apparatus. Not that our Cuban assets are good enough for us to seek confirmation. No matter. The point is, Smyslov told our American source that when the Soviets finished their secret project in Cuba, the United States would be as surprised as Levitzky against Marshall. Alas, before he could explain further, one of those beastly gorillas appeared, and Smyslov clapped the American on the back and said he would see him in Varna and tell him the rest of the story. The next day, Smyslov flew home."

She saw Margo's blank stare.

"Dear me. Where shall I begin? A famous chess game, my dear, played in 1912 at Breslau. Levitzky is doing fine, possibly heading for a win, when, out of the blue, Marshall's queen swoops down onto the most heavily defended square on the board. But it can't be captured. No matter which piece the queen is captured with, Marshall will checkmate Levitzky. Sudden, unexpected, forceful—some call it the most brilliant move ever played on the chessboard."

"I see," said Margo, utterly mystified.

"Except you don't see, do you, Miss Jensen? Let me explain. Smyslov had no reason to let slip anything about Cuba. But we know—and I suspect Smyslov knows we know—that, in addition to his chess, he does occasional odd jobs for the KGB. Pretty much all of them do, or they don't get to travel abroad. Our American source missed the point, but when he got home to New York, he mentioned the tale to one of his chess friends, who mentioned it to a friend of ours. We realized what our source didn't—that Smyslov was sending us a message. He very likely came to Curaçao with that very intention. He wanted us to know that the Soviets are planning something brilliant and unexpected in Cuba that will turn the game on its head." Harrington turned another page. "You wouldn't know this, of course, but Soviet ships have been offloading huge crates in Cuban ports for weeks now." That preposterous laugh. "Oh dear. Need I remind you that what I am about to disclose is highly classified? If you should ever share it with anyone, they'll send you to prison for simply years, my dear. You do understand, don't you, Miss Jensen?"

This time Harrington waited, and Margo realized that she had to respond, for the record. "I understand, Mrs. Harrington," she said, shrinking inside.

"It's Miss Harrington, my dear, or Doctor, if you find that more comfortable." The older woman slid a long printed form and pen across the table. The page carried a warning in large red capitals: YOUR SIGNATURE SUBJECTS YOU TO STATUTORY PENALTIES—DO NOT SIGN WITHOUT READING! But whatever the text might demand, Margo knew that she would sign anyway: having been brought this far inside, she found unbearable the thought of being escorted summarily from the room and sent back to Ithaca. And even as Margo signed—without reading—and added the date, it occurred to her that Harrington, for all her surface pomposity, was rather a wise psychologist, having chosen the perfect moment. For Margo stood at the precipice of the secret world, and longed to jump.

"Excellent! Oh, you're doing wonderfully well, my dear. I can see why Dr. Niemeyer admires you so. Well." Harrington checked the signature, then slipped the paper back into her folder. She was once more turning pages. "The crates being offloaded in Cuba. All we know about them is that the Soviets have code-named the operation Anadyr. That is the name of a river, and a town in one of the Soviet republics. The name was chosen in order to mislead us, Miss Jensen. Alas, our vaunted intelligence agencies have had no success in penetrating Anadyr, and so we have no idea what they are seeking to mislead us about. But the crates keep coming. They could hold tank shells or grain, automobile parts or Spanish-language copies of *Das Kapital*. Those are the optimistic scenarios, my dear. In light of what Smyslov said, and given the state of our relations with the Communist bloc at the moment, we are forced to assume the worst. There has long been a faction within the Central Committee urging Khrushchev to put nuclear warheads into Cuba. I'm sure Niemeyer has taught you that in the next war, warning time will be everything. With missiles in Cuba, we would have none. Washington and New York might disappear before anyone had the chance to tell the President that the Soviets had pushed the button. Oh." A motherly lift of eyebrows. "Why the long face, my dear? You needn't be worried. Most of our people think Khrushchev is too clever to try such a thing, because, if the Reds start a war, we would wipe the floor with them"—from her partisan delight she might have been discussing the Harvard-Yale game—"but one doesn't protect one's country by assuming the best of the enemy, does one? Naturally, then, we have to find out precisely what Operation Anadyr is. You see that, don't you, my dear? Probably there is no reason for concern, but Khrushchev is under enormous pressure, poor lamb. That's why he built that beastly wall in Berlin. He wants to prove that he's as tough as his predecessors, you see."

Harrington's gaze had intensified, and Margo, no longer able to meet its glow, was staring at the blank pad in front of her. The State Department logo was embossed in the blue leather.

"So, there we are," said the older woman. "We need information, don't we? We need to know whether the Soviets are offloading missiles or mosquito nets. At the moment, our only path to that information is to follow up the message from Smyslov. As I believe I mentioned, Vasily Smyslov is scheduled to be at the Olympiad in Varna, playing for the Soviet team. Our American source will be there as well, playing for the American team. We asked our fellow countryman if he would please rekindle the conversation with Smylsov, to find out what on earth he was talking about. He can talk to Smyslov, you see. Nobody else will be able to get past the security gorillas. Only, the little snot refused." Harrington chuckled in embarrassment at her own vulgarism. "Oh, dear me. He does bring out the worst in people, I'm afraid. Never mind." She folded her hands.

"I apologize, Dr. Harrington. I still don't see why you need me."

"My dear, it is evident that you are an innocent. You don't know men as one day you shall. When we asked our countryman to help us out, he told us no, absolutely not. We appealed to his love of country. He said the Russians would kill him. We said we'd give him a minder. He said talking to Smyslov about some Russian surprise in Cuba would distract him from his chess. We pointed out that the mission would require only one or two conversations over the course of three weeks. We offered him money, but money seems to bore him. We had friends of friends prevail upon him. Finally he said he would do it—he would meet Smyslov—but only if we pay him a great deal of money, *and* if you go. He appears to believe that you are his good-luck charm."

"Oh, no," said Margo, a terrible suspicion dawning.

"Oh, yes, Miss Jensen. Our American source seems to have developed quite the crush on you. I would congratulate you were Bobby Fischer anything other than the little monster we both know him to be."

<h1 style="text-align:center">II</h1>

If Harrington intended by her clever deployment of the identity of the source to get a rise out of her guest, she succeeded, quite literally, for Margo was on her feet, instinct causing her to back away from the table, as if to put physical space between herself and the memories evoked by the name. For a terrible moment, time flipped backward to last spring, and she heard voices raised in fury, shouting about life being wasted, together with layering insults about the intellectual capacity of women, who, as a group, ranked somewhere below the hated Russians in Bobby's bizarre cosmology. She saw Bobby's long, narrow face and those dark, pounding eyes as he screamed at her; saw the only man she had ever loved, squaring to slug his best friend in the world.

Because of her.

Bobby Fischer and Tom Jellinek were indeed friends, if a man like Bobby could be said to have friends. They had grown up together in Brooklyn, attending Erasmus Hall High School. Both had been chess-mad. Tom had been very, very good at the game; Bobby had been a true genius, who already at age thirteen had defeated one of the strongest players in America in what *Chess Review* labeled "The Game of the Century." Bobby dropped out of school to focus entirely on chess, and was now, at age nineteen, one of the best in the world, widely expected to win the championship before too long. Tom won a scholarship to Cornell. Margo got to know Bobby because he came up to Ithaca now and then to spend a few days sleeping on the floor of Tom's dorm room, to escape the Russian spies peering in his window, or the knife-wielding thugs hiding behind every lamppost, or the people coughing on him in the street, from whom he might catch some dreadful disease. Tom usually indulged his peculiar friend, so Margo did, too. For a while, she even developed a maternal attitude toward him, for Fischer projected the air of a sly child bewildered by the world and in need of protection. But then, the last time he visited—

"Do sit down, my dear," said Harrington, with a touch of bemused impatience. She was still turning pages in her folder. "I'm afraid we have not completed discussion of the mission parameters."

But Margo was shaking her head. "No," she said. "Absolutely not. I am not going to Bulgaria with that boy."

Harrington wore glasses on a chain around her neck. She put them on, and her eyes were all at once large and demanding. "I didn't ask you whether you are going to Bulgaria," she said. "I asked you to sit."

Plainly, the older woman had already realized that her guest had been raised to respect the authority of elders. Margo sat.

Warily.

"Now, then," said Harrington, ruffling her papers. "Shall we continue?"

"I don't think you understand. Bobby and I don't get along. He doesn't get along with anyone."

"So I gather. Nevertheless, Miss Jensen, you are his price, and your country has agreed to pay. The matter is out of our hands. You have no more choice than the rest of us." She did not wait for Margo to contradict her. "Mr. Fischer, as I said, seems to regard you as a good-luck charm. Evidently, he won some famous game in your presence?"

"Yes, in New York last December, against a man named Byrne, but—"

"Then it's settled, my dear. The mission parameters remain the same. There is no requirement that the two of you like each other, or even that you pretend to like each other. What Mr. Fischer has demanded is your company. He cannot demand that you enjoy his. Naturally, we will compensate you for your labors."

With every word out of Harrington's mouth, Margo felt diminished. The assurance of payment only heightened the sense of having been bartered by her own government. Quite against her raising, she put her elbows on the table and rubbed her palms over her eyes. A rising exhaustion battled a rising fury. No one had actually deceived her, but their refusal to tell her whom she was to accompany until now had much the same effect. They hadn't lied; they had simply deployed the truth rather cleverly.

"You don't know Bobby like I do," Margo finally said. "He's not just unpleasant or rude. I don't care how brilliantly he plays chess. He's crazy. That's not just a word. He's actually crazy. Half the time he's a perfect gentleman or a shy little boy, but the rest of the time he's seeing monsters under the bed. He thinks the Russians are going to murder him to keep him from winning the world championship. He isn't joking. He really believes it. He thinks people are poisoning his food. He thinks Communists, Jews, and homosexuals are in a conspiracy to rule the world. Do you know what book he brought to Ithaca the last time he visited Tom? *Mein Kampf*! Do you have any idea what kind of man he is?"

Again Harrington affected not to hear. "This is the way things are going to work, Miss Jensen. The Olympiad games begin every afternoon at three. Mr. Fischer sleeps late most mornings, I am given to understand, and rises for lunch. You will join him for lunch whenever possible, although I am told that he prefers to eat alone. In the afternoon, he likes to walk. You will walk with him. You will try to get him to talk to the Soviet players—Smyslov in particular. If he can get you past the security gorillas, you might even be introduced to Smyslov yourself. In any event, you will endeavor to listen to any conversation the two of them might hold, or between Mr. Fischer and any other Soviet or Iron Curtain player. We will not expect you to record the conversations, because there is no time to train you in the use of the proper equipment—and, besides, a microphone is precisely the sort of thing the gorillas will be looking for. You will listen as best you can, and then, when the round begins, you will return to your hotel room and make the best notes you can of what was said. Agatha will take possession of your notes each evening, and that will be the end of your responsibilities. You will fly home with the thanks of a grateful nation, along with a nice bit of cash, and you will resume your studies, and you will never again lay eyes on either Agatha or myself."

"Who's Agatha?"

"Your minder. Chaperone, if you like. You'll meet her this evening. I believe you will find that the two of you have a good deal in common."

Margo digested this. "Mr. Borkland said all I would be doing in Bulgaria is watching the chess and enjoying the beach."

"Bill Borkland is a sweet man, my dear, but not fully informed. In an operation of this sensitivity, one does tend to compartmentalize." Steepling her fingers. "Naturally, Miss Jensen, we would rather spare you this effort. But our analysts have judged Bobby Fischer wholly unreliable. Unfortunately, he is Smyslov's chosen conduit. And as you are the only individual Mr. Fischer is likely to allow in his vicinity, you are the one who will have to report back on what happens. Once more, my dear, there is no choice. We have to penetrate Operation Anadyr so that we will know whether to prepare for a war. Or, perhaps, prepare to start one." Closing the folder with a decisive snap. "And, to answer your earlier question, yes, Miss Jensen, I do know exactly what kind of a man Bobby Fischer is. I know about his mother's medical training in Moscow and her peace activism, and how he despises all women. I know that he doesn't trust President Kennedy because President Kennedy puts his hands in his pockets in public, and I know that he grows skittish and unmanageable when forced to sleep in the same place for more than a few nights running. I know that he is a paranoid, and, in the judgment of some of our wiser psychiatrists, is suffering from schizophrenia. I know the risk we are taking by using him for this mission, my dear. All the more reason that we were fortunate indeed that he insisted on your presence."

It was suddenly too much. Margo wanted none of these accolades. She wanted away from this airless room with its Marine guard, away from the web of secrets and conspiracies that just days ago had seduced her so willingly to its center. She wanted the simplicity of what she had had before.

She said none of this; but Harrington's pale eyes said she knew it all anyway.

"You leave in the morning, Miss Jensen. You will fly to New York, then to London, then to Vienna, then to Sofia. From there you will take the train to Varna. The entire journey will occupy the better part of two days."

Margo swallowed. "I'll be traveling all that time with—with Bobby?"

"Dear me, no. No, my dear. You'll travel with Agatha. Mr. Fischer is already on the way to Europe, along with the rest of the American team." Serene again. "Wouldn't fly with the others, poor lamb. Sailed on the *New Amsterdam*. Said he was worried the Russians might sabotage his plane."

SEVEN

A Brief History of Santa

I

Harrington stood in the hallway, watching Borkland escort Margo out. The dotty smile remained pasted to her face in case the poor young woman turned around for a last look. Harrington could be many things at once and often was; just now, she wanted Margo to remember her as she had pretended to be. But the child never turned, an omission that warmed Harrington's secret heart. There was more to the girl than the others suspected.

That was a relief.

Margo was now her agent, and therefore Harrington loved her like a daughter, as she loved them all. The chances of arrest were small, but, on the other hand, as Harrington pointed out sadly to her inner circle, if by some chance Margo did fall into the hands of the opposition, she was not the sort of prisoner whose release one negotiated. She was, as the Russians said, a *zaychik,* a little rabbit, meaning that she might be worth catching but wasn't worth selling. Both sides did a lot of trading in those days, exchanging one captured agent for another, but rabbits tended to be left out of the general commerce. Harrington had omitted this tidbit from Margo's briefing, and, as she told Borkland afterward, she felt occasional pangs of guilt about sending Margo off to possible incarceration. Although, even speaking to her intimates, Harrington never referred to her agent as anything but GREENHILL, the cryptonym she had been assigned for the duration of SANTA GREEN.

Harrington's own superior, an ugly little man called Gwynn, had been opposed to the operation from the start, and was bothered particularly by the role slated to be played by what he insisted on calling a nineteen-year-old child. He was unimpressed by Harrington's protest that she had run much younger agents during the war. The war, he pointed out, was twenty years ago: an unsubtle reference to Harrington's age. For, although Gwynn was always angry at every woman but at Harrington in particular, he was just now particularly furious at the clever way in which she had circumvented his authority in getting the operation cleared.

In time, she knew, he would find a way to exact vengeance.

Even now, watching GREENHILL vanish around the corner, Harrington wondered whether the recruitment had been too fast. When Margo Jensen had first come to her attention, she had been unsure what to make of the girl. There were signs, certainly, that she was indeed special, just as Professor Niemeyer insisted; and it was also true that Bobby Fischer seemed quite taken with her. Since she needed Bobby, she needed Margo.

Except that matters were not quite so cut-and-dried. Something was off about the case; Harrington had sensed it from the start.

She just wasn't sure what it was.

Later, in her final debriefing before separation from government employ, Harrington would tell the inquisitors that she had no regrets about fighting for the operation, notwithstanding its disastrous end.

What about the fate of your agent? they would ask. Any regrets about that? Would you change the plan if you could?

And she would look at them very straight and say: No. No regrets. War's war.

II

Alone again, Harrington tucked her papers beneath her arm and headed for the elevator. People looked up as she passed their desks, then glanced away. They all knew she had done a thing or two in the war, even if they didn't know exactly what. The junior officers in her department traded tales in hushed voices. One rumor said she had nearly been captured by the Gestapo in Vienna and had killed two men making her escape. Another had it that she had been the spotter on the ground in Prague when Kubiš and Gabčik, aided by British

Intelligence, assassinated Reinhard Heydrich. Harrington never said if any of the stories were true.

Although Margo had taken her for an academic, Harrington was a career intelligence officer, and had been decorated by three Allied governments for her service in the war. She was a soldier's sister and a soldier's daughter, and her great-uncle, a Union cavalry officer, had helped Philip Sheridan chase down Jubal Early's army in the Shenandoah Valley, sealing the fate of Richmond, and ending the Civil War. The only direction any member of her family ever moved was forward. And Harrington herself had been marching hard toward her goal since she first got wind of the message from Smyslov on Curaçao.

"Think of it this way," she might have said, were she given to explaining her motives, which she was not. "If a colonel had whispered in Napoleon's ear that he'd met a peasant who claimed to know a man who could tell them Nelson's plans for the Battle of Trafalgar, don't you think Napoleon might have sent someone to find out?"

She was fascinated—so fascinated that she put aside a really quite promising ploy involving a corrupt Indonesian general to look into it. Maybe there were missiles in Cuba, maybe there weren't. The Soviets were moving *something*—and everybody on Capitol Hill had an opinion. The Agency was getting nowhere.

A perfect opening for Harrington's contrarian talent.

By the time the Smyslov approach came to her attention, it had already been dismissed by the Agency, no further action to be taken. Fischer was unstable or Smyslov was a plant: in either case, the best way to deal with the proffer was to file and forget. Harrington at this time had no formal involvement in the case. But she was sufficiently intrigued to gather in her living room one evening three or four like-minded souls from agencies every bit as faceless as hers: like-minded in the sense that they shared her frustration at the bureaucratization of intelligence gathering. Her guests knew nothing about what had happened on Curaçao, and the only member of the group who had even heard Smyslov's name remembered him less for his chess than for his opera singing, for he had been a prodigy in both fields. But they knew that the Soviets were sending men and materiel and gigantic crates to Cuba, and they were as frantic as everyone else to learn what was inside.

"I believe I might be able to help," said Harrington.

She laid the case before them, and cajoled and argued and charmed and browbeat until they provided what she wanted. A young man from CIA Counterintelligence gave her access to certain "serials," as they were called: the scattered and disjointed bits of fact and conjecture that were supposed to add up to an index of Soviet intentions, and even operations. A fellow Radcliffe alumna and Harrington protégée provided certain records from HTLINGUAL, the Agency's secret program to intercept, open, and copy letters to and from specified targets within the United States, notwithstanding the prohibitions on domestic surveillance written into the Agency's charter. And a professor of something, an engineer from Purdue who spent his spare hours consulting for the newly created National Reconnaissance Office, was inveigled into providing her raw U-2 surveillance photographs of certain naval movements in the Black Sea, material up until then gathering dust because it lacked apparent significance.

It was from this modest start that Harrington went over to the offensive. She spent the month of June painstakingly crafting a brief in support of her position that the approach to Bobby Fischer was worth pursuing.

In early July, she shared the memorandum with her superior, Gwynn.

Who rejected it out of hand, scrawling unfavorable notations in blood-red ink all along the margins.

Harrington asked for a face-to-face meeting. Grudgingly granted. Last appointment of the day, and he had to depart in fifteen minutes for a Georgetown dinner party.

"This is the best shot we have," she said.

"Maybe if you're aiming for your foot," her superior smirked. Gwynn was no taller than five foot six and had come over from a position with one of the larger defense contractors. He approached life with an attitude of condescension, and had a reputation for wit.

"Do you have a better idea?"

"Yes. Leave it to the clowns across the river. Let them lay their heads on the block. One doesn't actually see the virtue in putting one's hoof in."

"Clowns across the river" being Gwynn's standard but entirely unoriginal put-down of the Central Intelligence Agency.

Harrington kept pressing. Gwynn listened to her arguments, and kept shaking his head. At the end of fifteen minutes, he locked his safe for the night, gathered up his coat and hat, and assured her that he would give her proposal a bit of thought; by morning, there was a letter on Harrington's desk, signed by Gwynn, copy to her personnel file, ordering her to get her head out of the clouds and do some serious work.

Harrington was an old hand—older by a decade and a half than her titular superior—and she knew that bureaucratic battles were never won but only lost. The key to avoiding defeat was carefully collecting markers, while always understanding the structure better than your adversary. She knew people; more important, people knew her, and some even owed her.

III

The rejection of her outline for SANTA GREEN did not slow Harrington down. She worshipped her great-uncle the Union cavalry officer, who'd had a tendency to ride off on missions of his own choosing, always pointing to poor lines of communication to explain why he had ignored orders. He got away with it because his mad schemes usually paid dividends. Harrington had inherited her ancestor's personality. In mid-July, without awaiting authorization, she sent an intermediary to meet Bobby Fischer in New York.

The intermediary—the very same Borkland who would later interview Margo in Niemeyer's office—returned that evening, as exhausted as if he had gone ten rounds with a champion boxer. Bobby was willing, said Borkland, but only on the condition that they pay him money—a great deal of money—and also arrange for a certain young lady to accompany him.

It is in Harrington's memorandum of this conversation for the SANTA GREEN file that the asset subsequently known as GREENHILL makes her first appearance. Within two days, Harrington had a bit of background on her, most of it the result of intermittent surveillance conducted by the Federal Bureau of Investigation on GREENHILL's roommate, a suspected radical. J. Edgar Hoover's grim men rarely shared material with the spies, but Harrington had done Hoover the occasional rather grubby favor, and in return he now and then sent her files that might be useful. The coincidence of the connection to Bobby might have been God's hand, or Harrington's good fortune, but she was not about to reject it merely because she couldn't explain it.

After that, she went up to Vermont to visit Lorenz Niemeyer at his summer cottage. They had sandwiches and lemonade on the porch, where the susurrating insects provided a natural cover for their conversation. He didn't want to hear operational details, said Niemeyer, although he still held his security clearance. And, no, he hadn't had GREENHILL in class yet, but he had heard not entirely bad reports of her, and she was enrolled in his course on Conflict Theory in the coming fall. In the meanwhile—said Niemeyer—Harrington should pull the file on GREENHILL's father.

"What file?"

"Just look. Donald Jensen was his name."

"Look where?"

He told her.

"Why would I want to do that?"

"Because some talents run in the blood."

"That's absurd."

"Just look."

Getting the file proved difficult. She had to cash in more favors, this time at the Defense Department. But at last she was able to see a redacted version. Even incomplete, the tale was impressive.

Back up to Vermont: none of this could be discussed on the telephone.

"You knew him?"

"I did."

"Even so. Those are the father's accomplishments. Not the daughter's. What makes her special?"

"I promised to look out for his family."

"Sending her into harm's way is looking out for her?"

Niemeyer had the good grace to look embarrassed: a thing that she had never before witnessed. "She's ambitious. She wants to be noticed. This will send her straight to the top of people's lists."

"Assuming she survives."

"That's your responsibility, not mine."

"There's more to this than you're telling me."

Niemeyer was his cool, diffident self again. "Use her or don't use her. It's entirely up to you."

Harrington hated him for that, as for many other sins, and for a week pretended that she might not need GREENHILL after all. But, no matter how hard she tried, she could not come up with a plausible alternative.

She gave in—and the rest of the operation fell into place. Within days, she had a rudimentary plan of attack. There was no point in going back to Gwynn, and so Harrington chose a tactic known in the jargon as "plowing around the tree." She stepped outside the chain of command and, ignoring Gwynn entirely, took her brief to Higher Authority: the undersecretary, at that time the second rank in the State Department, whom she had known in London during the war.

The undersecretary owed her a favor, and so gave her half an hour the very next afternoon.

And listened; and said no.

But, unlike Gwynn, the undersecretary gave reasons: Fischer is too unreliable. He needs a minder. No, his asking price is too high. No, a college sophomore is too young. Also, this particular sophomore is a girl. And a Negro. And has a radical roommate and probably smokes marijuana.

Harrington battled back. She had built her storied career on standing her ground, and if those with whom she worked disliked her at times and resented her always, they nevertheless admired both her fortitude and her stellar record. Her magic was the string of successes she had built upon similarly shaky operations. Harrington had enjoyed a marvelous war, much of it lived behind German lines, and although nobody ever talked about the details, everybody gave her a little extra maneuvering space. True, she had had her failures as well, most spectacularly the operation known as PBFORTUNE, aimed at bringing down the Guatemalan government by assassinating key leaders. But she was still the great Harrington, and when she spoke, even Higher Authority in the end had no choice but to listen.

Bobby was perfect, she said. The very nuttiness that had people worried made him an unlikely target of recruitment. Therefore, nobody would suspect him. As to the money, surely it was trivial when placed beside the value of the intelligence dividend.

"What about GREENHILL?" the undersecretary asked.

Nineteen years old was perfect, Harrington insisted. Young enough to be an idealist still, to believe that the world was fair, and therefore to take part willingly in the sort of mission that would frighten a more jaded soul out of her wits. Besides, Harrington herself had run younger agents in occupied France just twenty years ago, and not without success. "Needs must," she said.

The undersecretary frowned.

Female was perfect, Harrington gushed on. GREENHILL's gender provided natural cover as Fischer's supposed girlfriend. Negro was perfect, because she would be so prominent and obvious that nobody would imagine for a moment that her role was covert. Here again, her youthful innocence would help, for it was precisely what was needed to pull off her dual role of bucking up Fischer and keeping her ears open: a more mature and watchful young woman would have every secret policeman in Bulgaria on her tail within minutes. Even the radical roommate was perfect, said Harrington, because—

The undersecretary gave in.

By formal memorandum three days later—one copy up the chain of command, another to the file, a third to the Agency, and of course a copy for Gwynn—SANTA GREEN was born. But the delivery was not without complications.

The case was full of disturbing anomalies. Back at her desk now after briefing Margo Jensen, Harrington pondered the most troubling of them all: the body that had washed up on the shore of the East River in Flushing just this morning. It was very strange. The dead man was a habitué of the coffeehouses and chess clubs of the Lower East Side. He was also the one who had overheard Bobby Fischer one evening talking about his strange conversation on Curaçao with Smyslov, and had brought it to the attention of the proper authorities. He had apparently drowned—although how he had wound up in the river, nobody seemed to know. The remains had been in the water less than a day, but the fish had savaged his flesh.

Harrington saw no reason to burden her agent GREENHILL with the news.

IV

Viktor Vaganian was sitting on a bench in Dupont Circle, polishing his gold-rimmed glasses with a cheap cotton handkerchief. At a low stone table nearby, two old men were playing chess. Viktor slipped his glasses back on and watched the game as he fed the pigeons the remains of his sandwich. He marveled at the amount of food the Americans wasted. They were awash in luxury, and yet always wanted more. He was not surprised. Their empire was young, and yet already they were spoiled. Theirs was the only industrial nation left untouched by the Great Patriotic War. Naturally, the monopolists took advantage of this position, but the deluded workers believed their corrupt politicians, who told them that their advantage was a result of the capitalist system. It was lunch hour. He watched the men and women streaming through the park and wondered whether Marx was right, that in some peculiar way America might prove immune from the socialist tide that was bound to sweep the world—and if Lenin was right that, in time, the proper form of industrial relations would have to be forced upon them.

Some of his colleagues believed that Operation Anadyr was a necessary step in realizing Comrade Lenin's dream. Viktor hoped that this was true. The Americans were many things—decadent, greedy, oppressed, uncultured—but they were not cowards.

"Good afternoon."

Ziegler had arrived, and sat on the bench beside him, unwrapping a chicken sandwich and pretending to read a newspaper. They spoke in English, knowing that the crowds surrounding them provided the requisite anonymity.

"They found the body," the American continued in a murmur.

"What body is this, please?"

"The body of the man who heard Fischer talking about Smyslov's message and passed it on to our intelligence people. The man you cut up and left in the East River."

Viktor shrugged. "He did not wish to share what he knew."

"He didn't know anything. He was a conduit. And the body shouldn't have washed up for weeks. What exactly did you call yourself doing? I thought you were a professional."

"Perhaps the weighting was improperly done. I shall talk to my people."

"I need you to do more than talk to them, Viktor. Your people, as you call them, need a little more discipline, it seems to me."

The man called Viktor suppressed his anger. Typical bourgeois, he reminded himself: all impatience and disapproval, full of what Comrade Stalin used to call the jargon of the huckster—the use of words for effect on the listener, without proper attention to their meaning.

"Do you have any additional information for me?"

"I have the particulars on our agent. They're in my lunch bag."

"I have warned you what might happen to this agent at the hands of my colleagues. You will allow us to treat one of your citizens so?"

"I told you. Your territory. Your rules." Ziegler finished his sandwich. He brushed his hands on his shirt. "But I don't understand what you people are doing over there. You know the message came from Smyslov. Why isn't he arrested? I'm sure he'd tell you in two minutes who he got it from."

Viktor briefly removed his gold-rimmed spectacles. He marveled that so boorish a man as Ziegler could rise so high. This was among the most serious contradictions of bourgeois culture: it claimed to value music and art, but insufficiently rewarded refinement, and therefore often elevated the unrefined. Viktor suspected that the man sitting beside him had never been to the ballet in his life.

"You have no understanding of our system," said Viktor. He slipped the glasses back on. "You worked in intelligence, but you are subject to the same illusions as your deluded workers. We are a people's democracy, not a police state. We have laws and procedures. We cannot simply arrest and interrogate a man who four years ago was the chess champion of the world. In Soviet Russia, authority is divided and balanced. Smyslov has powerful protectors in the Party. This is as it should be, for he is a valuable national symbol. Until we have proof of his treachery, therefore, we must seek alternative measures."

"That's a very nice speech, Viktor, but you and I both know that if you really wanted him you could get him." Now he, too, was feeding the birds. "Because let's remember what's at stake here. We have a common interest."

"Indeed."

"Whoever sent Smyslov, that's who we have to stop."

"We cannot arrest a man like Smyslov," Viktor repeated, unhappily. "We cannot interrogate him. We can in certain ways inconvenience their conspiracy, but we must find the answer on this side of the ocean."

"I know. But look at it from our point of view. We can only cover for you so much. If you're going to do any damage, it's better if it's mainly Russians who get hurt."

Viktor frowned. Definitely *nyekulturny*. Uncultured. To speak so casually about violence. Typical of the sort of man who rose to authority in a country that had never faced extermination, as the Motherland had.

"It was you who came to us," he said. "Not we who came to you."

"Because we know what the Smyslov approach means. Because we don't trust our leaders any more than you trust yours. We didn't know you'd be torturing our citizens!"

Viktor wiped his hands and stuffed his napkin in the paper sack. His contact did the same. With a quick, deft motion, each wound up with the other's bag of trash. He stood up, looking down at the uncultured American.

"In Russia, we have a proverb," he said. "If you're afraid of the wolves, you shouldn't go into the woods."

EIGHT

Babysitting

I

"I'm thinking I might get married," said Bobby Fischer. His high-pitched voice was defiant with uneasy confidence. "But I don't know. Maybe I should buy a car instead. With a car, you get something for the money."

"Mmmm," said Margo, wishing that the young genius would, for just a moment, shut his mouth. They were strolling along the white sands behind the looming towers of their blocky socialist-modern hotel, where, as Agatha explained, you had to tip the maid an American dollar—quite against Bulgarian law—if you wanted such rudiments as recently laundered towels. That was the rule for Westerners. Those who flocked to Varna from various landlocked Iron Curtain nations often received no housekeeping services at all.

Agatha, Margo's mousy little minder, who so far seemed to know everything about everything.

"I want a Japanese wife," Bobby continued. "Maybe Korean." The sun was low and splendid in the cloudless afternoon sky. Margo was wearing slacks and sandals appropriate to the seashore, but Bobby was dressed in a tailored gray suit, complete with shiny hand-tooled leather shoes, white shirt, and dark tie. At nineteen, he was tall and gaunt, with a long chin and a narrow pink face that thrust itself insolently forward. His dark eyes were sparkling and intense: you could feel that remarkable brain ticking away. The ticking drew you. Bobby projected the peculiar magnetism of the rare man truly destined for greatness, and young women flocked to him wherever he went; what spoiled the aura was the words that spilled from his mouth. "American girls spend all their time at the hairdresser's," Bobby explained with a puzzled earnestness. "Women from Asia aren't like that. Also, they don't talk back. But the cost of bringing one of them to the States is about the same as the price of a car. And if I have to send her back, I'll lose money on the deal."

"I can see how that might be a problem."

He gave her a sidelong glance, not sure whether he was being mocked. "Are colored girls like that? Regina says that segregation is unfair. We went south when I was little. Regina showed me the water fountains and everything. I guess I wouldn't mind, if they'd let me play chess."

Regina being his beloved if occasionally hated mother.

"She used to come on Radio Moscow," he continued, in evident bewilderment. "The Russians cheated me out of the world championship—I proved it, I wrote a whole article about it in *Sports Illustrated*—and there was Regina, on the radio, talking about how Russia is a paradise for the workers. I mean, she used to. Who'd want to marry a woman like that? No wonder my father left. I would, too. Well, I did. I don't let her near me any more." He pointed to the massive hotel up the slope. "If she ever comes within six blocks of where I'm staying, I'm going home. All the organizers know that. I'm hoping she'll try sometime and get arrested." He brightened. "Hey, did you see my game against Unzicker? I'll bet I win the brilliancy prize."

Margo was in agony. This was her sixth day in Varna, and every afternoon was the same, walking with Bobby after lunch, listening to his views, usually about his game from the day before. His shy pride could be appealing or repulsive, depending on the nuances of expression and tone. There were times when he seemed so sweetly possessive that she nearly forgot they weren't a couple, and others when her every word annoyed him and he marched off in a huff. Margo persevered. This was why she was here. To listen to his conversations, to make her notes for Agatha, to wait until they met up with Smyslov and discovered what he was trying to tell them about Cuba: Margo Jensen, doing her patriotic duty. And the entire experience might have been almost bearable but for one small difficulty.

Smyslov wasn't in Varna.

Grandmaster Smyslov had fallen ill, the Soviet captain told the assembled journalists, and had been replaced by Grandmaster Yefim Geller.

Who, coincidentally, spoke no English.

Nobody had shared any of this with Margo until she arrived in Varna, although she suspected that Agatha knew, because at each stop along the two-day journey they had been met by a quiet man who had pressed pages from metal briefcases into the minder's hands, waited while she read, and locked the papers away again. The quiet men were all different, but they possessed the same rigid face and gazed at Margo with the same unashamedly suspicious eyes. One of the many reports Agatha read must have alerted her to Smyslov's absence; she simply had chosen not to pass the tidings on to Margo.

We follow the plan, Agatha said on the first night, after Margo read the news in the English version of the tournament bulletin. They were strolling in the surf, slacks rolled up, because, according to Agatha, even the best directional microphones were confounded by the waves.

I thought Smyslov was the plan, said Margo.

We don't give up, said Agatha. *We improvise. You're going to have to stay closer.*

To Bobby? No. I can't.

As close as you can, honey. As close as he'll let you. A message might still come, and he can't be relied on to pass it to us. She raised a warning finger, then pointed at the hotel. *And no names.*

Margo had reluctantly conceded the point. The crates, she reminded herself. Harrington's briefing. Anadyr. Finding out. This was what she had signed up for. Nana would say she had a duty; for that matter, so would Professor Niemeyer.

So Margo agreed. She would stick closer to Bobby.

And yet Agatha's command of the moment had come as a growing surprise. She was a small, prim woman, possessed of the inoffensive manner Margo associated with shopgirls and librarians. Agatha Milner seemed the perfect chaperone. Her brown hair was always in a bun, and she wore a pair of rimless glasses, which she called spectacles. She was perhaps thirty, although her meekness made her age difficult to judge: at times she seemed a good deal younger. Agatha was shy to the point of diffidence. She spoke little, and Margo found her singularly unimpressive, particularly in comparison with the ebullient brilliance of Dr. Harrington back at the State Department. But the quiet men who greeted them on their stops at airports and train stations all treated Agatha with an elaborate courtesy. Margo couldn't think why. In her own world, obsequiousness of that sort usually meant that a woman was related to or perhaps the wife of a powerful man, but here she sensed something else going on. They were in Vienna before the answer struck her.

The quiet men were all afraid of mousy little Agatha.

Margo wondered why.

II

"Did you see my game against Unzicker?" Fischer repeated, now in the proud-little-boy tones Margo much preferred. They were farther from the surf than she would have wished, but the beach was crowded down there, and Bobby hated crowds. "He should never have played bishop-takes on the fifteenth move, but I would have beaten him anyhow. And the rook sac at the end!" he crowed—"sac" being short for "sacrifice" in chess parlance. "You should have seen his face fall apart."

"It was a very nice move, Bobby," she said, knowing what he needed. She found a smile somewhere.

"I don't know. Maybe my rook sac against Najdorf the other day was better. What do you think?"

"You're the genius, Bobby," she said dutifully, and watched his face glow with a child's delight.

"We should celebrate," he declared, not meeting her gaze. "We should have dinner. In fact, why don't you come up to my room? I'll order a couple of steaks. We'll celebrate."

This was the sort of invitation Margo was learning to tiptoe around. "Don't you have to get ready for the next game?"

"Day off. Come on. You can even get wine if you want." This reluctantly, for Bobby didn't drink. Nor did he have much experience of the opposite sex, although another member of the American team, mistaking her, as everyone did, for Bobby's girlfriend, had regaled her with unwanted tales of a woman they had sneaked into the young man's room at a tournament in South America a couple of years ago. Margo had no way to tell whether a single word was true.

As it happened, Margo had visited Bobby's room at least once a day, according to Agatha's strict instructions, and he had yet to behave as anything but a gentleman.

"It would be my pleasure, Bobby," she said, resignedly.

"But not your friend Agatha. She can't come."

Margo was taken by surprise. "She's very nice."

"No, she isn't. She might say she's on a fellowship, but she looks to me like a cop. Those eyes of hers, the way they see everything."

"She's a graduate student," said Margo, hoping she was remembering the cover story right. "She studies languages—"

"She's not a student. I don't know what she is, but she's not a student. I'd be careful of her if I were you."

Margo stood looking at the sea—families bobbing; lone bathers farther out, sedately swimming. Here and there along the beach were hot springs, bubbling right through the rocks. She had heard that the sickly came from miles around for the cure. She spotted her minder up near the seawall, leafing through a local newspaper, and had to fight a grin. Agatha might fool the Bulgarians, but Bobby had seen through her at a glance.

"I'll try to remember," she said.

"You'll be there the day after tomorrow, right? To watch me play Botvinnik?"

"Of course."

"He's the world champion. But with my good-luck charm in the room, I can beat him."

"And if you beat him, you're world champion?"

Bobby eyed her disdainfully. "Of course not. Everybody loses games. You get to be world champion by beating the champion in a match. Best of twenty-four games. But the Russians cheated me out of the chance, because they're scared I'd win."

Not wanting to tempt Bobby down that road again, Margo hunted for a change of topic. "It was very nice of you to invite me to Varna," she said, with forced bonhomie. "I realized I haven't thanked you. So—thank you, Bobby. I'm having a lovely time."

Bobby had this way of twisting his head back and away to show skepticism. She'd seen him do it when analyzing the moves of lesser chess players. He did it now. "It wasn't my idea for you to come."

Margo stared. "You just said I was your good-luck charm."

"I was being nice. I'm not superstitious. I don't believe in luck. I believe in good moves." He was gazing out to sea. "I do like having you here. I like you. But they suggested it."

"Who did?"

"I don't know. The guy who asked me to talk to Smyslov. He drove down in this big car to see me." He rubbed his eyes. "I don't have time for this. I have to go study."

And he was away, striding fast on his long legs, leaving Margo alone and bewildered on the beach.

III

Night. She stood in the surf with Agatha, slacks hiked up, chilly water lapping at her ankles.

"I don't know what you're talking about," said Agatha for the third or fourth time. Her pale face floated in the darkness like a ghostly balloon. Her tone was as placid as the gentle waves, almost placating, so perhaps she was worried by the fire in Margo's eyes.

"Look. Dr. Harrington told me that I had to go to Bulgaria because Bobby asked for me. Mr. Borkland told me the same thing. And now Bobby says it isn't true. He says somebody told him to invite me. He was happy about it, sure—he calls me a good-luck charm—but it wasn't his idea. Do you get that? It wasn't his idea. Dr. Harrington lied to me."

The minder shook her head. The wind had blown a few strands of brown hair loose from her prim bun, but she made no effort to shove them back into place.

"It makes no difference who said what to whom," she said.

"How can you say that? Of course it makes a difference. Don't you realize that everything Dr. Harrington told me turned out to be wrong? Bobby was supposed to get a message from Smyslov, but Smyslov isn't here, and the man who took his place doesn't speak English. Bobby didn't ask for me. That was a lie. They wanted me to come. Why? Why me? What makes me so special?"

Agatha slipped off her glasses and polished them with a handkerchief. Margo had already learned that the minder's eyes were fine without them.

"It's not part of my job to help you figure out how you got here," said Agatha. "It's my job to help you carry out your mission."

"I thought it was Bobby's mission."

"He's the conduit. You're the carrier."

"I don't have the faintest idea what that means."

"Yes, you do." Agatha waved dismissively. Her hands were large and well controlled: you had the sense that she worked wonderfully with tools of all sorts. "And you can dump the wide-eyed innocent act. It's not charming and it's not necessary. There's confusion at the top of the tree? So what? It doesn't change the mission. Agents always encounter problems. They improvise."

"I'm not an agent." Somehow her protest seemed inadequate. "Come on, Agatha. I'm a college student. I don't have any training."

"If you had training, you'd be an officer. Officers are the ones who run agents. Agents are the people on the ground you recruit to do a specific job. They don't do this kind of thing full-time."

"I'm nineteen years old."

Agatha allowed herself a rare smile. "Dr. Harrington ran agents a lot younger than you in the war. She wouldn't have sent you if she didn't think you're ready."

Margo was intrigued. "How well do you know her?"

"Well enough to trust her judgment. If she thinks this is the way to find out whether there are missiles in Cuba, I believe her. If she says somebody is going to get a message to Bobby, then sooner or later somebody will. Sticking close to him might not be the most enjoyable job in the world, but he seems harmless, and he really does seem to like you a lot."

"That wasn't what I meant." Agatha was looking up at the hotel, so Margo looked, too. The whitewashed towers of the hotel were gauzy and ghostly in the night fog. "I guess what I meant was"—she had trouble formulating the question—"I guess I wondered what she's like. What makes her tick."

To Margo's surprise, Agatha answered. "If you're asking me how she got into this line of work, I have no idea. But if you want to know what she's like, well, I can tell you a story. I was the only girl in my class at the camp"—Margo was too savvy to ask which camp—"and the boys, well, as you can imagine, they weren't happy about it. Dr. Harrington was one of the instructors. She's a legend, believe me." Agatha's confident voice went gentle with awe. "Harrington's done everything in her time. Everything. The stories I could tell you. Can't tell you." A chuckle, and then the librarian was back. "Well. I wasn't going to put up with any nonsense. I went to Harrington to complain about the boys. She said if I couldn't get the better of those little snots—her very word—then I'd never be able to deal with the Reds. She told me to improvise. Then she threw me out of her office."

"What did you do?"

"I improvised. After that, the boys left me alone."

"Improvised how?"

Behind the rimless glasses, Agatha's clear eyes narrowed, and for a moment Margo thought she might actually explain.

"We should get back," the minder said firmly. "Bobby might be looking for you. Or some Russian might be looking for him."

The summons arrived two days later.

NINE

Bureaucratic Snafu

I

"We've got a little problem," said Gwynn without preamble, the instant Harrington stepped into his office and closed the door, and she knew at once what he meant: *she* had a problem. "Your agent's been in Varna for a week now, staying at the fanciest resort on the Black Sea at ferocious expense, with, so far, nothing to show for it. True?"

"The expense isn't ferocious," she said. "This is Bulgaria we're talking about."

But Gwynn on his high horse, charging up his bureaucratic mountains, had a tendency to trample common sense and leave it in the dust. "It's money, isn't it? Comes out of the taxes paid by the American people, doesn't it? Wasting pennies makes it easier to waste nickels, my late mother always said. And, by the way, Doctor, while we're on the subject, I've been looking at these confirmations from the clowns across the river"—fingers stabbing at the pink carbon flimsies on his desk—"and it seems that you've been requisitioning resources about which I know nothing. True?"

Until this moment, it had never occurred to Harrington that Gwynn might have a mother. "Clearance isn't required, as you know. It's my operation, as you keep reminding me, so the competence rests with—"

Again he ignored her. With one hand he held a flimsy aloft; the other made a fist, punctuating his points with heavy swipes at the air. "You requested three more watchers, in addition to the one the Agency was good enough to lend you." He put the page down, took up another.

"You requested vehicle surveillance, with audio as possible, whenever GREENHILL takes it upon herself to go into the city."

"I'm worried that the Bulgarians might arrest her, and—"

"And when the clowns across the river, through their logistics division, denied these requests, you went over their heads. Not to your superior in the chain of command. That would be my humble self, but this is the first I'm hearing of any of this. To someone higher up. Another friend from the war, no doubt. Which friend, by the way, backed the Agency entirely." His hands were folded now. His pug face was bright with satisfaction. "It is my inclination, Dr. Harrington, to terminate QKPARCHMENT as of this moment. Any thoughts?"

"SANTA GREEN," she said.

"I beg your pardon."

"On this side of the river, the operation is SANTA GREEN. Not QKPARCHMENT. If it blows up, the Agency will be more than happy to pretend they never assigned it a cryptonym."

Gwynn's smile was a cruel, thin-lipped line in the fleshy face. At least that was the only smile Harrington ever saw. He was said to have another. On the Georgetown cocktail-party circuit, Gwynn was received happily as a guest of considerable charm, even if none of his hosts knew precisely what his job entailed.

"Call the operation what you want, Dr. Harrington. I would like to know why exactly I shouldn't terminate it immediately."

Harrington composed herself. She had a tendency to temper, she knew, and although Gwynn was less powerful than he thought, it would not be wise to alienate him just now. He might be unpleasant, but he wasn't wrong. She *had* gone behind his back, the Central Intelligence Agency *was* getting annoyed at her shenanigans, and continuing support for SANTA GREEN *was* in jeopardy. So she skipped over the facts that she, not he, held the operational charter, and that the authority to end the mission did not actually rest in his hands.

"Alfred," she said pleasantly—or as pleasantly as she could manage—"we still don't know what's in those crates. Another cargo ship arrived in Cuba yesterday. The morning intelligence report says that the dockworkers who unloaded the crates were being supervised by Soviet troops. Not just military advisers. Infantry, openly displaying weapons. Whatever is being offloaded, the Soviets are taking no chances."

Gwynn sniffed. "Nobody believes there are missiles in those crates, Doctor. Nobody but you. The Reds aren't that stupid."

"They're not stupid at all, Alfred. They're frightened, and they're most likely calculating that we won't risk war over . . ." She saw his stony face and knew that she had made the case too many times, that persuasion was out of the question. "And, yes, you might be right. There's nothing there; I'm wrong. But the White House is screaming at all the agencies to find out. That's all I'm trying to do, Alfred. Help find out. I agree, SANTA GREEN is a shot in the dark. And, yes, I know, the Agency has any number of operations of its own in place. But the more feelers we put out, the sooner we'll know whether the security of the nation is at risk. This isn't about bureaucratic reward. This is about avoiding a war that could kill tens of millions of Americans."

Gwynn frowned, and went on frowning. He drummed his stubby fingers on the blotter. Harrington had thrown in the line about bureaucratic reward because advancement was all that kept her superior in Washington. He dreamed of escaping from the intelligence thicket and rising to undersecretary, or, failing that, a prestigious ambassadorship. It had happened to others. By making clear that she had no interest in moving up the hierarchy, Harrington was reminding him of his own interest in exactly that.

He fluffed the flimsies back into their folder. "Cards on the table, then. I suppose we can keep QKPARCHMENT—excuse me, SANTA GREEN—alive a little longer. But I want all requests for additional resources to flow through proper channels. That means I sign off before anything crosses the river. Clear?"

"Clear."

"And if you really expect the Agency to provide more bodies to keep your agent warm and comfortable, I strongly suggest that you dig up evidence to persuade them that the chances of success are significant. We need to know what's in those crates, but we also need to balance the likelihood of attaining our goal against the cost of the resources involved. Remember, it's the taxpayers whose money we're spending. It's not our own—it's a public trust. We're accountable," he proclaimed proudly. "Cuba isn't the only trouble spot we have to keep an eye on, you know. Now, I've learned through experience to pay attention to your hunches," he lied, rushing past her objections to his sophistry, "but the clowns across the river don't necessarily share my respect for your acumen. Clear?"

"Clear."

"Oh, and, Dr. Harrington, one more thing." The black eyes were hard and glittery. "If by chance some calamity does befall GREENHILL, she's on her own. This is the wrong time for a diplomatic incident. We don't trade for her, we don't acknowledge her, we don't do anything. Don't give me that look. The orders come from the highest levels."

"The highest levels? What does that mean, somebody you met at a party last night?"

The smile really was too self-satisfied. "It means the White House."

II

Captain Viktor Vaganian was exhausted. His body had always adjusted poorly to changes in sleep patterns. But you were bound to upset your cycle when you shuttled from one side of the globe to the other. What his investigation had uncovered worried him enough that two days ago he had flown home to Moscow to consult with his superiors. They had given him fresh orders and sent him right back to Washington. The new orders broadened his authority at the embassy. But that wasn't all.

So important had his investigation become to the success of Anadyr that he was now permitted, in his sole discretion, to use "direct action," a euphemism for lethal force—usually the province of Department T of the First Chief Directorate. And Viktor had the assurances of the hierarchy that his diplomatic immunity would protect him from legal processes even if he happened to kill an American or two along the way.

TEN

Priorities

I

The summons arrived on the day of the big game. When Agatha and Margo left their room to go down to breakfast, they turned left toward the stairs, because the elevator, which lay in the other direction, racketed and groaned as if in preparation for spectacular collapse. Their room was on the eighth floor, but when they climbed, Agatha never even seemed winded.

Bobby was on twelve.

They passed the floor concierge, a massive woman swathed in black crepe who usually dozed in alcoholic slumber, but on this occasion she roused herself and called after them, "Miss! Message! Miss!"

Agatha told Margo to stay where she was. She crossed the threadbare carpet to the desk, spoke a few words to the woman, and gave her a couple of coins. The concierge muttered her message, then returned to her somnolence. Back at Margo's side, Agatha translated.

"Bobby would like you to come to his room," she said.

"Now? He's never up this early."

"I guess he is today."

"Can I get breakfast first?" She saw Agatha's expression. "Oh. Right. Let's go."

The minder shook her head. "You know I can't go with you, honey. He didn't ask for me." She leaned close, whispered: "I'm not part of the story. You are."

And indeed, Margo knew nothing of the minder's story. Not where she came from, why her colleagues were afraid of her, even whether "Agatha Milner" was her real name. They had traveled together for two days and roomed together for the past week, and Margo knew her no better than the day they met in Washington. But she admired Agatha's calm in all situations, and the way Agatha never took no for an answer. She had begun to see in her minder someone to emulate.

II

"It's a trick," said Bobby. "They just want to take me away tonight."

His room was one of the largest in the resort—he had changed twice—and three different chess positions were set up on the desk and two rickety tables, another on the floor. There were chess books everywhere, many not in English: he traveled with a valise-full, and bought more at every stop. He was striding in circles on the dingy carpet, dressed in white shirt and dark slacks and slippers, hands tousling his hair into an angry mess. He had received a message, it seemed: a piece of paper stuffed under his door yesterday, during his game. Bobby had glanced at it last night but only sent word this morning. Margo held the paper in her hand now: the name of a restaurant, today's date, and the time: 2200.

"This must be the appointment for the interview," said Margo, very conscious of the microphones. "It's tonight at ten o'clock."

"I *know* that. But I'm playing Botvinnik today. He's the world champion. He's pretty good, so it'll take me a while to beat him. The game will be adjourned after five hours. That means we finish tomorrow morning. And *that* means I have to analyze the position tonight. That's why they want me to go off to some restaurant for an interview. So I'll do lousy analysis and mess up the endgame and lose. That's what the Russians do, Margo. They cheat. They've been working against me for years." All of this as he stomped around the room. He stopped at the grimy window, pointed. "See the water out there? Remember, when we checked in, how they had me on the other side, facing the tower? I was practically looking into somebody else's room. That's what they do. See, that way, they can look in my window and see what moves I'm studying. More Russian cheating. That's why I made you change my room."

"Yes, Bobby, but this is different—"

He had found the game he wanted and was moving the pieces, very fast. "If it's so important, you go. You can tell me about it tomorrow."

III

Agatha had a map. She marked the location of the restaurant, then had Margo write in her own hand the name, in English block capitals, painstakingly misspelled.

"Just in case," said Agatha.

"In case what?"

The minder shrugged. They were standing in the surf once more, slacks rolled up to their knees. "The map is camouflage. If you have the map, if you're constantly reading street signs, it's evidence that you're just a tourist."

"Does anybody suspect I'm not?" asked Margo, suddenly chilly, and not because of the waves. "What if the whole thing is a trap?"

"The whole thing might well be a trap."

"What am I supposed to do in that case?"

"That's what Bobby is for. The Bulgarians wouldn't dare arrest him. Their own chess fans would riot." Agatha smiled. "Bobby is your protection, Margo."

"I thought I was escorting him, not the other way around."

"And I thought by now you understood. You're the one who's going to carry the message. You're the one who matters. Bobby's a lunatic. His only function in the entire operation is to be at your side so that nobody will touch you."

Margo stared. "When were you planning to tell me this?"

The smile never wavered. "I just did."

"Bobby is my protection. Not the other way around."

"That's right."

"So—what do I do if he won't go tonight?"

Agatha's watchful brown eyes apologized. "You're a woman," she murmured, in eerie echo of Stilwell's taunts back in Ithaca. "Persuade him."

IV

Margo had seen quite a bit of Varna. In the mornings, while Bobby slept in or studied his chess, she spent the hours wandering the town, especially the older parts, the churches and monasteries and even occasional castles that had survived war, pestilence, and socialism—to say nothing of ordinary plunder, for the stone for many of the buildings constructed in the past half-century came from demolishing walls and bridges and even palaces in disused corners of the city. She had seen Euxinograd Palace, with its magnificent gardens, and the dank caves in the hills above the city, where aging monks guarded manuscripts and relics said to unlock the secrets of the universe. She had tried to attend Sunday services at the Dormition of the Theotokos Cathedral but had been prevented by the usher for reasons he had not seen fit to put into English, so she contented herself instead with taking photographs of the golden domes with her Kodak Instamatic. Another time, she went to one of the city's handful of private vineyards, where the proprietors were so delighted to see an American that they piled her with bottles to take home. Untouched, the bottles sat in the hotel room, although, on Agatha's advice, she had doled out a couple to the staff.

Sometimes Agatha joined her on these little jaunts. Margo's only other company was a young fellow in a red leather jacket, who materialized whenever she headed into town. He rode a motorcycle and managed constantly to stay on her tail. Even when she sauntered through an alley, he would show up at the other end. She was careful to keep looking at him; and never to try to escape him.

They will watch you night and day, Harrington had warned. *That's their beastly way, my dear. There's no time to train you in techniques for losing surveillance, and even if we did, your newfound abilities would only make you stand out. This way, it isn't personal. They think every Westerner is a spy, poor lambs. The more nervous you are around them, the more they'll be sure you're the rare one who isn't.*

The Bulgarians were fascinated by her blackness, particularly once they learned that she was not African—she was of the branch enslaved rather than colonized by the capitalists. People came up to her in the street to ask innocently aggressive questions about America: What was it like to live in a country ruled by the Central Intelligence Agency? Was it true that millionaires could have their servants flogged, or were they simply thrown in prison these days? Once a prosperous-looking family commanded her disdainfully to pose with them for a photograph, snapped by a stylish woman holding a Kodak camera that looked suspiciously like the one stolen from her hotel room the day before. But when she tried to inquire, the family's English, theretofore quite serviceable, deserted them.

Still, Margo loved the city. She adored the architecture and the art. The people were friendly despite the weight of history, for this was a land whose polyglot culture stood as testimony to its frequent occupation over the past thousand years by larger powers. And there was something else. During World War II, Bulgaria, under Tsar Boris III, had been one of the Axis powers. Following the Nazi lead, the country had enacted severe restrictions on its Jewish population, limiting everything from property rights to education to permissible names. But, unlike other Axis countries, Bulgaria had refused Nazi demands to send its Jews to the camps. Forty-eight thousand Jews lived in Bulgaria when the war began; nearly all of them survived the Holocaust.

The Bulgarians at their best were a brave and charitable people; Margo would be counting on those qualities tonight.

V

Bobby proved unbudgeable.

It was nearly nine, and time to leave. Margo had been waiting outside Bobby's room when he arrived from the first session of the game with Botvinnik. He didn't look so much at her as through her, and when he opened the door, he seemed surprised that she followed him in.

"Go away."

"The interview, Bobby. It's at ten. We have to hurry."

"Interview?" He was setting up the adjourned position on one of the boards. "You're out of your mind. Go away. I have to analyze."

"Bobby—"

"There isn't time for this!"

She fought the urge to grind her teeth. "We have to go, Bobby. This is why we're here."

"I'm not going anywhere. I'm here to play chess, and I have to analyze. This is *Botvinnik*. The world champion." Throwing up his hands. "Why are women so *stupid*?"

"This is important—"

"So is this." Waving a wild hand at the board. "I'm a pawn up, but he's just sitting there, so confident. I don't think I missed anything—I think I win—but I don't know for sure until I study it. That's why the meeting is tonight. I told you. They don't want me to analyze the position. They're trying to cheat me, the way they cheated me in Curaçao!"

She tried womanly persuasion, just as Agatha had suggested; she just didn't know how it was done, and had always looked down on those who did. She tried every line that popped into her head: *Come on, Bobby. . . . We can have a nice dinner, Bobby. . . . We'll get to spend time together, Bobby. . . . Don't you want to take a night off, Bobby?* None of it did any good. Either she wasn't very good at this, or Bobby was unpersuadable.

She returned to her room alone.

"Then you go," said Agatha.

"What?"

"You meet the interviewer yourself." Pointing at the walls. "At least you can find out what questions he wants to ask Bobby. Maybe arrange another time for him and Bobby to get together."

Margo was already shaking her head. "I can't go to the meeting by myself. You said it yourself. Bobby is my"—she almost slipped and said *protection,* but she saw Agatha's stony expression, and the discipline of the past week held—"he's the reason I'm here. I've been touring the city by myself for days. I'm not all that interested in going out at night alone."

"This is why you're here, Margo. To make things easier . . . for Bobby." Dissembling for the microphones. "That's your mission, and you have to carry out your mission. Tonight. This is it, honey. The big leagues."

Margo swallowed. Hard. "Can you come with me?"

"Sorry, honey. I can't. I have other plans." The minder leaned forward and murmured in her ear, "You won't see me, but I'll stay as close as I can."

VI

She took the tram—watching the streets and consulting the map, because that was what a tourist would do, but also because she had no idea where she was going. Her fellow passengers crowded close to try out their English and to find out whether black people smelled different, and a boy with quick fingers would certainly have lifted her wallet had not a snarling old woman slapped his wrist and waved her cane in menace. A thirtyish man in a leather jacket scolded the boy, then smacked his cheek with a newspaper.

"Thief," he explained to Margo. His hair was very blond, almost platinum.

She had figured that part out for herself.

"Thank you," she said.

"Bad thief," the man answered.

The boy got off at the next stop. The blond man moved farther down the tram. The old woman smiled an apology. Margo smiled back. The old woman reached into her cloak and pulled out a little notebook that she flashed furtively, turning her broad back to screen the move from the other passengers. Margo expected an introduction to the black market, or perhaps even a whispered code word, but what the old woman waved before her eyes was instead a picture of John Kennedy, snipped from a postcard. She pointed to the photo, then, still smiling, pointed to her heart.

Margo nodded. "I like him, too."

The old woman beamed, and the notebook disappeared.

"Your stop," grunted the blond man in the leather jacket.

"Thank you," said Margo.

But he had gone back to his newspaper.

She stepped down onto the cobblestones and consulted the map. She was in front of a church, across from a housing block. The street was in shadow. Half the street lamps were out. Cars were jammed everywhere, most of them battered. A stone memorial celebrated some act of wartime heroism, but the lettering on the plaque was Cyrillic. She walked down what seemed to be the right street, ignoring the whispered invitations from the darkness that sounded the same in any language. She was scared to death and determined not to falter. The desire to look around for her minder presented a constant temptation. She was furious at Bobby, but at everybody else, too. She was so lonely at this moment that she would have welcomed even the boy on the motorcycle: would have bought him a drink, kissed him, slept with him, married him, had eight children for him, done whatever he wanted, in return for the briefest glimpse of a familiar face. But she kept checking the map and kept on walking. She wanted Harrington to be proud of her; and Agatha; and Nana, too.

It occurred to Margo that she did not know what the contact looked like, or how she would recognize him. But there couldn't be too many young black women in Varna just now, and photographs of her strolling the beach with Bobby Fischer had been in the papers.

She hoped Nana never saw *those*.

Two blocks on, she found the address. She maneuvered between the triple-parked cars toward the restaurant. The building looked to be two hundred years old, and the windows were high and narrow, as if to provide lines of fire against the hordes, but the door was open, and loud music, some sort of folk tune, was spilling out, along with several drunks.

It was not a part of the city that drew the tourists.

On the sidewalk, she hesitated. Agatha had promised to stay close, and this time Margo could not resist a quick look, but when she scanned the street she saw no sign of the prim little minder. Margo told herself that not seeing Agatha was better than seeing her, because it meant that the minder was good at her job. Thinking about Agatha gave her the courage she needed just now, not least because she was pretty sure that the man with the blond hair and leather jacket hadn't been on the tram when the other passengers were helping her with the map, and therefore couldn't possibly have heard her mention her destination.

"Keep moving," she whispered.

She stepped inside, and it was every cheap after-hours restaurant in the world: bad lighting, decrepit wallpaper, a grimy bar, a very loud, very bored combo, playing dreary music to which nobody would ever dance. A clutch of heavily painted women off to the side looked her over and evidently decided that she was competition, because they began whispering and pointing. A grubby little man in a dirty shirt bustled over and tested her Bulgarian, then her German, then a couple of other languages she couldn't identify. He was unable to make heads or tails of her schoolroom French, so she tried English.

"I'm meeting someone," she said, slowly. "I just want a quiet table."

He frowned and gestured to one of the girls, for whom Margo repeated her request. After a bit of puzzling and dumb show, they reached vague if general agreement, and the little man sat her up front, near the band, where she couldn't hear herself think. A waiter slapped a badly printed menu on the table and vanished. A beer arrived, although she hadn't ordered one, and when she looked up, a very broad man over at the bar was smiling at her and lifting his own bottle.

Not the kind of contact she was looking for, she reflected as he eased his bulk in her direction; but any port in a storm.

"You are Ethiopian?" he demanded, seating himself without quite being asked. His necktie was askew; his eyes were very wet. "Studying at the university, right? No? Kenyan? Dominican? Ghanaian? They say the women from Ghana are very beautiful, and you are very beautiful."

"American," she said.

"And you come here? Why?"

"I'm meeting someone."

"You have a boyfriend? A husband?"

She shook her head, frantic now. "No, no, I'm meeting a—a journalist."

"And you come alone? To this part of town?" A laugh, loud and oppressive. "Maybe you need a protector. Maybe I wait with you. What do you say?"

"I think I'll be fine. Thank you."

"Maybe we meet this journalist together. Come on. Drink your beer. Let me order some food. What do you want? Sausage? Ham?"

"I don't need anything."

"Listen." He bounded to his feet with improbable energy. "There's a better place a few blocks away. Real jazz. Western-style. Meet some intellectuals. I take you there, okay?"

"I'm fine here. Thank you."

"Come on. You meet some great people. Artists, writers."

He had a hand on her arm. She shook it off. "I'd rather stay and wait."

"Maybe your journalist friend will be there. Lots of Westerners."

"No, thank you." Coldly now. "Please, leave me alone."

He marched off angrily. Three drunks playing cards at the next table raised their glasses in salute. Margo nodded back uneasily, and the men resumed their game.

The waitress returned, and made a great show of wiping off the table, but never asked Margo what she wanted. Huffing in annoyance, the woman vanished again. Two minutes later, she showed up to wipe the table again. Margo realized that the rule was the same as in the hotel: you had to tip in advance if you wanted service. She pulled a bill from her pocket, and it must have been the right size, because the waitress picked it daintily from her palm and more or less smiled.

"Mineral water," Margo said.

Another man arrived at the table, sad-faced and cadaverous, and she was about to say something rude, but there was in his posture a hint of importance, and even before he sat, she knew this was her contact—the messenger from Smyslov—the truth about Operation Anadyr and whatever was happening in Cuba—the mission that had brought her to Varna, come to life at last.

He slid gracelessly into the seat across from her and drew up the lapels of his heavy coat as though expecting a storm. He took off his glasses and polished them on a cotton handkerchief. His eyes were red-rimmed and hunted.

"Who are you, please?" he asked.

"My name is Margo Jensen."

He glanced around the room. "I was expecting to interview Mr. Fischer. Is he here?"

"He stayed at the hotel."

"At the hotel?" The stranger's air of disappointment intensified. He folded his arms. The thin wrists were a pasty white. "He will not be joining us?"

"No."

"Did he receive the message?"

"Yes." She looked around, nervousness growing. "He had to study the adjourned position."

One of the drunks from the card game was looking their way, remarkably clear-eyed. The stranger sighed and thrust his hands into his pockets. He looked like a gambler in the movies, planning to shoot the man across the table. "Very well. You will come with me, please."

"Where are we going?"

"Please, miss."

Margo stared. And noticed that the bar had gone very quiet. The musicians had put down their instruments and, like the rest of the patrons, were busily averting their eyes. A couple of men and one of the women were standing very close, and looked not at all drunk.

"I don't understand. What about the interview?"

"The interview was with Mr. Fischer. He has chosen to stay at the hotel. This was wise of him."

"Why?"

"Because, unlike you, Mr. Fischer is not breaking the law." He drew his hands from his pockets, and he was not holding a gun after all, but only a wallet, which he flipped open to display a grimy photograph and several lines of Cyrillic, cheaply printed but imposing. "My name is Ignatiev. I am a colonel of the Second Head Directorate of the Darzhavna Sigurnost, tasked with protecting the security of the decent and peace-loving citizens of the Bulgarian People's Republic against foreign spies. You are under arrest, miss."

The room swayed. The DS. The Committee for State Security. Agatha had told her scary jokes about it. The colonel put a steadying hand on Margo's arm. She heard her voice, weakly, asking what she was charged with.

"All shall be explained."

"I—I want to call my consulate."

"One shall see. You will please come with us."

Her knees trembled. Her feet weren't working right. Suddenly the sweat was not just on her face but everywhere. She shook her head; felt his grip tighten.

"Please, miss, make no effort to resist, or we shall be forced to restrain you."

The drunk stood at her other side, and one of the women who had been tending the pots guarded the side entrance. Margo looked around for Agatha, but saw only the decent and peace-loving citizens of Bulgaria, frowning their disapproval of the imperialist spy. Ignatiev led her out. A low, dark car was waiting, the driver already behind the wheel. The colonel got in the front. They sat Margo in the back, where the woman and the other man squeezed to either side of her. The car roared off into the cobbled darkness.

ELEVEN

How News Travels

I

In Washington, D.C., it was early evening. Harrington was in her office, paging through a fresh set of CIA serial reports on the interrogations of various minor defectors from the Soviet Union and its satellites. She needed more collateral. Gwynn was right. And not only Gwynn.

"Are you sure you have control of this thing?" Lorenz Niemeyer had asked over drinks at the Mayflower the other night. He was in town for a seminar at Georgetown and had dropped in to see how she was doing. Pudgier than ever, he still projected the easy hauteur that had headwaiters mistaking him for royalty. "Because they're already talking about you in the past tense."

That was his way of being clever. There were times when she found it difficult to believe that she had once been married to the man.

But the powers that be had chosen their messenger well. Gwynn's screeching Harrington could ignore; Lorenz Niemeyer still knew people. If he felt he had to warn her that her star was falling, it could only mean that Langley and the White House felt the same way. That was why she was pressing so hard for answers. And during the past few days, Harrington had more than once been sure she had found what she was looking for: a hint in the testimony of a former East German military attaché; a discrepancy in the confession of a former Hungarian prison guard; a peculiar omission in one unimportant answer by a former Czech communications officer. But each time, when Harrington tried to press further, she met a blank wall. Though there were clues everywhere, she was unable to piece them together.

Harrington rubbed her eyes. Time for a break. She took herself off to the ladies' room, washed her face, marveled at the pale, haggard woman glaring savagely from the mirror. She remembered, vaguely, having once been young.

Her moment of weakness dispensed with, she returned to her desk, and her research. She had just opened a fresh serial—the deposition of the estranged wife of a deputy commissar in Polish counterintelligence—when Borkland knocked and stepped in without waiting to be invited.

Harrington shut the folder with a snap and looked up . . . expectantly.

"A report, finally? It's been hours since GREENHILL left the resort."

"I'm sorry, ma'am. We have word from the Agency that GREENHILL has been arrested."

Harrington digested this. "Are they sure?"

"They have it from the West Germans, who have an asset in the DS."

Another beat. "And her minder?"

"Disappeared. She hasn't checked in. Presumed arrested as well."

She nodded. "Very well. Keep me informed."

"Shouldn't we—"

"I believe you saw the same memorandum I did, Bill." Her tone was bitter. "If GREENHILL is caught, we do nothing. Absolutely nothing." She read the reproach in his expression. She softened. "Don't worry. I'll make some calls."

II

And she did. She called Gwynn. She called Gwynn's boss. She called Gwynn's boss's boss. She called her friends at Langley. She called the office of the President's national security adviser.

Nobody took her calls. Nobody returned them.

Niemeyer was right. Her star was falling indeed, and it was Margo Jensen who would suffer as a result.

Harrington moved to the window. Washington was enduring one of its misty gray drizzles, the sort where your umbrella is useless because the rain doesn't so much fall as materialize. She lifted a hand to the heavy curtain, a war relic, as if to tug it closed, but hesitated. The gesture evoked a memory. The same wet fog had blanketed Vienna the night Carina disappeared. Carina was an agent Harrington had run during the war, a young Jewish woman who could pass for Aryan, and on the night in question, Harrington had waited in the wet, drafty safe house for hours past the appointed time. Carina never showed. She was never seen or heard from again, but it was easy to guess her fate.

Margo reminded her of Carina, not in appearance but in manner: the same swift intelligence, the same determination not to be bested by her fears. The difference was that Carina had a personal stake in her war. As for Margo, Harrington had played to her ambition and her vanity, to say nothing of her simple curiosity, and, as always, had played well. Yet she felt a punishing guilt that had never plagued her during the war, when she sent children much younger than Margo into battle.

TWELVE

Unsung

I

Margo wasn't sure what she had expected. A dank basement lined with shackles. Truncheons. Bright lights in her face. Even being marched to the parapets lining the roof: *Tell us your mission, or we throw you off!* Instead, she sat in a steamy office, the windows tightly shut. They had driven her to what Agatha called, half jokingly, the Forbidden City: a compound of broad, squat buildings on the outskirts of Varna, guarded by grim men in greatcoats. She was pretty sure she was on the first floor. The windows gave on a floodlit inner court where motorcycles and black ZIL automobiles were lined up as if waiting for the parade. For an hour or more they had left her alone with her fears, but her solitude was past. A blue-clad female guard stood near the door, at parade rest. She was not wearing a sidearm, but the deadness in her gaze said she could break Margo in half without a twinge of regret. The chair had a bad leg and wobbled every time Margo tried to get comfortable. The table was plain wood, and on the other side, the same colonel who had presided over her arrest offered foul cigarettes and a grape-flavored *rakia*, known locally as *grozdova*—"to calm your nerves, miss"—but she accepted only mineral water. She was frightened, certainly, but the fear seemed to sharpen her perceptions, and her mind was alert. She had talked her way out of trouble all her life, and was not about to turn teary and girlish.

"You are Fischer's girlfriend?"

"No."

"His wife?"

"No."

"His mistress?"

"*No.*"

"Then why do you keep going up to his room like a whore?"

There was no malice in his tone. He was scarcely looking at her, and never once raised his voice. Mostly, he wrote in a small notebook made with cheap paper and cardboard covers. The cigarettes smelled very bad in the airless room.

"We're friends," she finally said.

"You have known him long?"

"A year or so."

"What are his views about the socialist countries?"

Relief flooded her. It was Bobby who was under investigation, not she. And although she had been raised never to take pleasure in another's misfortune, she found herself gaining strength from the realization that she might not be in trouble after all.

"We don't discuss politics," she said. "All he talks about is chess."

"And money, naturally. He is a capitalist. All capitalists are greedy, are they not?"

"I wouldn't know."

"Because you are the descendant of enslaved Africans. You have no access to capital. Naturally, your people are forced to become the dregs of the West."

There was considerable truth in this observation, Margo admitted to herself, but she thought also of the old Negro families she knew, some of them with millions in the bank: the sort of family Nana expected her granddaughter to marry into. Few Americans, black or white, were aware of their existence. There was no reason to expect an officer of the Bulgarian secret police to know any better.

"Naturally," she said.

She wondered whether she sounded sarcastic, but the colonel seemed pleased by her agreement. "Are you comfortable? Do you need anything?"

"To contact the American consulate."

"We shall see."

A few more desultory questions, and then, without a word, the colonel closed the notebook and left. Margo was alone with the female guard, who had spoken not a word. The woman's hair was drawn severely back, much like Agatha's.

"How long do I have to stay here?" Margo asked.

The guard stared at a spot several feet above her prisoner's head.

"What's your name?" she tried. "I'm Margo Jensen."

No answer.

"Do you speak English?"

Nothing. The woman was so still, she might have been a waxwork, and being alone with her was like a child's nightmare.

Margo turned toward the window. She sipped. The mineral water was warm and tasted metallic. Her hands were trembling again, and she wondered whether she should have accepted a little *grozdova* after all.

To calm her nerves.

She shut her eyes and listed fifteen reasons why she should have listened to Tom. She would be in Ithaca right now, just another student hoping to attend a decent law school. She wondered where Agatha was, and why she hadn't ridden to the rescue. She wondered if they were going to send her to prison, and hoped Nana wouldn't take it too hard.

Suddenly the shivering was more than she could take. Her eyes blurred, and she wiped at them with her soiled sleeves. The guard looked on with the studied impassivity of someone who had seen it a hundred times. The green walls, badly plastered and badly painted, seemed to draw closer. The chips in the paint might have been fingernail marks, from the desperate scrabbling of some earlier prisoner. Margo knew that was insane, but all at once her brain wasn't going where it was told. They were never going to let her out of this room.

"Is it okay if I stand up?" she asked, voice shaking. "I have to stretch my legs."

Hearing no answer, she pushed the chair back and began to rise. The guard snarled at her in Bulgarian and made a furious gesture.

Margo dropped back into her seat.

The minutes ticked past. The heat was making her drowsy. She felt her eyelids droop and forced herself to sit straighter. She dozed anyway, and when she opened her eyes again, a different, younger man stood across the desk, arms folded as he studied her dispassionately.

Margo managed a glare.

"I demand to contact the consulate," she said.

The man said something to the guard, who marched out. Then the stranger stood across the desk from her, arms folded.

"No," he said, after a moment.

"I have the right—"

"Let me explain how this works, Miss Jensen. This is not America. You don't have any rights. If I decide our conversation isn't going the way I like, you might just cease to exist."

"You—you can't just—"

"My name is Fomin. I am a colonel in the Soviet intelligence apparatus. I have come a considerable distance to meet you, Miss Jensen. So let's not waste time."

II

Margo had thought she was frightened before, but Colonel Fomin's idiomatic English came as a terrifying surprise. She was in the hands of the expert now.

"You are a student of Niemeyer," he announced, still not seated. In his expensive tweed suit, he would have looked right at home on the Cornell campus. "Then, all at once, you leave campus and come here. That means you're probably a spy."

"That's not true." Panic. Deny, deny, deny.

"Then why are you here?"

"I came for the Olympiad. To watch the chess—"

Fomin finally sat. He leaned his chin on his large hand, a pose that twisted his mouth into something small and cruel. "What are your orders from American Intelligence?"

Down beneath the table, Margo was pinching the same fold of skin that had kept her calm during her interview with Borkland and Stilwell, but the trick wasn't working, for her voice was rising in pitch, and she could not seem to stop its trembling. "I don't have any orders. I don't know anything."

"You are here as part of an American intelligence operation to determine what my government is offloading in Cuba. There is no point in denying this fact." He had a brown folder under his arm. He laid it unopened on the table. "Margo Jensen. That's your name."

"Yes."

"You are from a family of spies, then." Her evident bewilderment amused him. "Please, Miss Jensen. There is no need for games. The American services are known to recruit family members of their officers. They have obviously done so in your case."

She was shaking her head. "I don't have any idea what you're talking about."

He flipped open the folder. Margo glanced down. The first few pages were in Cyrillic script. Fomin shoved them aside, withdrew a typewritten document in what looked like German.

"You are a student of Niemeyer," he repeated. "He was a spy in the war."

"He's not family!"

"No, he is not. However, according to the records of the Gestapo, he ran a *réseau*. Do you know this word? *Réseau*? You are studying French, are you not?"

Margo shook her head. She was only a B student in French, and in the panic of the moment the language seemed a meaningless jumble.

"Then I shall tell you," said Fomin, like an impatient tutor. He stabbed out the cigarette. "In the war, *réseau* was used as a synonym for a network of spies. Niemeyer was part of what became known as Operation Jedburgh. He ran a *réseau* across occupied France and even into Germany. Some intelligence gathering, but mainly sabotage. Very dangerous work, Miss Jensen. Over time, the Gestapo captured several members of this *réseau*. Naturally, they talked. They implicated not only Niemeyer but also a French-Algerian engineer, a black African called Rouane. He was possibly the best bomb-maker in the Resistance. He built portable but very powerful devices that killed many German soldiers." Fomin pulled something else from the folder—a photograph, which he kept facedown. But already she feared what it showed more than anything this man might do to her. "The Gestapo set a trap for this Rouane. He escaped, but a colleague of his, high in the French Resistance, was captured. Under intense interrogation, this man admitted that Rouane was actually an American agent."

He flipped the photograph over.

The image was yellowed and creased, as if copied many times. A man was lying on the muddy ground, a German soldier standing above him. The man on the ground was Margo's father. A bloody mess, but undeniably her father.

"He was cornered a week later, outside a farmhouse near Nancy. He blew himself up with a grenade to avoid capture and interrogation."

III

The hissing of the radiator seemed louder than ever, or perhaps it was her hearing that was off. Margo's clothes were sticky with sweat. She wondered whether she could pinch herself and wake from the nightmare, but when it didn't work, she picked up the photograph instead. Fomin made no effort to stop her. Her emotions warred with each other—anger versus pride, fear against joy—but beyond the turmoil, her rational faculty was less surprised than she would have imagined. Furious, yes; surprised, no. She twisted the photograph this way and that, matching the features to the snapshot in the top drawer of her dresser at Cornell. Well, yes. Maybe the chin a trifle more pointed? The hair a little thicker? And that ragged beard: where had that come from? But undeniably Donald Jensen. So this was it. The big secret nobody dared discuss. Daddy was a war hero. A spy who'd risked greatly to battle the Nazis, then blown himself to bits to protect other people. Well, of course, that was the kind of thing Nana would hide, she told herself bitterly: who'd want to burden a child with such knowledge? Let a daughter think well of her father? Heaven forbid!

And Niemeyer, with his teasing. He knew her father, but wouldn't say where. Then there was the hypothetical in class, the man who walks into a bank, threatening to blow himself up . . . with a hand grenade. It was as though he'd been testing, to discover how much Margo knew about her father's death. But just to come out and tell her directly—well, no, that wasn't the great man's style.

Fomin seemed to read her thoughts. "They never told you," he said, not unkindly. "Perhaps your grandmother herself does not know the entire truth. Perhaps Niemeyer was not sure that you are ready to hear. However, it is my understanding that you have lately been inquiring about his fate." He slipped the photograph gently from her grasp, returned it to the folder. "These are from the archives of the Gestapo, captured by the Red Army when Berlin fell. They are accurate."

Margo felt an absurd burst of gratitude, exactly what the Soviet no doubt intended. She was furious at those who had deceived her, and was certain he was counting on that, too. She needed a moment to quiet the hot whirl of emotion. "Why are you telling me this?" she finally managed.

"As I said, Miss Jensen, the Americans like to recruit from the families of their spies. Perhaps they believe that loyalty and perseverance are transmitted from generation to generation through our genes."

She hesitated. The hot worm of terror was still squirming, but somehow had been shoved back, back, back, as the pride had clawed its way to the surface. She didn't have the whole story yet—she suspected she never would—but one thing she was sure of was that Colonel Fomin hadn't told her about her father out of altruism. He *expected* her to feel betrayed by those she had trusted. He *expected* her fury at Professor Niemeyer. He *expected* her to confess everything.

Instead, he had given her reason not to.

"I don't know if I should believe you," she said.

Fomin was unimpressed. "You believe me, Miss Jensen. You need to believe me. You cannot bear to think that your father, so brilliant and accomplished, was an unimportant transport corporal who died when his truck crashed in North Africa."

"I can bear it if it's true."

"Come, Miss Jensen. You're not a child. Which of us truly longs for truth? We all of us live for the lies that make life bearable. Joyful, if we are lucky. Given the choice between two stories about your father, do you really wish to reject the one in which he is an unsung hero of the war?" He put the folder aside, took up another. "I, too, performed tasks of a clandestine nature in the war against fascist aggression. I therefore respect your father and his sacrifice. He was a great hero. You should be proud to follow in his footsteps." He turned a page. "You see now why I am interested in you. And why Niemeyer is interested. By the way, why did he take you to his office after class the week you left? Was it so that you could receive your instructions for this mission?"

Startled by the swift change of subject, Margo almost blurted what her captor wanted to hear. But in her mind's eye, her father was pulling the pin on a hand grenade and holding it to his chest, sacrificing himself to protect the members of his *réseau*.

"I don't know what you're talking about," she said. Although her voice was not as cool as she was hoping, she was relieved at how little it trembled. "I want to contact my consulate."

"After we discuss your mission. Your father would have been proud of you for undertaking this mission. Surely you see that."

Margo shook her head slowly, not sure what to say.

Fomin was growing impatient. "There is no point in lying further, Miss Jensen. It is perfectly plain that you are here as part of a conspiracy of the West against the socialist peoples of the world. You are here as part of an operation code-named QKPARCHMENT. Correct?"

This time her bewilderment was genuine. "I don't know what that is."

"Come, Miss Jensen. Let us be honest with one another. Your President believes his own side's propaganda that the Chairman has been forced to place offensive missiles in Cuba. This of course is capitalist fantasy, but your security apparatus will pretend to believe it in any case. You are here in Bulgaria to make contact with reactionary and revanchist elements for the purpose of provocation. You are a spy, and the Bulgarian People's Republic punishes spies severely."

"What is it you want me to say?" she asked when he paused for breath.

The dark eyes were unforgiving. "I want you to tell me the truth. I want you to describe your mission."

From somewhere she found a bit of sass, for she had started to think of Fomin the way she thought of her professors. "Which of us truly longs for truth?"

The Russian pursed heavy lips. "You seem unaware of how serious a crisis we face, Miss Jensen. Whatever we have done, we have done because we believe that your regime may be planning a surprise attack against the socialist countries. Naturally, we would be required to respond. Is it your wish to contribute to the horror that is sure to follow?"

Margo shook her head. She wasn't sure what to say, because she wasn't sure what her father would have said. She wanted to see the photograph again.

Fomin was pawing through his folder. "I have a copy of your application for the grant that has paid for your travel. Our experts tell me that this is not your handwriting."

"That's ridiculous."

"But going out by yourself in the middle of the night to meet a stranger in the roughest part of town—that isn't ridiculous?"

"I was trying to arrange an interview for Bobby. I don't know anything about the rest of what you—"

Fomin stood, very fast, and leaned over the table, mouth twisted, eyes blazing. He grabbed the front of her coat. Tugging at his wrist was like tugging steel. His face was so close she could feel the angry heat.

"You are not your father, Miss Jensen. You are not trained. You do not have his responsibilities, and this is not his war. Your father was fighting against the fascist aggressor. But it is your side that is the aggressor today. There is no reason for you to put yourself through any suffering for the sake of the capitalist gangsters who run your country." He let her go. Brushed his fingers on his tweeds. "You are nineteen years old, are you not?"

"Yes," she said, shakily.

"Your father briefed saboteurs your age during the war. He sent them out to blow up bridges and sabotage tanks. Some were younger. One was a girl of fifteen. Many were captured. The Gestapo were not kind. In time of war, youth is no protection against the rigors of interrogation."

"I'm not scared of you," she lied, determined to make her father proud.

"Yes, you are." Fomin made a show of patting his pockets, then drew from inside his coat a small pair of pliers. "In medieval times, under the ruthless hegemony of the bourgeois Western church, the prisoner sentenced to the Inquisition was first subjected to a ritual known as displaying the instruments. This was to give him the opportunity to repent." He dropped the tool on the desk. The clank was very loud. Margo couldn't pull her eyes away. "I will give you one hour to consider whether you wish to tell me the truth, or prefer to suffer the consequences."

He left.

THIRTEEN

Like Father . . .

I

Alone in the stifling room, Margo thought not of Cuba or of the grim possibilities of war outlined by Dr. Harrington, but only of her father. The fate she faced was the fate he had killed himself to avoid. True, no hand grenade was available. But it was just as well: she didn't want to end things the way her father had.

She wished Fomin had left the photograph. Cradling it close, or even gazing at her father's face, would give her strength. She was sure of it. She wanted to hold out. She didn't want to suffer, but she didn't want to talk. Not to protect the mission or even, as Harrington put it, the "security of the nation." Margo wanted to resist because she knew Donald Jensen would have resisted.

True, the situation seemed hopeless. She was a prisoner of the DS. She had, as Fomin had told her, no rights. They believed she was a spy and were determined to have the truth. And she was pretty sure she would have to end up telling them whatever they wanted.

Except for one thing.

The pliers were still on the desk.

The instruments, as Fomin called them, displayed for her to see. She wondered how it would feel if he tugged out a fingernail. Two fingernails. She tried to imagine the hot, shining pain. She shuddered, but briefly. Because, for all that she might wonder how badly the pliers could injure her, the really important question was whether they could pry open locked windows.

II

She stood by the window, hands clasped innocently behind her back, the pliers still lying where Fomin had dropped them, in case this was all a trick. Margo was not particularly mechanical, but she loved solving puzzles, and this was just another.

In addition to the usual swivel clasp, the window was secured by a metal hasp with a padlock threaded through it. She had no hope of breaking the lock itself. The hasp, however, was attached with screws. Though she had no screwdriver, she thought the pliers might be used as a lever to pry the hasp free, screws and all. The trick was getting some piece of the pliers underneath the edge—

Sound in the hallway.

She threw herself back into the chair, but the footsteps passed by.

Margo waited, then returned to the window, still studying, still not touching. She had left the pliers precisely where Fomin had dropped them, on the theory that if he caught her by the window she could say she was only looking out as she tried to make up her mind.

He'd said she had an hour, but she had no reason to trust him.

On the other hand, if she got caught, he could hardly threaten her with anything worse than what already loomed.

Donald Jensen wouldn't have hesitated; neither would his daughter.

So she snatched up the pliers and went to work.

III

The pliers were of the needle-nosed variety, and she tried to slip one of the metal points between the hasp and the frame. The fit was very tight. She kept wiggling and twisting the pliers, but could not budge the metal. The pliers slipped and pinched her finger. She cried out, then covered her mouth and stopped to listen; nobody seemed to be approaching. She wiped the sweat from her brow and started again.

This time, the point sank into the wood—not far, but enough to give her a space in which to try to lever. The point sank deeper. Beneath the badly painted surface, the wood was soft. She kept working. The hasp never budged, but the pliers kept sinking. Soon they sank too far. She tried to tug the tool out to keep levering, but now the point was stuck in the window.

Problem.

Not only could she not remove the hasp this way, but when Fomin returned, the pliers would be jammed into the window, and he would know she had tried to escape.

Panic.

No. Not allowed.

Margo took a breath. Okay. She was still Claudia Jensen's granddaughter and Donald Jensen's daughter. There was a solution, and she would find it. The pliers were stuck because the surface of the wood was hard and the interior was soft. Why was the interior soft? It had to be rotten. When trees rotted from the inside out, her grandmother liked to point out, they would come crashing down at unexpected moments, no matter how sturdy the exterior.

Okay.

On a table in a corner was a heavy book. The cover and contents were entirely in Cyrillic, but she wasn't going to read it. She carried it to the window. If the pliers would not come out, she would press-hammer them farther in. When they were in deeply enough, she would start to jimmy them back and forth, hoping to dislodge the hasp that way. She swung the book hard, like a mallet, and struck the pliers.

The tool barely budged.

A second hit, harder, made her arm sing with pain.

She swung a third time, and, to her astonishment, the entire window burst free of the frame, wood and glass blasting outward into the courtyard.

This time, the noise had to have been heard.

She put her hands on the sill and climbed out onto the cobbles. She felt her dress catch and knew she'd ripped it, felt her leg scrape and knew she had cut herself, but she was out of that terrible room and in the courtyard.

IV

Margo ran. She had no choice. They would be in the room in seconds.

The courtyard, as she had already observed, was full of cars and trucks and motorcycles. The building made a U-shape around three sides. She ran for the high wall separating the compound from the street. She had no hope of getting over, but the interior floodlights picked out a heavy double gate for the vehicles, flanked on either side by a pair of pedestrian entrances, both shut. Margo suspected that they would be locked on the street side but not necessarily on the inside.

In any case, Margo had to move. The rising bevy of angry voices behind her, and the searchlight beaming down from the tower, told her that her pursuers were close behind.

She pelted across the courtyard, hugging the shadows, dodging the parked cars and the crisscrossing beams, ignoring the pain from her wounded leg, attention riveted on the nearer pedestrian door. The cobbles were wet and slippery. She supposed it must have rained earlier but she couldn't remember just when. She heard a shout in the far corner of the courtyard. Two guards were running in the wrong direction.

Margo slowed. As children, she and her brother Corbin had been unbeatable at capture-the-flag. The reason was what Edgar Allan Poe called "evens and odds"—the ability to work out how clever their opponents were, and act just one level beyond it.

She reached the door, which was of heavy wood. A metal bar stretched across the surface, resting in a slot, making access from outside impossible. The bar wasn't locked in place, however, and Margo had no trouble lifting it. She put her shoulder into the door, budging it open, then took off the other way, back toward the shadows. She had spied an entrance to another part of the building, and that was her goal. Evens and odds. They would try to outthink her, so she had to outthink their outthinking. They knew she was in the courtyard. They would expect her to try for the gate, and guards would no doubt be posted on the other side. Indeed, no sooner had she slunk off into the shadows than the searchlights converged on the exits leading to the street.

The entrance she had spotted led into a kitchen. The scent of heavily cured meat was in the air. Two men in undershirts were smoking and arguing while one of them poured offal into a pot. Both were heavily muscled. One was older, and bearded. They looked up in surprise at the intruder. They didn't seem frightened, just confused.

The bearded man asked a question in Bulgarian, then in German. Margo said nothing. The men laughed. She sidestepped toward the hallway beyond the kitchen. The cooks looked at each other; then the younger moved into her path and put his hands on his hips. He stuck out his hand, palm upward.

She realized he wanted to see her pass. It occurred to her that he didn't know she was a prisoner. Agatha had said that some African revolutionaries were trained in Bulgaria; they must think she was one of them.

So she smiled and shook her head, spreading her own hands wide, explaining in her passable French that she was in a hurry, late for a meeting, and hoped that either from some rudimentary understanding of the language, or from her smile and her posture, they would accept that she belonged. The older one said something that made the younger laugh lasciviously, and pointed not down the hallway but to a different door.

Margo gave him a look that she hoped would convey irritated disdain, then slipped through the doorway to which she had been directed. The room was small and airless. A woman in uniform sat at a desk. She barely looked up before nodding Margo toward a curtained arch, cluck-clucking to herself as the younger woman passed.

Beyond the arch was a sort of dressing room with bunks included, and there Margo found six or seven women fixing their makeup and adjusting their clothing. They looked dressed for a party. They fixed furious appraising eyes on the newcomer. One of them pointed to Margo's disheveled clothing and made a comment that was plainly derisive. The others chuckled, then went back to their preening.

An hour or more passed. The women continued to ignore her. Eventually, a flabby man wearing a uniform stepped in, and the women leapt to their feet, Margo alongside. His froggy eyes lingered curiously on Margo before he pointed to another woman, a very tall redhead, who smoothed her gown and preceded him out the door. He pointed to another woman, who nodded and sat.

The other women shook their heads, picked up their purses, pulled on their coats, lit cigarettes.

Margo understood. The man had picked two, and the rest could leave.

She had no handbag, but she was still wearing her coat, and when the women filed out, she followed. A female guard materialized, led them down a concrete stairway and down a dank basement hallway with dripping water pipes along the ceiling. They went up another stair, at the top of which the guard unlocked a steel door and swung it wide.

The street.

Freedom.

A couple of women headed for the tram stop; the others walked off down the street, perhaps to ply their trade elsewhere. Nobody paid Margo any attention. She studied the neighborhood, trying to get her bearings. She dared not ask directions or take a taxi. Across from the DS headquarters was a park, and beyond the park were low buildings she did not recognize. Above the rooflines, she saw the distant, misty domes of the Dormition of the Theotokos Cathedral, which she had visited last week. If she could get there, she was fairly certain that she could find her hotel.

Except she didn't want the hotel.

If the ploy goes to pieces, Niemeyer had warned her, *you don't go back to your hotel. You march straight into the American consulate, nowhere else. Ask for a counselor named Ainsley. Mr. Ainsley is an associate of mine, and he'll take care of you.*

Right. Good plan. Margo would march straight into the consulate, and find this Ainsley. It was important that she not be caught—not only because she might face prison or worse, but because she was her father's daughter and she had a mission to complete.

She knew precisely what was going on in Cuba. Colonel Fomin had told her.

She started off down the street.

FOURTEEN

Officers

I

She hurried along the wide boulevard named for Georgi Dimitrov, the revered Bulgarian Stalinist arrested by the Nazis for supposed complicity in the Reichstag fire, although the locals still called the street Maria Luiza, after the wife of the late beloved Tsar Ferdinand I. The sky was heavy with pre-dawn grayness. She realized that she had spent most of the night in custody. Traffic was light. There were few pedestrians at this hour. Margo kept the hood of her raincoat up and her head down, in the hope that the night would disguise her blackness—a clue that would otherwise lead the DS to her in minutes. The cold, freshening rain helped. Nobody was making eye contact. Everyone was hurrying, umbrellas or newspapers over their heads.

She walked fast, but not too fast, keeping the cathedral's golden belfry ahead and to her right. She guessed the distance at about half a mile. From what she remembered, the consulate would be three blocks farther on. She had no idea whether it was staffed at this hour, but she had no other plan.

She wondered, in a vague way, why Agatha, the minder who scared well-trained intelligence officers, had left her to her fate rather than riding to her rescue. She wondered, too, whether Fomin realized how much he had told her by the questions he asked. Most of all, she wondered whether her father, if he knew, would be proud—

The sound of whispered conversation ahead made her lift her eyes.

Two policemen in dark ponchos were headed her way. Margo didn't break stride, but felt their hard gazes lift to her as they passed.

Caught, she told herself; they could hardly have overlooked her color.

But the policemen kept walking. They weren't particularly watchful. Routine, she told herself. They were just patrolling the street, and happened to be on the same sidewalk as she.

She passed a shuttered restaurant and a state commissary, crossed a pretty prewar bridge with an unpronounceable name, and there was the cathedral, diagonally across a well-tended park. As she entered the trees, someone whispered insinuatingly from the shadows, and she walked faster. She heard a footstep ahead of her and took a fork on the path. The trees closed up, and she could no longer see the cathedral: because of the rain there was no moon. Now, the same voice came from off to her right, the sort of nasty male challenge—half querulous, half threatening—that she needed no translation to understand.

She glanced over.

A drunk was pacing her, perhaps ten feet to the left, stumbling angrily through the trees. He was heavyset, and although beyond that Margo could see no details in the darkness, she could hear his angry growl.

When he called to her again, she broke into a near run. The drunk grunted in surprise, then took off after her.

The night had moved from tragedy to farce. Her arrest, her escape, and now being chased by a drunk. Full of hysterical energy, she found herself laughing. Then she burst from the trees, and was safe at last, finally on the grassland across from the cathedral. Through the misty air, the domes sparkled soft gold. She hurried forward, and the drunk brought her down in a tackle.

Margo cried out and kicked, then swung a hand as he tried to pin her. Either her aim was lucky or he was too drunk to react, but she made sharp, satisfying contact with his nose and saw blood spurt. She kicked again, struggled to her feet, and turned to run, only to find herself grabbed by one of the police officers she had passed just minutes before.

He spoke to her sharply, asking a question. His partner had the drunk cuffed.

"I'm sorry," she said, carefully. "I don't speak your language." She stood straighter. "Thank you for helping me."

The officer frowned. "Passport," he said, beckoning with his fingers.

Margo hesitated. She could hardly tell him that it was in her handbag back at the DS headquarters.

"I lost it," she said. "I'm an American. A tourist."

The policemen had a quick, sharp conversation. One of them took her arm. "You will come," he said.

She shook his hand off. "I lost my passport. I'm going to the consulate to get a new one." She pointed down the road past the cathedral. She had no idea how much time she had before there was an alarm throughout the city. "Please. It's just half a mile away."

He grabbed her again, more tightly. "You will come," he repeated, and it was evident that this was the extent of his English.

Then he let her go and snapped off an awkward salute. She followed his gaze and saw Colonel Fomin striding down the path. The trio held a swift conversation, after which the policemen left with the drunk, and Margo was alone with the Soviet intelligence officer.

II

"This was not the safest route," he said. His hands were in the pockets of his raincoat, and he looked terribly unhappy. "I assumed you would have stayed on the main thoroughfare."

She was busily catching her breath. "You were following me the whole time?"

"No. Your escape plan was clever. Your father would have been proud. That fool of a guard has admitted letting you leave with the other women, and I have no doubt that the Bulgarian savages will be punishing her severely. You have also done us a service. Ignatiev has suspected for some while that some of the senior officers are smuggling women into the building. Until tonight, he had no evidence. Now he does."

Margo managed to stand straight. "How did you find me?"

"The policemen. You will recall that they passed you earlier, on the street. When they returned to their radio car, they heard the bulletin.

We figured out where you were heading and asked them to detain you."

She felt scratchy, and angry, and ready to sleep for a thousand years.

"What happens now? Are we going back?"

"No. I have conferred with my superiors. Their judgment is that you should be released for lack of evidence, in order to avoid a diplomatic incident." He smiled wanly. "I myself do not concur in this judgment. I still believe that you are a spy, that you want to know about what is going on in Cuba, and that you have been sent here by Niemeyer. Your escape, I believe, is evidence for my view. But it will not sway my superiors. You violated Bulgarian law by leaving custody, and you did damage to public property. I am advised, however, that you will not be charged. There is consequently no reason to take you back into custody."

"You mean I'm free to go?"

"The People's Republic has revoked your entry visa. You must leave the country within twenty-four hours."

The unexpected reprieve left her relieved and heartsick at once; and puzzled. "I don't understand."

"You should not question your good fortune." He seemed to expect her to write this down. "You will need this."

He handed over her handbag. She checked. The passport was inside.

"My cash is missing."

"Perhaps you would like to remain in the country and file a complaint? No?" He nodded toward the cathedral. "I assume your destination is the consulate. You should ask them to put you on the earliest possible flight. Between now and the time of your departure, I shall endeavor to change the minds of my superiors and have you rearrested."

The rain had stopped, but the sky was still cloudy and moonless. Water dripped from leaves. Voices murmured just out of sight; she didn't know whether they were Fomin's people or someone else's.

"Thank you for . . . for just now," she said.

"Do not thank me too soon, Miss Jensen. The drunk was a hooligan, of the sort more common in the capitalist West than in the socialist countries. He will be treated according to the process of law. You, too, could have been arrested. I almost chose not to intervene. I do not consider spies entitled to the protection of the law. And now I would suggest that you go at once to your consulate, to avoid any further difficulty." He nodded toward a gap in the hedges. "That way. Don't worry. You will be perfectly safe, as long as you remain on the path."

"But—"

"Go, Miss Jensen. Now."

She went.

III

There was hardly any traffic. Half a mile to the consulate. As she crossed the road, she noticed a shiny blue Ford parked in front of the cathedral, the motor idling. A man bounded out, lithe as a dancer despite his broad shoulders, boyish blond hair flopping about. Margo jumped back. She could not be rearrested, not so near her goal.

The stranger intercepted her, a bright smile on his youthful face. "Oh, wonderful!" he cried, as he might to a long-lost friend. "There you are. So good to see you." A whisper: "Relax, you're fine now." Margo had not realized how hard she was trembling. He had an arm around her, moving her to the passenger side of the Ford. "I'm Ainsley. I'm with the consulate."

Despite her flooding relief, she had the presence of mind to push free of him and ask for identification.

He pulled out his wallet, showed her. "Would you like to ask me who won the World Series?" he asked, teeth gleaming. "It's not over yet, but the Yankees just won Game Five. Tom Tresh hit a three-run homer in the eighth inning. Okay?" He was leading her to the car. "Let's get you out of here."

"They said I have to leave the country," she mumbled.

"That's for later. All taken care of. Eleven a.m. flight to Vienna. Right now I'd guess you need some sleep."

"How did you know where to find me?"

His smile was as brilliant as a politician's. "A couple of us have been out looking for you. We heard you'd escaped. That's rather impressive."

"I think they let me go on purpose. It was too easy."

"Wanting to avoid a diplomatic incident? You could be right. Fischer is a big deal, and there's no reason to risk his wrath."

"Fomin said—"

His hand shot out, arresting her words. "Time for that later. You rest."

"I need to call my grandmother." The car moved off. The sad morning sun was a smeary gray, as if dawn had been forbidden. "I need to call Tom."

"You can call from the consulate, but remember, it's the middle of the night back home. We're seven hours ahead."

"I want to go back to the hotel."

"Out of the question," he said with an apologetic smile. His peculiar eyes flashed gold in the morning sun. "We sent someone for your things, but the DS has been through the room, and it was rather a mess."

For some reason, this violation seemed worse even than her treatment last night, and for a mad moment she found herself looking around for someone to hit. Ainsley drove smoothly, one hand on the wheel, the other gesturing as he laid out the rules.

"You can't talk to anybody about what happened. Not until your debriefing. You won't get a chance to say goodbye to Fischer or anybody else. They don't know you were arrested. Nobody knows but us, and we'd like to keep it that way."

"I'd prefer it."

"That includes your grandmother and your boyfriend."

Margo nodded stiffly, having half expected this command. She leaned against the seat and watched the city hurry by: the towers of fourteenth-century palaces mixed with the blocky practicality of socialist architecture. A tram buzzed past. A lone driver struggled over the cobbles, and Margo wondered automatically whose side he was on. She felt as though she had been in Varna a very long time.

"Where's Agatha?" she said suddenly.

"Who?"

"From the State Department. My"—she almost said "minder," then remembered about rooms and cars—"roommate. She's traveling with me."

"Oh, right. Right. Miss Milner." A shrug of the broad shoulders. "I don't know where she is. My understanding is that she's already left the country." A pause, as if he was weighing how much to tell. "I would suspect she's lying in a hospital somewhere. Germany, most likely." He didn't wait for Margo to ask. "She was mugged last night. The police found her unconscious in the street. I'm afraid they beat her up pretty badly."

IV

A few hours later, accompanied by Ainsley, Margo flew to Vienna. Actually, he had barely left her side all morning. His principal goal seemed to be keeping her away from the rest of the diplomatic personnel. Ainsley warned her at the start, via a handwritten note, that conversation inside the building was not secure, and signs on seemingly every wall reminded her again. She had expected a debriefing, or at least a question or two about her experiences in custody, but every time she tried to bring it up, Ainsley changed the subject. In Vienna, he saw her onto the late-afternoon flight to Paris. She sat beside an elegant Frenchman who smoked constantly and invited her to spend the weekend at his château, a man so voluble that she suspected that he, too, was there to keep an eye on her—or, more precisely, an ear. That flight was met by another American functionary, a young woman named Paula, who reminded her in manner but not appearance of the vanished Agatha. Paula kept Margo company in the transit lounge, smoking one cigarette after another while chatting garrulously about the coming referendum on whether the French President should be elected directly by the people rather than in an electoral college, and in this way managed not only to keep Margo from mentioning her experiences in Bulgaria but also to bore potential listeners to tears. Paula got her early to the gate and made sure she boarded the connection to Idlewild Airport in Queens.

Margo slept the whole way.

In New York, she stood in the passport line with everybody else until a plainclothes immigration officer flashed a badge and asked her to follow him. Under the curious stares of the crowd, they passed through a door marked NO ACCESS, down a dingy hallway, and into a private office.

"You did ever so splendidly, dear," cooed a familiar voice, as Harrington rose from the other side of the desk. "Goodness, but you've had a time," she continued, putting her hands on Margo's shoulders as if to brush her off. "Let's have a good look at you, dear, shall we?"

But Margo was in her arms, as the tears she had held in check for a day and a half finally poured out of her.

"That's all right, dear," Harrington murmured, patting her neck. "Everybody cries the first time."

PART II

Evens and Odds

October 6, 1962–October 20, 1962
Ithaca, New York | Washington, D.C.

FIFTEEN

The Larger Story

I

Margo spent the night with yet another female minder at a high-ceilinged apartment on Central Park West in the Sixties, and in the morning, beneath the gleaming dining-room chandelier, she was debriefed by a pair of hard-faced men she had never met before, neither of whom offered a name. They provided her with two days of newspapers to assure her that the American public knew nothing of her arrest. Reading the headlines, Margo learned that Bobby Fischer had ruined his adjournment analysis, and, from a superior position, allowed Botvinnik to slip away with a draw—a fact that seemed scarcely relevant at the time, but would turn out later to matter a great deal. Then the questions, fast and direct, although they wrote her answers into their notebooks with agonizing slowness while the minder lurked in the shadows like a bad conscience.

Margo spent a day and a half with them, all her needs provided for, but none of her many questions answered. Such as: Who told Bobby to invite her? Such as: How was Agatha? *Where* was Agatha? Such as: How did Fomin learn so much about Margo herself so fast? Such as: Didn't it seem to them that she escaped from the DS a little too easily? Such as: Didn't Fomin's questions to her suggest that there really were missiles in Cuba? Such as: Are we going to war? Is everyone going to be blown to bits?

The official debriefers made note of her questions but explained that they were not authorized to answer, only to ask. As for Harrington, upon arrival on the final morning, she said the same thing, in more flowery language: "It's not unusual at all, dear, for someone who's been through what you've experienced to think she's unlocked the secrets of the universe. Best to let it lie. All of this is being handled at higher levels, I assure you. As for you, my dear, it's time to return to your normal life."

Margo asked again about Agatha: "She's fine, dear, that's all that I can tell you." Only when Margo blurted that she might like to be like the minder one day did Harrington turn correcting: "No, dear, you wouldn't, I can assure you."

And then there was the matter of Margo's father and his fate. Harrington was dubious: "It's just exactly the sort of thing the Russians would dummy up, dear. To upset you, dear. To get you to love them more than you love us." But when Margo asked why on earth they would bother when they could have pulled out her fingernails instead, Harrington only shrugged and said there was no predicting the mind of a man like dear Aleks Fomin.

Until that moment it had not occurred to Margo that Fomin might have a first name, and she asked Harrington to repeat it.

"A-l-e-k-s-a-n-d-r."

After that there was paperwork for Margo to sign, concerning confidentiality (again), as well as her release of the federal government and its agencies and assigns and employees from any and all liability in return for a payment of ten thousand dollars into an account in her name at the Riggs National Bank across the street from the White House, to be turned over upon her attaining the age of twenty-one or receiving her degree, whichever came first, providing she kept the terms of—

Margo signed, not bothering to read the rest.

Harrington checked the signatures, filed the papers away, then launched into a lecture about how her part in this drama was officially over, and she should return to her normal life as swiftly as possible. And how she must never, under any circumstances, try to contact any of the people she had met during what Harrington insisted on calling "this little adventure."

Then Harrington gave Margo a hug, wished her well, and urged her to do her best to forget everything that had happened in Bulgaria.

"Suppose I can't."

"You'll do fine, my dear."

A moment later, Harrington was gone, the debriefers with her, and GREENHILL's minder was leading her down to the street, where a taxi was waiting, the driver paid in advance for the hour-long trip up to the house of Margo's youth, in the sleepy Hudson River town of Garrison, where Claudia Jensen would be waiting to scold her granddaughter back to health.

II

Margo spent the first day sleeping, and in the morning, over breakfast, asked her grandmother whether there had ever been a hint of a secret truth behind the official tale of how her father died. Nana was furious. She marched into her study, unlocked the drawer of her enormous claw-footed desk, and pulled out a red satin box Margo had seen a hundred times. Inside, resting on a bed of silk, was the European–African–Middle Eastern Campaign Medal awarded to Donald Jensen, together with two service stars, one for Tunisia, the other for Algeria. Margo stared at the bit of metal and multicolored cloth. As a child, she had been terribly impressed. Only in college had she discovered that the same decoration was awarded to every member of the armed forces who served in the theater.

"Do you want to take this away from him?" Nana snapped.

III

There was, of course, a larger history, of which Margo remained innocent. The simple facts, some even today not declassified, are these: Margo Jensen, American student, was arrested by the Darzhavna Sigurnost late on the night of Thursday, October 4—the day of the Botvinnik-Fischer contest at the Olympiad. Because of the time difference, the news of her arrest arrived in Washington early on the evening of the same day. By coincidence, on that very day the Air Force was in the midst of a determined effort to wrest control of the U-2 surveillance flights from the Central Intelligence Agency. The collapse of SANTA GREEN tipped the balance in the negotiations—the spies, said the airmen, could do nothing right—and a few days later, the President's national security adviser, McGeorge Bundy, finally agreed.

He had the President sign an order formally transferring authority to the Strategic Air Command. SAC immediately scheduled an overflight of Cuba for the next day, but it was postponed due to weather.

GREENHILL by this time had been back in the States nearly a week. She escaped from the DS early on the morning of Friday, October 5, and flew to Vienna with Ainsley later that morning. She went onward to Paris, where she boarded the flight for Idlewild Airport in Queens, arriving on October 6. She was debriefed, and the tapes and transcripts were sent off for analysis.

As for Harrington, with SANTA GREEN behind her, she flew to Florida to assist in the debriefing of a Cuban asset who had been exfiltrated by boat after another aborted effort to discover what the Russians were building ninety miles off the coast. Harrington was old-school, and believed passionately in human sources, but the United States, as it moved rapidly into the technological era, was raising a new breed of intelligence officer, of whom Gwynn was typical. The new breed disdained human sources—in ordinary language, spies—because spies, as mere mortals, could lie, make mistakes, get drunk, fall in or out of love, take bribes, get tortured, create diplomatic incidents. The new breed believed that the only reliable intelligence was culled from that which could be intercepted, detected, recorded, measured, or photographed. So it was that, six days after Margo arrived at her grandmother's house in Garrison—to be precise, Sunday, October 14—a U-2 lifted off from Laughlin Air Force Base in Texas. The plane was part of the 4080th Reconnaissance Wing, and the pilot, in accordance with the rules governing the U-2 program, had resigned his commission in the Air Force prior to undertaking surveillance over hostile territory. Flying at seventy thousand feet, he made the first American overflight of Cuba since the crisis began back in the spring with Smyslov's cryptic message on Curaçao. Onboard cameras snapped hundreds of photos of the target areas. The Soviet troops on the island were aware of the surveillance, but had difficulty tracking the plane; in any case, they had no orders to fire.

This would shortly change.

The pilot completed his mission safely. Although the U-2 flights were now controlled by SAC, the photographic analysis still took place at the Central Intelligence Agency's new headquarters in McLean, Virginia—often referred to, inaccurately, as Langley, which is an unincorporated community. By the following day, the Agency's experts had completed their analysis of the photographs. The supervisor of the photographic section briefed the deputy director of intelligence, who immediately called National Security Adviser McGeorge Bundy. They met that evening at Bundy's office in the basement of the West Wing. There was no longer any question, said the DDI: the Soviets were constructing launching sites for intermediate-range ballistic missiles.

"How do you know?" Bundy asked, because he possessed that rarity among politicians, a mind that was persuaded by evidence rather than by conclusory assertion. He was a short, thin-faced, scholarly man, in narrow tie and spectacles. At Yale he had studied mathematics, dazzling his professors, who urged him to enter the academy. For a while, he even had. He had been dean of arts and sciences at Harvard at the unheard-of age of thirty-four, and had almost single-handedly ended the system under which rich kids got in automatically. He liked things neat. He believed in logic. He believed in compartmentalization. He did not suffer fools. Despite his diminutive stature, he had dressed down more than one Cabinet secretary or senior senator. He had destroyed careers, but never casually. Bundy craved information, and the man sitting across from him was excellent at providing it.

"I'll show you," said the deputy director, an Air Force lieutenant general, and proceeded to draw from a file the photographs of a site near San Cristóbal: the missile trailers, the missile launchers, the antiaircraft batteries.

"Are you sure these trailers are carrying ballistic missiles?"

"At that size and with those launchers, the cargo can't be anything else."

"Missiles that could carry nuclear warheads to our shores."

"Yes, sir. Intermediate-range. Probably the R-12. What we call the Sandal."

Bundy nodded, outwardly calm but inwardly worried. The Sandal had an effective range of well over a thousand nautical miles. Fired from Cuba, the missile could probably carry a warhead as far north as Chicago or New York. Hitting Washington wouldn't pose any sort of problem. A nuclear war would end in five minutes.

"Are the missiles operational?" he asked.

"Not yet."

"How long?"

"We're not sure. We're working on it."

"And not a bluff, I take it—wooden missiles painted to look like the real thing."

"No, sir. Believe me, our people can tell the difference."

"Have you checked this with YOGA?" YOGA being the Agency's highest-ranking asset in the Kremlin, a colonel of military intelligence named Oleg Penkovsky.

"We're trying. But the indications are consistent with everything YOGA's told us about Soviet weaponry."

"Ah. He did that missile course at Dzerzhinsky, as I recall."

"Yes, sir."

Bundy looked at the evidence before him on the table. The deputy director would say later that he detected in the national security adviser's visage more sorrow than anger, and he would be right. Bundy, the DDI knew, had just today appeared on *Issues and Answers*, ABC's Sunday-morning news program, and told the nation that the Administration had yet to see any evidence that the Soviets had plans to install nuclear weapons in Cuba. This assurance was based on the CIA's own Special National Intelligence Estimate 85-3-62, forwarded to the White House in mid-September, which concluded that the placement of missiles in Cuba "would be incompatible with Soviet practice to date and with Soviet policy."

But public embarrassment was not the reason for Bundy's evident pain. The cause was the failure of his furious efforts to prevent just this occurrence.

President Kennedy had stressed repeatedly, in public and private alike, that the United States would never accept the introduction of strategic weapons anywhere else in the hemisphere. Ever since the Cuban Revolution, the American nightmare had been that the Soviets might put nuclear missiles on the island. The Administration had decided a year ago that the only way to prevent this from happening was to replace Castro with a friendly regime. The result was MONGOOSE, an Agency operation to use covert means, including sabotage and assassination, to topple the dictator. Bundy had been reluctant to go along but had seen the necessity: do nothing, and sooner or later the Soviets would be unable to resist the temptation.

But MONGOOSE had proved farcical, with nothing to show for the money spent—although a handful of clever Cuban exiles and a couple of Mafia kingpins were each several hundred thousand dollars richer.

"Thank you, General," Bundy finally said. "I'll get this to the President. I suspect we have a couple of busy weeks ahead of us."

IV

Elsewhere in the city, the man called Viktor was listening to the raving of his contact.

"You people had her and you let her go. Why would you do that?"

"It was not my decision," said Viktor, morosely. He adjusted the gold-rimmed glasses. They were sitting in the back of a noisy bar on Capitol Hill. Young men and women laughed together at adjoining tables.

His contact was unsatisifed. "I don't care whose decision it was. I want to know why the hell you let GREENHILL go."

"It was the judgment of my superiors. I do not fully understand."

"Well, I think I do." The American drained off his beer, signaled for another. "My government is split over how to deal with the missiles. The military, State, the intelligence agencies—everybody's split. Hawks against doves. Sounds like yours is, too."

Viktor shook his head. He pushed his glass away. The vodka was not nearly cold enough. He did not understand how Americans could manage without the bone-chilling crispness of a vodka properly served. "Her interrogator was the great Fomin himself. As you know, he is a legend in our services. He was also one of my teachers. It is not possible that he is among what you call the doves."

"Then it wasn't his decision."

"Perhaps not. He is always making plans and conspiracies of enormous complexity in order to confound your side. He would have fought hard against any order to release this GREENHILL. Therefore it is likely that her release will serve his purposes."

"Can you find out?"

"Fomin will not tell me. He keeps his secrets." Viktor wiped his mouth. "Perhaps I should meet this GREENHILL myself."

"I don't know if that's such a good idea," said his contact. "Besides, if she wouldn't talk to Fomin, why would she talk to you?"

"I am not Fomin." A grim smile. "Perhaps I shall leave her no choice."

SIXTEEN

Fire on the Water

I

The asset known as GREENHILL was standing on the widow's walk atop her grandmother's house in Garrison, up the Hudson River from New York City. Not that Margo knew her code name. She knew nothing of the contretemps set off by Harrington's wild idea, or the tug-of-war among the nation's intelligence agencies set off by the mission's collapse. She knew nothing of the CIA's confirmation that there were nuclear warheads in Cuba, although there at least she had her suspicions.

Especially after Varna.

Margo leaned her smooth brown face into the snapping wind off the river and looked south, where the Hudson vanished around a bend. Manhattan was a good fifty-odd miles away. She wondered whether it was really true, as Tom had told her, that even at this distance the bomb's glare could blind you.

The October sky was a delicate eggshell blue, perfect for cracking wide open. The clouds were high and wispy, and Margo imagined that she might any minute catch a glimpse of the Soviet bombers making their run, but she knew from Professor Niemeyer's course that the state-of-the-art method for delivering nuclear weapons was the stand-off position, the plane climbing and banking as the bomb was released, imparting an initial upward trajectory. By the time the weapon reached the top of its arc and began its final downward journey, the bomber was streaking in the opposite direction as fast as it could fly. Red Air

Force doctrine, Niemeyer had told them, mandated four planes to kill a large city, converging from different points of the compass, and one night their homework was to calculate the odds that two might collide as they struggled to get the lob angle just right.

Not that it would matter. A near miss counted the same as a hit to those whom the bomb would incinerate.

The past weeks had been nightmarish, and plagued by such horrid dreams that Margo no longer possessed a clear sense of the boundary between reality and fantasy. A month ago, she had been a student, a nobody, another sophomore political-science major at Cornell, worshipping along with the others the great Lorenz Niemeyer, who filled his frightening lectures on the mathematics of conflict with dozens of reasons why no sane leader would ever push the button, and no sane adviser would allow an insane leader within a mile of the nuclear codes. Then, for a wondrous instant, she had become an unexpected player in great events, part of the effort to prevent . . .

Well, to prevent what she was on this roof waiting to witness.

The radio said that the city was being evacuated, and Margo supposed it must be true, but no line of desperate families crammed into Fords and Chevies had made it this far north. Maybe the army was turning the traffic toward New England. Maybe her grandmother's house wasn't safe after all. From her perch on the roof, Margo could look across the gray autumn river toward West Point, and although Professor Niemeyer always said that nobody would ever survive the first strike to launch a second, she imagined that the military academy must be somewhere on the list of low-priority targets. In the classroom, all of this had seemed excitingly abstract. Niemeyer liked to tease them, asking how far down the list Ithaca, New York, would lie. His mockery generated an absurd competitiveness among the students, who vied with one another to invent reasons for the Russians to vaporize Cornell University. Niemeyer claimed that adults all over America played the same grim game. Margo had no parents to speak of, and she spent her vacations with her grandmother here in Garrison. Nana's idea of a good time was to cross the river and ride the tour bus up Bear Mountain for a picnic. When Margo asked Nana last summer whether she and her friends ever talked about Armageddon, the old woman seemed to think her granddaughter was referring to the final battle in the Book of Revelation. Margo said no, she meant the risk of nuclear war. Nana laughed and said not to worry—with Kennedy in the White House, everything was going to be fine. That was three months ago. Now it was fall, and Kennedy was still in the White House, and everything wasn't fine, because New York was about to explode. Margo had attended segregated public schools in both New York City and New Rochelle, but she had always imagined somehow that there would be time for the Movement to gather steam, so that her own family would live where she and her husband pleased. Despite the monthly classroom air-raid drills and the twice-yearly trips down to the fallout shelter, she never imagined, in those innocent days, that she would never have a family to worry about because the world was going to end in 1962. The schools she had attended, the parks where she had frolicked, the museums where she had passed her lonely days—all would be ash.

And five million people with them.

A hydrogen bomb, said Tom, worked by implosion, not explosion: what created the blast was the pieces all being pressed together in the right combination with enormous force. After that came the light, then the heat, then the wave. He always said it that way: light, heat, wave. The light was first, as bright as a hundred suns, and your blink reflex would never be fast enough to stop the glare from blinding you. Next came the heat, but that was only local, setting fire to everything within a mile or two of the implosion. Finally came the blast wave, the wall of force knocking down everything it touched—trees, buildings, bridges, dams. In the Nevada highlands, said Tom, one bomb test had hollowed out an entire mountain peak. The military had built whole towns out there, complete with mannequins and televisions, and the blast wave had crushed them flat. You could shield yourself from the glare. You could escape the heat. But the only protection against the blast wave, said Tom, was the inverse-square law.

"Get as far away from ground zero as possible," he said. "Figure out where the targets are, and be somewhere else."

Niemeyer scoffed at this strategy. Nobody had ever launched an intercontinental missile in anger, he said, and nobody knew if they would hit their targets. The earth wasn't perfectly round, the magnetic field wasn't perfectly uniform, and the multiple launches and explosions would themselves do incalculable damage to the calculations. Some would likely hit, but the errors would be enormous. If the Russians lobbed six missiles at Washington, wrote Niemeyer in one of the books that made him famous, the chances were that at least three of them would miss by a hundred miles, blowing up shoe factories in Pennsylvania and farms in Virginia instead.

Maybe Nana's house wasn't far enough, after all——

There was the promised flash, a flicker, an eyeblink, more white than gold, then swift, leaping yellow, and Margo didn't go blind or feel the heat or feel anything, really, not least because her strong, fluid body was roiling soot——

And as she died she heard Niemeyer's mocking laughter——

Because she had failed——

II

Margo opened her eyes with a silent scream on her lips. It was two in the morning, the windows were open to the autumn chill, but her slim body was drenched with perspiration. This was her second night in the room where she had spent more than half her life, and she already knew it was time to go. If the dream that had troubled her sleep since Varna could chase her even here to Garrison, it could follow her anywhere. Better, then, to dream in Ithaca, where at least she had friends. Her Nana was many wonderful things, but she was neither warm nor comforting. Her recipe for dealing with terror was to scare it out of you.

She wondered what her father's recipe had been.

Margo climbed from the bed and padded barefoot to the casement window with its involute leading. She cranked the pane farther open, hoping the sweat would evaporate. Her nightgown billowed in the breeze. She had a sense that she was thinner. Since Varna, she had almost stopped eating, a peculiar reaction given that she was hungry all the time. At her bedside was the cup of cocoa Nana had insisted would help her sleep. Margo hadn't touched it.

Her window gave on the side of the house, the yard where remnants of the small wooden castle of her youth still stood, the secret hideaway salvaged from the yard in New Rochelle after her mother died. In the old days, Margo and her brother used to sit inside with their milk and cookies and books, during the one hour of reading their mother required every day after school. Now, in her mind's eye, she saw not the wreck that sat on her grandmother's lawn, but the lively playhouse of her New Rochelle childhood. The playhouse was where Margo would seek her own company after a scolding; it was where, after church one Christmas, her brother, Corbin, had gulled her into believing that there existed a country called "Orient Tar"; and where she and seven-year-old Kirby McKinley from down the block had shared what was for both a first kiss.

The rosy images faded, replaced by the starkness of the present moment.

She crossed to the bed, sat down, sipped at the chocolate. It had gone cold. Everything did, sooner or later. She sipped again anyway, for Nana's sake. A third sip. She licked her lips. There was a peculiar bitterness to the mixture. She sniffed at it. Felt dizziness coming on. Her fingers fluttered. The cup tumbled to the floor, and Margo collapsed on the bed.

Aleksandr Fomin loomed from the darkness.

"Surely you didn't think we were through with you, Miss Jensen."

III

Margo opened her eyes, and remembered.

She was back in Ithaca, in her dormitory room, Jerri in the bed opposite, snoring loudly in her drug-induced haze. This at last was the reality; but it was no happier than the dreams.

SEVENTEEN

The Midnight Oil

I

On Tuesday morning, October 16, National Security Adviser McGeorge Bundy went into the Oval Office to tell the President that the Soviets were installing missiles in Cuba. For a moment, Kennedy just stared at him. Bundy waited. He had been around politicians a long time, and was prepared for the sort of outburst—*"How did this happen without anybody knowing?"*—that masks with anger the determination to show that it isn't the speaker's fault.

Kennedy surprised him.

"Well, I guess we'll just have to get them out of there, won't we?" Then the crooked smile. "And I don't suppose words are going to do it." The smile faded. The President was in his rocker, and Bundy could tell that his back was particularly bad today. "You've seen the evidence, Mac?"

"Yes, Mr. President."

"You're persuaded?"

"Entirely, Mr. President."

Kennedy nodded. His gaze drifted out toward the Rose Garden, where his children were playing, and Bundy wondered whether he was thinking of the millions of children on both sides whose fates hung suddenly in the balance. "I warned them," said the President. "I said that strategic missiles in Cuba would have the gravest consequences. They didn't listen. They think because of the Bay of Pigs . . ." He trailed off.

"There's no doubt they're testing us, sir."

"Testing *me,* you mean." He shook his head. "Khrushchev thinks I'm a weak little boy, doesn't he?"

"I'm sure he doesn't, sir."

"It doesn't matter what he thinks, though, does it? It's the policy of this government that no other country in this hemisphere can have strategic missiles. Period. And it's not just me who's said it. Ike said it. And Congress—what was it, two weeks ago? three?—Congress even adopted a resolution along that line—not unanimous, but almost—"

"In the House, three hundred eighty-six to seven, in the Senate, eighty-six to one."

"So the missiles have to go. We're not negotiating on that."

Bundy wondered whether this was decisiveness or bluster. "Yes, Mr. President."

"Do the Sovs understand this could mean war? Nuclear war? I mean, how do they know we won't just bomb the missile sites?"

"I assume they're hoping to present us with a fait accompli. The missiles aren't yet operational. Most likely, their plan was that we wouldn't discover the missiles until they could be fired at us."

Kennedy chewed this over. "And they think I'm gun-shy. I wouldn't bomb Cuba to help the invasion at the Bay of Pigs, so I won't bomb now? Something like that?"

The question was rhetorical, and Bundy said nothing.

"We don't go public, Mac. And we don't tell the Reds what we know. Not just yet. Let's kick this around a little. Figure out what we can *do.* Not just what we can *say.* Get some people in. Get the agencies working overtime. We hold the knowledge to the people who absolutely need to know, but those people work the hell out of it. Nobody's on vacation. Nobody's on leave. Nobody's out sick." The eyes swiveled back to Bundy, and hardened. "And nobody talks. We still have the Espionage Act, right?"

"We do."

"Good. Anybody who leaks, I want in prison. For life. I don't care who it is."

"Yes, Mr. President."

"And, Mac?"

"Yes, sir."

"We start today. Get them in this morning. We'll meet daily until this is resolved."

"Yes, Mr. President." Packing up his file. "But I think you should still make your Midwest campaign trip at the end of the week."

"Why would I do that?"

"If we don't want anyone to know something's going on, we can't act like something's going on."

Kennedy smiled. "You know future historians will say that when I heard about the missiles, the first thing I did was go off to raise money for our congressional candidates. They'll think it shows how irresponsible I was."

"With all due respect, Mr. President, this isn't about your reputation. Our job right now is to make sure that there *are* future historians."

The grin widened. "What a charmer. I can't imagine why Harvard ever let you go."

II

Doris Harrington sat in her cramped office, glasses for once on her nose. Unclassified files were heaped everywhere. The heavy green safe stood open. Borkland sat across from her. They had divided up the transcripts of GREENHILL's debriefing, searching for any clue, however small, to explain the twin mysteries of why the Bulgarians arrested her and why they let her go. They had just switched halves, so that he was now reading the pages she'd read, and vice versa. It was a bit past ten when she spotted something.

"Look at this," she said. "Page seventeen. Top. A line she attributes to Fomin."

> Q *Please tell us again, Miss Jensen. What exactly did he say about the President?*
> A *He said, "Your President believes his own side's propaganda that the Chairman has been forced to place offensive missiles in Cuba."*
> Q *Were those his precise words?*
> A *I think so. I'm pretty sure.*

Borkland was puzzled. "I don't see what you're driving at."

Harrington snorted. "Oh, Bill, I had no idea you were such a dunce. Why exactly did I hire you?"

"For my good looks, I imagine."

"Dear boy. You really don't see it, do you? It's all there. In this single word."

She tapped the page. He followed her finger. "*Forced,*" he read aloud.

"That's right."

"What does it mean?"

"It means that Khrushchev may not be in control of things. It means somebody over there is sending us a message."

Borkland looked at the page again. "That's a lot to read into one word."

"I agree."

"You think they arrested her to send us a message?" His turn to tap the paragraph. "How could he be sure she'd remember the words right? How can we be sure?"

Harrington's tone was placid. "*I'm* sure, Bill." She turned a page. "Look. It all fits together. See? He keeps asking about her mission. But he insists that he already knows. The mission is to find out what is happening in Cuba. But then he essentially tells her what's happening: it only matters whether Khrushchev has been 'forced' to place missiles in Cuba, if there are in fact missiles in Cuba. He goes to a lot of trouble to make sure she understands the importance. He even tells her he came 'a considerable distance' to meet her. See? Page eleven. He doesn't want her to forget. He hammers home the message five different ways." She closes the folder. "And notice that they don't interrogate the minder—the person they have to know is an actual intelligence officer. They knock her around a bit, they break her wrist, but in the end they leave her in the street. They only interrogate GREENHILL. But they give her more information than they get from her. Fomin even mentions the missiles. And then she escapes. Isn't it likely that Fomin intended to let her go all along? It all adds up, Bill. It all adds up."

Her deputy sighed. "Fine. Say you're right. What do we do about it?"

"Nothing."

"I beg your pardon?"

"There's nothing *to* do. There's something off about this whole case. Can't you feel it?"

"Sorry, boss," said Borkland tartly. "I haven't had the chance to peek at the answers in the back of the book."

Harrington smiled. "You mean that as a criticism. Fair enough. I don't have facts to back up my worries. But I've been around long enough to trust my instincts, and so have you. The other questions she raised in her debriefing are good questions. How did Fomin tumble to her mission? Where did he get the file on her so fast? Why didn't he re-arrest her when he had the chance? He could have found a thousand excuses to keep her."

"If somebody's sending a message, that's why he let her go."

"And why he arrested her. Yes. But that's the problem, Bill. Why her? Why GREENHILL? And why Bulgaria? If Fomin has a message for us, there are hundreds of diplomats and reporters he could call right here in Washington." She sighed and shut her eyes briefly: age was beginning to play its games. "No, Bill. We do nothing. Not yet. It's not our move."

"With the missiles in Cuba, we just sit and wait?"

"Exactly." She waved an admonishing finger. "And not a word of this goes into any report. No hint passes outside this office."

"You don't think the Secretary should hear this? Or maybe the President? Or the fifty analysts Langley has on Cuba just now?"

"Again, not yet. Let's see how things play out."

Borkland was uncomfortable. "Time is short, boss."

A beatific smile. "Then I suspect our wait shan't be very long."

EIGHTEEN

The Elusive Peace

I

"Let's talk about fallout shelters," said the great Lorenz Niemeyer, striding across the stage. It was the same Tuesday, October 16, and Margo had been back since Saturday. "If you've spent any time in Washington or New York or Chicago, you've seen the signs everywhere. But imagine the weapon targeted on those cities. Possibly thirty megatons. The Soviets build them that big, I seem to recall. A thirty-megaton warhead would leave a crater nine hundred feet deep and a mile across. Even the White House bomb shelter would be ash."

He snorted and executed a rather fine pirouette for a man of his bulk. Margo frowned at his antics. She had switched seats since her return to campus and now sat near the back. She admired Niemeyer a good deal less than she had before her little jaunt behind the Iron Curtain. It didn't seem fair that he'd survived the war and her father had blown himself to bits.

"We spend a fortune building shelters where they're least needed," Niemeyer continued, punching the air with his tiny fist. "Nobody in the big cities is going to survive anyway. They're needed in the hinterlands, where the fallout, not the bombs, will be the killer. And, of course, up here we don't have enough. Why is that?" The mocking gaze moved around the lecture hall, brushed past Margo without lingering, settled on a nearer target. "Miss Seaver. Tell us, please. Why are there so many shelters in the cities?"

Annalise struggled through a halting explanation. From her perch
at the rear, Margo tried to take an interest in her best friend's answer,
but couldn't hold the words in her head. She was too busy being angry
at Niemeyer. A part of her wanted to march right up to the lectern and
demand to know whether or not he had really known Donald Jensen in the OSS, even though she knew perfectly well—the civil-rights
leaders still talked about it—that American Intelligence during World
War II had not recruited Negroes.

"Not even wrong," said Niemeyer when Annalise was done. With a
theatrical sigh of disappointment, the great man moved on to someone
else, who offered at least a fragment of the response he was seeking:
the purpose of the shelters was to make people believe they would survive. Another acolyte supplied the rest: at the same time, the shelters
provided a unifying force, a way of reminding us that we're all in this
together, and—

Margo decided she'd had enough. She rose from her seat and hurried up the aisle toward the door. She felt Niemeyer's eyes on her, but
that might have been her imagination. "Most fallout shelters are little
more than holes in the ground," he was saying as she fled. "They aren't
built to the proper specifications. For example, the entrances should be
constructed with a particular set of complex angles to make penetration by wind-borne fallout less likely, but instead we tend to . . ."

She was out. Mercifully. She let the door slam, probably on purpose. The sound echoed in the corridor, where the teaching assistants kept their gloomy vigil against unwanted listening. Margo could
hardly believe that a month ago she would have given anything to be
one of them. She could take little more of Niemeyer and his acolytes.
Every time she heard his voice, she was plunged back into precisely
the memories she was trying to forget. Harrington had said to put it
behind her, and Margo wanted to. Desperately.

But as one October day shivered into the next, Margo found herself
unable to follow Harrington's advice. She would sit in a sunlit classroom as the professor discoursed, in elegant French, on the wonders
of Lamartine, and for a moment she would forget herself; but when
the hour ended, out in the bustle of the corridor, her eyes would lift
automatically to the sign on the wall, three inverted yellow pyramids,
touching at the vertices, emblazoned on a black circle—the symbol for

a fallout shelter—and that night she would dream sleeplessly, plagued by visions of her classmates banging pitifully on the locked shelter door as they breathed their last.

Or she would be downtown with Annalise and Jerri, sipping ice cream sodas at the counter and exchanging superior comments about the high school girls who flitted in and out, trying to draw the eyes of the Cornell men, when she would catch sight of some fellow who reminded her, in manner if not in appearance, of Aleksandr Fomin, and suddenly she would begin to tremble, quite badly, and excuse herself. Naturally, her girlfriends would insist on driving her back to campus. Annalise would tell her she needed to lie down, and Jerri would offer her something to calm her down, but she would break free of them and stalk up the hill on foot, hoping to use the afternoon chill to drive the memories away. It never worked; but at least her friends would not be around to see the tears.

The worst time of all occurred with Tom, who had at first tried to comfort her over the trauma she had suffered in Bulgaria, but her refusal to discuss the details finally put him off. They quarreled. Tom said he knew that it was something to do with Bobby. Margo insisted that this was untrue, but Tom refused to let it go. From the wounded and occasionally angry hints he dropped, Margo finally realized that he thought she had slept with Bobby during the Olympiad, even though, for reasons of either pride or propriety, he refused to come out and ask. In all the scenarios she had imagined for their reunion, it had never occurred to her that her boyfriend might be jealous. The reproach in his voice even as they held each other began to weigh on her. On the second night, as they stood together outside her dormitory after pizza, Tom made the mistake of forgiving her for, as he put it, whatever she had done.

Margo stiffened, and Tom hastily tried to make amends. "I'm just worried about you, sweetheart. You're not yourself."

"I'm fine," she said, but couldn't meet his injured gaze. She glanced at the building. "I have to get inside. Parietals."

Now she stood in the hallway outside Niemeyer's classroom—coincidentally, beneath the yellow-and-black triangles of the fallout-shelter sign—and tried to slow her whirling and disobedient mind. She might never have gone to Varna at all had not Niemeyer manipulated her with that mention of her father. She had yet to confront him about that, and she told herself that her reluctance was because she didn't want to invite him to lie to her any further. But another part of her knew that she didn't want him to burst her bubble. Harrington had sown doubt about Fomin's tale, and the last thing Margo wanted was for Niemeyer to say: Yes, sure, I knew your father because he drove for me when I was in Tunisia to see Eisenhower. Sorry about the way he died, Miss Jensen, but of course history doesn't give all of us the opportunity to be heroic. Still, you can take pride in—

"Margie. Hey."

Phil Littlejohn had a hand on her shoulder. She realized that she had been standing with her head tipped against the chipped hardwood paneling of the corridor.

"I saw you run out. You okay?"

"I'm fine," she said, shaking off his touch and turning around.

"It's just, you've been acting spooked since you got back from Bulgaria."

Margo studied his patrician face, searching for any hint of the cruel mockery of which she knew he was capable. She remembered their confrontation under the stands at the stadium, and his teasing invitation to inspect the mattresses of the shelter back at his frat. But this time she saw a genuine concern, and, in his eyes, a twinkle that seemed to her to mark some sort of secret knowledge.

"I'm fine, Phil," she repeated, more gently than she intended.

"Look. I wanted to apologize for the way I behaved last month. Too much beer. I'm sorry, Margo. See? I got your name right."

"I have to be somewhere—"

He leaned closer. "It's okay, Margo. I know all about what happened over there."

The doors burst open. The crowd was filing out. Now somebody would tell Tom that she'd been whispering with Phil Littlejohn in the hallway, and there would be yet another fire to put out. But she had to hear the rest. She took Phil by the sleeve and drew him away from the main entrance.

"What are you talking about, Phil? What do you think happened?"

"That the scholarship was just a cover. The way I heard it, you went to Bulgaria on official business. I think something went wrong and you got arrested." He grinned. "But you're back. So they let you go. You're safe. You should relax and put it behind you."

She tightened her grip on his arm. "Where did you hear that story?"

"My family knows people who know people. That's all I'm going to say."

"Phil, you can't tell anybody. I'm not saying if you're right or wrong, but you can't—"

"Ah, Miss Jensen," an all-too-familiar voice boomed. "Is this your young man, then? Or do you require rescue from his clutches?"

Niemeyer had come up behind them, trailed by a brace of graduate students.

"No, no," she began. "We just—"

But the great man as usual spoke right over her. "The way you went racing out of class, I was worried. For no reason, I see. You seem to be in good hands."

This was too much for her. She made her awkward excuses and hurried from the building, nearly colliding with a man she took to be another professor, because of his pipe, tweeds, and flannels. She scarcely noticed his gold-rimmed glasses.

II

After dinner, from a phone booth in the dorm lobby, she made a collect call to her brother, Corbin, in Ohio. They passed a few pleasantries, but the truth was they were nearly strangers by now. Corbin had attended a small college in the Midwest, met a young woman, and settled down. He taught history at an Episcopal academy near Cleveland. He seemed happy, but he never came home to Garrison. A part of her longed to share her experiences in Bulgaria, and another part of her wanted to warn him about Cuba, but she remembered about telephones and didn't dare. Finally, she asked him straight out whether he had ever heard any stories about Daddy doing more in the war than drive a truck. He was four years older, after all, and might have knowledge she lacked.

"What are you talking about?" His voice was warm with sympathy. "What's the matter, sis?"

"I just wondered."

He laughed softly. "I know. I used to want it to be true, too. But he did what he did. There's no changing that."

"I see."

A pause: they really had little to say to each other. She decided to make her excuses and promise to consider his insincere invitation to visit, and then she would hang up and—

"Although, now that you mention it, there was one funny thing," said Corbin. "After the war ended—I think about 1946—I remember because I'd just turned seven, so you would have been, I guess, three—this man came to the house to see Mom. Caucasian. He said he knew Dad in the war, and that he wanted her to know how brave he'd been, and how he'd done important work, even though he wasn't at liberty to tell her why." The gentle laugh again. "I remember those words—'not at liberty'—because I'd never heard that phrase before, and I had to ask Nana what it meant."

"Do you remember anything else about him? What he looked like?"

"Just that he was a pudgy little fellow. Oh, and there was something wrong with his hand."

"Something like what?"

"Come on, sis. It's been a long time."

"Please. Whatever you can remember."

"Mmmm. Let me see. I think maybe it was his fingers. They were all bent, like they'd been broken or something."

III

That night, she went with Jerri and Annalise to hear a speaker on the subject of the Freedom Rides that had begun last year. Jerri went in the hope of hearing evidence that the revolution was near. Margo went because Annalise dragged her: Niemeyer had hinted in class that he might ask them on next week's midterm exam to use the tools of conflict theory to analyze the civil-rights demonstrations. There weren't many black students at Cornell, but nearly all were in attendance tonight, and some few had gone South as Riders. Margo had talked about joining, but Nana forbade her: *Nothing's more important than your studies, child. You didn't see the white kids skipping class to ride those buses down South. Let the cops beat on some other fool.* Actually, a lot of white kids had gone, but arguing with Nana was like arguing with the weather. Sitting in the auditorium now, listening as the young Negro man in white shirt and dark tie described being beaten savagely for sitting in the wrong section of an interstate bus, and then spending a night in jail, Margo experienced none of the guilt she had anticipated. Instead, she sat serenely. She saw up on the stage not an individual who had made sacrifices she hadn't, but a fellow sufferer. She was proud of him; but of herself, too.

Then she looked across the auditorium and spotted Phil Littlejohn looking back, and her mood faded.

"What's he doing here?" she asked her friends as they left.

"Maybe he's interested in race relations," said Jerri, fumbling for a smoke.

"Or some kind of relations," said Annalise. She smiled at Margo's surprise. "He's got a little crush on you."

"He has a creepy way of showing it."

"He's accustomed to getting what he wants. He doesn't know how to deal with a girl who says no."

"How about taking her at her word?"

After the lecture, Margo split off from the others and headed for the library, where she was supposed to meet Tom to study together. She wasn't sure whether she wanted to, because she was tired of fighting and also tired of his treating her as if she had betrayed his trust. But she had never quite been able to shed the dependability her grandmother had drilled into her.

She was passing the statue of Andrew Dickson White when a tall man materialized from the shadows and fell into step beside her. When Margo heard the voice, she wondered if she might be asleep.

"Don't look at me, Miss Jensen," said Aleksandr Fomin. "There's someone following you. Don't turn around. It is important that we talk. Don't go into the library. Just keep walking as if you're headed into town. I will pick you up on the street. Look for a brown Chevy."

She was about to rebuke him, but he had already melted into the night.

II

They walked, along a path leading past the shuttered ice-cream stand, through the young trees, toward Cayuga Lake. Margo expected whoever else was out there to follow like a faithful guard dog, in the manner of Niemeyer's teaching assistants, but when she looked over her shoulder there was only darkness.

"I have sought you out because I trust you," Fomin said. "There is no other reason. I am here because there are very few who can be trusted, on either side. It was difficult to get here," he repeated.

She glanced at him. The calm was still with her. Class reunion. Old friends' day. "Because you're not allowed this far north," she said, remembering the fact from some book Niemeyer had assigned. "You're a Soviet diplomat. You're only allowed in certain cities, or to travel between them, or within ninety miles of them."

"This is correct." His tone was rueful. "But I am ignoring the restrictions. I came here to find you, Miss Jensen. Our two countries are about to go to war, and you and I have to stop it."

Margo stared. Her aplomb never faded. So. The dream at last. Her grandmother's roof, the perfect blue sky, the bombs falling invisibly, the world an incinerated ruin.

"I'm not a spy," she pointed out, the same line she had repeated ad nauseam in Bulgaria.

"Perhaps that is the reason I trust you," he repeated. He gestured with the cigarette. In the darkness, the tip described a bright red arc. "An interrogation, Miss Jensen, is only in the second instance an effort to uncover information. It is, in the first instance, an effort to study another human being. To understand his strengths and weaknesses, his fears and his dreams, his degree of resilience. Or hers, as the case may be. I have interrogated you, Miss Jensen, and I trust you. There is no other American I trust."

"Trust to do what?"

"Please, listen carefully. I have a message for your President."

This brought her up short. They were standing in the sand now, a few covered boats bobbing nearby. Yellow moonlight flirted and played on the flat black water.

"My President. You mean Kennedy."

"Yes."

She felt slow and stupid. "If you have a message for the President, maybe you should be at the White House."

"I wish you to deliver it."

Again she shut her eyes, worrying that same fold of skin. She said nothing. Most of her didn't believe him.

"There are missiles in Cuba," Fomin said. "Actual missiles," he continued, as the world did flip-flops. "They are intermediate-range missiles, type R-12 Dvina. Your military designates this as the SS-4, or the Sandal, the successor to what you previously labeled the SS-3, or the Shyster. Range, about two thousand kilometers. There are also R-14 missiles on the way. Your military calls these the SS-5, or Skean. Range, about four thousand kilometers, maybe a bit more. Has Niemeyer taught you these types?"

She heard her voice as if over a great distance. The shadows seemed to thicken, gathering a shuddery substance. She imagined capering demons just out of sight. "No. No, he hasn't."

"Listen, then. These missiles would be able to deliver warheads in the megaton range to more than half of your country. There would be very little warning. Less even than if you were to use your Jupiter missiles in Turkey, or the Polaris submarines. They are a first-strike weapon, Miss Jensen. Do you understand?"

Margo was gazing at the dark water. Niemeyer had shown them declassified films of thermonuclear tests. One of the explosions had been set off at sea. The water had boiled into what the narrator called, with understatement, a "water column." The column weighed millions of tons. To Margo it had looked like the hand of some sea god, whose sudden lurch from beneath the surface caused a tsunami. The wave had knocked over heavy ships as if they were tin cans. The spray, felt at a distance of miles, was intensely radioactive. She supposed that Cayuga Lake would cease to exist.

"I understand," she said, voice faint, remembering the dream.

"The President knows about the missiles, Miss Jensen. Your spy aircraft have been overflying Cuba for several days. He is presumably in the process of deciding how best to respond."

"Okay," she said, only because Fomin had paused, and seemed to expect some response.

"He has already met with our foreign minister, who of course denied everything, but our foreign minister is not fully informed. Our side expects that your President will shortly offer negotiations, probably in Washington. We will attend, naturally. Everyone will declare their desire for a peaceful solution to the issues that divide us. But here is the important part, Miss Jensen. Are you listening?"

She was listening.

"The negotiations will fail. There will be war." She glanced at his face, but his gloomy visage was turned toward the water. "Thermonuclear war, Miss Jensen. The last war, very probably, that the planet will ever endure."

III

The fog was lifting. She could dimly pick out lights on the far shore: houses, a car or two crawling along the road.

"This is why you had me arrested," she said. Her throat felt clotted, perhaps with nuclear ash. "You wanted to find out if you could trust me."

Fomin did not answer directly. "You are an extraordinary young woman. Much as your father was an extraordinary man." He was walking again, taking long strides like a man late for an appointment. "It is difficult to trust someone not raised to doctrine, but you seem quite unsullied by bourgeois so-called freedom. You are young. You are of an oppressed minority. You are not part of the ruling class, despite your ambition. You are not a part of the war clique, despite your admiration for Niemeyer, who is among its leaders."

"Even if you're right about any of that, you couldn't have known it at the time of my arrest. Not unless you were already investigating me."

Again he ignored her challenge. "You are Niemeyer's student. Therefore, tell me, please, the first rule of negotiation."

The direct inquiry popped her back into A-student mode. "Each side must have something the other wants."

"Exactly. The Soviet side has something you want: the removal of the missiles. But, Miss Jensen, at the moment, your side has nothing we want. There is nothing you are able to offer that would satisfy us. Not around a negotiation table." He let out a sigh; flicked the cigarette away. "Yours is such a beautiful country, Miss Jensen. So large and rich and powerful. Your people are full of confidence. Your homeland has not been battered and brutalized as ours has, and so you cannot possibly appreciate the suspicion with which we look upon powerful neighbors."

"We're not neighbors," Margo protested. The night shadows were whirling close now, enclosing her in empty darkness.

"In a world of nuclear missiles, Miss Jensen, we must behave as though we are. And this is the point. We lost twenty million people in the Great Patriotic War. Try to imagine it, Miss Jensen. Twenty *million*. After such devastation, we dare not trust any nation in the world. We cannot abide America's growing military might. We cannot allow you to possess more power than we. This has nothing to do with your actual intentions. Our history has taught us to assume that everyone is ranged against us, no matter what words they use, no matter what terms they offer. Do you understand?"

"Yes, but—"

"Miss Jensen, let us be frank. You have many more missiles than we do. Your President told the country during his campaign that you are behind us, but this is not so. You have always had more. More missiles, more warheads, more planes. And, if we are honest, we must admit that your technology is advancing much faster than ours. Our long-range economic forecasts—the private ones presented to our leaders—are also not good. In ten years, perhaps even five, your country will have consolidated its technological and economic advantages. You will be so far ahead that we will be past the point where it is even possible to speak of a balance. You will be able to dictate, and we will have to follow. This, of course, is unsupportable."

"I can't believe—"

"This is our last chance, Miss Jensen. Either we strike you now, or we content ourselves to accept the failure of our great socialist experiment. That is why there are missiles in Cuba. And that is why we cannot withdraw them."

She needed a moment to slow her heart, and to remember to breathe. "Are you saying that your side *wants* a nuclear war?"

"Perhaps some on your side, too."

We're the good guys! she shouted—but only in her mind. Aloud she said, "I still don't understand what you want me to do about it."

Fomin was on the move again, along the lake, toward the boat-houses that lined the western shore. For a while they marched in silence. He stopped near a small inlet where a slim one-man sailboat had been beached.

"This is a child's boat," he said, after a brief study.

"I guess so."

"Do you wish to have children, Miss Jensen?"

"One day. Of course."

He nodded. "I myself have three children. I see them rarely because of my duties, but I would like them to live. That is why I do the work that I do."

"I understand," she said, although she didn't.

Fomin's voice grew weary. "What I have told you is the truth, but it is only one version of the truth—the version that is believed by the party ideologues, by the leaders of our military, and even by many in our diplomatic corps. War with the Main Enemy is inevitable, and it is better to fight it sooner, on our terms, than later, on yours." He was in motion again, the worried soldier unable to rest. "Those are the people who will dominate the negotiation. The Comrade General Secretary cannot act publicly without their support. Do you understand?"

"Yes."

"But their view is not his view. The Comrade General Secretary is a good Communist, but he is also a pragmatist. He believes that your system will collapse in time because of its own contradictions. He believes it is an error to try to force matters now. So he would prefer to find a peaceful solution to the problem presented by the missiles in Cuba. The difficulty is that it cannot be pursued in the course of public negotiation. The ideologues will not allow it. If the public negotiation is the only one that takes place, there will be war. Do you understand, Miss Jensen?"

"Yes."

"We must therefore arrange another negotiation. Through you to me."

The shadows were back; and the thickness in her throat. She felt feverish, and really hoped she would wake up soon. She wondered if she had tried some of Jerri's mezzroll after all: this whole thing could be a hallucination.

"This is some kind of joke," she muttered. "It's not real. It's a trick."

"No joke. No trick. I have nothing to gain by conning you, Miss Jensen, and, as you point out, I have taken a significant risk coming here. I trust no one else. I trust you, my superior trusts me, his superior trusts him, and that superior is the General Secretary. Two layers between the Comrade General Secretary and you. Then you go to your President, and bring back his answer, and so on. You must meet with the President personally. No envoy. No opportunity for the war clique to interfere." She listened, but the air of unreality was back. None of this was real, and soon she would wake. "The official negotiations will continue," Fomin said. "And they should be played out as though they reflect reality. But they do not. Too many of our madmen are involved. Perhaps too many of yours as well. The only true negotiation will be between your President and the Comrade General Secretary, through you and me. That is the negotiation that will save the world."

IV

Despite the night chill, Margo's dress was damp with perspiration. She didn't believe a word he said, and yet she believed it all. She didn't know what he really wanted, and yet she did. She shook her head. "I don't understand," she said for the third or tenth time. "What am I supposed to do? Walk up to the White House and ring the bell?"

"You are a resourceful young woman, Miss Jensen. You proved that in Varna. You are only nineteen years old, but you survived interrogation by the Darzhavna Sigurnost, and even escaped their custody, a thing that is unheard of, and all of this without ever admitting your true role—"

"I had no true role—"

Fomin waved this away, indulging a pedant. They were standing together in the silt near a ruined dock, listening to the slow lapping of the black waves. "Fine, Miss Jensen. Have it your way. You were an innocent tourist. A student on a fellowship. Whatever you like. My point remains the same. You are resourceful. Courageous. Inventive. Much like your father. You will surely work out some means of communicating the Comrade General Secretary's message to your President. But that I leave in your hands."

"You have the wrong girl."

"On the contrary, Miss Jensen. You are the only one I trust to do this thing."

Still watching the placid water, she let out a long breath. Dust thou art, and to dust thou shall return, said the traditional funeral service. Maybe so. But Margo had always hoped she would die near the water; better, in it.

"What's the message?" she finally asked.

Fomin was lighting another foul cigarette. "You are," he said.

V

Viktor Vaganian sat in his car on a downtown street that looked up at the waterfall. He was using a flashlight to study the Esso road map unfolded on the steering wheel. He was unfamiliar with this town and had lost Fomin's car in the darkness. Odd that Fomin knew the twists and turns so well.

But Fomin's presence in Ithaca was itself a surprise. Viktor had trouble working it out. Was this Margo Jensen the colonel's agent now? Had he somehow turned her in Bulgaria, as in his time the legendary recruiter had turned the Rosenbergs and Fuchs and so many others? If so, the inexplicable decision to release her from custody would at last find a logic.

Of course, there were other, less attractive explanations available. Viktor was reluctant to embrace them. He did not want to believe that his own teacher could be the traitor he sought. But he would have to investigate the possibility.

He refolded the map, every crease perfect, and headed out of town.

TWENTY

The Recluse

I

Lorenz Niemeyer lived alone, in a small cottage on a bluff to the north of Fall Creek. Trees shrouded the house from the road. The winding driveway was marked with signs against trespassers and warning of vicious dogs, although in practice his mongrel, Demeter—half poodle, half something unknown—was more likely to do her business on a stranger's leg than bite him. Around the bend, another sign, quite old, informed the unwary of land mines in four languages: a souvenir, it was said, from a dicey nighttime jaunt across the border between the two Germanies back in the days before the Wall. The great man wanted all the world to know that he preferred to remain undisturbed, but when she pushed the bell, three chimes rang loud enough to wake the dead, and although it was well past eleven, the butler, Vale, opened the door at once.

"Miss Jensen," he murmured in his funereal tones, contriving to recognize her without ever looking anywhere but above her head.

"I know it's late," she said, conscious of the tremor in her voice. "I'm sorry to disturb you. I need to see Professor Niemeyer. It's urgent."

Still Vale did not look at her. He was tall and broad-shouldered and heavy-waisted, and his eyes had the dull and distant cast of a man on drugs. People said he had worked with Niemeyer in the war and was suffering from shell shock, or perhaps the aftereffects of his treatment by the Gestapo; because it was common ground that *something* terrible must have happened to him. Now he inclined his long head and stepped to the side. Despite the hour, he was fully dressed. "Do come in."

She stepped past him into the foyer, which was large but low-ceilinged, and decorated with indifferent seascapes collected by a previous owner. She remembered her only previous visit to the house, early in September, when Niemeyer threw the annual party for his students. She had been one of two hundred young people crowding the lawn and spilling onto the porch and into the cottage proper, although a makeshift barrier of twinned chairs arrested the progress of the guests at the hallway leading deeper into the house. Now Vale led her down that very corridor to a cozy book-lined study, where, late as it was, a small fire burned in the grate. A book of chess games was open on a side table, where a position had been set up on a board.

"Please, wait here, Miss Jensen," the butler said.

"Thank you."

Vale pulled the double doors closed behind him. Alone again, Margo squeezed her hands together to try to control the shakes. Vale had seemed so calm; but, then, from what she understood, it was not unusual for undergraduates to visit the house at all hours.

Female undergraduates: or so the rumor mill had it.

Unable to sit still, Margo moved to the window. Niemeyer's cottage backed on the woods. The night had gone overcast, but there was wind, and now and then the skittering clouds cleared for a moment, allowing silver shafts of moonlight to brush the trees. She wondered who was out there watching, for she had come to believe somebody always was. Harrington had told her to resume her normal life, but she wasn't sure Harrington would know a normal life if it sat down for dinner. Margo nibbled her lip. A part of her mind still was not entirely sure that she wasn't still in the dream. The borderline between this world and that was harder to find in the dark, and had been ever since—

The double doors opened, slowly but loudly, and even as Margo turned, she realized that Niemeyer wanted her to hear the sound so that she would not be startled when he entered the room. A dream Niemeyer, she decided, would not be nearly so considerate.

"Good evening, my dear," he said. "This is indeed a delight."

He was wearing pajamas and a robe and floppy slippers. His hair was disordered, and the bad hand was in his pocket, and it was plain that she had roused him from his sleep. His eyes were guarded. The bonhomie seemed forced. She could not at first put a name to what she read in his tired face. Then it occurred to her that he might be nearly as frightened as she.

"Good evening, Professor," she said. Her voice still shook. "I'm sorry to disturb you."

His smile was tentative but wry. "There was a time when visits by comely young women such as yourself to my humble abode were a more common occurrence. But nowadays, I'm afraid I need my rest."

She didn't trust her voice this time, so she only nodded.

"You would appear to be in need of a drink, Miss Jensen." He crossed to the sideboard, uncapped a decanter, sniffed. "Sherry, you know, doesn't have an actual vintage the way other wines do, but this is a good one." Another sniff, followed by a frown. "Fairly good, anyway."

He poured two glasses, offered her one. She hesitated. "I insist," he said.

"No, um, thank you, no." Margo found herself babbling. "The drinking age for women—"

"There is a medicinal exception, Miss Jensen." The humor was forced, the grin a ghastly imitation of the pompous smile that accompanied the worst of his jokes. "You need this. It will calm you down. Good. Now sit."

She did as bidden. She had been doing as she was bidden quite a bit lately, but, in this stuffy library, began to feel somewhere deep down the banked fires of a rebellion.

"Better. One more sip. Good. Now, my dear. It's the middle of the night, and you arrived here terribly upset. Now that you're relatively calm, why don't you tell me what you're doing here?"

"I didn't know where else to go. Who else to talk to." He waited. Her mind was galloping ahead of her mouth, or perhaps stumbling behind. Finally, she was able to form the words. "I think Dr. Harrington is working with Soviet Intelligence."

II

Now it was Niemeyer's turn to go mute. He had told them in class that the key to a successful interrogation was for the interrogator never to seem surprised. He did not seem surprised now, just thoughtful. He returned to the sideboard and unstopped the crystal decanter once more, taking his time, then topped up her glass and his own. He sat again, this time beside her on the sofa. He crossed those plump legs and sipped, watching her.

And Margo responded. She had not realized until tonight how badly she needed to tell the story. The story of her experiences. The reasons for her suspicions of Harrington came tumbling out: That she was being followed on campus even before Stilwell and Borkland visited. That Fomin seemed to know she was coming, to be waiting for her. That he already had a thick file on her. That he had a copy of the forged application the State Department had prepared. That he'd had her arrested and then, when he caught up with her after her escape, released her. It had to be a test, Margo said: a test to see whether she would be capable of carrying secret messages. But there was no way Fomin could have heard of her unless Harrington had been in touch with him . . .

And she wound down.

"I didn't know where else to go," she repeated, not liking the weariness in her tone.

"Not a dream, I suppose," he said after a moment. "And not a scheme to winkle yourself into my bed, hoping for a better grade, one supposes. Pity, that." But the humor failed to rouse the slightest fury. Niemeyer took a longer drink. "This meeting with Fomin really happened, then."

"Yes, sir." The "sir" sounded odd in light of the occasion, but the habits of the classroom die hard. "But about Dr. Harrington—"

"First things first, Miss Jensen."

"I thought it might be you," Margo went on, eyes downcast, missing the point. "Who was in league with Fomin, I mean. But that didn't jibe with the access to the State Department files, or with the detailed knowledge of my mission."

"Unless I'm working with Dr. Harrington." She looked up sharply. "Or maybe there's another mole. It needn't be me. It needn't be Dr. Harrington. It needn't be anybody. I wonder whether you're allowing your imagination to run away with you, Miss Jensen. When you're in the field, everything that goes wrong looks like conspiracy."

"That's what Agatha said."

"And who's Agatha when she's at home? I don't believe we've had an Agatha in the story."

"My minder. She got hurt the night I got arrested. Nobody will tell me where she is, or even how she's doing."

"I can check, if you like." He was topping off her glass, using his good hand. "Now, listen to me, Miss Jensen. There will be plenty of time to go mole hunting once the crisis is successfully resolved. For the moment, why don't we stick to the facts and put the speculations to one side?"

"I— yes. Okay."

"The basic information is this. In Bulgaria, you were interrogated by a man identifying himself as Fomin, who claimed to be a colonel in the KGB. Tonight you saw him again, he confirmed the presence of missiles in Cuba, and he asked you to serve as his conduit to the President of the United States. Fair summary?"

"Not his conduit. Khrushchev's conduit."

"Indeed." A sip. "Granting that emendation, Miss Jensen, why precisely do you come to me?"

She was, for a moment, wordstruck. Wasn't it obvious? "You're the only one I know who can help. You know people in Washington. I assumed you'd know what I should do next."

"I see." He swirled his glass, studying the liquid, but Margo knew it was the quality of her story, not the quality of the sherry, that was under scrutiny. "Would it trouble you terribly were I to ask a few pertinent questions? By way of clarification, let us say?"

"You mean, to figure out whether I'm lying."

He didn't smile, or bother to respond.

"You came here straight from wherever this was?"

"Stewart Park. There was another man there, too. Also, Fomin said somebody was following me, and—"

Niemeyer raised a hand and actually covered her mouth. "An old trick. He says somebody's watching you, and, just like that, you're on the same side against the mysterious watcher."

"He was lying?"

"No idea. Makes no difference. Now, listen carefully, Miss Jensen. I don't want those details. Not yet. First, we establish the provenance of the information. Then we hear the story."

His face had gone serious, and Margo knew this was his element, the real Lorenz Niemeyer beneath the flannel: she was face-to-face with the ice-cold spymaster he was reputed to have been, and some said still was.

"I came straight here," she said.

"How?"

"I guess I walked."

"You guess?"

The hard truth: "I don't remember all the details. I was sort of in a fog."

"Call your boyfriend? That Jellinek fellow?"

"No."

"Your drug-addled roommate? Your friend Annalise? Littlejohn, or the other silly fools from your study group? Anybody?"

She registered no surprise that he knew her life as well as she did. "Nobody."

"Anybody see you on the way here?"

"I don't know. I walked all the way from Stewart Park."

"That's over a mile, mostly uphill. Cars must have passed you."

"Probably. I don't remember."

"Did you change your clothes? Buy a soda?"

"No."

"Wait here." He stood up and walked toward the door. Vale opened it at once from the outside. Margo wondered how the butler knew his master wanted him; and, for that matter, how he had known her name when she rang the bell. In the hall, the two men had a whispered conversation. Vale vanished, and Niemeyer resumed his place.

"Did he give you any warnings? Not to talk about this—that kind of thing?"

"He said not to tell anybody but the President."

Niemeyer's face hardened. "So it's been less than an hour, and you're already breaking the rules."

"I didn't know what else to do. I tried to explain to Fomin. I can't just walk up to the White House and knock on the door and ask for an appointment."

"And what did Fomin say to that?"

She found herself reciting Fomin's theory with a certain pride. "He said that any girl resourceful enough to escape custody at the DS headquarters could surely talk her way into the White House."

The great man thought this over. His frown deepened. The misshapen hand toyed with what remained of his hair. "Suppose you were able to reach the White House and persuade them to accept you as the conduit to Khrushchev. Did Fomin tell you what to do next?"

"He said I'd be contacted."

"Did he say through whom?"

"No."

"Did he say when?"

"No."

"Did he say how you'd know the contact was authentic? Did he give you a word code, anything like that?"

"No."

"Sometimes, after an experience like you had in Varna, people make things up. Trying to get attention. You wouldn't be doing that, would you, Miss Jensen?"

"No." The rhythm Niemeyer had established left her little choice but to keep giving the same answer.

"Exaggerating at all?"

"No."

"Are you omitting any details?"

"No."

"Fomin. What was he wearing?"

She shut her eyes, saw him in the darkness, heard the squeal of the unoiled swings. "A turtleneck sweater. A sports coat. Some kind of dark pants."

"Was he smoking?"

"Yes," she said, very surprised.

"What brand?"

"I didn't see the pack. They smelled terrible. I never looked at the pack."

A knock on the door. Vale stepped inside, crossed the room on silent feet, whispered in his master's ear. The great man nodded. The butler went out.

Niemeyer resumed as if the interruption had never occurred.

"You're sure Fomin said missiles—plural."

"Yes."

"Did he say how many?"

"No."

"He told you the types."

"Yes."

"But he did say that the official negotiations wouldn't go anywhere?"

"He said Khrushchev couldn't afford to lose face."

Niemeyer nodded. "We model the Kremlin as a zero-sum game. There's only so much authority to go around. Whatever flows out of one set of hands flows into another. The General Secretary never holds all the power. Not even Stalin could act entirely unilaterally, although he had more freedom than the poor bastards who've held the office since." He was talking to fill the void while he thought. "We saw this coming, you know—the missiles. We told Eisenhower. We told Kennedy. Nobody would listen. We have our water borders, we've never been successfully invaded—if you don't count that small unpleasantness in 1812, when the Brits burned the White House—and, come to think of it, that particular unpleasantness is celebrating its sesquicentennial this year, isn't it?"

Automatically, her mind recorded the six-syllable word with the accent on the fourth syllable, but tonight she derived no pleasure from adding to her list.

"And that tale has an instructive provenance." Niemeyer was still racing out ahead of her. "Consider, Miss Jensen. Have you ever wondered *why* precisely the Brits were able to burn the White House? Because we saw the troops coming up through Maryland and thought they were headed to Baltimore. Because the President's military advisers were sure that any attack on Washington would come from the west or the southwest. Nobody had them coming from the southeast, and there wasn't enough army to defend every approach. They chose our soft underbelly while we looked the wrong way, Miss Jensen, and they're doing it again. We have early-warning radars in Alaska and all across Canada, we have listening stations in Greenland, England, Europe, Japan, the Philippines, Guam, and none of it—none of it—would be of the slightest utility should the attack come from Cuba. It's the oldest story of warfare, and it's been true all through history. Nobody ever defeated the enemy by building walls to keep him out. When you retreat behind your walls, you've already lost. Ask Athens. Ask Carthage. Ask France, twice in this century alone. Ask anybody." He nodded his heavy head, the way he did in class when confirming his own analysis. "You go after your enemy in his lair. If you sit back and wait for him to come, the war's as good as over."

Margo said nothing. She wasn't sure whether she was supposed to respond. Her own preternatural calm continued to surprise her. Harrington was right: having once experienced the excitement of the secret world, she found it more real than the rest of life.

"This is what we're going to do," said Niemeyer. His contemplative moment had passed; he was the spymaster again. "Vale will drive you back to your dormitory. You won't tell anybody about Fomin, or about our conversation. Not a word. I'll do a little bit of checking, and Vale or Mrs. Khorozian will get a message to you tomorrow or, at the latest, the day after. Do you understand?"

"Yes." She restrained an urge to thank him.

"Until you get the message, you live your normal life."

"I will."

"Including with your friends, with young Jellinek, with everyone." He was up again, striding, unable to sit still. He took the poker, prodded the fire. The cinders made a red swirl. "And don't lie in bed, sick with worry. Don't ditch your classes. You have to behave as if this never happened. Do you understand me, Miss Jensen?"

"Yes, sir."

"Do you know who Aleksandr Fomin is?" He didn't wait for an answer as he continued toying with the fire. "He is the head of the KGB's Washington station. Formerly he headed up their spying operation out of the United Nations. We believe that he was involved in that Rosenberg business. The point is, he's as high as the KGB goes over here. This is the top table, Miss Jensen. Oh, and Fomin isn't his real name. Alas, we haven't worked that one out yet."

"The top table," she echoed.

"Indeed. If he says he has the General Secretary's ear, he might actually be telling the truth." He put the poker down, sat beside her on the sofa. "Doubtless you are wondering why Fomin came to you. I'll tell you. He interrogated you in Varna. He trusts you, by which I mean he knows you're unofficial, and brave, and dependable. Those are the qualities he needs to run a back channel."

"A what?"

"Back channel. An unofficial negotiation that runs parallel to the official one. Typically, the official negotiators know nothing about it." He touched her knee, but his mien was fatherly. "If things work out as I expect, Miss Jensen, this won't be the only message you'll carry."

"But—but—"

"The missiles in Cuba are now a crisis, Miss Jensen. The crisis could lead to the planet's last war. Like it or not, you're in the middle of it." That curt nod. "*You* are the back channel."

"I'm not the right person."

"On the contrary, Miss Jensen. Aleks Fomin's presence in upstate New York proves exactly the opposite. By coming here, he is as much as instructing the President that he will deal with no one else. The back channel will be through you, or there will be no back channel." He was on his feet again. "Now, go back to your dorm and leave matters in my hands. Such events as these are measured in hours, not days."

In the foyer, it was her turn to ask a question.

"Can you tell me about my father?"

"Tell you what, Miss Jensen?"

"How you came to work together. Why it's all still such a big secret." She hesitated. "If he really died the way Fomin said."

He considered. "I met your father in North Africa. He was a corporal in a transport battalion, just as you've been told. A colleague of mine and I had to . . . well, we had to go on a mission. Our usual driver had just been shot, and your father's lieutenant recommended him as the best they had. The journey was long, and very dangerous. The truck was attacked by the Luftwaffe. My colleague was killed. He had a specialized function that I was not trained to fulfill. Your father was an engineer. I hadn't realized this. There was a device. It had been damaged in the attack. He examined it and announced that he could make it work. I told him to go ahead. He took about fifteen minutes. We completed the mission. The device worked as designed, perhaps a bit better. I swore him to secrecy. When we got back, I hopped the next plane to SHAEF in Tunisia, and I asked for his transfer to my unit. They insisted that the transfer be informal, as OSS field units were not permitted to have Negroes. I was angry, but your father said it made no difference to him. He joined me in Europe, and we did some things I can't talk about. Your father received several secret commendations and two secret medals. But when he died, he was still formally a corporal in the transport battalion."

"But why the secrecy even now? I don't understand."

"I am not at liberty to discuss the matter further, Miss Jensen. I've probably told you already more than I should."

She considered. "And the way he died?"

"That I cannot discuss."

"But if he was a hero—"

"He was, Miss Jensen. You will have to take my word for it." He had the door open. "And as to the other matter you raised, I have known Doris Harrington for twenty years. She is a thorough patriot. You haven't even persuaded me that there was a leak. But if you're right, you must look elsewhere for the culprit."

"If I was betrayed—and if I do wind up functioning as the—the back channel—then it's possible I'll be betrayed again."

"Indeed. For that reason, I would be careful to remain well clear of anyone with whom you worked on SANTA GREEN."

III

The car was grand and shiny and old, a Cadillac Imperial Landau, vintage 1930s: Nana had a photograph of one just like it that her cousin used to drive. The green fenders sparkled. The headlights were as big as portholes. The engine, Margo knew, was an improbable V16. As she climbed in, the gray mist swirled like an encircling army. She had no idea how Vale could see where they were going, but he never faltered.

Like it or not, you're in the middle of it.

True, some part of her had always longed to be at the center of great events, but now that she was there, she was frightened half to death. She had spent those terrible hours at DS headquarters in Bulgaria, she had the dream almost every night, and she jumped at every shadow. She wanted to be a little girl again. She wanted Nana. No, that was a lie. She wanted Tom. She had missed their study date tonight, and to make things worse she would never be able to tell him why. He would be hurt. Probably angry. Still, just now she craved the comfort of another human being who wanted her back. The two of them had never slept together, but if she were headed to his place rather than her dorm, she had no doubt that tonight would be the night.

Which was why it was a good thing she was heading to the dorm.

Sort of a good thing.

Riding with Vale was like being driven by a ghost. Not only because of his alabaster flesh and distant, sepulchral manner; not only because he neither addressed a single word to her nor turned his face in her direction; not only because he drove with such gentle skill that the car seemed to glide through the October night without actually touching the road, and at times, even as he sped along Ithaca's winding lanes, seemed not to move at all; but also because Vale's very presence somehow reached down to some ancient and atavistic part of her brain and chilled her, exciting her fight-or-flight reflex—for Vale, like every incorporeal creature of her nightmares, exuded an aura of being able to do enormous harm even though he himself could never be touched.

She realized, as she climbed out at her dormitory, that in certain ways the chauffeur reminded her of Agatha, whom she suddenly missed: Agatha, of whom everyone on the intelligence side seemed unreasonably frightened, even though she struck Margo as mousy and benignant; Agatha, who had been beaten badly the night Margo was arrested, and whom she had neither seen nor heard from since.

"Good night, miss," said Vale in his reedy voice, his first words since she had climbed in. He was holding the door for her and even touched his cap. She watched the shiny Landau until the luteous glow of its lamps grew faint and finally vanished in the mist.

She slept poorly, and dreamed about the bomb.

TWENTY-ONE

The Committee

I

"The President is considering three options," said Jack Ziegler. "His advisers seem deeply divided. Some of them favor a blockade of Cuba, except that they'd call it a quarantine, to get around certain problems in international law. Some of them want to attack immediately, to blow the launchers to kingdom come before your people can finish assembling them. And a couple are willing to remove our Jupiter missiles from Italy and Turkey if you'll remove yours from Cuba." He took a bite of his hot dog. They were walking through the zoo, nearly deserted on an autumn weekday afternoon. "I'm told that the President was furious about that last suggestion. He considers it tantamount to blackmail. It isn't going to happen."

Viktor Vaganian's English was excellent but not perfect, and it took him several seconds to work out such words as *quarantine* and *tantamount*. He suspected that Ziegler used complicated constructions just to annoy him.

"Your sources in the ExComm are quite competent," the Russian said: "ExComm" being the Executive Committee of the National Security Council, the body the President had empaneled to advise him in the crisis.

"More than competent," bragged Ziegler. "I have sources in the room."

Viktor frowned to hide his satisfaction. The fool shared information too casually. Viktor decided to toss out a little more bait.

"In the Soviet Union, we would find the traitors and shoot them."

Ziegler chuckled. "Here, we'd strap them into the electric chair." Serious again. "But nobody's going to get caught. A lot of people are worried about the direction this thing is going to take. People in powerful positions. They'll protect each other, believe me."

Viktor considered. They were in the monkey house now, and the American was making faces at the creatures. "There is no word of negotiations?"

"Not yet."

"Preventing a successful negotiation is the purpose of our collaboration."

Ziegler was still clowning for the apes. A few were up against the bars, baring their teeth. He spoke without turning around. "I don't think I'm likely to forget, Viktor. Don't worry so much. As soon as they start talking, I'll know about it, and then you . . . well, you can do what you do."

II

That same evening, Harrington was in Gwynn's office. As usual, he had made her wait until the end of the day. As usual, he had only a moment to spare, because he was due on the Georgetown party circuit. This time, he had added another device to keep her in her proper place. When she walked in, he smiled and told her to have a seat, he would only be a second. Then he resumed studying the file that was open on his otherwise uncluttered desktop. Precious seconds ticked past. He turned a page, made a note, turned another. Harrington understood the technique entirely; she used it herself. The idea was to create a growing impatience in the visitor, and then to use that agitation to gain control of the conversation. You knew you'd won when your visitor spoke first, thus becoming a supplicant.

But knowing how the technique worked did nothing to reduce its effectiveness. Once she realized that Gwynn was prepared to read and wait until it was time for him to go, she finally spoke up.

"You win," she said. "You can put the file away now."

He turned a page. "In a minute, Doctor. Just be patient."

"Alfred," she said.

He made a note.

"Alfred!"

Finally, the clever eyes lifted to hers. "Sorry, Doctor. I have to be up to speed. Been going to the White House for the ExComm, you see. Have to keep up with the reports."

So now she knew why he had agreed to meet: to rub his little surprise in her face.

"I'm pleased to hear it," said Harrington, remaining as calm as she could. No matter what she might think of Gwynn, he was deputy assistant secretary for intelligence and analysis. It made perfect sense that he would accompany the secretary. "How do things look?"

"You know I can't tell you that, Doctor."

"Well, that's why I'm here. I want in." She circled a finger to indicate the rest of the floor. "Half the analysts in this department are working on Cuba. And you have me doing corruption in the Diem regime."

"Vietnam's important. We could be heading for war there."

"Not if we go to war with the Soviets first."

He shrugged. "That's not your problem any more, Dr. Harrington."

"I've been on Cuba since January, as you're perfectly aware. I know as much about what's been going on there as anybody."

"Maybe you did before. You don't now. You're not cleared for these details." Spreading his fingers lovingly over the red-bordered folder. "This is strictly need-to-know. I'm sure you understand, Doctor. You were in the war."

Drawling the last word.

"You seem to be forgetting that it was my operation that—"

"Your operation blew up in your face. I warned you that would happen, and I was right."

Harrington took her time. This was her last shot, and she knew it. In the intelligence world just now, Cuba was the only industry: anybody working on something else might as well have been unemployed. You could tell who was on the way out by checking the subscription lists on the Cuba material and seeing which names were omitted.

Hers, for instance.

"Have you even looked at GREENHILL's debriefing, Alfred? It contains priceless information—"

"I can't tell you what we have and haven't looked at."

She chafed at the plural pronoun. "Don't make this personal

between us. We haven't always gotten along, and that's more my fault than yours. There's still a tremendous amount I could contribute—"

But Gwynn was tucking the folder into his briefcase and locking it with a key. "You're out of the loop, Doctor. It's been decided at the highest levels." He reached for his coat. "Oh, and a word to the wise. I wouldn't try going to my friends this time. I've warned them, and they agree. Nobody's interested in bureaucratic battles just now. Not when there's a nuclear war to avert."

"You wicked little horror," she whispered, but he was already out the door.

III

On Wednesday morning at ten, the ExComm reassembled in the Cabinet Room. Mostly, the members went over the same ground as yesterday: the President could attack the missile sites, or declare a blockade, or rely on diplomacy. The fact that the options never changed confirmed Bundy's secret belief that the ExComm was a waste of time, that a very few senior people should be meeting, without staff, to thrash this out. Half the comments around the table seemed aimed at getting the speaker a mention in the minutes. McGeorge Bundy, the President's special assistant for national security affairs, tried to hide his frustration. He sat with his head down, taking scrupulous notes with his gold pen.

Bundy knew committees well—from academia, from industry, from government—and he loathed them. A committee is like crabgrass, he told himself: it sits forever, swaying with every breeze, and is impossible to eliminate once it takes root. He had urged the President to avoid too large a group of advisers on how to deal with the missiles in Cuba. Great men made swift, reasoned decisions after consulting a few trusted advisers, not after batting ideas around for hours with a dozen or more egomaniacs.

President Kennedy, however, had an almost childlike belief in the importance of hearing everybody out. Must come from growing up in a large family, Bundy decided.

Last night's meeting had been dominated by the generals and their reasons for preferring an invasion. This morning, Secretary of State Rusk did most of the talking. Bundy had some difficulty figuring out the secretary's position, and the expressions of others around the table suggested that he was not the only one confused. A blockade would violate international law and show that we wouldn't be intimidated, and an attack would be illegal and might be the only way to . . .

Bundy tuned him out, and spent the time outlining the memorandum of the meeting he would later place in his classified files. The inability to work out a plan worried him. The United States was the mightiest power on the planet, but was dithering and dickering over how to handle the installation of nuclear missiles a few miles off its shore. The President of the United States sat serenely, if a bit embarrassed, a bystander at a stranger's family quarrel.

Bundy continued to write. Involuntarily, the thought came to him: the President he served might not be up to the job.

When the group broke for lunch, Bundy tugged Bobby Kennedy aside.

"What's he doing? The missiles can't be talked out of existence."

The attorney general's tone was mild. "The lions need their chance to roar, Mac. These are powerful men. The President can't act without their support."

"And when the time comes, can your brother tame the lions?"

They could talk this way to each other. They knew each other well. Bundy was one of the handful of government officials who received regular invitations to the private seminars the attorney general held at Hickory Hill, his estate in McLean, where the great writers and thinkers of the generation were regularly on display. Bobby was smart and curious and charismatic. There were days, even, when Bundy thought Bobby would have made a better President than his big brother Jack—not least because Bobby was as true as steel to his marriage vows, whereas Jack . . . wasn't.

"You worry too much, Mac," said the attorney general. "The President will do fine."

But it was family loyalty speaking, and they both knew it.

IV

When the ExComm resumed that afternoon, the argument turned bitter. The Pentagon, in the persons of Defense Secretary McNamara and General Maxwell Taylor, newly appointed chairman of the Joint Chiefs, presented a united front: the United States had to invade Cuba, right now, immediately, before any of the nuclear sites became active.

The President was astonished, and said so: just two days back, McNamara had been all for caution.

"What if they use their nukes?" the President asked.

"The Soviets won't do that. They might retaliate in Berlin, say, but it won't come to war." The defense secretary considered, then modified his answer. "It's possible some nuclear weapons might be used without permission, and we'll obviously take some losses, but it won't come to a full-scale exchange."

A murmur of alarm around the table. Even Bundy was surprised at how cavalier McNamara sounded. But they both knew what most in the room did not, that the report had come from YOGA, their top source inside the Kremlin.

General Taylor took up the cudgel. "The secretary is right, Mr. President. You can't do this with air power alone. If you want to end this threat, you have to end it. Really end it."

Somebody asked how many Soviets would die in a surprise air strike.

As always, McNamara had figures at hand. "At least several hundred. Possibly more. Khrushchev will have to strike back. We have to decide what the level of losses we're willing to incur to get those missiles out of Cuba."

"They won't hit us," said another voice. "They wouldn't dare."

Bundy was about to ask what on earth would lead anyone to believe that Khrushchev would stand aside while the United States military killed hundreds of his soldiers, but at that moment his assistant stepped in to hand him a note. Even as the conversation continued, the others looked on curiously, no doubt wondering what bit of urgent news they were about to learn.

The national security adviser read the note twice. He hesitated. The ExComm seemed to be coalescing around immediate military action, a path, he was certain, that would lead to nuclear war. The President, although still skittish about the invasion, was listening closely to the arguments. Already trains full of troops were converging on Florida, just in case. Over three thousand Marines had been airlifted to Guantanamo. Multiple squadrons of fighter-bombers and interceptors had been relocated to Homestead, McCoy, and Tyndall Air Force Bases. The attack could be launched within hours of a decision. But Bundy knew these men. They loved the sound of their own voices. No decision would be reached any time soon.

He hopped to his feet, and even interrupted John McCone, director of central intelligence, an act that always gave him a secret frisson of delight. "Excuse me, Director. Mr. President, if you will excuse me for a moment, I have an important call."

Maxwell Taylor fixed him with the famous glare that left three-stars quivering. "Whatever it is, Mr. Bundy, it can't be more urgent than what we are doing here."

Bundy was unruffled. "Actually, General, it can."

The national security adviser slipped from the room, his mystery intact.

V

Bundy took the call in his office. He loathed Lorenz Niemeyer, whom he saw as a bloodless calculator of lives and a narcissistic self-aggrandizer into the bargain, but he could not deny the man's strategic brilliance. Niemeyer wasn't like many others who longed to revolve in the orbits of power. He didn't fawn. He didn't drop by the White House for coffee in order to stay on the Administration's radar, the way so many amateur strategists did. He knew that he was needed. And the fact that the man had driven two hours to Griffiss Air Force Base in order to make the call on a secure line told Bundy that it must be important.

"I had a visit from GREENHILL last night," Niemeyer began, without preamble. The relationship between the two men was built on a decade of mutual loathing, and neither any longer bothered with pleasantries.

"And?" Bundy prompted.

Niemeyer spoke. Bundy listened. And listened some more.

"No," he finally said.

Niemeyer argued.

"Out of the question."

Niemeyer wouldn't stop.

"Enough, Professor. I'm telling you, officially, we are not interested. Not in the slightest. Calm her down any way you can, keep an eye on her if you think you must, but leave this matter entirely alone. Do you understand me?"

Niemeyer's answer was unprintable.

As usual, the two competed to see who could hang up on the other fastest.

Bundy took a moment to compose his thoughts. He knew he had to get back to the ExComm before the hawks bullied the President into an irretrievable decision. But he also knew that he couldn't just bluff them into silence. He needed an alternative, a plausible case to put before Kennedy, an idea sufficiently compelling that it just might slow down the juggernaut.

He drummed his fingers, considering Niemeyer's crazy idea. And he found himself wondering whether it was the idea that was crazy, or just Niemeyer.

Bundy buzzed his secretary, asked her to step in.

"Janet, I need Dr. Harrington in my office in one hour."

"Who?"

A beat. "Harrington. Doris Harrington. She's an analyst at State."

"An analyst?" Janet echoed, her cocked eyebrow and questioning tone intended to remind him that the national security adviser did not waste time dawdling with mid-level bureaucrats.

"The truth is, I'm not precisely sure what her title is. But I want her waiting when I get back from the ExComm."

"Yes, Mr. Bundy."

"Also, if Professor Niemeyer calls back, I'm not available."

"Yes, sir."

"After that, I want every file we have on SANTA GREEN."

Again the eyebrow went up. "I believe those have been archived, Mr. Bundy. The operation was a failure."

"I'm not so sure." He was talking to himself as much as to her. "I think maybe that's what we were meant to believe."

TWENTY-TWO

Cut Off

I

Wednesday was agony. She had to wait for Niemeyer, and waiting was one of her pet hates. In the interrogation room in Varna, for all that she was terrified, she at least had been able to take action; here in Ithaca, in relative safety, she was unable to advance her cause through her own actions, and the inertia was making her crazy. Not even her studies diverted her. Niemeyer's class was canceled, which she found odd. She botched a translation in French, and when she looked at her notes from Professor Hadley's course on political anthropology, they were gibberish. After Systems Theory, Littlejohn accosted her again.

"Hey, look. I didn't mean—"

She interrupted him. "About Bulgaria. You haven't told anyone, right?"

He bowed and put a hand over his heart in a pantomime of gallantry. "You have my word. Like I said, I can keep a secret." Then he straightened. "But I want to make sure you're taking care of yourself. You've made arrangements and everything?"

She didn't know what he was talking about; she didn't care. She had her own agenda. "Did your source tell you anything else?"

Littlejohn's expression grew somber. "They think you were betrayed. That's why you got arrested."

As she hurried away, she gave a quick thanks that the secret was still safe, because a student who'd been arrested behind the Iron Curtain could hardly serve as a back channel: the entire point was to remain anonymous. But mostly she worried about whether Phil Littlejohn could possibly be right.

They think you were betrayed.

Betrayed why? For what? She didn't know anything, and had been unable to find out anything. Maybe Littlejohn was what he pretended to be, a spoiled rich boy with a silly crush. Maybe he was working for somebody. Maybe he had been sent to upset her. Sent by Fomin. Sent by Harrington. Sent by Niemeyer.

Or maybe he didn't know anything. Maybe he had just heard a couple of rumors and made a couple of good guesses.

And maybe tonight she would grow wings and fly to the moon.

In the late afternoon, she tracked Tom down and offered a wooden apology for missing their study date last night. They went for their usual pizza, and it was like attending a funeral.

And all day, no word from Niemeyer.

II

If Wednesday was agony, Thursday was worse. Margo rose early, not least because she had hardly slept, but also because, when she did manage moments or hours of escape from the world, she spent them fighting off the clutching hands of the swarms of those who had relied upon her and were now trying to pull her off the roof of Nana's house, down into the Hudson, where they kept the most dangerous prisoners in Bulgaria. Lying in bed with her eyes open was no better than lying there with her eyes closed. Today she would hear from Niemeyer.

Dressing, Margo picked a pointless fight with Jerri, who had as usual used her shampoo without asking. She marched off to breakfast, where she picked an equally pointless fight with Annalise, and afterward could not recall what they had argued about.

"What's the matter, sweetie?" Annalise asked, blue eyes wide. "What's going on?"

But Margo had no way to explain her swirling emotions. Harrington had warned her about this part, too. *Nobody likes a spy*, she had said. *Least of all her friends.*

She went to the library, found a carrel in the corner, dawdled. It was Thursday morning, and Thursday morning was the deadline. Thursday morning she was supposed to hear something from Niemeyer, via Vale or Mrs. Khorozian. The morning was ticking past, and he had said that in the current crisis time was counted in hours, not days. At nine-thirty, Margo gave up waiting and hurried over to the government department.

Niemeyer's suite was locked.

She cupped her eyes and pressed her face against the frosted glass. She could see, dimly, the light from the window opposite. She was quite certain that the office was empty. That Niemeyer was absent meant nothing: a seminar, a woman, an urgent summons to Washington for consultation. But Margo could not remember a weekday when Mrs. Khorozian hadn't been guarding the door with all the fierceness at her command. And if by some chance she was ill, the graduate assistants were always fluttering about.

Always until today.

Never mind. The great Lorenz Niemeyer surely had matters in hand. She would return to her dormitory and find a note from Mrs. Khorozian. Or perhaps Vale, the chauffeur, would be outside in the shiny green Landau, ready to whisk her off to wherever the negotiations were being held. But there was no Landau, and no note, either, unless she counted the envelope from Tom Jellinek, who seemed to think that they should talk, and wanted to know if she would meet him for coffee at four this afternoon, after his physics lab.

The kindly, protective woman behind the desk in the dorm lobby was called Flo. Flo asked whether she wanted to leave him a return note: the way things were done. Margo shook her head. She could think of nothing to say.

"He's really sweet, your young man," said Flo.

"I know he is."

"You should leave him a note, honey. You know how men are."

"Later," said Margo. Heading for the door, she could feel Flo's eyes censuring her for her rudeness.

She skipped French, Niemeyer's warning notwithstanding. She knew she would never be able to concentrate, and didn't want to embarrass herself again. She headed for the library and found a free carrel up in the stacks, quite near the bound back-issues of periodicals she needed for her term paper for Professor Hadley. But she wasn't working. She had chosen a spot overlooking the windows of Niemeyer's suite in the government department. She was watching for the moment his lights went on. She waited. People entered and left the building, but his windows remained dark.

Surveillance, she realized. She was undertaking surveillance. Watching without anyone's knowing. The notion in some peculiar way reassured her: better to wait actively than passively. And it surely mirrored, in some small way, what her father would have done.

Besides, her classes were less important to her than they had been. That was the perhaps predictable side-effect of Varna; and, now, of Fomin. Margo had spent her life following the rules, but had also found exhilarating her rare moments of disobedience and risk. She remembered a silly night back in eleventh grade when she and three other girls borrowed a car and a bottle and drove down to the shore to go skinny-dipping, Margo not really approving but desperate to belong. They were spotted by a couple walking a dog, and the police arrived. Fortunately, one of the other girls had an uncle who was minority leader of the State Assembly, and there weren't any charges, even against the lone black girl. Nana, of course, exacted her own punishment, and except at school Margo had seen none of her friends for two months.

But the mad moment of rebellion had been worth it. That was the secret truth behind Margo's surface obedience, and probably the real reason she had succumbed to Harrington's blandishments and gone to Varna with Bobby Fischer in the first place. Margo had always led a highly structured life, protected by but also imprisoned within the cold, unassailable bars of familial expectation. She broke the bonds only rarely. When she did, the results were usually painful, but occasionally worth it.

As they were worth it now.

Because, down below, one of Niemeyer's teaching assistants was hurrying up the front steps of the government department.

III

She ran. There were elevators, but Margo took the stairs. She raced across the Quad and was in the corridor no more than two minutes after spotting the TA. But even as her footfalls echoed on the grand tiles, she knew she was too late. Sure enough, Niemeyer's suite was locked and dark.

The TA was at the other end of the hall, headed for the rear exit.

What was his name? Mitch? Matt? No, Mark.

"Mark!"

He swung around. He was a second-year graduate student, diffident and dead-eyed.

"Yes?"

"Where's Professor Niemeyer?"

The question seemed beneath him. Like the other Conflict Theory TA's, he had absorbed something of the great man's hauteur. "Who are you, please?"

"Margo Jensen. I'm in the course. Class was canceled again today, so I wondered——"

He spoke right over her. "We don't go sharing the professor's privacies with every sophomore who crawls out of the woodwork. Now, if you don't mind, I have things to do."

"Wait." She actually put a hand on his arm. She could tell Mark didn't like it, so she left it as a goad. "I spoke to him night before last. He was supposed to leave a message for me by this morning."

"Then I suppose he changed his mind."

"Can you at least tell me what you were doing here? Or is that also classified?"

He was unmoved by her sass. "I was making sure the cabinets were all padlocked, if you must know. We do that when he's out of town. It's really Mrs. Khorozian's job, not mine. Now, if you'll excuse me."

He marched away.

She considered what he had told her while trying to tell her nothing. That Mrs. Khorozian wasn't in today. That Niemeyer was out of town, probably for a while. And that, although Mark spoke as though he had no idea who Margo was, he had known she was a sophomore.

Quite a haul for ninety seconds. Donald Jensen would be proud.

IV

She tracked down the department receptionist, who insisted that nobody but the one grad student had been in the suite all day.

Margo's eye fell on the department directory. Without asking permission, she picked it up and leafed through. The receptionist ignored her.

A minute later, Margo was on her bicycle. She headed west, downhill to Stewart Avenue, crossed the bridge over Fall Creek, and pedaled north along Cayuga Heights Road. Finding the little side street was easier in the daylight than it had been the night before last. Margo arrived at the cottage shaking and sweaty. Once more she ignored the posted warnings. She climbed to the creaky porch, but nobody answered her ring or her knock, and when she went around the side and peered through the kitchen window, she saw no sign of life. She stepped down into the side yard. Through the little squares of glass cut into the garage door she saw the mighty Landau standing where it should, but the practical Buick that Niemeyer used to get around town was gone.

She heard a rustle in the trees. Turning, she saw a heavy shape moving in the woods. A deer? A bear? Surveillance? Littlejohn again? Or just a crazed murderer, which at this point would almost be welcome? Maybe this is what Nietzsche was getting at: when you spent too long jumping at shadows, they started to jump back.

On her bike once more, Margo headed east again. It took her a good half-hour to reach the address she had found in the directory, way up the Dryden Road. It turned out to be not a house, but Mr. Khorozian's antiques business. As if they didn't want people knowing where they lived. The storefront was shuttered. At the auto-repair shop on the corner, the mechanic gave her what Nana called the twice-over and offered a crafty smile. Using a soiled cloth to clean grease from his hands, he told her she could try the Khorozians at home.

"Sometimes Mr. K works from there. Sometimes he don't come in."

Her sweetest smile: forced, but it still counted. "Would you happen to know their address?"

He did, and, leering, led her into the cluttered office. He grabbed a grimy card file, found the one he wanted, held it out for her to memorize. "But you won't find them up there," he added. "Not today."

"Why not?"

"They left in a hurry yesterday morning. Big black car came for them." He was still wiping grease from his fingers; and still looking at her all wrong. "Driver spoke one of those foreign languages. Maybe Russian."

V

There was an emergency number at the State Department. Harrington had vouchsafed it to Margo before sending her into the lions' den, and made her repeat it back until she had it cold. Margo used it now, from the telephone in the back of the repair shop. She had offered to pay for the call, but the mechanic had magnanimously told her to go ahead, while he stood out in the shop ogling her backside through the smeary glass. Her sweaty fingers fumbled at the dial, and she had to try three times before she got it right.

"D.O.," said the laconic voice at the other end.

Margo recited precisely from her script. She felt idiotic, but the rules were the rules. "This is Hyacinth calling for Miriam."

She heard pages turning as the duty officer looked up "Hyacinth" and "Miriam" in his codebook. His response, she remembered, should be *Miriam's not here right now. Can Gwendolyn help you?*

Finally, the answer came back. "We don't have a Miriam," he said.

Margo stared at the phone. "How about Gwendolyn?" she finally said. "Maybe Gwendolyn can help."

This time the response was instantaneous.

"We don't have a Gwendolyn."

Had she gotten it wrong? Misremembered, as Nana liked to say? Was it Glynis, perhaps, or Guinevere? No. She remembered perfectly. This was something else. They were cutting her off. She didn't know why, but no other answer made sense.

Margo glanced out the window at the mechanic, who was looking pointedly at the clock above her head. She had promised that the call would only take a minute. She smiled at him, but he didn't smile back. Plainly he thought he'd been had.

She made another try. "Can you connect me with Dr. Harrington?"

"We don't have a Harrington."

"Listen to me," she said. "My name is Margo Jensen. I was in the building last month. I met a Dr. Harrington. I don't know her first name, but she must have a desk or an assistant or a supervisor or somebody you can connect me with."

"We don't have a Harrington," he repeated.

"I don't think you understand. My message is urgent. That's why I called this number. I'm in trouble. There must be somebody who can help in an emergency."

"Impossible," said the duty officer, and hung up.

TWENTY-THREE

Plans Within Plans

I

In Washington, it was the same Thursday afternoon, and the ExComm was on the verge of voting for war. The mood in the Cabinet Room was somber. CIA Director McCone had just reported that a handful of the MRBM sites were probably operational, and the President's advisers were facing the real possibility of their own extinction, perhaps within days. McCone's announcement had lent to the proceedings an air of reality that had previously been lacking. Until today, the ExComm might have been an academic seminar.

No longer.

Bundy glanced around the table. McCone had said "probably," but he could see from their faces that the group had missed the qualifier. It was entirely possible that this very afternoon, without waiting for authorization from Congress, the President would allow a dozen or so worried advisers to persuade him to push the button.

"'Operational' meaning what?" asked Bobby Kennedy, who saw the same danger.

McCone looked straight at him. "Meaning, from launch order to missile away would be about eight hours."

"Why so long?" asked Gwynn, from State.

All eyes swung his way. The poor man didn't seem to understand that his job was to shut up and take notes. Watching him, Bundy wondered whether his own alternative plan had any chance of swaying the

President: especially given that he wasn't quite ready to share it. In a crisis, time was always the enemy.

"Because they use liquid fuel," said General Curtis LeMay, Air Force chief of staff, whose task it would be to execute the attacks on the missiles if and when they were ordered. He toyed with his slate-gray mustache. He was rarely seen not chomping on his trademark cigar, but had forsaken it for the afternoon. "Ours use solid fuel. That's another advantage we have over the Reds. We can have a bird in the air on fifteen minutes' warning. A few years from now"—this almost wistful—"well, that advantage just might have disappeared. It might be a good thing this is happening now instead of later."

The President frowned. Bundy knew what was going through his mind: McCone said some of the launchers were operative, but the truth was that the Agency didn't know for sure. In the bureaucratic competition to get information to the table, they were reaching the point where unanalyzed rumor was being passed along as fact.

"Let's come back to this later," said Bundy. "I understand the Joint Chiefs have prepared attack plans."

Taylor and LeMay presented the scenarios together. They would begin with two waves of air attacks, the first aimed at destroying the surface-to-air missiles, the second to take out the MRBM launchers. The ideal follow-up would be a ground assault on the launch positions, just to be sure. The discussion went on for a good forty-five minutes. Most of those at the table seemed inclined toward an attack. Then McNamara threw cold water on the whole thing with a chilly reminder that any attack on the missiles would entail significant Soviet casualties—and, since the attack would have to include napalm to be sure that the launching sites were destroyed, the manner of many of those deaths would be quite horrible.

"So, you still think they'd retaliate," somebody clarified.

"They'd go nuclear," said McNamara. "They'd have no choice."

"We could handle them," said LeMay. He was one of the most respected commanders in the military, but Kennedy loathed him, and the feeling was mutual. Yet Bundy had to admit that LeMay, for all his bellicosity, had been responsible for building the Strategic Air Command into the serious deterrent force it had become. "Believe me, Mr. President, they don't want war with us."

"We don't want war with them, either," Ted Sorensen shot back. But it was plain that the ExComm was inclined in LeMay's direction. The man was an aggressive spellbinder. The Kennedys were about to lose control of the table.

"I had a conversation with President Eisenhower," McCone offered. "He proposes ignoring the missile sites and attacking the Castro regime instead."

It took the group a moment to appreciate the distinction, but Bundy immediately saw the appeal. First, an attack on Havana was less likely to entail Soviet casualties. Second, once a new regime was installed, the Cuban government itself could demand the removal of the missiles, and if the Soviets refused, they would then be committing the act of war against Cuba.

Bundy thought the plan had merit, but Kennedy seemed uninterested, maybe because he had now twice burned his fingers trying to unseat the Castro regime, maybe because the suggestion came from his still-popular predecessor.

Or maybe because, for all his Cold Warrior credentials, Kennedy still believed in the power of words. That was the part that worried Bundy most.

Bundy stood. "The President has a meeting," he said. "Let's resume in ninety minutes."

II

From the Cabinet Room, the President returned to the Oval Office to meet Andrei Gromyko, the Soviet ambassador. Bundy had to be there, but first he stopped Alfred Gwynn in the corridor, drew him away from the others.

"You've been pestering your superiors about Dr. Harrington," he said without preamble. "She's your problem. How you handle her is entirely up to you."

Gwynn was cautious. "She has powerful friends."

"They won't interfere."

Bundy turned away, but not before noting with satisfaction the leap of delight in the little man's eyes. A fundamental principle of Washington life was never to let ambition blind you to manipulation. By that measure, poor Alfred Gwynn was as blind as they come.

The question was whether the same could be said of Doris Harrington.

TWENTY-FOUR

The Grand Illusion

I

The New York Central had a six-thirty train running south from the depot in Syracuse, more than an hour's drive away, and even with Annalise driving full-tilt, Margo almost missed it. The train reached Garrison a little past eleven. There were no taxis at that hour, but from Syracuse she had called the Paxtons, the only other Negro family of means in the town, and their batman, as Mr. Paxton insisted on calling him, was waiting. The ride to Nana's house from the station was all of five minutes. Margo could have walked, but arriving sweaty would have been taken by Claudia Jensen as a sign of disrespect and even what she referred to as disrepute: the sort of thing associated with the riffraff.

They turned past the crumbling stone lion—its mate had vanished long before Margo moved in—and entered the pitted drive that wound its way up Nana's hill. Another corner, and suddenly the house loomed out of the darkness, a hulking shadow against the night sky. It was an Irish Palladian, sprawling and tumbledown, a granite monstrosity with chimneys and balconies and clever stone carvings everywhere you looked: one of those grand mansions built along the river at the turn of the century by the great industrialists—the barons, Nana called them—who used to shuttle between city and country by private barge, or, in a few cases of obscene wealth, private railway. The barons were long gone, and half the grand palaces stood empty and dying. Thus the wheel of history: the spectacular achievements of one age became the forgotten detritus of the next. Margo had learned this history at her grandmother's feet, because Nana wanted the little girl she raised as her own to be the brightest child in every classroom she would ever enter.

Knocking took as much courage as stepping alone onto that tram in Varna.

The heavy door opened at once: Muriel, the maid, had waited up. She told Margo that Mrs. Jensen had retired but would join her at breakfast. There was hot chocolate in the kitchen. Margo thanked her and told her to go to bed. She made a cup, then stood for a while on the stone portico around the back of the house. The hot chocolate warmed her against the autumn night. Once upon a time, Claudia Jensen had hosted grand parties out here. Now the stonework was cracked and the metal furniture sagging. Down below was a field of rushes that Nana always said would poison you should you get a scratch. Margo had never believed the story, and never tested it. Beyond the rushes was a mud-bound, bashed-in dock to which nobody would ever tie up a boat, and beyond the dock was the river. Ripples of moonlight teased their way toward the city. A distant thrumming marked the passage of a barge, gentled northward by a tug. In daylight the barge would be rusted and ugly, but by night it was majestic, braving the current. Margo thought of Fitzgerald, and wondered how you avoided being borne back into your own past. She nibbled at her lower lip. She hated this house, and for much of her life she had hated her grandmother, too, but no other route was available. Robert Frost was right in "Death of the Hired Man": Home was indeed where, when you had to go there, they had to take you in.

Margo had nowhere else to go; and so had gone home.

She had told nobody other than Annalise that she was leaving campus, and nobody at all her reason: she had run out of ideas she could pursue from Ithaca. Nana represented her last hope. In a way, she always had. Claudia Jensen had never been kind to her granddaughter, but she had also never admitted that a single problem existed that was unfixable. That attitude had evidently rubbed off on her son, and perhaps a bit on Margo as well. Nana always claimed to know everybody who was anybody. Tomorrow Margo planned to put that claim to the test.

She had no choice. Fomin was counting on her, and if a part of her knew perfectly well that the fate of the world could not possibly rest on her slim nineteen-year-old shoulders, another part of her hoped that history had thrown up a chance for the daughter to complete the work the father had begun.

The wind freshened. Margo sipped her cocoa and lifted her eyes to the lighted spires of West Point across the river. She remembered the dream. Was Garrison far enough from New York? Niemeyer would have said that was the wrong question. She knew because Littlejohn had asked in class whether Ithaca was far enough from some military base in upstate New York.

Niemeyer had smiled benignly, the way he did in the face of lesser minds.

"Stop being a ninny," he'd said. "Remember, we're stronger than they are. We might not be stronger tomorrow, but we are today. They're more frightened of us than we are of them. The right question, children, is whether Dubna or Kaliningrad or Yaroslavl—or wherever they plan to hide the Central Committee in case of war—is far enough from Moscow."

"Are you saying you want a war?" another acolyte had asked, for the sheer pleasure of hearing Niemeyer's response.

The great man waddled to the center of the stage. "Nobody wants a war," he announced, and if he had told them he held the survey results in his hand, they would have believed him. "But if we're going to fight one, the time to do it is now, when we can still win. Ten years from now, fifteen, God alone knows what the correlation of forces will be." He flipped his hand dismissively. "When you children get to run things, I'm sure the first thing you'll cut will be our military. Good luck scaring the Bear or the next bogeyman after you're done beating your guns into butter."

The memory of classroom banter had almost warmed her, but the bitter chill riding the river breezes reminded her of reality. Niemeyer was gone. He had abandoned her; and so had the State Department. The duty officer had paged through his codebook until he found the notation telling him to cut her off. Margo could not begin to fathom Niemeyer's sudden flit, or the abrupt severing of her connection to Harrington, but she had to press on. Others in her position would have accepted that the world would likely be able to save itself without their urgent assistance, but for Margo the matter had nothing to do with choice. It had to do with expectation.

Claudia Jensen had not raised her granddaughter to retreat; and Donald Jensen would never have given up.

Margo lay awake in the room of her youth, window open to catch the distant lapping of the waves, wondering whether tonight she would have the dream.

On Friday morning, she got down to business.

II

"The White House? You mean, the Kennedys?"

"Yes, Nana. The Kennedys. I'd like to meet the President."

"Mmmm."

"This weekend," Margo added, feeling at once idiotic and determined. They were in what Claudia Jensen called the morning room, a glass-walled atrium off the kitchen, added well after the house was built. Potted monkey-puzzle trees guarded the corners. The view was of the sloping brown lawn down to the playhouse. The rosebushes had been covered in burlap for the season.

"Oh, well, of course, then," said Nana, quite loud. She was a tall, imperious woman, whose idea of raising children had been to bark orders and then tell you to go away. If you ran to her because you had fallen and scraped your knee, she upbraided you for carelessness and called the maid to take care of the problem. A long time ago, she had been the first Negro to serve as a deputy mayor in New York City. The money was her late husband's, because, in addition to practicing medicine, Arturo Jensen had owned a small piece of the largest black life insurer in the country.

Not that there was as much money left as Nana liked to pretend.

"Of course," said Nana again. She took a long gulp of orange juice. She was unaware that Margo had known for years where Nana hid the gin she always had Muriel mix in. "Meet the President. I'll call him up. How's that? Call him up, tell him to make time in his schedule."

"Nana—"

But Claudia Jensen's sarcasm was as awesome as her disapproval, and, once launched upon the project of your humiliation, she never stopped until your mortification was complete. If you cried, that was bonus.

"Mr. President, my dear old friend, how lovely to hear your voice. How's Jackie and the little ones? Marvelous. Yes, I'm fighting fit, so terribly good of you to ask. Now, Jack, I'm afraid I need a little favor. Yes, another one. What can I tell you? I'm a soft touch, everyone knows it, so everyone asks. But if you might oblige me one last time, my fool of a granddaughter wants to visit the White House this weekend. Would you be available to give her a personal guided tour? You will? First thing tomorrow? I am so very grateful, Mr. President. I am forever in your debt. If you need any help against the Russkies in Berlin, or against the heathen Chinese wherever they might be making trouble, give a call."

"Are you finished?" said Margo.

"What did you think I was going to say? Do you think I'm a magician?"

"Sometimes you are. Yes."

The old woman smiled at this. "Well, well," she said; and nothing more. Her heavily powdered face was almost pale enough to pass for white.

"I'm serious, Nana. I really do need to meet the President. Not want to. Need to. And I can't tell you why."

"Mmmm," said Nana again. She spooned her oatmeal, looked around suspiciously, then grabbed the syrup and poured a healthy tot. "Well, I do grant that you've been acting strange since you made that fool trip to Hungary."

"Bulgaria."

"Where?"

"Bulgaria!"

"No need to shout. Besides, it's all the same, dear, isn't it? They're all Commies, aren't they? But I must say, you're being very mysterious."

Half the truth: because Claudia Jensen, whatever airs she might put on, was no fool. "I wish I could tell you, Nana. All I can say is that it's a—a security thing. It has to do with what happened over there."

"*What* happened to your hair?"

"*Security,* Nana. The security of the United States. I wish I could tell you more."

"Imagine that. Margo Jensen is going to save the world. Well, well."

But something in her granddaughter's face impressed her. "Very well, dear. Maybe you're not the silly little girl you seem. The security of the nation. And you have to see the President. Well, well."

"Yes, ma'am."

"Mmmm. The President. Kennedy. I never took to the Kennedys. New money. I hate new money. Always putting on airs. Now, the Roosevelts. That was a family. Eleanor Roosevelt and I used to have tea now and then. Did you know that, dear?"

"Yes, but—"

"Eleanor's very ill just now. She lives right up in Hyde Park. Not in the big house. She stays in that little cottage. It's really been too long. I should get up to see her before it's too late. She isn't long for this world, I'm afraid. Maybe you could come with me. You've never met her, dear. I'm sure she'd adore you." Another long drink of orange juice. "So—what exactly is this magic you expect of me, dear? How am I supposed to arrange for you to meet the President?"

"Your godson."

"I have thirteen godchildren—"

"I'm talking about Uncle Eddie. Eddie Wesley. He was something big in the campaign, right? Doesn't he work in the White House?"

"Not any more."

This brought Margo up short. Another one of her master plans shot to bits.

"He resigned a few months ago," Nana was saying. "I'm sure it was some matter of principle. All the Wesleys are that way. And the most dreadful social climbers. Muriel. Muriel!"

The maid raced in.

"This is cold. Freezing cold. And the syrup is a clotted mess. Look. Look! Take it, dump it, eat it yourself. I don't care. Hot. Bring it hot." Lifting her chin toward her granddaughter. "Take hers, too. I can't imagine what they feed them up there in Ithaca, but it's bound to be better than this."

"I'm fine, Nana."

"See? She hates it, too. Bring her something else. Cereal. Cold cereal. That's the ticket. Cornflakes. We do have cornflakes, don't we? And milk, I take it? Then bring her cornflakes and milk. She can put the sugar on it, same as she did when she was a girl. And I'll have more orange juice." Alone again. "Now, dear. Where were we?"

Margo was having trouble keeping up. Each time she visited Nana, Nana was worse than before.

"Your godson. Uncle Eddie. He must still know people in the Administration."

"I really wouldn't have any idea." Nana gave her a calculating look. "But I suppose I might give him a call."

III

Doris Harrington stood by the window, watching as two security officers emptied her safe and searched the other cabinets and shelves for classified material. She would keep her security clearance while she served her thirty-day notice period, Gwynn had assured her, but he had also made clear that she wasn't expected to do any work of actual significance, adding that if she chose to spend her time at home, the State Department would have no objection, and would of course continue her salary and benefits. As a matter of fact—he had added, blank-faced—that might turn out to be the best idea.

She had known this day would come, of course. In her business, everybody flamed out sooner or later, and taking the blame for failed operations was one of the risks of the trade. Lorenz Niemeyer had tried to warn her that the balance of opinion was starting to run against her, and their uneasy marriage, whatever its pains, had taught her to trust his political judgment. So she had not been entirely surprised to learn yesterday evening that she was finished. But to lose out to a little snake like Gwynn: that had indeed surprised her. Even more surprising had been the way all her fabled links to people of influence had gone dead: she had telephoned everyone she knew, and nobody had taken her calls.

"I think this is everything, Doctor," said one of the security officers.

"I believe it is, Walter."

"Do you have any classified materials at your house?" At least he had the good grace to look embarrassed: Harrington had known him for ten years.

"No."

"You realize we'll have to check?"

"Of course."

Another awkward moment. "Well, good luck, Doctor. Sorry about all this."

Walter and his partner rolled their shopping carts out the door and off down the hall. As soon as they were gone, she dialed Borkland, her assistant, but there was no answer. The receptionist told her that he was in a meeting.

With his new boss.

Embarrassed afresh, Harrington rang off. Gwynn didn't have the reach to pull this off, she told herself. The ambition, surely, but not the ability. On the other hand, McGeorge Bundy did. Crossing back to her now pristine desk, she wondered, not for the first time, why the President's national security adviser, a man she had never before met, had summoned her to his West Wing office three nights ago and proceeded to grill her about every aspect of SANTA GREEN. Bundy might have simply been getting his facts straight as he sharpened his knife for her, but that seemed like a task several levels below his pay grade, particularly when he had the missiles in Cuba to worry about.

That was the proverbial joker in the deck: the missile crisis. Why on earth would a man with Bundy's responsibilities waste a precious hour nailing down the details of what went wrong in Bulgaria? And why so many questions about her assessment of her agent, GREENHILL? It made no sense that Doris Harrington could see.

No matter, she told herself, grimly. Not her problem any more. She felt, suddenly, old. And alone. Her brother had died in the war. She hadn't seen her sister in years. The agents she ran were all the family she had. And the last of them was now off limits, forever.

TWENTY-FIVE

Double Dactyl

I

While Nana made her calls, Margo waited in the high-ceilinged library, long her favorite room, even though it had been forbidden to her as a child. The windows gave on two sides of the house. She stood in the front, studying the gravel drive as it made its winding way past the hedgerows. She wondered whether anybody was watching the house. Fomin had told her somebody was following her on campus the other night, but—as the vanished Niemeyer had pointed out—he might well have been lying. She half expected to see his battered brown Chevy climbing the hill toward the house. Or, if not Fomin, maybe Ainsley, or even Agatha, about whose fate Margo worried constantly, secretly blaming herself for whatever had happened.

Ainsley had called it a mugging, but the club of those who had deceived her grew larger by the hour.

She tipped her head against the glass, wondering. She realized that a part of her actually wanted someone to be watching, as a signal of her significance: just as somebody would surely have been watching her father. She studied the hedges. She saw movement, but it was only a squirrel. Beyond the bushes lay the gravel lane that didn't appear on the maps, guarded by a PRIVATE WAY—NO TRESPASSING sign where it reached the county road. There were only six houses, all of them old and enormous, and after all these years the townspeople were still astonished that one of the owners was a Negro.

Even though Margo had lived in this mansion for considerably more than half her life, she never felt that she belonged. Home to her was still her parents' small house on Lincoln Avenue in New Rochelle. Growing up with Nana had been like being a visitor, a tourist in a foreign world. Niemeyer liked to describe spying as looking out of somebody else's eyes. That was how Margo had spent her childhood after her parents died, concealed deep in her own head while somebody else used her mouth to say, "Yes, Nana," and "Thank you, Nana," and went to the fancy dinner parties and the ladies' teas so that Claudia Jensen could show off her granddaughter's exemplary poise and manners.

Margo had hated it here.

She crossed to the desk. There were two telephone lines in the house, and she used the second to call the operator. Several minutes later, she had the numbers for eleven Harringtons in Washington, D.C., and its environs. Margo tried them one by one. None of the seven that answered owned to knowing a Doris, although one belonged to a rather breathless gentleman who complimented her on her lovely voice and suggested that they get together for a drink.

She tried the State Department emergency number again. This time the duty officer was female, but she still acknowledged none of the code words, and insisted afresh that they had no Harrington.

Stymied.

It occurred to her to try Bobby Fischer. After all, it was one of Bobby's acquaintances who had passed on to American intelligence the original contact from Smyslov. But according to Tom, Bobby was furious at her for deserting him in Varna, and considered it her fault that he'd messed up his analysis of the adjourned position against Botvinnik.

"I don't think he wants to hear from you right now," Tom had said, and the reproach in his voice suggested that he still wasn't ready to believe that nothing had happened between them.

She'd asked him to let Bobby know she wanted to talk to him, but she knew nothing would come of it. Another avenue closed. And so she was left with a bizarre truth: three nights ago, a colonel in Soviet Intelligence had driven her through the streets of Ithaca, and today she could find nobody who wanted to hear the story.

Maybe she should just walk up to the White House gate and tell the guard she has an urgent message for the President.

Margo laughed but didn't like the sound of it—screechy and

overdone—and she might seriously have started to wonder whether something was wrong with her had not Muriel chosen that moment to summon her to the kitchen telephone.

"Is it Uncle Eddie?" Margo asked as they walked along the hallway.

"No, Miss Margo. Mrs. Jensen says she can't reach Mr. Wesley. He's in Europe or one of those places."

Another hope broken.

"She's gone to her nap," Muriel added, handing her the phone.

"Hello?"

The breathless, familiar voice of her best friend. "Margo, it's Annalise. Listen. Something's happened."

"What is it? Is it Tom?"

"You should sit down."

"Just tell me. Please."

"It's Phil Littlejohn. Somebody ran him over with a car outside his frat last night. He's dead."

II

Down the grassy slope to the south of the mansion was the small playhouse where her brother used to tease her so relentlessly. Inside was a little bench, and that was where Margo sat, hunched so that she couldn't be seen from the house, the same way she used to sit when her grandmother's wrath would chase her away, setting off dark-red storms of fear and self-loathing in her young brain. She felt the echoes even now.

"It was an accident," she whispered, voice tinny and distant to her own ear. "Just an accident. Nothing to do with you. Nothing."

An accident. A coincidence. A tragedy, but not because—

Not because—

"He was following me around. Asking questions. But that's not why it happened. It's not."

A hit-and-run, Annalise had said.

No, there weren't any leads.

Yes, just last night, around midnight: that is, about the time Margo was standing on the portico sipping hot chocolate.

"Nothing to do with you," she told herself again.

Margo had to believe it, because the alternative was incomprehensible.

"Incomprehensible," she said aloud, then laughed, remembering.

She had sat on this very bench in high school, too old for the playhouse but not too old to seek out a spot where she could be alone when the pain of being ignored or despised by the white students became too much for her. The word *incomprehensible* sparked the memory because it had six syllables, and six-syllable words had been her passion, ever since Mrs. Hochberg, her tenth-grade English teacher, had introduced them to the double dactyl, a form of comic verse with precise rules of rhyme and meter, beginning with two nonsense words and containing a real word of six syllables, with a stress on the fourth. They were called double-dactyl words. Double-dactyl words, double-dactyl poems: Margo had been hooked from the first—not least because her instant mastery of the complicated game had altered her destiny.

In those days, Margo's most hated adversary had been a tall blonde cheerleader named Melody Davidson, chased by all the boys Margo secretly liked. Back then, Margo had been quiet rather than combative, and Melody zinged her at will, knowing she would never fight back. Margo was one of the two or three best students by class rank, but submissive in the face of confrontation, and therefore an ideal target for bullies. She remembered the day they had read aloud in English class the double dactyls they'd composed as homework. Most of them were poorly done and didn't begin to follow the very precise rules, but Melody's was brilliant:

> *Higgledy Piggledy,*
> *Margo of Garrison,*
> *merrily teasing the*
> *boys at the dance.*
>
> *She'll soon be losing her*
> *marriageability,*
> *unless she swiftly gives*
> *some guy a chance!*

The class was stunned. Mrs. Hochberg was angrily commanding Melody to stay after school to do the assignment over, reminding her that personal attacks were not permitted in the classroom, and threatening a note to her parents, but Melody's cold blue eyes, fixed on Margo, glittered malicious delight at her successful coup.

Margo did what in those days she always did at moments of confrontation: she dropped her gaze, as if her notes were suddenly of the most surpassing interest. She scribbled nonsense as the heat rose in her face, and she felt the judgmental stares of her classmates, her humiliation not in the least assuaged by Mrs. Hochberg's lecturing her tormentor. Then she looked at the page and realized that what she had written wasn't nonsense at all. She blinked. Years of slights and mockery by the white kids—and now, suddenly, a way to fight back.

At that moment, Margo's life changed.

"Wait," she'd said, very loud.

Mrs. Hochberg adjusted her thick glasses. "It's okay, Margo. You don't need to say anything. This wasn't your fault, and you should ignore it. It's my responsibility—"

For the first time in her life, but not the last, Margo interrupted a teacher. She was writing hard. An idea had come to her. "I'm not offended, Mrs. Hochberg. I thought Melody's double dactyl was funny. I'd like to read mine now, if that's okay."

"Oh, um, of course, that's fine," said Mrs. Hochberg, quite taken aback.

And so Margo had marched to the front of the room, holding in trembling fingers the lined paper on which she had just rewritten her own double dactyl:

> *Melody Shmelody,*
> *high school queen Davidson,*
> *never does homework or*
> *gets the top grade.*
>
> *Not in the running for*
> *valedictorian,*
> *she will be no one when*
> *beauty doth fade.*

Stunned silence. Melody's mouth hung open. Then the laughter began. Even some hooting. Mrs. Hochberg was on her feet, bellowing her rule against personal attacks and telling both girls to see her after school.

Margo always thought of that afternoon as the moment she went over to the attack. She was still an outcast, to be sure, but she generally managed to give back as good as she got, and became known for her scary sharp tongue. After a while, the others teased her less. Some of them—not Melody, but others—even befriended her. That was why, when first Professor Bacon and then Professor Niemeyer began to talk about the theory of deterrence, Margo already had an instinctive appreciation of its intricacies. Even her answer on the fateful afternoon when Niemeyer asked whether she would put missiles in Cuba, was informed by her own experience. Niemeyer was wrong. She wasn't being methodological. She was being, as one would put it in a double dactyl, autobiographal. When she answered his question, she was imagining herself as the United States and her tormentors as the Soviets. That was why she had said the likely American response would be reason enough not to put the missiles in. Only now did she admit the truth: a brilliant mind, even when combined with a sharp tongue, didn't guarantee success.

As Phil Littlejohn could testify.

All at once, sitting still was too much. It was Mrs. Hochberg's classroom all over again. She had been pushed around by the bullies—first Niemeyer, then Stilwell, then Harrington, now Fomin—but the time for submissiveness was done. This time, a double dactyl wouldn't be enough. Her mind, on the other hand, was always available. She could think her way out.

As her father would have done.

Margo was on her feet. She all but ran back up to the house, and asked Muriel to tell Nana that she was borrowing the car.

"Mrs. Jensen will want to know where you're going."

"Out," said Margo, like the teenager she still was.

III

She drove north along Route 9, not quite able to believe her own destination. Nana's car was an old Cadillac, fiery red, with winged fenders and lots of chrome. Margo stepped hard on the gas. A part of her even hoped to get pulled over, but the one state police car she spotted didn't seem to care. She passed through Fishkill and Wappingers Falls, where she stopped to buy coffee and a newspaper. The dark-blue Chevy stopped, too, which scarcely surprised her, because it had locked onto her tail half a mile beyond the gates of Nana's estate and never strayed more than two or three car lengths behind.

Margo almost smiled—she was still in the game after all—and then she remembered Littlejohn, and her buoyant mood died. She had forgotten to ask Annalise whether there were any arrangements yet.

In Hyde Park, she drove right past the cottage where Nana's friend Eleanor Roosevelt lay dying. She found a diner and had lunch and read the paper. No mention of any missiles in Cuba. The press seemed more worried about the prospect of war between India and China than between the United States and the Soviet Union. Of course: the missiles were still a secret. Margo turned the page. In New York, *Who's Afraid of Virginia Woolf?* was drawing record audiences. She and Tom had talked about going, but Nana would have been appalled that her granddaughter wanted to see such filth.

Still, Hyde Park wasn't Margo's true destination: she was teasing herself.

As she resumed her drive north, a black Chrysler replaced the blue Chevy. Fine. If they knew, they knew. It could scarcely make any difference. She got off in Poughkeepsie, and stopped at a lunch counter near the edge of the Vassar campus because the sign outside, a blue bell in a blue circle, told her the restaurant boasted a phone booth. By a miracle, the phone book was intact. By a further miracle, the name was listed: LITTLEJOHN, WM & SUSAN—with an address on Lockerman Avenue. She had to ask directions twice, but finally found the place, a sprawling Dutch Colonial set well back from the street.

And the last thing she expected, as she pulled into the driveway, was the gray-uniformed men carrying paintings and crates into a moving truck out front.

A stylish convertible was parked in a turnaround. Margo pulled the Cadillac beside it and hurried up the steps. The movers ignored her as she walked to the open door. Maybe they thought she was staff.

She stepped into the foyer. Pale rectangles on the dark wood marked places where art had been removed. Two men were trundling a large seascape down the stairs. From what Margo could tell, the furniture was untouched. Only the art was going.

"Mr. Littlejohn?" she called out. "Mrs. Littlejohn?"

No answer.

She grabbed the sleeve of one of the movers, asked the obvious question.

"I just do what I'm told, lady," he said, and continued out the door, a bust of Shakespeare cradled in his arms.

The living room had views of the woods behind. A man was taping shut the drawers of a beautiful antique desk.

"May I help you?"

Margo turned. Behind her was a stout woman perhaps five years her senior, with the same flaming red hair and bulbous chin as the young man who had accosted her so regularly these last few weeks.

"I'm sorry. I didn't mean to barge in. My name is Margo Jensen. I was a—a friend of Phil's. A classmate at Cornell. I came to pay my respects."

The stout woman looked her up and down. "You're the one he talked about, then," she said. She stuck out a pale, fleshy hand. "My name is Priscilla. I'm his big sister. Would you care for a cup of coffee?"

TWENTY-SIX

Risk Assessment

I

The President was furious. Not at Bundy or Bobby—the only ones present for his outburst—and for once not at Khrushchev, either. He was furious at the ExComm, his own handpicked advisers, who at today's meeting had scarcely bothered to hide a growing frustration, bordering on disrespect.

Kennedy had told the group that he was increasingly uneasy about attacking Cuba, because the Soviets would likely respond in Berlin. The comment had enraged General LeMay, who shot back that the best way to invite the Soviets to move in Germany would be to do nothing about the missiles. To refrain from invading, he'd added, would be "almost as bad as the appeasement at Munich"—a thinly veiled reference to the President's ailing father, Joseph Kennedy, who had argued for placating Hitler and staying out of the war.

The other members of the Joint Chiefs, in more muted and respectful language, had said much the same; and several of the civilians present joined in.

Although Kennedy maintained his aplomb in the meeting, afterward he exploded. Bundy was seriously worried that the President might actually try to dismiss his top military officials in the midst of the crisis.

"Who do they think they're talking to?" Kennedy fumed. "Who do they think they are?"

"They're frustrated," said his brother. "We all are. We need a decision, Jack. We're out of time."

The President was stung. "*Et tu,* Bobby?"

The attorney general stood his ground. "We should at least set a deadline for action. Let the Joint Chiefs start planning."

"Maybe. We'll see." Kennedy turned to Bundy. "You know what the real problem is, Mac? Our vaunted intelligence agencies aren't supplying any useful information. They can count missile launchers but not votes in the Politburo. This would all be a lot easier if we knew what was going on in Khrushchev's head."

"I'll see what I can do," said Bundy.

"Do it fast, Mac. If we don't come up with something in a couple of days, I'm going to have to let the brass have their war."

II

Back at his desk, Bundy called Langley. After a wrangle, the Agency agreed to send over all of its material on Oleg Penkovsky, code name YOGA, the West's top Kremlin source. The files arrived within the hour, in an armored vehicle accompanied by an armed guard who was sitting even now in the anteroom, waiting for the national security adviser to finish his reading so that he could return the papers to the Agency vaults.

Bundy read fast, and the more he read, the more he worried. Although Penkovsky was a British source, the Agency paid his hefty "salary." Yet the man was mostly bluff and bluster, and often seemed almost to agitate for war. There was that peculiar line in YOGA's first serious debriefing, back when the fear was that Khrushchev would give the Cuban regime conventional weapons: "I must report to you that the Soviet Union is definitely not prepared at this time for war. . . . With Cuba for example, I simply can't understand why Khrushchev should not be sharply rebuked. . . . Kennedy should be firm. Khrushchev is not going to fire any rockets. He is not ready for any war." In the same conversation, Penkovsky kept telling his handlers how easy it would be to eliminate the entire Soviet general staff in case of war—including details of where they would disperse and how much explosive it would take to get them. Almost as if he wanted them gone.

Or at least wanted the West to try.

Bundy put the file aside. Whatever YOGA's agenda, he wasn't the solution to the President's demand for a line into Khrushchev's thinking. They needed something better, something more direct.

He asked his secretary to step in. "Do we still have the file on GREENHILL?"

"Yes, Mr. Bundy."

"Please check and see if she has any relatives or close family friends in Washington." He considered. "And I need to see the head of the White House Secret Service detail. Right now."

"Concerning?" Pen poised.

"Presidential security."

TWENTY-SEVEN

A Word to the Wise

I

"My brother liked you a lot," said Priscilla, puttering around the kitchen. "The way he talked, I think he had a little crush on you."

"I can't believe that," said Margo.

Priscilla's mourning was just hours old. Her smile was wan and forced. The cabinets were cherry, polished to a high sheen. Most of the dishes were packed, but a tea service stood on a trolley, as if awaiting this very moment. The cups were by Versailles Bavaria. "He could be a pain in the ass," Priscilla was saying, "but he could also be sweet. He said you had a boyfriend. I think he counted that his loss."

"We were just in a couple of classes together. He was a—a friend. A good guy."

"Not really. He was a spoiled brat. But he had his moments." She blew out a lot of air, like a patient getting ready to hold her breath for the needle. "My folks will be sorry they missed you. They're up in Maine. Well, Dad actually went up to Ithaca, to claim the body, but he'll be back in Maine soon. Phil—Phil would have—he would have been up there, too." But for the momentary catch in her voice, she seemed entirely unruffled. "Mom's family has a compound twenty miles north of Bangor. Twelve hundred acres. Most of the relatives will be arriving there in the next day or two. I'll be heading up as soon as the truck leaves."

"I notice they're taking mainly art."

She nodded as she poured the tea. "The art, the valuables. Dad's collection of rare books. Plus the gold coins, of course." She saw Margo's puzzlement. "It was one of Grandpa's rules. Everybody in the family has to have a couple of thousand dollars' worth of gold stashed somewhere, in case of emergency."

Margo found it odd that the family would respond to the death of their son by heading off to Maine with their gold and artwork, but she supposed that the manner of their mourning was none of her business.

"Miss Littlejohn—"

"Priscilla. Please."

"And I'm Margo. About your brother—"

The pudgy woman waved a hand. "You don't need to offer more condolences. If you're wondering why I'm not wearing black or sitting around sobbing, well, that's not who we are. We've lost relatives before. We know how it's done. We're old New Englanders, Margo. We aren't public in our grief." She played with her cup. "So, you. Where are you going?"

"I'm sorry?"

"Phil said your grandmother lives down in Westchester somewhere."

"In Garrison."

"Wow. That's really close."

Margo was more mystified than ever. "Um, yes. I suppose."

"You do have some kind of plan, right? From what Phil says, you're the kind who always does." That diffident smile again. "Oh, never mind. My family doesn't pry. Well, except for Phil, I suppose. Oh! I almost forgot. Where are my manners?" She sprang to her feet, crossed to the counter, put some cookies on a tray. She set the tray on the table, curled into her chair once more, and immediately began to munch. "Mmmm. Chocolate-chip. These are the best. From a bakery down the road. Want one?"

"Um, no, thank you."

"Come on. Why should I get fat by myself?" Shoving the platter her way. "And anyway, who knows when there'll be more?"

Margo dutifully selected a small one. It was as delicious as promised, and, not quite against her will, she was soon eating another.

"Poor Phil. He wanted to run for office. Did you know that? It's kind of a family tradition. Public service. My dad did all sorts of things before he settled down to teach. He wanted to be President one day. Not Dad. Phil. And why not? We've had Senators in the family. A governor of Connecticut. A Supreme Court justice. Cabinet secretaries. Three or four ambassadors. A couple of generals. But no President Littlejohn. Not yet. One of my less attractive duties is to marry a rising star in some political field and have lots of children who'll grow up and keep the family famous. Dad was furious that I wanted to have a career. I told him I'd meet a better class of men in New York. Not my dream, of course. In my family, we don't have choices. We have our assigned roles to play." As if caught by a fugitive emotion, the round face for a moment looked ordinary, and sad, and woefully tired. Then the smooth aristocrat was back. "Not that the girls aren't allowed to work. Why, Aunt Beverly is private secretary to Mamie Eisenhower. And I have a cousin who's some kind of senior accountant for the Rockefellers."

"Very impressive," said Margo, once she realized that Priscilla was waiting for some sort of response. "That's quite a family tree."

Priscilla flapped a soft hand, as if to show she didn't care about her own pedigree, although if that were true there would have been no reason to describe it in such detail. "But you, Margo. It's so interesting that you would turn up today. Phil and I were just talking about you——oh, Wednesday, it must have been. The night before he died." She sipped her coffee. "He was fascinated. He said he didn't know they made Negroes that smart. I'm sorry if I give offense, but that's what he said. And there's something else that he mentioned. Oh, you're done. Here. Another cookie. No, I insist. Look. I'll have one, too."

One of the movers came in with a question. Priscilla got up and followed him out of the kitchen. She left the tray practically in her guest's lap, and it occurred to Margo, as she considered her host's sweet but relentless pushiness, that Nana must have been like this once. Margo herself tended to be self-effacing; she had always let her grades speak for her. But now, as she bit into another delicious cookie, she wondered, not for the first time, whether this instinctive assertiveness, rather than intelligence or hard work, might be the true key to success.

"Sorry," said Priscilla. "Some people can't find their own shoes unless you hold their hands. And rude! Did you see how he didn't step aside to let me precede him from the room?" Sliding into her seat, she took back the conversation. "You, on the other hand. Your manners are impeccable. We're not racists here. Not my family. We've been for the civil-rights thing since 1948, when Humphrey gave that speech.

A couple of my relatives were there. I'm sure Phil must have mentioned that. And of course one of my uncles drafted Truman's order to desegregate the armed forces. I don't mean I'm for those marches and boycotts and sit-ins and all that. No sensible person supports that kind of behavior. We're a nation of laws. Yes, we should be changing the laws, but we shouldn't break them to do it. Some of those civil-rights preachers are real rabble-rousers. That's dangerous. Hey, did you leave me any cookies? Oh, good. Now. Where were we?"

Margo stifled a retort to her host's peculiarly limited enthusiasm. Priscilla once more sounded like Nana. "You were saying that your brother told you something else about me."

Priscilla's mouth was full. She nodded. "He said he thought you were in some kind of trouble." She laughed, sprayed crumbs, mopped them embarrassedly with a napkin. "Sorry. Sorry. And I said, of course you're in trouble, given what happened." She put the napkin aside. "In Bulgaria."

II

Margo tensed. Finally, she was where she had intended to wind up, without having to be the one to raise the subject. "What about Bulgaria? How do you even know about that?"

"Oh, well." Flapping an impatient hand. "Dad's a banker. He worked at the Treasury. He was on General Marshall's staff in the war. Afterward, he worked for the Economic Cooperation Administration—they handled the Marshall Plan—and then he went to Wall Street for a while. Uncle Donnan used to run the bank where I work. That's after he was Secretary of Commerce. Anyway, Eisenhower put Dad on the Forty Committee for a while"—a momentary flicker of the eyes, as if wondering whether a Negro would know what this was; in the end, Priscilla compromised—"and, as you probably know, they advise the President on intelligence operations and so on and so forth. Dad still has friends down there. Anyway, last weekend, Phil and I were up here for our folks' anniversary. Over dinner, Dad told us that the State Department had sent a college student to Eastern Europe on some damn-fool mission to find out what the Soviets were up to in Cuba, and she'd been arrested, and Phil said one of his classmates had just gone to Bulgaria. Dad wouldn't say any more, but Phil knew it was you, of course. He said Professor Niemeyer pulled you out of class one day, and the next day you were gone. And Dad said, 'Niemeyer? Really?' And he laughed. He said, 'Well, Niemeyer's not the craziest of the bunch'—something like that."

Niemeyer thought the crowd in Washington was crazy, and they thought he was crazy. Maybe both sides were right. But Margo's mind had leapt ahead.

"That's not all your dad said, was it? This wasn't just about the anniversary."

"I don't know what you mean."

"He didn't just bring up Eastern Europe and Cuba out of the blue. It must have been part of a larger conversation." Priscilla was staring at her, as if recognizing at last the peculiar intelligence her brother had described. "You said he invited you and Phil home specially. And it wasn't to share gossip about Bulgaria. He wanted to warn you, didn't he? Just like his friends down at Forty warned him. That's why everybody's going off to Maine. That's why you're shipping the paintings and the gold."

Priscilla was gazing out the window, on a landscape she might never see again. "Oh, you mean, did Dad tell us there are missiles in Cuba? Of course he did. He said it wouldn't stay secret for long. He said Kennedy and Khrushchev were both so insecure that neither one would have the good sense to blink. He said there's going to be a war. He said Stewart Airport is an emergency dispersal site for the Air Force, and we're practically around the corner, and, well, a near miss . . . Anyway, he said we should get moving." She was on her feet again, collecting the crockery. "Only Phil wouldn't go. Maybe because of you. Maybe some other reason. Mom begged him, and he said he'd drive up if things looked really bad, but in the meantime he'd be safe enough in Ithaca." Her laugh was harsh and tinny. "You know what? He wasn't."

Margo joined her at the sink, taking the dishes and drying them. "Again, I'm so sorry."

Priscilla seemed not to hear. "Phil was worried about you," she said, distantly. "Especially after Dad said you were in over your head. He told us that some of the people involved with the operation—the operation that I guess sent you over there?—he said some of them, well, it was kind of hard to be sure which side they were on."

They think you were betrayed. Margo stiffened, but Priscilla Littlejohn, deep in her story, didn't seem to notice. She picked up another cookie, took a bite, and resumed talking.

"I don't want you to get the wrong idea. Dad wasn't the sort to tell tales out of school. It came up because he was warning us. He wanted us to understand what kind of harebrained schemes the Administration had approved to try to find out what was going on in Cuba. That's what he said, word for word—'harebrained schemes.' And when the Bulgaria ploy blew up, well, he said the woman in charge might lose her job. Bad operational security. Then Dad said something about how it was different in the old days, how everybody knew how to keep the secrets. And then it got funny." She was still scrubbing dishes, her gaze fixed on the middle distance. "Phil was upset. He asked Dad if he was saying that you—well, he said 'the student'—if the student in question had been double-crossed. Dad just shrugged. He said, 'These days, who knows?' Then he said the details didn't matter. What mattered was that war was coming, and we had to get to Maine. Phil wouldn't go; he said he had things to do in Ithaca first."

Margo's face burned. Her words dried up. Now she understood what Phil Littlejohn had been leading up to. He had been trying to find a way to invite her to join his family up in Maine. He wanted her safe.

The women stood side by side in the kitchen, each alone with her private grief. Margo had come to obtain information, but would leave with more than she wanted. Phil wasn't one of the bad guys. He had been trying to help. Guilt and responsibility threatened to overwhelm her, and no matter how hard she tried to tell herself that it wasn't her fault—that she had never flirted back or encouraged him in any way—she had to accept the bizarre truth. Had she never met Phil Littlejohn, he might still be alive.

"I'm sorry," Margo said again, just to break the crushing silence. "I'm so sorry for your loss."

Finally, Priscilla's eyes sought out her guest once more. "I'm sorry, too, Margo. And it was good of you to come by, but I think it's time you left. I have things to do, and, well, the truth is, you're starting to give me the creeps."

Priscilla walked her briskly to the door. One of the movers, stepping hastily out of her angry way, dropped a box of framed photographs, presumably from her father's study. The glass on one shattered. Priscilla let loose a stream of firm but quiet invective as the man stooped to collect the pieces.

"Just step over him," Priscilla commanded.

"Wait," said Margo, crouching.

"He doesn't need help."

But Margo wasn't trying to help. She was tugging another photo from the box, one that had caught her eye.

"Who's this?"

"Oh. Well. That's Phil, obviously. That's me. Way too fat for shorts in those days. I tried to get Dad not to frame it. And the good-looking fellow in the captain's hat is our cousin Jerry. This was on Nantucket, I think two years ago."

"Jerry," Margo echoed.

"First cousin on my mother's side. He works for the State Department." Priscilla looked at her strangely. "Family black sheep. He got in some kind of trouble overseas. He's riding a desk at Foggy Bottom while they decide what to do with him."

Margo looked up. They recruit families, Fomin had said. "Do you know how to get in touch with him?"

TWENTY-EIGHT

Jerry

I

Doris Harrington wondered whether somebody was playing a bad joke. It was nearly ten o'clock, and she was sitting alone in a booth at an all-night diner in Bethesda. The phone call that found her at her house two hours ago included all the proper code words, and when she tried to protest that she was on the verge of retirement, the male caller, who declined to give his name, replied that her "immediate plans" made no difference.

So here she sat, still on her first slice of pie but sipping her third cup of coffee, watching the parking lot through the wide front windows. The diner announced its name in huge flashing neon letters, and the light played hypnotically over the shiny cars. The waitress poured more coffee without being asked. Harrington needed the coffee to stay awake, but knew she would regret it later on, when she tried to sleep.

The place the caller had chosen was well off the usual State Department path, and that was the only mercy, because, had anyone she knew spotted her, Harrington would have been mortified—not because she was in some hole-in-the-wall diner but because the only explanation for her presence at this time of night would be that she was involved in some sort of—

She sat straight. A young man had come in and was heading toward her. He was slim and towheaded and had eyes of a strange orange-gold. Smiling, he slid into the booth, across from her.

"Thank you for coming, Dr. Harrington. My name is Jerry Ainsley. I work for the State Department——"

"May I see your identification?" she asked coolly.

He opened his wallet, showed the laminated photograph threaded with blue.

"Very well, Mr. Ainsley. Would you mind telling me what I'm doing here?"

"A friend of yours would like to see you."

"Oh?"

"She's waiting in the car. I gather that she has quite the story to tell, but for some reason, Dr. Harrington, she won't tell it to anybody but you."

II

They were in the woods, walking along a path of hard, pitted dirt in Wheaton Regional Park. The park was closed for the evening, but Jerry knew a side way in. The first frost had come early. Leaves crunched beneath their feet. Ainsley was off in the trees, moving silently as he guarded their backs. Harrington was unsurprised at his evident skill: she had guessed almost from the moment they met that State might cut his paychecks but his orders came from the clowns across the river.

She had been somehow unsurprised to find Margo Jensen in the front seat of Ainsley's Mercedes. She did not believe in fate, but she did believe in her distant Anglican God, and she had suspected that her path and GREENHILL's might be crossing again. In unconscious mimicry of her former husband, Harrington had first rehearsed her onetime agent on the details of how she had wound up in Bethesda: the condolence call on the Littlejohns, the discovery that Ainsley was a cousin, cajoling Priscilla Littlejohn into calling with the cryptic message that "the person you met in front of the cathedral has to meet you urgently"—and Ainsley's message back fifteen minutes later, that she should take the two o'clock train to New York City, where a friend of his would drive her to Baltimore, where in turn he would be waiting.

"He sounds very swift and well organized," said Harrington, all skepticism. "Maybe too well organized."

Margo spread her hands. "I don't know how I'm supposed to answer that."

"You're not. I'm thinking aloud."

"I'm telling you the truth."

"I know you are, dear."

The wind had changed direction. It had been swirling gently at their backs. Now, all at once, they were walking into an icy breeze. Harrington hoped it wasn't a portent.

"Why don't you tell me what this is all about," Harrington finally said. "After that, we can worry about the logistics of your journey."

In an instant, Margo was off. It was obvious that she needed to talk, and that Harrington was her chosen confessor. The older woman had seen this before in agents, and she fought not to be so swept up in the narrative that she failed to search for the tiny hesitations and inconsistencies that might suggest that GREENHILL was romancing, or nuts—or, recalling a couple of unfortunate cases, had been instructed to memorize a script.

She heard nothing but a desperate fluency, and relief in the telling.

When Margo at last ran down, they walked together in silence for a bit. Harrington was remembering what was known in the trade as the second rule of intelligence—when you're out, you're out. She'd preached it herself in her lectures to the kiddies, and now and then to people she'd fired. When you're out, you're out. No matter how much you miss it, no matter what the temptation, you don't get involved. Period. No contact. No clever ploys. You're done, and you can't buy your way back in with information. You shouldn't even want to. If an old agent comes alive once more, you don't debrief him yourself: you turn him over to your ex-employers and go back to bed.

Therefore, the first words out of Harrington's mouth should have been a warning to say no more, and the second words should have summoned Jerry Ainsley, followed by crisp instructions to take GREENHILL and her story straight to Langley. Here was the key to resolving the Cuban missile crisis, and Margo belonged with the people who were on the inside, not with a washed-up former agent runner whose career had ended when her final operation was blown to pieces.

She opened her mouth, meaning to explain these things, but what came out was "Well, you are in a pickle, my dear. Let's see what we can do to get you out of it, shall we?"

Because suddenly it all made sense. The late-night interview with Bundy. Her exclusion from the discussions about Cuba, and now her summary dismissal from State. The way her contacts went dead on her. Even—rough justice—the way Fomin had so cleverly manipulated matters that Margo had briefly suspected Harrington herself of being a Soviet agent.

"They gave you a lot of obstacles to overcome, dear. Checking to see if you're really the right conduit, one supposes." They were standing now, on a low bluff from which they could look down at the highway and the scattered lights of houses beyond. Harrington reached up and tucked a few loose strands of hair behind Margo's ear. "I want you to come home with me now," she said. "You can get some rest, and I'm going to make a couple of calls. Tomorrow is Saturday, and I suspect they'll want to bring you in and brief you and so forth. But understand one thing." Her voice hardened. "I won't be your case officer. I won't be involved at all."

"But I came to you—"

"Listen, Miss Jensen. Listen carefully, my dear. This has been scripted. Your part in this whole contretemps. I don't know by whom, but it doesn't matter. You are going to be playing on a much larger stage now. A stage where the Harringtons and the Niemeyers and the Ainsleys of the world never tread. The people who will run the operation will likely be from the very top. They will keep this knowledge close. They won't want second-level bureaucrats like me involved at all. Do you understand?"

"Yes, but—"

Harrington talked right over her. The lessons took hold after all. "What they want you to do is going to be dangerous. What Fomin told you is true. There are people on both sides who, should they discover the back-channel negotiations, will do whatever they can to keep them from succeeding. Secrecy will be your only protection. Do you still want to proceed?"

Margo swallowed but didn't drop her gaze. "Yes."

"Don't just say what you think I want to hear."

"I'm not. I've thought it through. I'm doing this."

Harrington was impressed by the girl's resolution, but she had heard the same determination in Carina's voice the night she'd disappeared in Vienna. "Very well," she said after a moment. "This, then, is how things are going to work. I will make the calls on your behalf. I will ensure that your information gets to the right individuals. Once that task is done, I shall be stepping out of the picture." To her surprise, she choked on the next words. "And you, my dear, must promise, absolutely promise, never, for any reason whatsoever, to contact me again."

III

Margo spent the night at Doris Harrington's small row house on P Street in Georgetown. She didn't expect to sleep. Her day had been too full. Priscilla had telephoned Ainsley for her, and his swift, confident response had both exhilarated and frightened her. Within ten minutes he was back with instructions: catch such-and-such a train, look for such-and-such a car. Returning to Garrison, Margo had squared for a battle with Nana, but Claudia Jensen was surprisingly complaisant, only making her granddaughter promise not to leave Washington without calling on various family friends.

Now, as Margo tried to get comfortable in the narrow attic guestroom, she found her thoughts back in Poughkeepsie. During the conversation with Priscilla, an idea had teased at the corner of her mind, a question about the accident that had killed Phil Littlejohn. Something vital that she had missed. The key to the mystery. Alas, the harder she tried to grab the thought, the more tantalizingly it eluded her, and when Margo opened her eyes, it was nine in the morning, and she didn't even remember trying.

TWENTY-NINE

Indecision

I

McGeorge Bundy was irritated, a trait he manifested only by a slight tightening of his fingers on his gold-plated pen. It was late morning of Saturday, October 20. Yesterday, he had told the President that he had changed his mind. He no longer believed a blockade would be adequate. They had to go in and get the missiles. It wasn't that Bundy wanted war; he simply had no other option ready to hand.

Now, suddenly, he did. An opportunity had been handed to them; but he couldn't mention it in the meeting.

And so he kept listening and taking notes. His intention when he spoke to the President had been to support only a limited air strike. But now, as he listened to the other members of the ExComm, Bundy realized that his reluctant switch in position had only hardened the line of the hard-liners. General Taylor thought an air strike would work. Robert Kennedy called an immediate attack their final chance to destroy the missiles.

Then the director of central intelligence reported that at least eight and possibly as many as sixteen of the launchers were now active. Silence fell.

"What that means," said McCone, "is that they can now fire off the R-12s on about eight hours' notice. And those missiles, as you know, can strike anywhere on the East Coast."

Everyone looked expectantly at the President, waiting for him to instruct the Joint Chiefs to take out the launch sites.

But Kennedy kept going back and forth. He saw points in favor of the strikes; he saw points in favor of the blockade. One minute he seemed inclined toward Maxwell Taylor and the Joint Chiefs, who wanted to attack at once. The next he was nodding in apparent agreement as McNamara, backed up by United Nations Ambassador Adlai Stevenson, insisted that diplomacy could resolve the crisis.

"That's crazy," said Taylor. "If we make the first offer, we look weak."

"All that matters is getting those missiles out," said Stevenson. "What difference does it make how we look?"

"When they launch those R-12s at Washington and New York, you'll find out what difference it makes."

"You can't possibly hit all the missiles in the first attack. They'll launch whatever they have left."

"Once you start thinking that way," growled Taylor, "you've already lost."

The general's furious gaze was focused on Stevenson, but Bundy knew that the true object of his anger was his commander in chief. The President's indecisiveness was costing him respect around the table. A lot of these men had served under Eisenhower, and still considered Kennedy an unproven boy.

Other voices, equally passionate, weighed in. Discussion was turning into argument. Finally, at Kennedy's signal, Bundy rapped on the table for silence.

"We go with the blockade," said Kennedy.

Several members of the ExComm suppressed groans: the President had chosen to split the difference.

"Let's at least call it a quarantine," said Dean Rusk, unhappily. "A blockade violates international law."

"Quarantine, then," said Kennedy. He turned to Bundy. "And let's do something to make sure that, no matter what happens, nobody fires the Jupiter missiles in Turkey without my direct order."

"We've taken care of that already," said an irritated General Taylor. "We've sent out clear instructions."

"Let's just make double sure," said the President.

As the ExComm broke up, Bundy hurried into the hallway, catching up with the Kennedy brothers just before they entered the Oval Office.

"Mr. President, if I might have a minute."

"I have to talk to Bobby and Sorensen—"

"Yes, sir. Your brother should probably hear this anyway. But nobody else at this point."

Kennedy gave him a look. He hated Bundy's penchant for secrecy, but could not deny its dividends.

"Let's go in the office," he said.

II

The President sat in the rocker, with the attorney general frowning behind him like a bodyguard. Bundy sat to attention on the sofa.

"Go ahead," said Kennedy.

"Sir, I had a call early this morning from President Eisenhower—"

The President's brother interrupted. "Well, call him back, Mac. Tell him we're grateful for his advice, and we'll let him know if he can help."

But Jack Kennedy only waited, fingers steepled as he rocked. "This isn't Ike being a busybody again, Bobby. This isn't Ike tossing off ideas to remind me that I commanded a little wooden patrol boat and he commanded D-Day. This is different, isn't it, Mac?"

Bundy's eyes never left the President's face. "Yes, sir."

"Well, then, what is it? What did Ike say that you can't say in front of the whole ExComm?"

"Sir, it's about SANTA GREEN."

Again the attorney general intervened. "I've told you before, Mac, we don't want to hear any more about that operation. This office has to be protected from it."

Still Bundy spoke only to his commander in chief. "Mr. President, it seems that the operation may have borne unexpected fruit. I believe that we may have our back channel. That was the subject of President Eisenhower's call."

All at once, neither Kennedy looked bored. "Go on," said the President, eyes narrowing.

"Sir, President Eisenhower was calling to give me his enthusiastic endorsement of a woman named Harrington. She's an analyst at State—"

"She's the one who just got fired," said Bobby, to the President.

"The one who came up with the idea for SANTA GREEN in the first place."

Bundy would not be deterred. "Sir, I also had a call late last night from Dr. Harrington. President Eisenhower's purpose was to tell me that I should trust what she told me."

"Why on earth——" the attorney general began, but his brother waved him silent.

"Let him finish, Bobby."

"Sir, GREENHILL got in touch with Dr. Harrington last night. She claims to have been contacted directly by the Soviets. The General Secretary is offering to negotiate through her to you, as a back channel, separate from the negotiations at the embassy, which he does not expect to bear fruit. One of our leading academic analysts believes her story to be credible. So does Dr. Harrington. And the claim is also consistent with certain information the Agency has developed concerning the movements of the KGB's top man in the United States. In short, we should take it seriously."

Bundy paused, testing their reaction. The Kennedy brothers were intelligent, courageous men. True, they were a bit arrogant, and too self-certain and self-satisfied for Bundy's taste. But they respected his judgment, and knew he would not waste their time unless he thought the idea worth trying.

Finally, the President smiled. "Ike has never really liked me that much. He didn't like my tax cuts, and he's worried I'm spending too much on defense. But I'll tell you something. After the Bay of Pigs went south, I asked him to come down to Camp David for a talk. Sent the helicopter. We spent a couple of hours together." The rocking slowed, then picked up again. "We talked about what went wrong. He said I should have given the invasion air cover. I said I was worried about everybody knowing it was us. Ike laughed. He told me the invasion force had boats, weapons, radios—where else would they have gotten all that? He said it's impossible for the United States to hide its hand in the world. Whatever we do, everybody will always know it's us. And then he gave me some advice. He said, never go into battle unless we plan to do whatever is necessary to win."

"Yes, Mr. President."

"And you think this woman—this GREENHILL—can help us win?"

"I do, sir. But it's going to be tricky. If word leaks out, the Soviets will run for cover and the back channel will shut down. We'll have to exclude the ExComm."

The attorney general was flabbergasted. "Why would we do that?"

Still Bundy kept his solemn gaze on the President. "Sir, I am going to make a proposal. It won't be in writing. Nothing will be in writing. I would like to run an operation involving three principals, and nobody in the White House, aside from the three of us and the director of the Secret Service, will be aware of what is going on."

The attorney general started to ask what the operation was, but his older brother got in the first question: "Who are the principals?"

"One, a Soviet intelligence officer," said Bundy. "Two, a college student."

"Who's the third?"

"You, sir. You'd have to be part of the operation for it to work."

Kennedy stopped rocking. "In case you've forgotten, Mac, I'm the President of the United States—"

"Yes, sir. And that's why only you can do it."

"What exactly would I have to do?"

"Provide ample grounds for Washington rumor, sir. Unflattering rumor, I'm afraid. Your reputation will be hurt, but the country will be saved."

The Kennedy brothers exchanged a wary glance. It was the attorney general who said, curtly: "I think you'd better explain that."

Bundy never cracked a smile. "Well, for one thing, I understand she's a real beauty."

"Who is?"

"GREENHILL."

THIRTY

Washington Rumor

I

The two women shared a late breakfast, in the course of which Harrington asked Margo about her hopes and her dreams and her young man, and kept the conversation carefully clear of Varna and Fomin and the missiles in Cuba. Afterward, they went for a walk along narrow Georgetown streets while Ainsley trailed a block behind, watching for surveillance. At three-thirty in the afternoon, a car called for her, a dark Ford that practically screamed official business. The driver's name was Warren. He was brown-haired and broad-shouldered and sported a crew cut and an ill-fitting suit, and even if his identification, demanded by Harrington, had not said "Secret Service," Margo suspected that she would have recognized him a mile away.

"We won't speak again, dear," said Harrington on the front step.

"I understand."

"You'll do fine."

"I'll do my best," Margo said, and felt somehow that her answer had let Harrington down.

Sitting in the back as the dark sedan sailed through the Saturday traffic, Margo was at once nervous and proud. This was it. She had what she wanted. Harrington had warned her back in September that being on the inside could be an addiction, and Margo understood entirely, because the rush that had her trembling was anticipation, not fear. Her body felt loose and hot, her clothes scraped uncomfortably against her skin, and she supposed this is what it must feel like when you're sneaking off to meet your lover.

She was righter than she knew.

II

Warren drove swiftly across town. Twice she asked where they were going. Twice he answered with boyish diffidence that they were almost there. Finally, he pulled up outside an aging apartment build ing on Columbia Road, just off Sixteenth Street. Warren parked on a side street and, holding the door, directed her to what looked like the service entrance.

"Just ring the bell, miss. Oh, and don't forget your bag."

The man who answered might have been Warren's twin, in affect if not in appearance, for he, too, was tall and crew-cut, although his hair was black to Warren's brown, and Margo guessed he was somebody's bodyguard even before he had her remove her hood and then held up a photograph, comparing the likeness. He stepped aside and invited her in, but never offered to take her bag, she supposed to leave his hands free in case she pulled a weapon.

"Please, follow me," he said, his voice surprisingly soft in a man so obviously tough. He led the way along a narrow corridor. The walls were sagging with damp. At the back of the apartment, he knocked at a door, opened it, waved her through, shut it from the outside.

The man waiting inside was small and professorial, right down to the regulation tweeds. The steel frames of his spectacles glistened. His eyes were very dark, and very serious.

"My name is McGeorge Bundy," he said, taking the bag from her hand and setting it aside. He seemed distant and distracted. Behind the polished lenses, his sharp eyes flashed with the anger of unresolved tragedy, like a man who had just lost a relative and wondered whether you were to blame. "I work at the White House. I am special assistant to the President for national security affairs."

A larger stage indeed.

"I've seen you on television," Margo said, and immediately felt like an idiot.

But Bundy was in any case not a man for small talk. "We have very little time, Miss Jensen. I'm going to explain what happens next, and then, God willing, you're never going to see me again."

Steam gurgled behind a wall. Clothes, tools, and empty beer bottles competed for floor space. She suspected that the building super lived here, when the President's national security adviser wasn't borrowing the place.

For half an hour, he laid out the scheme—she would have a cover job at the Labor Department, housing had been secured for her—and then he explained the procedure for arranging her meetings with Kennedy.

"I'll be meeting him personally?" she asked, very surprised.

"That seems to be what Fomin expects. He doesn't want intermediaries. He sounds ready to see conspiracies everywhere. The only way to reassure him is if you carry messages directly to and from the President."

"I'm just going to walk into the Oval Office and meet the President?"

"Not exactly. We'll get to those details in a moment."

There was more to the briefing—contact numbers, addresses—and then Bundy apologized handsomely for drawing her into the middle of this. But he kept looking at his watch, and she wondered what he was late for.

"That covers it, Miss Jensen. Any questions?"

"Yes, sir."

"Please."

"I've been asking, but nobody will tell me what happened to Agatha. Agatha Milner. She was with me in Varna—"

"We're not discussing Varna," he said firmly. "Next."

The swiftness and finality of this dismissal left her momentarily dizzy. As simple as that, Bundy was able to conjure Agatha into the ether.

"How long will I be in Washington?"

"Until the crisis is over, or until we persuade Fomin to deal with us directly. And that last is unlikely, I might add. Next."

"Are the missiles a real threat? They really could hit Washington and New York, like the press is saying?"

"Yes. Next."

"You said we'd come back to how I'm going to meet the President."

"Yes. Well, this is where the plan gets complicated." As if the rest were not. "Let me explain the cover story."

He did. And as she listened, her fists clenched with anger and her eyes grew wide with dread.

PART III

Prisoner's Dilemma

October 23, 1962–October 29, 1962
Washington, D.C.

THIRTY-ONE

Ground Zero

I

On Tuesday, October 23, just past seven in the evening, Margo Jensen stood in a bleak urban rain waiting miserably for the D.C. Transit bus. The stop was on Fourth Street in Southwest Washington, just north of G. Her red Cornell umbrella shielded her from the downpour but not from the autumn night that chilled her bones; although the weather was not the cause of her trembling. Twenty-four hours ago, President Kennedy had told the nation that the Soviet Union had placed missiles with nuclear warheads in Cuba. Now Margo was off to her first meeting with Aleksandr Fomin, to help Kennedy and Khrushchev figure out what to do about them.

Margo cupped a hand above her eyes, peering into the downpour in search of the bus. Earlier today, as she crossed the street after work, a skidding car had nearly run her down; her nerves were so stretched that she had caught herself wondering whether the driver might have been trying to hit her. Everybody in the city seemed jangly. In her apartment building after Kennedy's speech last night, people were thronging the hallways, arguing and shouting, talking about where they were from, and where they had friends, and where they intended to go with their families once the station wagon was packed. The two propositions on which they all agreed were that Washington, D.C., was Ground Zero, and that Ground Zero might not be the best place to be.

Margo had watched the President's address with the two roommates she had met only Saturday night, when she moved in. Hope and

Patsy were interns in dull federal departments, just as Margo herself was: for her cover work was in an obscure corner in the Labor Department, in the office of a woman named Torie Elden, principal deputy to the functionary charged with calculating unemployment numbers each month. Torie was in her thirties, and unmarried, and what was known at this time as a woman of speed. She was also, via the tentacular relations of the old Negro families, a distant cousin, a key factor in the selection of her office as Margo's destination, for the fiction at every point had to be plausible. Anyone dogging her steps would suppose that Margo, exhausted and distracted following the events in Bulgaria, had chosen to take a leave of absence from school, opting instead to use family connections to gain an instant, and fairly easy, internship deep in the labyrinth of federal bureaucracy. And if Torie persisted in giving her peculiar looks all through that first morning, as she explained which reports went into which folders and when, there was behind the surface fiction a second fiction that, through the operation of the Washington rumor mill, would soon provide the indelicate explanation for the sudden White House command that Torie find her cousin a place.

Margo dutifully took notes, and spent the rest of Monday filing and fetching (as Nana huffily referred to secretarial work), all the while waiting for the promised contact. Fomin had not said how he would get in touch with her, but the vanished Niemeyer had assured her that the Soviet spy would figure it out. At her briefing on Saturday, Mr. Bundy had said much the same.

"How will he know where to find me?"

"He'll know."

As for Hope and Patsy, they were madly curious about her but had evidently been warned not to ask too many questions. Dark-haired Hope was a Midwesterner, quiet and studious; blond Patsy, a loud, rangy Californian. But the oddest part was that when she arrived they said they had been expecting her since Friday.

You are going to be playing on a much larger stage now, Harrington had said. *The people who will run the operation will likely be from the very top.*

That much Margo understood. It explained why they had cut off her access to the State Department, and why Niemeyer had done his vanishing act. But, the more she pondered, the more the chain of events escaped her. Fomin had visited her on Tuesday. Niemeyer had disappeared on Wednesday. Her emergency codes had been cut off on Thursday, and Torie Elden had evidently been contacted on Friday morning.

Yet her reunion with Harrington had not come until Friday night. What was going on?

II

She was on the bus now, headed north on Fourth Street. Every few blocks, the bus bumped over the tracks of the city's vanished streetcars. The apartment they'd found for her was in a development of townhouses and residential towers known popularly as "the new Southwest." In the morning, the bus would have been crowded with bureaucrats heading to work, but this time of night, the clientele was harder, and darker, and angrier. As the bus crossed the Mall, the Capitol dome shimmered murkily through the night rain. Soon she was passing thickly clustered federal office buildings. Gazing out the window, she remembered yesterday morning's briefing by a highly curious Torie Elden, who was busily trying to figure out why she had a second intern, even though the budget provided for just one.

"Either you know somebody or you are somebody," Torie had murmured in genuine admiration. "Your application never even got to my desk."

"It was a last-minute thing," said Margo, lamely, because the briefing had not covered that particularly detail.

"My boss told me not to ask too many questions."

"That's probably a good idea."

"We don't really have an office for you. You'll have to sit in the file room. It doesn't have a window." Striking a saucy pose, hand on ample hip. "Does that meet your approval? Or are you going to complain to somebody who'll call up my boss and make him give you my office instead?"

"Of course not," said Margo, blushing. The briefing hadn't covered that issue, either.

An awkward pause. "I thought your side of the family was all Republicans."

"I'm a Democrat."

"You're not even old enough to vote."

"I'm old enough to serve my country."

Torie laughed. "Margo, honey, you'll be working as a file clerk. If you want to call that serving your country, that's up to you. But there are people out there who risk their lives. Don't put yourself in their category."

"No, ma'am. I won't."

III

The Labor Department was housed in a granite monstrosity, occupying two blocks north of Constitution Avenue, fronting on Fourteenth Street. Its somber gray walls were decorated with enough pillars and pilasters for half a dozen government buildings of more ordinary dimensions. It was constructed in the 1930s, an era when size and elaboration were often mistaken for importance.

On Tuesday, Margo lunched with a brace of fellow interns: the one who worked for Torie, and four or five others from around her floor. The group had taken the newcomer to the basement cafeteria, to lay out what they called the rules of the road. The linoleum was colorless with age. The vast room smelled vaguely of cat. As Margo struggled with her overdone chicken breast, they peppered her with advice: Never let Mr. Baldwin get you alone in his office, or anywhere else. Don't talk about civil rights. And don't mind what anybody says about you: They're just jealous.

Jealous of what? Margo asked.

"Of your obvious friends in high places," they said, scarcely bothering to hide their snickers.

Margo didn't know where to put her eyes. "It's just that Miss Elden is my cousin," she said, but this wasn't enough to get her off the hook.

As they crossed the room to bus their trays, an older man bumped into her, spilling his tray but, oddly, not hers. As he crouched to pick up his food, she heard his papery voice close to her ear. "Yenching Palace. Tonight. Eight. Alone."

She might have ignored him, or even assumed that she'd misunderstood him, except that the last time she saw him he was wearing a Cornell hat and snapping her picture.

All of which explained how Margo had come to be riding the bus through the chilly night rain, wishing Mother Nature hated her a little less.

IV

Margo stepped off the bus at last, on Connecticut Avenue at Macomb Street. The public library was directly across the street. The Yenching Palace, a Chinese restaurant, was two blocks north of the library. She wanted the two blocks, hoping the walk might calm her. The neighborhood was called Cleveland Park, and Margo knew it well. During high school, she had spent a couple of weeks in Cleveland Park each summer, because one of her white girlfriends was the daughter of a congressman who had houses both here and in Westchester County. Margo wondered whether Fomin, in choosing the restaurant, was aware of her familiarity, and decided arbitrarily that he must have been.

Trudging north, leaning into the wind, Margo cinched her coat more tightly around her neck. The umbrella was inside out and useless. She felt the same way. Instincts honed over the past month led her eyes into alleys and doorways, but she didn't know what she was looking for. Bundy had told her that no American agencies would have surveillance on her. Margo wasn't sure whether to believe him; or, for that matter, whether he meant his words in warning or reassurance.

Connecticut Avenue in this part of the city was nearly all commercial, but the leafy lanes crisscrossing it were filled with the large, elegant homes of the city's well-to-do. No Negroes lived in Cleveland Park. She wondered how long that change would be in coming. Both Congress and the White House were in the hands of the Democratic Party, but the chances of passing an open-housing law were near zero. These were the pressing matters on which Margo Jensen focused as she continued across Newark Street. She was determined to think about anything except what was really happening: Kennedy's speech, and her own role in preventing what the people thronging the hallway of her building were worried would happen next. The dream was now the reality.

Margo stopped beside Engine Company 28. The roll-up door was open, and a couple of firefighters watched her as she stood in the rain. Next door, the Yenching Palace announced itself in bright neon letters, yellow rimmed with red. The outer wall was an odd shiny bluish-green.

Behind a low wrought-iron fence, a scattering of tables stood outside, but in this weather nobody was seated at them.

She stood a moment, working on her breathing. She felt as madly determined as she had in Varna, and conquered her nerves the same way: by remembering Claudia Jensen's expectations of her grand-daughter.

You have to wow them, Nana always said.

She would.

She plunged through the doors.

THIRTY-TWO

Checks and Balances

I

In his mind, McGeorge Bundy followed GREENHILL's progress up the avenue. He had only imagination to guide him. He knew she was going to the Yenching Palace—she'd called the assigned number to say so—but beyond that bit of information lay only mystery. Bobby Kennedy had wanted her watched every minute, but Bundy rejected the idea out of hand. Fomin would notice. He was among the best the Soviets had, and he was bound to spot surveillance. And, given that the back-channel negotiations were supposed to be secret from each side's security apparatus, he would take any sort of observation as a sign of bad faith.

Though the attorney general had argued, the President had backed his national security adviser's judgment. But it was a near thing. With midterm congressional elections two weeks away, the President wanted to look decisive.

"Decisive," in the ExComm, being a code word for bombing and invasion.

Then, today—Tuesday—the group had discussed what to do should one of the U-2 surveillance planes be shot down. Here the Joint Chiefs were adamant. The men who were asked to go up on those over-flights had to know they were protected. A couple of voices protested that any sovereign had the right to shoot down planes over its airspace. But the ExComm supported the JCS. So did Kennedy. The decision was clear: If a U-2 was shot down, the surface-to-air missile sites would be bombed. This, of course, would mean killing Russians—all the SAM sites had Soviet crews—and would certainly lead to war.

Emotions around the table were running too high. Bundy didn't know how much longer he could hold this thing together.

II

Back in his office, the national security adviser considered his options. His various worries were beginning to intertwine. There was the risk that Kennedy would act rashly. There was the risk that the back channel wouldn't work. There was the risk that SANTA GREEN had been betrayed from within. If they had a leak, there was no reason to think that the leaking had stopped. He didn't think the back channel was at risk, but the rest of their planning Kennedy discussed two or three times a day with a dozen or more advisers, all of whom had deputies and assistants and wives and mistresses and who knew what else. If the President ordered an attack, it was entirely possible that the Soviets would know about it before the orders were delivered to Homestead Air Force Base. Yet he couldn't seek help from, say, the Federal Bureau of Investigation—not in the middle of the Margo Jensen–Aleks Fomin show.

Bundy weighed his options, then called in his favorite deputy, a chubby postgraduate named Esman. "Go to Langley, then go to State. I want you to look at every scrap of paper on SANTA GREEN."

Esman wore thick glasses. His dark hair was shaggy. His sports coat needed pressing. He lacked small talk and, for the most part, affect. He was utterly unprepossessing. He was also one of the two or three brightest people Bundy had ever met.

"Are you sure they'll show me everything?"

"I'll get you a presidential order."

"That might not do it," said Esman tonelessly. "Remember the JSCP?"

A studied silence. Bundy did not like being reminded of the embarrassing incident, a year ago, when he had demanded, in the President's name, to see the Joint Strategic Capabilities Plan, the entire nuclear attack strategy worked out by the Joint Chiefs of Staff—and had been refused. Eventually, the Pentagon had agreed to send over not the entire plan but a brief summary—and for the President's eyes only.

Which the White House was not permitted to keep.

Few Americans probably realized the extent to which the military had become a law unto itself, in effect a separate branch of government. The Congress controlled its budget but gave the generals whatever they wanted, and the President was the commander in chief when he had time and they had the inclination. The system worked because the American military was run by men of unparalleled integrity.

Most of the time.

"I don't think you'll have any trouble," Bundy finally said. He rolled the gold pen in his fingers. "The President isn't about to take on the Pentagon. Not in this climate. But the spies are another story. Anybody who gets in your way, I'll fire."

Esman might have been impressed; he might not have. As usual, neither his face nor his tone betrayed his feelings—if indeed he possessed any.

"And I'm looking for what exactly?"

"The names, positions, and clearances of every individual who had access to any part of the files."

"The subscription list has about forty names."

"Let's see who actually subscribed."

Esman tilted his pudgy head back and tapped a finger against his front teeth. The habit annoyed Bundy unreasonably, but it seemed to help the young man think. Esman himself was, as usual, quite unconscious of anybody's reaction. "You think the operation was blown. You don't think GREENHILL made a mistake. You don't agree with Langley's assessment that things went wrong in the field." The head came down again. "You think it was leaked to the opposition, and you want to see who had access to which pieces of information so that you can tell who might have been able to leak it."

"That's correct," said Bundy, both amused and alarmed by the young man's swift perception. "How long will it take you?"

"Three or four hours."

"Three or four hours from when you get the materials?"

"Three or four hours from now. I already have the files I need. I ordered them up last week."

"And how exactly did you manage that?"

"I told them that anybody who got in my way, you'd fire."

Bundy permitted himself a smile. "You're going to go far, Nate."

"True," said Esman. He rumbled to his feet, and left without a word.

Bundy liked to unwind with his martini of an evening, but at the office he drank only Scotch. He went to the cupboard and took down the bottle. He was missing something, and it annoyed him. He didn't miss much. True, he had overlooked the missiles going into Cuba, but gathering intelligence wasn't his job. He was in the White House to ensure that the President adopted the right policies with respect to the security of the country. In a few minutes, the ExComm would resume—

His secretary buzzed again. Langley was coming through on the secure line.

"Who?"

"Head of Plans." Plans. Clandestine operations. The happy end of the business, as some of the old-timers called it. "Mr. Bundy? He says it's an emergency."

III

Bundy wasn't a man for physical exercise, but he sprinted up the marble stair. Having first called the President's private secretary and warned her that Kennedy was under no circumstances to walk into the ExComm meeting until he'd spoken to Bundy. He shouldn't even have a conversation with any member of the group.

In the Oval Office, the President was behind his desk, Bobby standing off to the side, snapping out a stream of orders to a trio of aides. The aides took one look at Bundy's face and fled.

Bundy shut the door.

"What is it, Mac?" asked Kennedy, the half-smile two-thirds forced. "Where's the fire? Or are you here to tell me that GREENHILL is even more gorgeous than I've been led to believe?"

"Bad news, Mr. President. YOGA's been arrested."

"What!"

"Langley doesn't have the details yet. They're waiting to hear from the Brits. But there's no question about the arrest. Penkovsky is a full colonel of military intelligence, and technically shouldn't come under KGB jurisdiction, but they dragged him out of his apartment all the same, and our understanding is that they weren't gentle."

"How long did they suspect him?" Kennedy asked.

"I'm sorry. We don't know."

"Penkovsky gave us crucial information just last week." The attorney general's voice lacked his usual fire. The timbre was one Bundy had never heard from him before: less than panic but more than anxiety. "He's the reason we're sure those missiles aren't ready to fire. Are you telling me we don't know if he was telling the truth?"

"I'm sorry, Bobby. Yes, it's possible that the information is bad. If they already suspected him, they might have been feeding him disinformation."

"So those missiles might be operational!"

"I'm afraid so."

The attorney general turned to his brother. "When the ExComm hears this, support for an attack will go right through the roof. They'll say Penkovsky was programmed to tell us the wrong number of days until the missiles would be ready to go so we wouldn't do anything and the Soviets would have time to get them ready. They'll demand action by yesterday."

The President was doodling. "And you'll be with them, won't you, Bobby?" He laughed, and Bundy was relieved at the evident ease of his manner. "What about you, Mac? Which side will you be on?"

"We simply lack the data to draw any conclusions."

"Come on, Mac," said Bobby, suddenly angry. "You can't spend your life on the fence."

Bundy's voice was mild. "I won't do the President much good if I shoot from the hip." He turned back to the older brother. "In any case, Bobby is worrying unnecessarily. The ExComm won't be told of YOGA's arrest. Remember, aside from the three of us, McCone and McNamara are the only ones in that room who even know of YOGA's existence." He let this sink in. "We have to keep it that way, Mr. President, at least until we get the back channel going and see whether Khrushchev is prepared to negotiate seriously."

The President was dubious. "If Khrushchev wants to negotiate, why arrest Penkovsky? What kind of signal does that send?"

"Maybe he's not even in charge," said Bobby, darkly: a theory already floated in the ExComm by LeMay and others. The attorney general leaned close to his brother, and spoke with a soft urgency. "Maybe Khrushchev's fanatics have taken control. Maybe they arrested Penkovsky because they don't care about consequences. If those missiles are active, they could be getting ready for a pre-emptive strike as we speak."

"There's another possibility," said Bundy. "Khrushchev might have allowed Penkovsky to operate just long enough to get us truthful intelligence about when the missiles would be operational."

"Then why arrest him now?" the attorney general demanded. "Why not keep him in place in case he's needed again?"

"This could be Khrushchev's way of making clear that from now on there will be one and only one means of genuine communication. This could be his way of forcing us to rely on the back channel."

"That's pretty ruthless," said the President. "Letting his own man be tortured and probably executed just to send us a message." He pondered. "Okay. We'll stick with the back channel. But only for a couple of days. We'll wait for Langley to confirm that the missiles have gone operational. Once that happens, I'll have to decide what to do next. But I'll tell you right now, my inclination is to go in and take them out."

"You'll start a war, Mr. President."

"Khrushchev already did."

THIRTY-THREE

Cover Story

I

In the foyer of the restaurant, she checked her coat. She had assumed that Fomin would take a shadowed table at the back, but when she walked into the dining room he was sitting alone in the first booth on the right. His expression as he stared was amiable, and he even stood politely as she sat down across from him.

"I feel conspicuous," Margo muttered.

"Good." He was seated again. "Sometimes the most visible secret agent is the one who tries too hard to be surreptitious." He summoned the waiter with an imperious gesture that would have done a capitalist proud. "Will you drink? Are you hungry?"

"Just water," she said. Fomin, she noticed, had a half-finished plate in front of him: remnants of egg rolls and chow mein. Her older brother, who had spent time studying in Asia, heaped scorn on what he called American-style Chinese food.

"Was it difficult getting here? Have you spoken to Kennedy?"

Straight to the point. Bundy had instructed her to withhold nothing—except what he told her to. "I met his national security adviser. I'm supposed to meet the President only if you have a substantive offer to place on the table. Otherwise, I go back to the apartment and wait for you to contact me again."

"How will they know?" asked Fomin, as if this were the usual way of doing business.

"I have a number to call."

"Will you tell me the number?"

"No."

The waiter was back. He had brought more egg rolls without being asked. Fomin grabbed a pair with his hands, but for Margo, family lessons held. She used her fork to put one on her plate, then cut into it delicately.

"I am pleased that you managed to make contact with your President," the Russian said. "I was confident that you would."

"I didn't think things would move this fast."

"The times demand haste. Did you listen to Kennedy's speech last night?"

"Yes."

"What did you think of it?"

She shook her head. "I don't know, Mr. Fomin."

Another nod, but his gaze became less sympathetic. Perhaps he was at last regretting his chosen conduit. "Bundy briefed you personally?"

"Yes."

"You will contact him later also?"

She remembered Bundy's language. "I shouldn't share operational details."

"Who else knows about your mission?" he asked between bites. "You didn't arrange all of this yourself. You had to talk to people in order to make your way to the White House. So—who else knows?"

"Only two people. One in Ithaca, one here."

"Who in Washington?"

"I'd rather not say."

That frown again. There were men who took defiance in women as a challenge to their charm, and there were men who took it as an affront to their dignity. Fomin was in the second category.

"I mean no harm, Miss Jensen. I would simply like to know the extent of our risk." Back to the food. "I say 'our risk' advisedly. I have told you that there are hotheads on my side, but perhaps there are hotheads on your side, too. If they become aware of your mission, they will try to disrupt it. Violently, if necessary."

"Why would they do that?"

"Because they want war. They believe your country would prevail in a general nuclear exchange. Perhaps they are wrong." A very Slavic shrug. "Certainly your technology is more advanced than ours, but our country is much larger. Less of the Soviet Union would be contaminated." Again he was windmilling food into his mouth. "Of course, we are here because we do not wish to test this theory. You understand the need for haste."

"I do, Mr. Fomin."

"Good. Because I have a message for your President. But first, let us discuss the matter of operational security."

"I'm not sure what you mean."

"Please tell me by what means your side is concealing your meetings with the President."

Margo hesitated. As the blush rose in her cheeks, Fomin read the truth on her face. His frozen demeanor softened into humor. "Ah. I see. Well. You are to be congratulated, my dear. Such a sacrifice for the peace of the world. To place your reputation at risk."

Margo dropped her eyes, for he was speaking into the fears of her heart; she imagined Nana's shocked fury, were she ever to learn the fictional version of her granddaughter's reasons for going to Washington.

Fomin wasn't finished. His wolfish expression told her that he was enjoying himself. "Then, one day, long after the events of the moment are done, when you are married and have grandchildren, an ambitious historian will discover your liaisons with President Kennedy. He will knock on your door and demand the details. He will want to know whether you seduced the President or the President seduced you, and what Kennedy was like as a lover. And even then, you will be expected to lie, to pretend that the affair was real. Because your reporters are like the birds who eat carrion. They produce little of value, and feed off the remains of what others have left. They will destroy the reputation of your President for profit. The First Amendment is the tragedy of your system. In my country, we protect the reputations of our leaders, because in that way we protect the reputation and integrity of the Party, and therefore of the country and the people. We would know how to take care of such a fool."

Margo could not meet his gaze. She had no way of knowing that she would shortly see his words as prescient.

II

Ten minutes later, she was back on Connecticut Avenue. She walked south along the wet pavement, low heels clopping loudly in the empty darkness. The rain had stopped during her meeting with Fomin. Traffic was thin. At the public library, she turned right and proceeded uphill on Macomb, a tree-lined street of quiet homes. On her left was Tregaron, the fabled estate of Marjorie Merriwether Post. Behind a high fence, trees rose in darkly beautiful ranks. No cars passed. No other pedestrians climbed the twisted cobbles. She was back in high school, sneaking up the driveway after Nana's curfew. She was back in Varna, tromping toward the restaurant where Colonel Ignatiev would arrest her. She was in the Yenching Palace, squirming at Fomin's snide insinuations about how future historians would view her. She wasn't sure why the Soviet's words had so disturbed her. He had told her nothing she didn't know. She understood that she would never be able to tell what had really happened. She saw the possibility that someone would find out, and word would travel back to Garrison, and Nana would keel over from a stroke.

"Stop it," she chided herself, and focused her attention on the street. Just below Thirty-third Place, a car flashed its lights twice, and the double flash was the signal. Margo climbed into the front seat. Behind the wheel sat Warren, the Secret Service agent who had driven her from Harrington's townhouse.

"All set?" he asked, but Margo had barely closed her door before the car was barreling up the empty street. At Thirty-fourth they turned left. A few minutes later, they passed the floodlit Gothic splendor of the unfinished National Cathedral, then turned left again onto Massachusetts Avenue, cruising southeast past the embassies.

"Where are we going?" Margo finally asked.

"Not the White House, if that's what you mean."

She supposed that she might well have meant exactly that. She didn't know what she was supposed to say. As far as the agent knew, she was a young woman on her way to an assignation with the President of the United States.

Margo shut her eyes. She tried to rehearse Fomin's message, but somehow what she kept hearing was his studious inquiry into the cover story for her meetings with President Kennedy.

"Almost there," said Warren after a moment.

Margo sat up and blinked. They were cruising east along Constitution Avenue. To their right was the Mall. She must have dozed.

"Sorry," she said, a bit stupidly.

"Don't worry about it."

She watched the museums pass. She decided not to let Fomin's bad jokes upset her. The man was a clever psychologist. He had said so. Fomin had tested her in Bulgaria, he had tested her at Stewart Park, he had probably tested her half a dozen other times without showing his hand. He was testing her now.

A subject who's angry makes mistakes, Harrington had counseled her, back when Margo had imagined that going off to Varna would be a lark. *You have to stay calm or you'll lose your way.*

Thanks, Dr. H. Thanks a lot. That's helpful.

Fear is different. Fear you can't avoid. In the field, you'll be afraid all the time. Fear will become so constant a companion that if it ever goes away, you'll crave the adrenaline. That's the moment to start worrying, my dear. Not when you're afraid. When you stop being afraid.

She smiled ruefully. "I haven't stopped yet, Doctor."

Warren's head turned slightly. "I'm sorry, miss. Did you need something?"

"No, no. I'm fine."

They circled the Capitol, then headed along East Capitol Street. After five or six blocks, the driver began to slow. A limousine sat outside a small townhouse. A dark sedan much like the one she was in stood just behind, with another across the street.

Warren glided to a stop beside the limousine. He helped her from the car.

"Just walk in," he said, pointing along the bluestone path. "It's not locked."

"Thank you," she said, embarrassment creeping up again.

Longest walk of her life.

An agent stood in the yard, watching her approach, and another opened the door from the inside.

"Go on up," he said, averting his eyes in disapproval. "Second door on the right."

"Thank you," she said, but he had already turned away.

THIRTY-FOUR

The Presence

I

"Miss Jensen. It's a great pleasure to see you again." The President was busily shaking her hand. The agent outside the door pulled it shut.

"I didn't—didn't think you remembered," she stammered. "The campaign film was two years ago."

He flashed the world-famous smile, all of it for her. "Of course I'd remember."

But the smoothness in Kennedy's voice told her he had no idea what she was talking about. The bedroom was large and plush, decorated in bright colors. The canopied bed was fit for an emperor. The heavy comforter had been turned down. Margo could hardly look at it. On a polished sideboard stood glasses, an ice bucket, and several bottles. The sofa was brocaded in gold. "Please, Miss Jensen. Sit."

"Thank you, sir."

For a moment they sized each other up. The President's jacket was off and his tie was loose. His collar was unbuttoned, and there was stubble on his chin. He looked like what he was: a hardworking executive at the end of a long day. His next word confirmed the image.

"Drink?"

"No, sir. Um, thank you, no."

Kennedy had a glass already. He swirled the smooth brown liquid, sipped, pulled a face. He stood looking down at her. "You're a very brave young woman, Miss Jensen: Bulgaria. Now this. Has anyone bothered to say thank you? I'll say it now. On behalf of a grateful nation. Thank you."

The swift move beyond pleasantries momentarily threw her. "I— I don't know what to say, Mr. President."

"Try 'You're welcome.' That usually works."

She found a weak half-smile somewhere. "You're welcome."

"All those adventures and you're just nineteen. You'll have a lot to write about one day."

"I would never—I mean, I signed a nondisclosure agreement."

"Oh, *that*." The President took another swallow. "They tell me you're quite the student. Straight A's your freshman year. Well, other than that B in French." He waved his glass. "Is this what you want to do when you graduate? Politics? Government? National security?"

"I—I haven't decided, Mr. President."

"Get married? Have a family?"

"Eventually. Of course."

"Of course," he echoed, and Margo realized that her answer had amused him. "It turns out I knew your great-uncle a bit. Your father's uncle, I suppose he would have been. Your grandfather's brother. Pierce Jensen. I didn't know you were related."

"Oh. Yes." She didn't know where to put her eyes. Her mother had rarely spoken of Uncle Pierce, and Nana never did. He had been an accountant, a graduate of Northwestern, but had wound up in prison for helping the wrong sort of people evade taxes. She was afraid to ask how Kennedy could know such a man. "I never met him," she said, sounding to her own ear arch and unpersuasive.

"I didn't know him well," said the President, catching her mood. "It's just that Pierce and my father did some business together a long time ago."

"Oh. I see."

"Thick as thieves," he said, and winked. When Margo didn't reply, he realized that his effort at small talk had misfired. "Tell me, Miss Jensen. What's your impression of Aleksandr Fomin?"

Again the change of subject caught her short. "I'm not sure yet."

"Bundy tells me he's a smooth so-and-so. Dangerous. Never tells you what he's really thinking. Great poker face." Kennedy settled beside her, so close she could feel his warmth. And his anxiety. "But the times are dangerous, aren't they? At times like these, maybe we need dangerous men."

"Yes, sir."

"Do you feel you can trust him?"

"I don't know. I think he trusts me."

"That's a good answer. Very good." He yawned. "You look very nice. That's a lovely dress."

Her face burned, and she dropped her eyes. "Oh, um, thank you. Thank you, sir."

The President's arm was stretched along the back of the sofa. Her shoulders were bare, and if his fingers touched her she would jump out of her skin. But he only sipped at his drink.

"You need to try to relax, Miss Jensen. If we're going to be meeting like this, you need to relax."

"Yes, sir."

"Remember, honey. Our cover is that we're having a fling. It won't work if everybody thinks you're afraid of me."

Margo was feeling trapped and panicky. "Yes, sir."

"Like when you came in just now. They have to see that you're happy to see me. A little nervousness, sure. But don't overdo it. You have to glow with anticipation. Excitement. Do you understand?"

"Yes, sir. I do, sir."

"You're an innocent girl." His eyes were huge and strangely warm as they bored in on her. "Very pretty, but innocent. Young. So— remember. Being with me like this is the biggest thrill of your young life." He touched her cheek. She flinched. "You love every minute," he said.

II

The Soviet Embassy was located in an ornate mansion at 1125 Sixteenth Street, just blocks from the White House. Half a century earlier, before the Russian Revolution, the house had been considered the fanciest in the city. Nowadays, it was a cramped rabbit warren of subdivided rooms, especially on the fourth floor, given over entirely to the activities of the Committee on State Security. It was there on the fourth floor that same night that Viktor Vaganian knocked on the door of Aleksandr Fomin's long, narrow office, then stepped inside without waiting to be admitted.

Fomin glanced up from the file to which he was appending a note. Those thick eyebrows knitted briefly, and then he returned to his reading.

"What can I do for you, Comrade Captain?"

"I am here in my counterintelligence capacity—"

"I asked what I can do for you."

"You met an American woman tonight at a restaurant on Connecticut Avenue."

The pen continued moving across the page. "And?"

"You met this same woman earlier, in Ithaca. She is the woman you also interrogated in Varna."

"And?"

"I should like to know, please, the subjects of your conversations."

"No."

Vaganian had to tread carefully. Fomin, like Smyslov, had powerful protectors. "As you know, Comrade, I am tasked with discovering how the Americans got word of Anadyr. I have full powers in this matter."

"I already told you, no." Fomin's flat tone offered no clue to his response to the implied accusation. "Listen to me, Viktor Borisovich. It is not the task of Counterintelligence to tell me how to do my job. I will gather intelligence in any way that I see fit. I don't care what jurisdiction you think you have. Interfere with my operations, and you will wind up in Siberia."

He picked up the pen and returned to his work.

III

"Is there a problem, Miss Jensen?" Kennedy murmured, still far too close. "Is there something you want to say?"

"No. No, Mr. President."

"Then try to act like you're enjoying yourself. At least pretend."

She bit her lip, trying not to cry. In some ways, this was worse than Varna. "I understand," she managed. "I'll try, sir."

Her compliance seemed to bother him. He drained his glass, sprang to his feet, only to stop, make a sound, rub his lower back. "Never mind," he said, now annoyed, although at whom was unclear. "I assume he gave you a message for me."

"Yes, Mr. President." She took a moment to compose herself, wanting to make no error. "He said that the General Secretary cannot afford to lose face just now. He said that the missiles are defensive only, but nevertheless the General Secretary might be willing to consider reducing the number if you are able to give him something in return. A show of good faith, so he'll know you're serious about negotiating."

Kennedy turned toward her, hand still massaging the same spot. "Did he say what?"

"No, sir. He, um, he said you'd know what the General Secretary had in mind."

"Oh, yes. I do." All business again. "I know exactly what he has in mind. Is that all he said?"

She felt a rising alarm. "Yes, sir. That's all."

"That bastard," said the President with sudden vehemence. "Wait. Don't tell Fomin what I just said." He was shaking with anger. Margo couldn't think why. "Just tell him that I am willing to help Khrushchev to save face, but he'll have to be more specific about what he's asking. Tell him I don't want a war, but I also can't give much. America can't send the message to the world that it's open season, that all you have to do is threaten us and we'll give you what you want."

"Yes, sir."

Lightning flashed outside. Kennedy was still angry. He put his glass down too hard. Scotch sloshed onto the sideboard. "Tell me, Miss Jensen. Did Fomin happen to mention what Ambassador Dobrynin, in the official negotiations, is asking for? They want us to take our Jupiter missiles out of Turkey and Italy. That's the official position of the Soviet government. That's the show of good faith Khrushchev wants. What good is a back channel if they take the same position as in the formal negotiations?"

"It might not be the same position," she said.

Kennedy spun around. "What did you say?"

"I said, he might not be taking the same position. You said that in the official negotiations they're insisting that we remove the Jupiters. But all Fomin said was that Khrushchev needs something in return. He didn't say what."

The President's eyes narrowed. "Go on."

"Maybe there's another way Khrushchev can save face. Maybe he's hoping, if you won't move the Jupiters, you'll offer something else."

"Something like what?"

She shook her head. More yellowy flashes from the window. She remembered how Nana liked to close the curtains during a thunderstorm so the lightning couldn't find you. "I don't know, Mr. President. Something."

A faint smile. "Now I see how you got those A's. And why Niemeyer is so high on you. That's what Bundy says, anyway. He and Niemeyer have known each other a long time. I don't think they like each other very much, but there's a lot of respect there." The smile vanished. "Okay. When do you see Fomin next?"

"He's supposed to contact me."

"Well, let's hope it's tomorrow. Tell him we're working on it. Tell him we're perfectly willing to help Khrushchev save face, but those missiles in Cuba have to go, and he can't expect us to dismantle the Jupiters in return. Do you understand?"

"Yes, sir."

"Tell him we need Khrushchev to be very specific in explaining what he wants. I'm not saying he can have it—I'm not saying he can have anything at all—but I'm perfectly happy to listen to his proposals. After all, the back channel was his idea."

"Yes, sir."

"And remind him"—a moment's hesitation, and on the President's face a shadow of something—mistrust, maybe, or even uncertainty—"remind him that they started this. They snuck the missiles in and lied to us about them. Say it just like that. Snuck. Lied. Understand?"

"Yes, Mr. President."

He was back at the sideboard. This time he poured but didn't drink. "Anyway, that's not what Khrushchev really wants to know." His craggy profile had gone reflective again. "He's trying to measure my will, Miss Jensen. What he wants to know—what that probe is about—maybe what this whole back channel is about—is whether I'm willing to go to war."

Margo swallowed. "Are you?"

Kennedy was a long time answering. It occurred to her that at this moment she was, paradoxically, calmer than the President of the United States. Not that he was in any sense panicky: he simply bore the weight of decision. Her actions made little difference; his mattered enormously.

And he knew it.

When at last he spoke, his voice was sharp and determined. "Oh, yes, Miss Jensen. I am. We are. In the end, either Khrushchev removes those missiles or we do it for him. Is that clear?"

"Yes, Mr. President."

"I suppose I said quite a bit, but I want you to take it all to Fomin."

"Yes, sir."

"You can remember all that?"

"Yes, sir."

Kennedy was leaning against the sill now, arms crossed. He examined her, head to toe and back, taking his time. Her skin felt warm. She realized that his gaze, like his manner, had once more lost its professional distance. She stood his scrutiny. She took hold of that fold of skin and pinched, but she stood his scrutiny.

"You don't need to write it down?" he asked.

"Um, no. Mr. Bundy said not to."

"That's right. You're smart. Everybody says how smart you are."

She blushed. "They're kind, sir."

"Don't be a shrinking violet, Miss Jensen. You know you're smart. Don't look away. Admit it. You're smart and you know it."

"I guess so, sir."

"You guess so?"

"I— yes, sir. I'm smart."

"Good. Now, come over here."

She rose to her feet, approached him gingerly.

"Closer," said the President.

"Sir, I—"

"Here," he said, and drew her roughly into an embrace. She gasped and, instinctively, pushed at him. "Stop it. No. Stop. Stand still. Don't worry. This is just for effect. I need you to kiss my collar and my cheek. For the lipstick smears."

Margo stiffened. She imagined Nana peering in the window in disgust. "Mr. President, please. Tell me you're not serious."

"The Secret Service has to believe it's an affair, Miss Jensen." He leaned in. "Come on. Let's go."

"But—but I—"

"In for a penny, in for a pound." He pointed to his cheek. "I don't have all night, Miss Jensen. I have a roomful of advisers back at the White House waiting for me to tell them what we're going to do. Hurry up."

Trembling, she kissed his collar. He smelled of expensive cologne. She kissed his stubbly cheek. Her eyes teared up and she wiped her mouth on the back of her hand.

"Good girl," he said, grinning again. He chucked her chin. "Sorry, honey. Now, try to relax next time. Remember. For as long as this lasts, you'll have to do that and maybe more pretty much every night."

And then I'll go home and throw up.

But she said only: "Yes, Mr. President."

IV

The storm had passed. Margo lay half awake in the lumpy twin bed. The apartment had two bedrooms. Before Margo's arrival, each girl had her own. Margo shared with Hope, who told her, without going into detail, that rooming with Patsy would be awkward. Above Hope's bed was a window. The blackness without was broken by a scattering of distant twinkles. Not long ago, Kennedy had promised the nation that an American would walk on the moon within a decade. Tom told her that the technology had been understood for years; all that was lacking was the money and the will. To the Toms of the world, the march of science was equivalent to the march of civilization. The future belonged to those who could build the best machines. But building machines capable of killing tens of millions of people in a single afternoon didn't seem very civilized to her.

Margo shut her eyes. Still sleep eluded her. She knew why. Blaming Tom or technology—those were excuses. It was Fomin who had gotten under her skin, with his clever insinuations about how history would judge her, as just another Kennedy woman. She hated the thought. She had hated it when Bundy explained it, and she hated it when Fomin made her face it, and she hated the President for forcing her to play to the role. Even though she knew why Kennedy made her kiss his collar and muss her dress, she felt filthy doing it.

Worse, Margo had the sense that maybe, just maybe, Kennedy was enjoying the fiction a little more than was proper. It was as if he wasn't just trying to fool the Secret Service into thinking they were having an actual affair: he seemed to want to fool Margo, too.

She turned her face to the wall, opened her eyes, remembered the burning humiliation of that day back in tenth grade when Melody Davidson had read that horrible double dactyl to the class. She had fought back; but the years had taught her that no amount of struggle back quite banished the pain.

There were many things in life that Margo hated or feared, but first on the list was humiliation—especially in front of white peers she knew she ought to best. Melody's poem had hurt less than her class-mates' eager laughter. She had been fleeing their mockery ever since. Getting straight A's didn't help her escape the demons who pursued her, and she had a hunch that helping to save the world wouldn't, either. She wasn't supposed to lose to the Melody Davidsons of the world, but too often she did. Fomin was right. Margo was only nine-teen, but even if the world survived, her own reputation would be destroyed. Half dozing now, she allowed her sleepy but agile mind to compose another double dactyl:

> *Washington Poshington,*
> *future historians,*
> *trying to figure out*
> *who Margo was.*

> *Bound to dismiss her as*
> *extracurricular:*
> *Kennedy doing what*
> *Kennedy does.*

Margo smiled wanly through her tears. She'd long had the sense that she was called to do something special. She'd dreamed since mov-ing in with Nana of leaving her mark on the world. Before this week, she would never have guessed that her footnote in the history books would expose her as the lowest kind of—

She slept.

THIRTY-FIVE

Premature Celebration

I

On Wednesday morning, October 24, Attorney General Robert Kennedy read to the ExComm the chilling letter from Khrushchev that Ambassador Dobrynin had handed him last night at the embassy. The blockade, said Khrushchev, constituted "outright banditry or, if you like, the folly of degenerate imperialism."

Kennedy smiled. "Well, he's not the first man to call me a degenerate."

Nobody laughed. Bobby read on: "The Soviet Government considers that the violation of the freedom to use international waters and international air space is an act of aggression which pushes mankind toward the abyss of a world nuclear-missile war. Therefore, the Soviet Government cannot instruct the captains of Soviet vessels bound for Cuba to observe the orders of American naval forces blockading that island."

"I see," said the President, his humor fading.

"Mr. President, he concludes by insisting that the Soviet ship captains will protect their rights. He says they have—quoting again now—'everything necessary to do so.'"

"It's practically a declaration of war," said McNamara.

Now other voices competed. Everyone had a suggestion. But Kennedy asked for quiet.

"Okay. That's the face Khrushchev has decided to put on. Is he just posturing, to keep his own fanatics in line? Or is this a real threat?"

He was looking at McCone, the director of central intelligence, who cleared his throat and shuffled his papers. "Sir, as far as we can tell, work on the launchers isn't slowing down. It's speeding up."

The President turned to Maxwell Taylor, the chairman of the Joint Chiefs. "General?"

"Mr. President, our naval forces on station inform us that the trawlers headed for Cuba are now being escorted by submarines."

Kennedy turned back to McCone. "Are their missiles ready for launch?"

"No, sir. Our best estimate is at least three more days."

Somebody from the State Department asked how good the intelligence was. McCone said it was excellently sourced and deemed highly reliable, but Bundy wondered. The arrest of Penkovsky left in limbo all their Soviet sources.

"So, in three days, they'll be able to hit our cities with nukes?" asked someone else.

"They can hit our cities already," growled General LeMay.

"Well, in three days they'll be able to hit us from a lot closer," a worried voice put in.

"Exactly," said LeMay.

As Bundy watched, the mood in the room began subtly to shift. Before, only the Joint Chiefs had seemed to favor invasion. Now the entire table was moving in that direction.

The President evidently sensed the change as well. He waved the others silent. "I don't want to put Khrushchev in a corner from which he can't escape."

But Bundy wondered. On Monday, the President had briefed congressional leaders, who, almost to a man, wanted swift military action. Kennedy had been stunned by their belligerence, but Bundy hadn't. He worried that the President he served, in his determination to listen to every argument and consider every option, was missing the response of the man in the street. Millions were leaving the cities, afraid of war; but many of those same millions considered war inevitable, even desirable. If their President decided to take military action against the missiles in Cuba, the great majority of the American people were angrily ready to support him.

The President asked what would happen if a submarine were to fire on an American vessel.

"What do you think?" one of the military men near Bundy muttered, but too softly for the commander in chief to hear.

Bundy made a note of his name.

There were small depth charges, McNamara answered, that could be dropped and even hit a submarine without doing damage. The captain would interpret this as an order to surface or be destroyed.

"How can we know for a fact that we won't damage the submarine?" asked Bobby. "It's not like we've tested these things on Soviet hulls."

"We know," said McNamara, jaw thrust forward belligerently.

The President, still driven by a concern about retaliation, answered that he would rather attack a merchant vessel than a submarine. McNamara corrected him gently. Maritime warfare could never be entirely accurate. He was skeptical that the Navy could put enough separation between the cargo ship and its submarine escort to take on one without fighting the other.

"Okay," Kennedy said, but he didn't sound persuaded.

The conversation turned to various ways to stop the Soviet ships if they refused to turn at the quarantine line—warning shots? taking out their rudders?—and it was left to Robert Kennedy to ask whether anybody had bothered to make sure that each American ship had a Russian speaker on board.

Silence.

Just before the meeting broke up, an aide handed McCone a note. "Mr. President, the Soviet ships are slowing. They are not challenging the blockade line."

There was a moment of disbelief; then, if not a cheer, at least a relaxation of tension. A smiling Dean Rusk went so far as to say that the other side had blinked.

Bundy was reluctant to join the celebration. Khrushchev had slowed the ships to gain time to consider his options. The ExComm seemed to have forgotten McCone's earlier report that work on preparing the missiles had actually accelerated. The Soviets were not backing down. Sooner or later, they would send at least one ship toward the line. They had to. Until that happened, neither side knew how far the other was prepared to go.

Nothing had changed.

They needed GREENHILL and the back channel more than ever.

II

Margo Jensen had not so much settled into a routine as come to experience her life as a single unbroken nightmare. Some of the girls were going out after work and invited the newcomer along. Her polite refusal only added to their suspicion that she was in town for the pleasure of someone powerful, especially after her furtive telephone conversation earlier in the day. A man had called the office looking for her—that's what they said when they came down to her cubby to get her, "a man"—and as Margo made her way along the hallway to the reception desk, she sensed the curious and disapproving scrutiny of everyone she passed. The receptionist was a thickset, unpleasant woman named Sylvie who wet her lips constantly with her tongue. She held out the phone and told Margo that she had almost hung up, so please don't take so long next time. Margo asked politely whether it would be possible to transfer the call to an empty office.

"No," said Sylvie with cruel satisfaction.

Defeated, Margo took the handset. An unfamiliar male voice began talking some nonsense about how a book she had requested from the Library of Congress had gone missing, and it would likely be weeks or more before they could find another copy.

"It wasn't that important," she said, because the code word was *library*, and meant an unscheduled meeting tonight. "I can wait."

Sylvie took the phone back. She licked her lips. "Everything all right, sweetie?"

"Fine, thanks."

"He can't make it?"

"There isn't any he."

"We're both women here." A horrendous wink. "Don't you worry. That's how men are. It doesn't mean he's tired of you. He's probably just busy."

Walking back to her cubicle, Margo kept her head high. She was now more puzzled than embarrassed. This was Wednesday. She had been in the city only since Saturday night. She had made no friends, confided in nobody, least of all her roommates or fellow interns. Despite that, everybody seemed to think she was in Washington at the command of a powerful man.

The rumor had spread awfully fast.

THIRTY-SIX

Premature Panic

I

On that same Wednesday, at about the same time that Margo was receiving her call, a scene of a different kind was playing out a mile away, in Foggy Bottom. "Comes to all of us sooner or later," Gwynn was saying as he perched against his desk, studying Harrington's separation papers. His voice was almost kindly, but dripped with malicious respect. "You've compiled a remarkable record, Dr. Harrington. You've sacrificed a lot for your country. Nobody could possibly ask you for any more. Time to get out there and enjoy life."

"You already fired me, Alfred." She sat easily in an armchair, projecting far less turmoil than she felt. "You've given me my thirty days' notice. I no longer have a security clearance. Frankly, I'm not entirely sure why you wanted to see me."

But Gwynn was having too much fun to slow down. "We've worked out the details," he continued happily. "Terms of severance will naturally be generous. And of course we'll be indulging the usual festivities to mark the occasion—formal dinner and so forth. Testimonials from old friends." Subtle emphasis on *old*. "You're a legend," he added, pressing the knife more deeply into her soul. "Irreplaceable. Well, you'll hear all of that at the dinner."

"Sounds glorious." Harrington knew that he was relishing this final opportunity to gloat before her departure. But she was buoyed by the knowledge that, although she herself might no longer be in the game, her chosen agent was still in play; and, although she would never admit it, the fact that her titular superior knew nothing of the revived operation constituted a source of particular pleasure.

Gwynn put the papers down. He smiled placatingly. "You've had a magnificent career, Doctor. So few of us can truly be called legends in our own time. You are certainly among that fabled few."

She found a little of the old fire. "Is there an actual purpose for this meeting, Alfred?"

But she could not shake his good humor. "Relax, Doctor. I'm not as wicked as you seem to think. I just wanted to make sure that you understand how much everyone here admires you." A wise nod, as though she, rather than he, had made the point. A folder on the Cuba crisis was open on his desk: a breach of regulations, given her lack of a clearance, but likely placed there intentionally, to remind her of who was who. "Now, it's true, if you were to press me, I suppose, given the committee's findings, we could have dismissed you for cause. SANTA GREEN was a mess. We nearly lost two people, and poor Ainsley at the consulate had his cover blown and had to come home. That could all be laid at your feet, Doctor. Your operation, your competence, your charter." He sounded positively jolly. "Nobody wants that. You've done yeoman service for your country—yeowoman—and I think I speak for the entire committee when I say that we would rather see you retired with every honor you deserve. There's even talk of an Intelligence Cross, and, as you know, that's as high as you can get."

Harrington, as it happened, had been awarded her second cross years ago. She opened her mouth to deliver a suitable rebuke, and that was when the alarm klaxon sounded.

And went on sounding.

Gwynn looked around in panic. "What is that?" he shouted over the piercing din.

"Evacuation," said Harrington calmly. She stood. "Come on, Alfred. We have to get to the bomb shelter."

II

The President was in his helicopter, heading for Site R, the command post tunneled out of Raven Rock Mountain in Pennsylvania. Jackie and the kids had already enplaned for a more distant location.

"What do we know?" he asked Bundy, seated just behind him.

This was the first chance they'd had to talk since the Secret Service barged into Kennedy's meeting with Commerce and Treasury on trade negotiations and all but carried him out the door, heading first for the bunker, and then, at a crisply radioed order, changing direction and rushing him onto the lawn as the helicopter landed.

Bundy leaned close. Two other aides and four Secret Service agents were with them. A Marine captain sat near the cockpit, handling communication.

Bundy spoke in a furred but clear whisper. "Mr. President, approximately twenty minutes ago, one early-warning satellite and two ground stations detected what appears to be a detonation in near space. The track suggests that it was a man-made vehicle, launched from inside the Soviet Union."

Kennedy's face was slack and gray. "You're saying it's an ICBM?"

"I've told you what we know, sir. The other DEW stations aren't reporting any activity, but three of them are off-line." The communications officer handed him a tear sheet. "General LeMay has the fighters and bombers at Homestead ready to take off on your order."

"Are the missiles in Cuba—"

"There was an overflight this morning. There's another U-2 in the air now. If they shoot the plane down, it's a good bet that we're at war."

The President turned to the window. Bundy sympathized. Maybe he was worrying about his wife and children; maybe his brother and his family; maybe the many ways he must surely feel he'd failed the country he served. As for Bundy, his own calm was a growing surprise. At Harvard they used to say his heart was an IBM computing machine. Only now did it occur to him that they might be right.

The communications officer handed over another tear sheet. Kennedy glanced across expectantly.

"Sir, warning site Laredo is tracking two possible inbound missiles over the Atlantic Coast. The Joint Chiefs recommend you set DefCon One and activate Emergency War Warnings to all commands."

The President was ashen. One of the Secret Service men overheard, and his hand moved instinctively toward his gun.

"My family—"

"They've been transferred to a second plane, Mr. President. They're heading for the dispersal site in Wisconsin."

Kennedy digested this. "Where's Bobby?"

"I believe he should be at Mount Weather by now."

"Can we get him on the radio?"

Bundy was irritated. The President's brother was smart and tough, but he wasn't in the chain of command. The Joint Chiefs would have been furious to learn that Kennedy couldn't make up his mind without talking to Bobby. Nevertheless, Bundy dutifully conferred with the communications officer. "Mr. President, I am advised that the channel isn't fully secure. The recommendation is to wait until we land to contact Mount Weather."

"If the missiles are nearing the coast, we can't wait that long."

"Yes, sir, that's why we—"

The helicopter banked hard. Bundy peered down but saw only trees. They couldn't be over Pennsylvania yet. The craft described a half-circle and headed back the way they had come.

The communications officer tore off another message. Bundy scanned the first few lines, then leaned close to Kennedy. "It was a satellite, Mr. President. Launched this morning, exploded as it reached parking orbit."

"What about the two missiles?"

"Believe it or not, sir, two more satellites. They didn't explode. Their observed motion happened to match predicted missile tracks. A remarkable coincidence, Mr. President, but a false alarm."

III

"Well, that was an unusually embarrassing episode, I must say." They were in the elevator, heading back up to Gwynn's office on the fifth floor. Three or four other functionaries were crowded in with them, and Harrington noticed how they avoided looking at her. The same thing had happened in the shelter. Word, it seemed, had gotten around. Gwynn, meanwhile, raved on, not caring who overheard. "Crowded into a sardine can with the secretaries and the messengers and goodness knows who. Can you imagine weeks or months like that? It staggers the imagination."

"It would only have been a few minutes," said Harrington as they stepped off.

"What?"

"In the sardine can, Alfred. We'd only have been there a few minutes."

He cocked an eyebrow as if suspecting insolence. "And why's that, Doctor? Would they be whisking us off to some other location? One of the President's secret hideaways, perhaps?"

"No. But the shelter's only four levels down. If this had been a real attack, we'd be dead."

At the entrance to his suite, he turned. His expression was oddly sheepish. "I know you think I'm against you, Dr. Harrington. I'm not. I argued your case in committee."

And next week, on Halloween, the Easter Bunny is coming down my chimney with presents, she said—but not aloud.

"I'm hoping that you'll be staying in town," he continued. "So that we can call on you from time to time. If we need counsel and advice."

She smiled. Coldly. "What you're saying is, you're afraid of my ex-husband, because even now he has better contacts than you do."

Gwynn began to stutter an angry response, but Harrington was already striding down the hall. She marveled afresh at her own aplomb. She had no children to fear for, and no family other than a sister she never saw. Down in the shelter, waiting to die, all her thoughts had been of GREENHILL.

THIRTY-SEVEN

A Brief Series of Errors

I

Margo was attending to her makeup when Patsy knocked impatiently. Margo groaned. Patsy, on the rare evenings she spent at home, practically lived in the bathroom, and tended toward annoyance at ever having to wait. This was the second evening in a row when Margo, to use Nana's argot, had gotten herself dolled up. No doubt Patsy considered her a kindred spirit. Again the fiction: her roommates knew she was getting dolled up *for* somebody, even if they hadn't guessed who.

"One minute," Margo called. She had never been much good with lipstick. She didn't understand how some women applied it so fast.

"It's the phone, Margo. It's for you."

She rubbed her forehead. Of all the times . . .

The only phone in the apartment hung on the kitchen wall above the counter; and, like the counter, it was yellow and oddly clammy. Margo didn't like touching it, and in fact had used it only once, to tell Nana where she was staying and what the number was. Patsy was holding the receiver out, jiggling it vaguely in Margo's direction.

"I like his voice," the Californian whispered with a saucy wink. She disappeared into her bedroom, but Hope continued to sit at the small table, reading her book.

Margo turned her back and hunched over, in the pretense that the conversation would be harder for her roommates to overhear. She said, "Hi, honey," and he said, "Hi, honey," back. She said she was sorry she hadn't called, and he said he was thinking about her, and she said something equally insipid. She wondered what it meant when you and your boyfriend ran out of things to talk about. Just weeks ago, she had thought herself the luckiest girl in the world to have a brilliant young man like Tom Jellinek at her side. She had sat willingly at his feet as he discoursed on mathematics or politics or whatever he chose at any given moment to dispense. It occurred to her now that Tom, for all his gentle sweetness, rarely asked her opinion.

On anything.

"So—what did you do today?" he asked.

"I was at work."

"And what are you doing tonight?"

Her breath caught. She knew he heard the sound, and probably was wounded by it. "Going out. Seeing friends."

Tom digested this. "Anybody I know?"

"I don't think so. No."

"Try me."

She held the phone away from her ear. She sensed without looking that Hope was no longer reading, but studying her instead.

"I need you to trust me," Margo finally said, voice pitched low, although Hope no doubt could hear. "Will you do that for me? Trust me?"

Even at a distance of three hundred miles, Tom came back hard and fast. "Are you doing something that requires my trust?" She said nothing. "I'm only asking because I care about you," he hurried on. "Does whatever you're doing have to do with what happened in Bulgaria?"

Oh, no! Not on an open phone line!

"No, of course not."

"Then why did you have to go to Washington so fast?"

"The job just became available. I didn't hear about it until Friday."

"But you left on Thursday. You have to admit, it's pretty strange. Tuesday you stand me up for our study date, Thursday you stand me up for coffee, and the next day you have an internship in Washington? That's one heck of a coincidence."

He was making it worse, and she had no way to stop him, because he didn't know about telephones and walls and cars, and how they could listen to you anywhere except the surf.

"Honey, look. I'll be back in a few weeks. Can all this wait until then? Please?"

Again he was a long time answering. "I don't like all these secrets," he said.

"There aren't any secrets," she lied. She felt Hope's judgmental gaze boring at the back of her head. "But there are things that are hard to talk about on the telephone."

"Is that a fancy way of saying you don't want to see me any more?"

Margo began to bristle. "Tom, please. Not everything is about you."

"Then who's it about?"

"Please, honey. When I get back."

They rang off inconclusively.

II

Again the Yenching Palace. Again Fomin. Tonight the Soviet was brusque to the point of rudeness. He had anticipated Kennedy's message, and had his reply ready. It was short. And angry.

Margo's anger was rising, too, but she had yet to find a target her own size. She needed Melody Davidson. She needed poor Phil Littlejohn. She needed someone she could defeat with a double dactyl. But with Fomin and Khrushchev on one side, and Bundy and the President on the other, she was a pygmy in the land of the giants.

Only she wasn't. That's what Margo kept telling herself as she left the restaurant with the message and headed for the bus stop. This time she would ride all the way down to the Federal Triangle to meet her driver. She wasn't a pygmy, she whispered into the night wind that whipped her long coat around her ankles. She was Donald Jensen's daughter, and they needed her. She hadn't sought out her role as intermediary, but she wasn't involved in the negotiation merely on the sufferance of the powerful men around her.

She was here because they needed her.

III

Bundy was in his office when his secretary buzzed. He ignored her. He was studying Nate Esman's report. Although the SANTA GREEN subscription list ran to forty-seven names, only nine people actually possessed enough information to have blown the operation. Of those, only four knew the actual identities of both GREENHILL and GREENDAY, the cryptonym for Agatha Milner. Someone could, of course, have alerted the Soviets without having that knowledge, but the precision with which the DS acted strongly suggested that they had hard information. Not even Bundy himself, who had approved the mission, had been privy to their identities. The four who had complete knowledge were Harrington; her boss, Gwynn; her assistant, Borkland; and, from the Agency, Jerry Ainsley, who had been the point man in Bulgaria.

Borkland he decided to exclude. In the wake of Harrington's forced retirement, Borkland had opted to resign from government service as a protest—hardly the act of a spy. He had a law degree, and planned to join a Washington firm.

Bundy was also inclined to put aside Alfred Gwynn. Gwynn seemed too much the fool, although that could be cover. But his ambitions were too openly and honestly worn. It was obvious to everyone that he was destined to crash and burn.

The buzzer went off again, and again Bundy ignored it. He turned to the next page of Esman's report.

That left two suspects—Ainsley and Harrington—who, between them, had engineered GREENHILL's return to Washington.

Bundy was tempted to dismiss Ainsley, largely because, as Esman's memorandum noted, his cover had been blown by the collapse of SANTA GREEN: his career in the field was over. On the other hand, the Soviets might have reasoned that a man of Ainsley's prospects could serve them better from Washington. And although Ainsley had virtuously refused to listen to GREENHILL's story, he surely could figure out why she was in such a hurry to get to Washington.

Harrington was so decorated and respected that Bundy could not imagine her as a fruitful target for Soviet recruitment. But Esman's report pointed out that the KGB's predecessor, the NKVD, had a significant presence in Vienna during the war years. Was it possible that she had been a Soviet agent since—

His secretary buzzed a third time.

"Yes, Janet?"

"Sir, Lorenz Niemeyer is in the West Wing lobby."

"In the lobby? He's at the White House? Now?"

"Yes, Mr. Bundy."

The national security adviser glanced at his watch. In half an hour he had to see McCone and McNamara—to talk about not Cuba but Southeast Asia, the other corner of the globe where America was on the verge of war. Bundy was skeptical that anything much could be accomplished, but the President seemed determined to try. At least Bundy would be spared his usual fight with Bobby: the attorney general was consulting with his staff about the security of James Meredith, who had recently become the first Negro ever to enroll at the University of Mississippi. The President was insistent that his Administration continue to do the work of the nation while awaiting the Soviet response.

Kennedy himself was on his way to the townhouse on East Capitol Street to hear GREENHILL's latest report. Afterward, Bundy and Bobby would join him in the Oval Office to analyze whatever news she brought.

Niemeyer had certainly picked a bad time to drop in.

"Bring him down," Bundy said, unaccountably worried.

IV

Bundy cleared his desk. He locked Esman's report in his safe. When the professor arrived, Bundy greeted him with a courteous diffidence that conveyed, if not quite affection, certainly respect. They made small talk for a few minutes, and Bundy poured his guest a glass of Scotch from the bottle on the credenza. Niemeyer was in town for a conference at Georgetown, and wanted to pay his respects. Bundy, just as disingenuously, assured the professor that not dropping in would have been a crime.

"I won't take much of your time," said Niemeyer when the pleasantries were done. He shifted his bulk. The wooden chair creaked. "I quite understand that this is a difficult moment."

"Indeed," said Bundy, dryly. "And so, just to save time, let me say right at the start, if this is about Dr. Harrington—"

"It isn't."

"Go ahead, then."

"From what I read in the press, Soviet ships are approaching the blockade line."

"I know you keep your contacts in the intelligence apparatus, Professor. You needn't pretend that your sources are limited to the papers."

Niemeyer toyed with his glass. "I would imagine that every amateur strategist in the Western Hemisphere is offering you advice. I'm mainly here to pay my respects, and to tell you I think the President is handling matters exactly right."

"But," invited Bundy.

"But," his guest agreed, "I'm a little worried, to be frank." He hunched forward. "Kennedy has made plain that he's willing to go to war over the missiles."

"That isn't what we've been saying."

"It's the implication, Mr. Bundy. Let's be honest. The President's statements may be cautiously worded, but they amount to a threat to wage war. The American public certainly understands his meaning. That's why you can't find any canned goods in the stores. That's why people in Washington and the other big cities are suddenly finding excuses to visit relatives in the Midwest. That's why those same relatives are digging shelters in their back yards."

"You're saying we're causing a panic."

"No. The missiles are doing that. And it doesn't really matter what your own people think. It matters what the Soviets think."

"Go on," said Bundy, eyes narrowing.

"The President's determination has frightened America. The question is whether it's frightened Khrushchev." Nodding toward the bottle. "Maybe I could have another drop."

Bundy crossed to the sideboard and poured. "Please continue, Professor."

"Think about a game of chicken," said Niemeyer. "The kids play it. I assume you know the rules. Two young men go zipping toward each other in their cars, fast as they can, and the one who swerves first loses. And if nobody swerves, they both die, so they both lose. If you want to win, the trick is to get the other fellow to believe that you're so crazy you won't swerve. At the same time, you need him to stay rational enough that, once he realizes you're crazy, he'll swerve."

"I know the theory, Professor."

"Do you?" Sardonically. "Well, then, maybe you've thought about the winning strategy. How do you persuade the other fellow that you're crazy? Not just by driving straight at him fast as you can. He's doing the same. You have to give him a stronger signal than that. Something unmistakable. Throw beer bottles out the window so the other fellow will think you're drunk. Better still, throw the steering wheel out the window. But I think there's an even better idea."

"What's that?" asked Bundy, only because he knew it was expected of him.

"Run over somebody."

"I beg your pardon."

Niemeyer grinned. Savagely. He knew he'd made an impression. "On the way to the collision. Hit one of the spectators and keep on going."

"Hit a spectator."

"Hard. And make sure the other fellow knows you don't give a damn." He took a long swig from the glass. "When we drop a bomb in wartime, we accept that there will be civilian casualties. We always say it's okay because we don't target them intentionally. But we targeted them in Japan and we won the war. We made them see how crazy we were. That's the point. The other side has to think you're a little crazy. The best evidence that you're crazy is to act crazy."

"Let me be clear, Professor. Are you advising us to blow a Soviet ship out of the water just to make a point? Because if that's what—"

"I'm advising you to do something crazy."

Bundy watched him closely. "Can you be a little more specific?"

"I told you already. Run down a spectator. A bystander."

"A bystander."

"Not as a rule. Only if that's what it takes to make your adversary believe you're sufficiently irrational not to swerve."

"Thank you, Professor," said Bundy. He stood. "Now, if you'll excuse me."

Niemeyer didn't budge. "How's she doing?"

"Who?"

The pudgy man shifted his bulk. "Miss Margo Jensen. GREENHILL. I assume by now you have her running between wickets." Toying with his glass. "Only you won't tell me, will you? Operational security. All that."

"I'm sorry, Professor Niemeyer. I'm afraid I don't know what you're talking about."

The old man ignored the attempt at deflection. "She's taken a sudden leave. One minute Fomin shows up, and the next GREENHILL is in Washington. It's not difficult to make the connection." He put the drink down and folded his pudgy hands across that ample stomach. "I'm sure she told you I disappeared on her. Ordered my staff to tell her nothing. You understand that it was necessary. After I called you to convey Fomin's offer, and you turned it down, I had to find a way to force GREENHILL to act. If she was half the girl I thought she was, she'd fight her way up the ladder. She did, didn't she?"

"You know I can't—"

"After GREENHILL managed that feat, her utility would be obvious. You'd have no choice but to use her, and I suspect that you're doing exactly that. Precisely as Aleks Fomin planned." Niemeyer, too, was now on his feet. "Ah, well. Thank you for your time, Mr. Bundy. I'm afraid I've chewed your ear enough. You must be about your duties. But do bear in mind one detail."

"What's that?"

"You remember what I said about playing chicken."

"Yes."

"Excellent. Because I think you should bear in mind that GREEN-HILL isn't one of the drivers. She's a spectator. A bystander. I'm sure Fomin and his masters accept that."

"You're a coldhearted bastard. Did anyone ever tell you that?"

"This is war, Mr. Bundy. A war we need to win without fighting."

The two men exchanged a hard look of professional understanding. Bundy extended a hand. "Thank you for coming by, Professor Niemeyer."

V

"What happened to you was operational," said Lorenz Niemeyer. "Bundy as much as told me that."

Doris Harrington's fingers tightened on her coffee cup. She was sitting on her living-room sofa. Niemeyer was in the chair opposite, drinking brandy.

"I'd figured that out," she said. "As soon as that nice young man showed up with GREENHILL in tow, it was plain that they wanted me out of the way." She sipped, watched his face for the old telltales. "Bundy must have spent days in preparation. Before he ever heard from me—before GREENHILL ever arrived in Washington—he had the plan ready."

"He's an amateur," the great man murmured, "but he's not without certain skills."

She shook her head. "I took orders from amateurs in the war. We lost good people because the amateurs wouldn't listen to those of us in the field."

"Including GREENHILL's father. He was one of the best."

"Well, I've been wanting to ask you about that." She put the cup down. "You said you promised him you'd look after his family."

"I did."

"I suppose you pulled a string or two to help GREENHILL's brother get his job at that private academy in Ohio. Turns out that the head-master was a colleague of yours in the war." Harrington waited, but Niemeyer offered no reply. "Then there's the grandmother," she continued. "My research suggests she's been through the money her husband left. She couldn't possibly have had enough left to maintain that palace of hers. So I suppose you've been helping the family financially. At several removes, to be sure. Untraceably."

A smile, faint but proud. "Perhaps."

"All because of your promise to Donald Jensen."

"Precisely."

"A conversation that took place when?"

Niemeyer swirled his brandy. "I don't think I understand."

The telltales: the curled contemptuous lip, the rising disdain in the cultured voice.

"I've been thinking about this, Lore. You told me you promised to look after Donald Jensen's family. It seems unlikely that you had that conversation with every agent you sent out. Or, if you did, it seems unlikely that you took it this seriously. Between us, we lost dozens of agents." She put her cup down. "That means Donald Jensen was special. The promise to him was special. Why would that be?"

"Suppose you tell me."

"I don't need to. It's obvious. He didn't blow himself up with a grenade, did he?"

"Fomin showed GREENHILL the Gestapo photograph. We have a copy. It's in the files."

"I saw it." Her finger jabbed at him. "The photograph only told us that he was blown to bits. It doesn't tell us where the grenade came from."

"The Gestapo report is very clear."

"The Gestapo report is based on an assumption. They surrounded the farmhouse. They heard the explosion. They went in and found the body."

"A sequence that seems to fit the narrative."

"Of course it fits. Except that the same report said that, after the explosion, at least one other member of the Resistance was seen racing away. A heavyset man, Lore. A man like you."

The clever face hardened. "And?"

"You were there. You threw the grenade."

"Not exactly. I'm not a monster, Doris. I was there. I handed him the grenade after pulling the pin. Then I ran out." His eyes focused on the middle distance. "He'd been wounded. Two in the chest, another that almost took his arm off. He couldn't escape. He couldn't blow himself up. He asked me to do it for him. We both knew that if they caught him, even if they patched him up, he had no strength left. Donald was a tough man, but in his condition he couldn't have resisted torture for five minutes. Probably he'd have been dead in ten. He asked me to take care of his family, and he asked me to pull the pin."

"That's not in the official report."

"No."

"Why? And why couldn't you tell Margo?"

"You mean GREENHILL." At some point during the conversation, he had moved from the chair. He was beside her on the sofa. "The story was heroic enough as it was, but people don't understand what it's like out there. I altered the events a bit, and, in doing so, made him an even greater hero."

"And spared yourself some difficult questions."

"Oh, I live with the difficult questions, my dear." He was stroking her hair. She allowed it. "I live with them every day. Every night. They haunt me. All the people I sent to their deaths, but Donald especially. They whisper in my dreams." He leaned closer. "As they whisper to you."

"They do," she said, tight-lipped, her mind on Carina.

"Doris."

"Stop it, Lore. You don't want to do this, and neither do I. Can't you find some willing undergraduate to take care of your needs?"

"I'm not interested in undergraduates, willing or not."

"Well, that's a change." She shoved at his hands. "No. Listen to me. We're going to talk about this. You shouldn't have involved her. And this isn't about your promise or what you owe." Harrington wasn't sure what she was going to say until the words popped out. "This is about making it right. Your mistake all those years ago. But you can't, Lore. She's not her father. He's dead. You pulled the pin and handed him the grenade. For all I know, you threw it. No. Stop that. You can't fix the past by tossing his daughter to the wolves and bringing her back. This whole thing was a mistake."

"They're using her, Doris. She's their back channel. It's working fine. And her career will be splendid."

"You're using her, too. This is one of your schemes, Lore. I see it in your eyes. She's playing a part, and you'd let her die if it would further the plan."

"Greenhill understands the risks."

"I'm sure you explained them to her."

"Indeed I did. And I've no doubt that you did, too."

She grabbed the burned, misshapen hand. "And what about this, Lore? Have you told her the truth?"

"What do you mean?"

"Your students. The people in Washington. The acolytes who worship you. They all think it was the Gestapo. I thought that, too. Because you never wanted to talk about it." She kissed the mangled fingers. "But that wasn't true, was it? You never lied to us. You just let us live with our illusions. Even your wife." She tugged on the stub of his thumb. "You didn't get out of the farmhouse in time, did you? After you threw the grenade. This is your own little souvenir of the night you killed Donald Jensen to keep him from being arrested."

"You always did have a vivid imagination, Doris."

"Tell me where I'm wrong." He said nothing. She gave him his hand back. "I care about that girl, Lore."

"So do I."

"No. You care about Lorenz Niemeyer."

"What I care about is the success of the operation. I care about getting those missiles out of Cuba without a war. Just now, nothing is more important. I thought you'd feel the same."

"What about the people, Lore? The ones we send out to die for the sake of our operations?"

"I balance their lives against the lives we save."

"That's very cold-blooded."

"You're just the same, Doris. That's what makes you so good at this work."

Harrington stood. "I think you should go, Lore."

At the door, he turned to her, kissed her cheek. "GREENHILL will be fine, Doris."

"I wish I could believe that."

"You'll have to trust me."

"Because that's worked out so well over the years."

Harrington stood at the window, watching him depart: the best man she had ever known, and also the worst. He was as brilliant and funny and charming and handsome as ever. And when there were decisions to make in the interest of the nation's security, he was a wall of ice, a human computer to whom individuals were factors in an equation. At such moments—tonight was typical—she hated him completely. And if she had known that they would never see each other again, she would have run down the street, taken his pudgy body in her slender arms, and hugged him close for the rest of their mutual lives.

THIRTY-EIGHT

The Visitor

I

"That's his answer?" said the President. "If we won't take the Jupiters out of Turkey and Italy, we have to give up the gravity bomb?"

"Yes, sir. Fomin said a prototype is being constructed at the Los Alamos National Laboratory under the top-secret designation TX-61, and that you would know the details. He said you asked for alternatives to the Jupiters. The gravity bomb is a suggestion. He said you might have other ideas, but you have to give Khrushchev a sign of good faith that he can show his hard-liners."

"Or else what?"

Margo was once more seated primly on the plush sofa. She fidgeted under Kennedy's scrutiny. "He didn't say, Mr. President. I got the impression that Khrushchev's position is precarious."

"Precarious."

"Yes, sir."

"And he wants a show of *our* good faith."

"Yes, sir," said Margo again, looking down at her fancy shoes. The clingy blue dress, too, was more alluring than anything that she would have bought for herself; or that Nana would have allowed her to wear. Bundy had presented it to her, along with three others, at their briefing. Margo's roommates had teased her about making herself pretty for the mystery man they were certain had moved mountains to bring her to Washington. It was no less humiliating for being part of the fiction.

"Did you happen to remind him that they started this whole

thing?" Kennedy's face was thundery. "Who the hell is Khrushchev to ask *us* to prove *our* good faith?"

Margo swallowed. "Mr. President, my job is just to carry messages."

"Right. You have no position. You don't care who wins."

Stung. "Of course I do. Why would you say that?"

Kennedy had been pacing, but now he paused. "Mmmm. Nice to see there's a little fire under all that ice."

"Sir?"

"I've been waiting to see who's really in there, is all."

"I—Mr. President—"

"Have a drink, Miss Jensen. You look like you need one."

"I'm fine, sir."

He went over to the champagne bucket anyway and filled two flutes halfway to the top. He handed her one. "Remember, honey, it's part of the job. The Secret Service has to smell it on your breath."

She took the glass, sipped, made a face, swallowed. Then she sipped some more.

Kennedy sat beside her. "Feel better?"

"Yes, sir. Thank you, sir."

"Good. I assume you remember the rest." He laughed at her blankly nervous stare. "My collar, honey. The lipstick."

"Mr. President—"

"Come on. You know the drill."

"Yes, sir."

They completed that ritual, too.

"Now you just need to muss your hair a little. And your dress." The crooked smile. "That is, unless you want me to do it."

Margo slipped into the adjoining bathroom, shut the door, tried to make herself look a little less presentable. She smeared her lipstick, eased down a shoulder strap, tugged and squeezed the hem to give it a wrinkled look. In the mirror she looked like exactly what her roommates thought she was.

The President knocked. "Are you okay in there?"

"Yes, sir. I'll be right out."

"Good. I have to get back."

When she emerged, she saw to her horror that the door to the hallway was open. Kennedy was whispering to a Secret Service agent. The President's tie was still undone. The bedclothes were half on the floor, the sheets wrinkled and disordered. The agent nodded, glanced at Margo without expression, nodded again, then left, pulling the door shut.

The President had switched to bourbon. "I was telling him to call my people to say I'm on the way." He looked her up and down. "Not that I have to go this instant. We should talk a little."

Margo swallowed. "Yes, sir."

"We're only meeting tomorrow if you see Fomin."

"Yes, Mr. President."

"You have to make him understand that his side started this whole thing. They're not really in a position to make demands. What I want to hear is a concrete offer."

"Yes, sir."

"You can stop all the 'Yes, sir, no, sir.' If we're going to be spending time together, we have to get used to each other." Kennedy stepped close. He took her hand in both of his. For a mad moment she thought he was going to kiss her. "Now, listen. You're worried about screwing up. I understand that, believe me. When I was in the Pacific, that's exactly what I worried about, every day. But you're doing just fine, Miss Jensen. Okay?"

Margo swallowed. "Yes, sir. Thank you, sir."

He released her hand and walked to the window. His fingers massaged his lower back. Pain and exhaustion played across the handsome face.

"Let me ask you something, Miss Jensen. Do you know what happens in the event of a nuclear attack on Washington?"

"No, sir."

"I'll tell you. The 2857th Test Squadron helicopters down from Olmstead Air Force Base. If the White House is intact, they load me and my family on board and take off. If the building's wrecked, we're supposed to be in the bunker, which might or might not survive the attack. Say it does. We can't get out, because the building's collapsed on top of us. Know what the brave men of 2857th do then? They bring in cranes and drills, and break through and pull us out. All this after a nuclear attack. How likely does that sound to you?"

"I don't know. I guess it's possible."

"That they'll stay in the blast zone, getting showered with fallout, on the off chance my family and I are alive?" Kennedy took a long pull of bourbon. "I'd say it's damned unlikely, Miss Jensen. I think we probably wind up entombed down there. There's power, water, food, everything. But sooner or later, it runs out. Then we starve to death or die of asphyxiation. How's that for a bitter ending? No," he continued, as if she'd been arguing the contrary. "No, I don't think that's how I want to go out. So—what do you say you and I solve this thing?"

"Yes, sir. I agree, sir."

He swung around, the moment of weakness gone. His energy was improbable, but admirable. "Tomorrow night, Ambassador Stevenson is addressing the United Nations. We've told the world about the missiles, Miss Jensen. Tomorrow Stevenson will show them our evidence." He was buttoning his collar. "People are scared already. They're going to be a whole lot scareder."

"Yes, sir."

"We're at the crisis point, Miss Jensen." He lifted a hand, thumb and forefinger millimeters apart. "We're this close to war."

She swallowed. "I—yes, sir."

He went to the mirror, tied his tie. He slung his jacket over his shoulder, and then, with his hand on the doorknob, turned to glance at her again. But not appraisingly this time. He was the commander in chief again. "Wait at least ten minutes before you leave. Fifteen is better."

"I remember, Mr. President."

"And, Miss Jensen . . ."

"Yes, sir?"

"Have another drink. You look like you need it."

He went out.

II

Sitting outside the apartment building in Southwest, Captain Viktor Vaganian pondered what he had learned. So the young woman who was meeting Fomin was also meeting the President. Well, well. Perhaps he had misjudged his colleague. Kennedy was said to be decadent. Suppose matters were as they appeared. This GREENHILL could be the President's mistress. In that case, she likely was Fomin's agent, and Viktor dared not endanger a highly sensitive operation by pursuing an investigation that might expose the relationship.

On the other hand, suppose this was all a clever camouflage, as Jack Ziegler continued to insist. That a back channel existed was not in doubt. The question was whether a man of Fomin's experience would hand such responsibility to a black girl of nineteen years. It could all be a decoy.

Vaganian saw only one way to find out. He hurried back to the embassy, where he sent an enciphered message to his superiors—or, as the Comrade General Secretary would presumably call them, his fellow conspirators.

<h1 style="text-align:center">III</h1>

"He wants us to give him a sign of good faith. Us!" The President was furious—striding, gesticulating. "He's the one who started this whole thing, and now he thinks it's up to us to make the first move. It's blackmail. I won't do it."

They were alone in the Oval Office, reviewing tonight's meeting with GREENHILL.

"I'm not so sure, Mr. President," said Bundy from his familiar place on the sofa. "We might be able to come up with something to give him."

"The country will never stand for it."

"The country doesn't need to know."

The President glared, then dropped into his rocker, looking spent and sixty. His hair was a mess. His collar was askew. He hadn't wiped off GREENHILL's lipstick. Bundy considered this quite untoward, and wondered whether Kennedy even knew how bad he looked.

"Tell me," the President said, and a sharp gesture ordered his national security adviser to make it fast.

"Sir, Khrushchev is paranoid. In the Soviet leadership, that's what keeps you alive. We know from Fomin's conversation with GREENHILL in Ithaca that Khrushchev is under enormous pressure from his hard-liners. He wants to reach an agreement, but he needs to buy off his Boyars, as it were. He also needs to believe that we're not preparing to launch an attack of our own. Not on Cuba. On Moscow. After seeing our false alarms, he has to be getting jittery. I'm sure his hard-liners are telling him that those were readiness drills."

"I'm not going to let him push me around," said Kennedy, wearily.

"No, sir. No question of that. Nevertheless, with your permission, I'd like to take at least until tomorrow morning to figure out whether there's anything we can safely offer without losing face. Maybe something we can give in secret." He didn't wait for an answer. He was remembering the curious interview with Niemeyer. "Tomorrow evening, Mr. President, you'll be seeing GREENHILL only if she sees Fomin. Just in case, let's try to come up with a message that at least gives Khrushchev some reassurance. She'll deliver it to Fomin at their next meeting, and then we'll see."

"Fine, fine," said the President, the dark mood still upon him. The aftereffects, perhaps, of the adrenaline rush of the flight from the White House under fear of nuclear attack. That was Bundy's first thought. But Kennedy's next words gave him pause. "What do you think of her? Margo Jensen? Do you really believe we can trust her?"

"Sir, with respect, inside these walls, we should use her code name."

"Fine. GREENHILL, then. Do you really believe we can trust GREENHILL?"

"Fomin trusts her. He chose her."

"That's not really an answer, Mac." Kennedy, seated behind the desk, didn't make eye contact. Bundy was standing alongside. "I don't know about this girl. She seems kind of nervous to me." His fingers combed absently through his thick but now unruly hair. "She's awfully young. And she's—I don't know—awkward. Stiff."

A small light went on. The national security adviser was remembering a certain young woman he had been obliged to add to his staff for a time last year. "Mr. President, ah, did something happen tonight that I should know about?"

The President finally looked up, and there was the mischievous, crooked smile, although it seemed to Bundy a little forced. "Whatever do you mean, Mac? What are you accusing me of?"

"I didn't mean—"

"Sure you did. But GREENHILL isn't that kind of girl. She told me." He laughed. "Besides, I'd never mix business with—well, with whatever you're accusing me of. I'm not a total degenerate, no matter what Khrushchev thinks. Anyway, I'm a happily married man," he added with a wink. Then his mood grew sober again. "Mac, look. I'm serious. This seems like a lot for some nineteen-year-old to go through. Now that we know the back channel works, maybe we should get somebody else to run between wickets."

"Mr. President, with respect. I see all the same risks you do. Yes, she's young. Yes, she's a college student. But so far she's been worthy of our trust, and, before us, Dr. Harrington's. I think she's up to it." He addressed himself to the glittering pen he was rolling between his fingers. "Besides, sir, we can't send somebody else. Fomin chose her. Fomin trusts her. He put her through a great deal to be sure she was worthy of that trust. If we send someone else, he'll get suspicious. He might blow up the back-channel negotiations and go home to die with his family."

"We're stuck with her? Is that what you're saying?"

"Yes, Mr. President."

"And if it turns out that I'm right and Fomin's wrong? If GREEN-HILL's not up to the job? What happens then?"

"Then, sir, we find out whether the White House bomb shelter is deep enough."

THIRTY-NINE

An Exclusive Interview

I

On Thursday, October 25, Margo went to lunch with a gaggle of girls from the office. The autumn weather had turned fine, so they walked the several blocks to the National Gallery of Art to eat in the basement cafeteria. A lot of the FBI guys ate there, one of the girls said confidently. Margo was distracted. She kept looking over her shoulder. There was no way she could have spotted a follower in the thronging midday crowds along the Mall, but the prickling hair at the nape of her neck told her things weren't right.

At the museum, Margo paid seventy-five cents for meatloaf and vegetables and joined the other girls at a long table. They were chattering about a new record somebody's cousin had brought back from England, "Love Me Do," by some group Margo had never heard of. She was frustrated, and puzzled. Three days ago, the President had announced the presence of Soviet missiles in Cuba. She had been waiting ever since for any sign that her co-workers were bothered by the news. But the one time she had raised the topic, they had all but engaged in a collective shrug, assuring her that there was no reason to worry, because JFK, as they familiarly called him, would fix it.

But Margo had noticed an unspoken change. She had started work on Monday, and Kennedy's speech had been Monday night. Here it was Thursday, and people were leaving the city. Grocery stores were sold out of canned goods. Of the six interns on her floor, three had left the city. The girls who had stayed might not want to talk about the crisis, but they could hardly ignore the rising swirl of panic. As her luncheon partners chattered on about music and men, Margo could not help wondering whether this desperate gabble was simply their way of coping: sticking to the mundane to cover the fears—

She sat up very straight.

A tubby little middle-aged man was waddling toward her across the cafeteria. He had a camera in his hand.

II

Margo was through running. She excused herself, leaped to her feet, and marched straight toward him. His hair was unkempt, there were food stains on his collar, and he wore his weight like an insolent challenge to a world he despised. His lips were set in a pout of disapproval. His eyes were pouchy and dissatisfied. Behind her, the girls were giggling and pointing, thinking, maybe, that this odd-looking creature was the secret explanation for Margo's sudden presence among them.

"Oh, good," he said, his voice as gratingly disagreeable as his face. "I was afraid I'd have to drag you away. You showed some sense."

"Who are you? What do you want?"

"Name's Haar. Erroll Haar. My card," he said, handing it over.

Margo looked. And looked again. He was a staff reporter for one of the sleazier supermarket tabloids.

"And what exactly do you want with me, Mr. Haar?"

"I want you to look at these."

From the folds of his coat, he produced a manila envelope. He handed it over. She opened it up, and slid out several glossy photographs.

And died inside.

There she was, dressed to kill, slinking into the townhouse on East Capitol Street.

There she was, leaving later, clothes and hair mussed, being assisted by a Secret Service agent.

And there was the President of the United States, head down, hands in his pockets, hurrying into the same door.

"No," she whispered. "No. Oh, no. God. No."

"Mmmm. First words out of her mouth are a blasphemy. Can I quote you?"

"It was a prayer," she muttered.

"Good. I'll quote you that way, then." Scribbling eagerly. He caught her expression, and his own became wolfish. "Sorry, sweetie," he said. "No real secrets in this town."

She didn't understand. How could they have been so careless? Bundy, or the Secret Service, or whoever was in charge of this madness: how was it possible that they had allowed a photographer to get pictures? It made no sense, but just now nothing did, because her brain had gone sludgy and soft. She felt the reporter's greedy gaze. She hated being on display. She knew the girls from work were watching, too, but she was gripped by the horrible paralysis that clutched her so tightly in the dream, when the fate of the world rested on her shoulders, and yet she was helpless.

No. She wasn't.

According to Niemeyer, outwardly irrational behavior often signaled a willingness to bargain. Haar wasn't here for a quote. He was here because he wanted something.

She squeezed the skin on the inside of her wrist and managed a semblance of control. She lifted her head. "Let's go outside," she said.

"Fine by me."

They took the marble steps to the lobby, not exchanging a word, and exited at the back of the museum. She looked up and down Constitution Avenue, wondering whether, despite Bundy's assurances, somebody was watching.

Half hoping.

"Okay," said Haar. He coughed twice. Climbing the stairs had winded him. "That's far enough. We're outside. Now. Any comment?"

"No. Absolutely not." She handed the envelope back. "I think you're filthy. You should be ashamed of yourself."

"Can I quote you on that?"

"Just leave me alone," she said, turning away.

"Whatever you say, Miss Jensen." The pudgy man laughed. "I don't really need a comment from you. The photos sort of speak for themselves. You getting out of the car, you leaving the house so drunk a Secret Service man has to help you. I also have a very nice telephoto shot through the upstairs window. I have pretty much everything I need." He had her attention again and knew it. "The only question at this point is what I should do with it."

During this peroration, Margo had swiveled partway back toward him. She hesitated, frightened and torn. "You can't publish anything," she said, trying to keep her voice from cracking. "Take my word, Mr. Haar. You cannot publish this story."

"Care to offer a reason?"

"Because of what's at stake. I can't tell you. I'm sorry. But it's more important than—than"—she searched for a comparison, found none, and finished insipidly—"than you can imagine."

"You mean, Kennedy's reputation? Every reporter in this town knows about his little flings. They're just protecting him." That grating laugh again. "Or is it your own reputation you're thinking about? Afraid you'll ruin your future? Be known as just one of JFK's girls?"

"This isn't about me. It isn't about the President. It's about—it's about larger issues than that."

"Right. And I suppose you'd do anything to get me not to publish, wouldn't you?"

"What?"

"I know about girls like you, Miss Jensen. I see you all the time. You think your body and your face will get you whatever you want." He coughed again, the sound hollow and wet. "Well, I've got news for you. My tastes don't run to dark flesh. You don't have anything I want. I'm publishing."

This, finally, was too much. She didn't slap his face, but only because they were standing on the sidewalk and had drawn too much attention already.

"You're filthy," she said again, and made to stalk away.

"Go ahead!" he called after her, not caring who heard. "Tell the Kennedys! That's great! They know how this works!"

That caught her attention. Margo didn't turn around, but she did stop. The breeze freshened, brushing fallen leaves along the sidewalk in a mocking dance. She heard his footsteps nearing.

"You don't know, do you?" he said from close behind. His breath was very bad. If he touched her she would scream. "They'll send somebody who's empowered to negotiate. They always do. I'll make more money from them than I'd ever make selling the photos." His rheumy, satisfied laugh got her moving again. "If you didn't know that, honey, you're in the wrong line of work."

III

Margo told nobody. Not at first. She had an emergency number to call, but wasn't sure whether this qualified. Besides, she was afraid of wrecking the negotiation. That was what she told herself. She didn't want the back channel to collapse. Hurrying back to the office, Margo tried to weigh things out. She didn't yet know whether she was seeing Fomin tonight. If there was no meeting with Fomin, there was none with Kennedy. She didn't need to decide yet, she kept assuring herself as she spent the rest of the afternoon plucking files and sorting them and delivering them. She ignored the now less discreet stares of her fellow interns. If they had heard the shouting on the street, there was nothing to do about it. Margo fretted nevertheless, and was even grateful for the worry over who knew what, because it kept her tortured mind away from what seemed to her a hauntingly likely explanation.

The reporter hadn't been following the President and happened to stumble on the townhouse on East Capitol Street.

He had been guided there.

Somebody had leaked the supposed affair, and Margo—deep down inside, where she kept truths she would rather not face—harbored the suspicion that the leaker was Bundy.

No better way to preserve the fiction than to multiply the number of people who thought it was fact.

IV

At the end of the day, her boss stopped by her cubbyhole, perched herself on the file cabinet, and folded her smooth brown arms.

"Is everything okay, Margo?"

"Everything's fine, Miss Elden."

"Some of the girls said you got into an argument with some guy this afternoon."

"It was nothing."

Torie nodded. "A lot of people are tense. We had a memo around lunch. One out of four folks in the department didn't come in today. Did you notice how empty the place is? Everybody's scared. I can't tell you how many big arguments I've overheard today, all of them over nothing. Those missiles have all of us on edge."

"I guess they do."

Nana liked to say that Torie Elden was the loosest thing on two legs, but Margo had learned already that she was no fool. Torie had caught something in her young cousin's voice, and now sat there with a frown on her face, swinging a leg back and forth to some unheard beat, hands clasped together as if in prayer.

"I don't know what's going on with you," she finally said. "And I don't know what connections you think you have. But you are not going to embarrass this office. Is that clear?"

"Of course. I would never do anything—"

"I worked on Kennedy's campaign, Margo." A girls-in-it-together tone. "I worked for Stevenson in '56. I know what it's like to be young and pretty, on your own for the first time, and having all the guys chase you. May I give you some advice?"

"I would appreciate it," said Margo, truthfully.

"Stay away from the guys. Especially the powerful ones. They'll show you a great time, they'll make all kinds of promises, but in the end"—a brief hesitation as some secret pain played over her face—"in the end, you'll wind up even lonelier than when you started. Because, once a girl gets a certain kind of reputation, she can't get rid of it. And the really good guys don't want to be with that kind of girl. Do you follow what I'm saying?"

"I understand," Margo said. "Thank you," she added, because she knew Torie meant well.

"You're a sweet girl," said Torie. She reached out and tousled Margo's hair, the caress warm and womanly. Her voice was soft. "You don't have to let some guy treat you this way. There are other men out there."

"I know," said Margo; and said no more.

Torie gave her a look. Probably she thought her cousin was being haughty, because, without another word, she shook her head and marched out. But the reason Margo hadn't responded to the advice was that her mind was on Torie's words: *they'll make all kinds of promises . . . once a girl gets a certain kind of reputation, she can't get rid of it.* Again, basic conflict theory: negotiations were pointless unless each side was able to trust the other. Commitments had to be credible. And establishing credibility sometimes required sacrifice.

Margo was beginning to wonder if she would turn out to be the sacrifice.

V

"There's a passenger ship nearing the blockade line," the secretary of defense was saying. "It's carrying five hundred technicians. Czechs."

The President had been doodling but now looked across the table. It was past six, and the lowering clouds glowed redly in the west. "To work on the missiles?"

"It's a good bet," McNamara said.

"Do we stop them?" asked the attorney general.

"It's a passenger ship," McNamara repeated. "There's the issue of civilian casualties."

The President looked at his watch. Bundy understood. He wanted to get back to the Oval Office and catch the Security Council debate on television. But they needed a decision first on the ship, and Kennedy would follow his natural inclination to let all sides argue for pretty much as long as they chose.

"If we stop them, we show we mean business," said Bobby. "We're calling it a quarantine, but we haven't actually stopped anybody yet."

"Fifteen ships have turned back without challenging the line," McNamara reminded the group. "That's a bigger victory than one symbolic stop."

"What about the *Grozny*?" asked the President. "We know it's carrying military equipment, right?"

"The *Grozny* will be at the blockade line late sometime tomorrow," McNamara said.

General Taylor wanted to return the conversation to where it had stalled this morning: the possibility of attacking the missile sites.

"I thought we were going to wait on that," said Gwynn, who was representing State this evening. "I thought the idea was to see how the blockade went first."

Silence greeted the remark. Poor Gwynn was bewildered. Bundy hid a smile. Yes, the man had made a good point, but it wasn't his point to make. He didn't understand his role here. He was somebody's deputy—not even an undersecretary—and here he was, trying to argue with the chairman of the Joint Chiefs of Staff. Bundy gave him high marks for courage but no marks for bureaucratic intelligence.

Maxwell Taylor was the sort who wouldn't forget, and who would, on some fitter occasion, visit retribution on him.

"Let's remember this morning's intelligence brief," said Taylor, as if Gwynn had never spoken. "Langley's sources say the Russian anti-aircraft crews have orders not to fire on our surveillance planes, right? So we could fly in bombers at high altitude. The Russians would think it was a reconnaissance mission. They wouldn't know it was an attack until the bombs were falling."

"At which point they'd fire back," said McNamara, clearly irritated.

"I still want to be prepared to go in there at a moment's notice," said Kennedy. "How much notice do we need?"

"Half an hour to hit the SAMs." Taylor always had precise facts at his fingertips, a talent Bundy appreciated. "Two hours to hit the missiles."

The President nodded. He stood up, and the room with him. "Don't turn the passenger liner. Let it go." He glanced at Maxwell Taylor. "But I want a plan to intercept the *Grozny* if it doesn't turn."

"What do we do then?" asked Gwynn, once more out of turn: the President had already announced his decision.

"Then we shoot," said General Taylor.

The President left, and the others filed out in twos and threes. Bundy stood with the attorney general in the private foyer connecting the Cabinet Room and the Oval Office. Two of the three secretarial desks stood empty, typewriters covered for the night. A young woman sat filing behind the third desk, on call in case she was needed.

"Is she seeing Fomin tonight?" asked Bobby.

"I don't know. I haven't heard."

"We need Khrushchev's answer," Bobby persisted. "You heard the President in there. He's wavering. We need something fast, or he's going to bomb those missile sites."

"I thought you were in favor of an attack."

"Devil's advocate. The President didn't tell you? He asked me to take that side in the meetings, then wait and see who piles on. I assumed you knew."

Bundy had his arms crossed. He was peering into the Cabinet Room, where Maxwell Taylor and Curtis LeMay were whispering with CIA Director McCone. Kennedy had been trying for a year and a half to get the military and the Agency to do a better job of coordinating their efforts. That they seemed to be getting along should have struck the national security adviser as good news.

Only it didn't. The sight chilled him, though he couldn't say why.

"Mac? Did you hear me?"

"Sorry, Bobby. Yes. She'll call when Fomin gets in touch. We have to be patient. Khrushchev is making a momentous decision."

"So are we. And I don't know if everybody's willing to wait."

And he joined Bundy in watching worriedly as the generals and the spies plotted together.

FORTY

An Invitation to Escape

I

That night was dinner at the Madisons': old friends of Nana, who had made her granddaughter promise to visit them while in Washington. Miles Madison was a major in the Marine Corps, a boisterous Jamaican with dreams of becoming a real-estate investor. His wife, Vera, was among Nana's many godchildren. Vera was from one of what Nana called the old families, and it was her family money that had mainly paid for their rambling house on Sheperd Street, not far from Rock Creek Park, in an enclave of well-to-do Negroes known as the Gold Coast.

Margo arrived, still shaken from her twin encounters, first with Erroll Haar, then with Torie Elden. The secret was obviously out. She rang the doorbell not entirely sure what to expect from so prominent and proper a couple. But the Madisons enfolded her in a warmth so unexpected and reassuring that Margo found herself, within minutes, relaxed and very nearly happy. They were a study in contrast, Miles Madison tall and broad, his wife so delicate you feared to breathe hard in her presence, lest she crumple to dust. But her laugh was full and hearty, belonging to a larger woman.

While Vera got dinner together and the Major, as he was known, chomped on his cigar and took occasional telephone calls in his study, Margo sat on the living-room floor playing with the children, the two-year-old Kimberly and the ten-month-old Marilyn, the pair of them already declared the princesses of a world of colored privilege that Margo had frequently observed but never quite inhabited. A sitter materialized to put the children to bed while the grown-ups sat down to eat. The Madisons peppered her with questions about job and friends and school, all slightly intrusive without being in the least offensive. Vera told stories about a much younger and rather wilder Claudia Jensen, and on any other occasion Margo would have been riveted. But tonight it was the Major's descriptions of his work in a bunker beneath the Pentagon that caught her interest. Vera explained that Miles Madison was part of a small group of military men with top security clearances who routed orders and messages around the world.

"If we do go to war over Cuba," she said, "it will be the Major who transmits the orders."

II

Dinner was over; and so was Adlai Stevenson's address to the United Nations Security Council, which they had watched together. Miles Madison crossed the carpet and turned down the volume knob. He glanced toward the alcove, and Margo realized that he had been waiting until they were alone.

"I'm sending the family to Ohio tomorrow. My wife has people near Cincinnati." His usually humor-lit face was all at once careworn. The raucous storyteller of an hour ago might never have existed. His tone was grimly serious. "It's only a precaution, Margo. Just for a few days, I hope. Until this thing blows over, as I'm sure it will." He was still standing near the television. He cocked his head: in the next room, the phone was ringing. "If it doesn't, those of us in uniform will have to start earning our pay the hard way." The sad eyes flicked over her face. "Maybe you should go, too. Not to Garrison," he added hastily. "That's not really far enough if . . ."

He trailed off. Margo was sitting very straight. From studying with Niemeyer, she had this part off pat; the nightmares filled in the rest.

"If there's a near miss on Manhattan," she said, voice like straw.

The Major nodded. "Exactly. Sorry. That's the way it is." He tilted his head toward the alcove. "You're welcome to go with Vera and the girls if you want. Cincinnati would be a low-priority target, so you should be safe. Again, it's just for a few days. I'm sure your internship will wait, and it's the least I could do for your grandmother. She asked me to keep an eye on you, make sure nothing happened, and, to be honest—"

He shut up at once, because Kimmie came hurtling back into the room, chased by her shrieking sister Marilyn. Their mother bustled in after, somehow stately despite her rush. Tension pinched the long planes of Vera Madison's elegant face, but she managed a smile.

"The phone is for you, dear," she said.

It took Margo a moment to realize which of them was being addressed.

III

The telephone, a blue Trimline, sat on a three-legged table in the alcove. A notepad lay handily beside it, the Bic pen attached with prudent string. Lifting the receiver, Margo caught her reflection in the oval mirror with its pretty gilt trim. Haggard. There was no other word. She was looking haggard, and a decade older than she had a few weeks ago. Pretty soon, it would be "ma'am" instead of "miss."

If there was a pretty soon.

"Hello," she ventured.

"Margo, honey, it's Carol," the familiar voice gushed. "I'm really sorry to bother you. You said you might be at the Madisons' tonight, and I thought I'd take a chance." A beat for the listeners, if any, to work that out. "Anyway, I have to cancel. I can't do lunch tomorrow. Will Monday work for you?"

For a mad moment Margo found that she couldn't play her role any more. Major Madison had awakened in her the fears that haunted her dreams, and what she wanted more than anything was to hop on the train to New York, change for Garrison, and hide her head in her grandmother's skirts; or, better still, her late mother's. Failing that, she wanted someone to disqualify her, to find a better actress; and better liar. And so, ignoring the lines she had so painstakingly memorized, she answered with great umbrage.

"You called me here to tell me that? Couldn't it have waited until morning?"

But Carol, whoever she really was, kept her cool. "I'm sorry, honey. I don't mean to spoil your dinner. If the Monday won't work, how about next Tuesday?"

"No, no, it's fine," said Margo with a theatrical sigh. The plan was really clever, fiction within fiction within fiction: anyone who looked at her life closely enough to discover that she had no friend Carol would think the calls were arranged by insiders at the White House to cover her affair with Kennedy. Nobody would imagine that she might actually be talking to a Russian spy. "Monday, at the usual place," she muttered. "I'll be there."

"Great," chirped Carol with the same brightness. "You sound tired, honey. Try to get some rest."

"Thanks," said Margo, bitterly, but the other woman had already hung up.

IV

She returned briefly to the parlor. Her hosts were standing near the fireplace, whispering. From their guilty expressions as she entered, Margo knew that the subject was herself.

"Mrs. Madison?"

"Yes, dear?"

"May I use your phone to make another call? I'm sorry."

Vera smiled indulgently. "Of course, dear. It's local, isn't it?"

"Yes, ma'am. Thank you."

Margo walked back to the alcove, reviewing her lines. She felt no excitement and no fear. She felt robotic, controlled, spoken for. As she lifted the receiver, she glanced in the mirror again and saw not Vera but the Major standing in the doorway, smoking his cigar, yellowy eyes narrowed as he regarded her thoughtfully. Margo shut her eyes. She had muffed it. She had said the wrong thing, given away the secret—or at least that there was a secret. As soon as she was off the phone, Major Madison would renew his offer to send her to Ohio, and then, when she declined, begin to wonder why. He would ask around, and before too long he would be on the phone to Nana, warning that her innocent little granddaughter was spending a little too much time alone with the President of the United States.

All of this flashed through her mind in an instant, but when her eyes fluttered open again, the Major was gone.

She let her shoulders sag and dialed.

"Yes?" said a growling male voice.

"Is Crystal there?"

"Crystal? Who is this?"

"This is Margo. I'm a friend of hers."

"I think you have the wrong number."

"Isn't this 5502?"

"It's 5505."

Click.

She opened her purse, took out the worn address book McCone had given her—full of names and numbers in her handwriting, but penned by others!—and flipped to the "S" page. The code was in the "05." She added two, making it "07," and ran her fingers down to the seventh name, someone she'd never met. An address on Brandywine Street. She turned the page, counted seven entries up from the bottom: this time, somebody she did know, a cousin, address on Mayflower Avenue in New Rochelle. The last two digits were a pair of ones.

The car would pick her up on Brandywine Street tonight at eleven.

She had an hour to get down to the restaurant, and then it was back up Connecticut Avenue to meet her driver.

The President would be waiting.

V

Doris Harrington, too, was out that night. She had dined with a prominent journalistic couple who lived two blocks away. She had tested carefully for relevant rumors, and found none. Now, walking home through the misty Washington night, she could almost imagine that the years were rolling away, and the cobbles of Georgetown were the pavements of Vienna during the war. The teenagers making out in an alley were Gestapo informants; the bus trundling northward on Wisconsin Avenue was the stinking, belching tram; the White Castle restaurant on M Street was a Viennese café where the habitués stayed up half the night playing chess and murmuring revolutionary slogans and state secrets.

What sparked the overlap of memory and reality was a silent scream that told her she was being followed, not just tonight but all the time now. She tried to blame it on Gwynn, but he had neither the cleverness nor the entrepreneurial spirit. Instinct told her that whoever was out there was malevolent. Whoever was out there was also skilled at surveillance, so that she rarely caught anything but the merest breath of their presence.

She walked faster.

FORTY-ONE

The Threat

I

"Tell the President that the Comrade General Secretary cannot turn the ship."

"What ship is that?"

She expected to be slapped down. Fomin, as she had already learned, hated questions, particularly from women. And he was fanatical on matters of security. So it surprised her when he answered.

"There is a cargo ship, the *Grozny,* that will arrive at the blockade line tomorrow. Your Navy will try to stop the ship and board her. The Comrade General Secretary cannot allow either of these actions, Miss Jensen. The loss of face would be too great. Tell President Kennedy, please, that if they attempt to intercept the ship, the captain will not stop. If they disable the ship in order to board, they will have committed an act of aggressive warfare against the peace-loving peoples of the Soviet Union." His broad face furrowed. "You are not persuaded, I see. You have a further question?"

She was remembering a report on the news. "Isn't it the position of your government that the blockade itself is an act of war?"

"Miss Jensen, if a single Soviet soldier were to get drunk and stumble across to the Western side of the Berlin Wall, he would be committing an act of war against the fascist German regime in Bonn. But unless he opens fire, the matter can likely be resolved without a fight. Do you begin to understand?"

"Yes."

Fomin devoted himself to his food once more. He had insisted this time that Margot eat, and she picked listlessly at a chicken dish she would on another occasion have relished.

"You will convey the message?" he asked suddenly. "About the *Grozny*?"

"Yes, but"—she hesitated, unsure whether it was her place, but a part of her would always be the eager student determined to impress—"but don't you think it's likely that President Kennedy will face the same dilemma? How can he back down?"

The Soviet's eyes were lidded. "It is not a matter of backing down, and the decision is not in your hands. You must tell your President that the Comrade General Secretary cannot turn the ship."

Margo remembered Kennedy's implicit expectation that she would not only convey his position but argue in favor of it.

"Mr. Fomin, the problem I believe the President has is that you keep asking him for things, or even demanding them—but you're not offering anything in return. I think it's fair to say that the President believes that America is the aggrieved party."

"It makes no difference. The Comrade General Secretary cannot be the first to back down. He cannot lose face."

"I don't think President Kennedy can be the first to back down, either."

Fomin signaled the waiter for another beer. "You are saying there is no solution. The negotiation is a waste of time."

"Not exactly." The idea sprang to mind, and she wanted to kick herself for not thinking of it before: textbook conflict theory. "It's a classic example of what's called the prisoner's dilemma."

Again Fomin cocked an eyebrow. "What is a prisoner's dilemma?" he asked, still chewing.

For a moment, Margo was back in the classroom. Breezy. Confident. "Say that the sheriff knows that one of two suspects has committed a crime and arrests them both. Then he tells them—" she saw the Russian's expression. "Um, never mind. Explaining it would take too long. But look at the situation. That ship is approaching the quarantine line. It can stop voluntarily; it can be forced to stop; or it can sail right through, untouched. If it stops voluntarily, Khrushchev loses. If it sails right through, Kennedy loses. If it's forced to stop, that's the worst of all, because that's when you could have the kind of accident that leads to war."

"I see. This prisoner's dilemma is the name you give to a problem with no solution?"

"The solution to the prisoner's dilemma typically requires mutual trust, and a degree of sacrifice—"

"Yes. We will sacrifice, and you will break your word. That is how the world has always dealt with Mother Russia."

"That's what makes it a prisoner's dilemma. Both men have to sacrifice a little. Each side has to trust that the other will do as he promises. Otherwise, both will break their promises, and the cost to both will be a lot higher."

"This is what Niemeyer teaches you? These abstractions?" Fomin's hand made a chopping motion. "Do you know that the West has broken every promise it has ever made to us? Does Niemeyer teach you this, too? How, in the Great Patriotic War, your President Roosevelt promised to open a Western front by 1943, then left Russia to fight for its life in the East for another entire year? How, after the war, you promised us aid, but attached so many strings that to accept it would have meant an end to socialism in our country? How you swore you would never place offensive nuclear weapons in Turkey? And yet there they sit."

She felt as if they had gone in a circle. "Mr. Fomin, if your side has nothing to offer—"

"The Comrade General Secretary has informed your President that he considers your naval blockade of our Cuban ally an unacceptable act of aggression. Naturally, we would not cooperate by allowing your country to stop or inspect our ships."

About to reply, Margo sensed that more was coming. She took a small bite, and waited.

"I have told you that there are those in the Kremlin who seek a war with the Main Enemy, who believe that it is better to fight now, on our terms, rather than later, on yours. This faction is powerful, and the Comrade General Secretary must placate them. This is what you must tell your President, Miss Jensen. Wolves need fresh meat. Do you understand?"

"I'm not sure I do."

"At times it is necessary to behave irrationally, in order to make one's point. I am sure Niemeyer taught you this principle."

"He did."

"Very well. Then please inform your President that it may become necessary for the Comrade General Secretary to engage in a small act of irrationality, in order to placate his war faction." He took a long swallow of beer, wiped his mouth with his sleeve. "At the same time, it is vital that your President control his own war faction. Otherwise he will force upon the Comrade General Secretary an unthinkable choice."

Margo put her chopsticks down with a snap. "Are you saying that you're going to launch some kind of attack?"

"Your President will understand the message, Miss Jensen. It is not required that you understand it as well."

But she did. She understood perfectly; and was frightened out of her wits.

II

At the townhouse, the scene felt wrong. There were no agents inside this time, and she heard the music even before she reached the top of the stairs. The room was the same—the same hideously ornate bed, the same champagne on ice—but the sounds of Sinatra from the wooden stereo beneath the bar seemed inappropriate to the moment.

Also, the President had his shoes off.

She tried to talk about Fomin, but he kept telling her it would keep. He took her coat and told her how nice she smelled; he handed her a glass and watched until she'd drained half.

"Mr. President, about Fomin. He says Khrushchev is in trouble with his hard-liners and—"

"Hush. Listen." He hummed a couple of bars. "He's singing 'Come Dance with Me.' Hear it?"

"Yes, sir, but—"

"Then dance with me. Come on, Miss Jensen. Margo." A wink as he topped off her glass. "It'll help with the fiction."

Kennedy was courteous but pushy, and finally she asked him, straight out, if he wanted to hear what Fomin had to say.

He smiled. "Dance first. Then you can tell me the whole story."

"For a minute," she said, as she had said to so many pushy men before—even if this pushy man was the President of the United States.

"Try to relax," he said, as he gently put his arms around her.

Margo swallowed. It was the fiction; that was all. His arms tightened, and she allowed it. For a minute, she told herself. Just one more minute, and then they would stop and talk, and everything would be fine again. Another minute, maybe two. The President was just being careful. He had no other purpose—

"Mr. President, I really think we—"

"Ssssh. Relax, Miss Jensen. Margo. Margo. A lovely name."

"Sir, please. Listen. Fomin said—"

"We can get to Fomin in a minute. Relax. It's a dance." He patted the back of her neck. "Come on. Head down on the shoulder. You know how this works."

She felt a lethargy taking her. A delicious, dizzying warmth. A sense of relief that events were spinning out of her control. She felt his strong arms, his chest, the urgent pressure of his body. His scent. The sound of his humming. She nestled closer. He stroked her shoulder, and she heard the sigh before she realized that it was hers. He kissed her hair and she shivered. His hands moved—

"No," she gasped, pushing free of him. "Stop. Don't."

The crooked smile. "It's all part of the fiction."

"I—Mr. President—"

"Come on. Let's at least finish the dance."

He stood not two feet from her, collar undone, handsome face flushed, hand held out toward her. How easy it would be to lose herself. A part of her wanted to.

With an effort, Margo took another step away. Kennedy was talking again, voice low and syrupy and persuasive, but she hardly noticed the words. And when she spoke again, she brought him up short.

"Mr. President, I think the Soviets are getting ready to shoot down one of our planes."

III

For as long as it takes to switch gears, the President stared. "Did Fomin tell you that?"

"Not exactly." She drew a breath: the A student, back on stage. "He said that you mustn't stop the *Grozny*. He implied that the command and control that Khrushchev exercises over his forces aren't as strong as you might imagine. He said that you must accept that it is necessary for him to give something to what he called his war faction. And that you must control your war faction. I think he was saying that if they shoot down a plane you mustn't retaliate."

"Is that so? Maybe you should tell him that we have a plan in place. If they shoot down a U-2, we'll blow up the SAM site that fired the missile. No question, no negotiation. He leaves our planes alone."

"Mr. President, I think what he was trying to say was that if you retaliate—even just against the SAMs—Khrushchev will be under enormous pressure to—"

"To strike back. We know, Miss Jensen. We've reasoned all this out. Our people figure that we'll face some difficulties elsewhere, maybe Turkey, most likely Berlin. A proportionate response."

"I think that's what he was getting at." She could not believe her own calm. Perhaps it was shock. "He said retaliation would force upon the General Secretary 'an unthinkable choice.'"

"He said that? 'Unthinkable'?"

"Yes, sir."

Kennedy shook his head. "Taylor and LeMay and that crowd are going to just love this." He put down his glass, too hard, and the champagne slopped onto the polished wood. He didn't notice. "I have to go."

FORTY-TWO

A Credible Commitment

I

"Let's assume she's right," said Bobby Kennedy. It was Friday afternoon. Last night they had agreed to sleep on Margo's theory. The *Grozny* was still steaming toward the blockade line, but slowly. There was time to think. This morning's ExComm was devoted to discussing disturbing new U-2 images that showed work proceeding on the missiles at an accelerated pace. There was talk of strengthening the blockade, but also of going in fast, perhaps as soon as Monday, to take out the launch sites. Neither the President, his brother, nor Bundy—the only three in the room aware of the back channel—had said a word about the possibility that one of the U-2s might be shot down. Now, in the Oval Office, the President wanted to talk it out.

"Let's assume that the Soviets plan to shoot down one of our U-2s," Bobby continued. "Fomin can't seriously expect us to just sit here and do nothing."

"Well, let's slow down a minute," Bundy began, but the attorney general rolled right over him.

"The ExComm has already discussed this, Mr. President. We have a protocol in place. If they shoot down a U-2, we attack their antiaircraft sites. We have to be able to keep eyes on the missiles, and they have to know that we'll protect our ability to do so." He was striding, gesturing, eyes bright with anger. "Taylor, LeMay, even McNamara—they'd hit the roof if we didn't take action. Frankly, I wouldn't put it past LeMay to order retaliation on his own initiative."

"He has the delegated authority to do that," said Bundy. "Unless, of course, the President should withdraw that authority."

Kennedy was standing at the window, to all appearances studying the Rose Garden while his advisers fought this one out. "And why would I do that, Mac?" he asked, not turning.

"To avoid starting a war."

Again Bobby cut in. "If the Reds shoot down one of our planes, they're the ones who are committing an act of war."

Bundy shook his head. "With respect, that's not so. They've shot down our surveillance aircraft in other parts of the world. We've shot down theirs. Nobody's thought that we have to fight. Our planes are over the sovereign territory of another country. Our pilots resign their commissions before they fly, precisely so that our overflights aren't military incursions." Back to the President: "Sir, I'm not saying we should do what Khrushchev seems to be suggesting. I do think that we should give it serious consideration."

"You're talking about sending an American pilot to his death and doing nothing," said the attorney general.

Bundy ignored this sally. "The test is very simple, Mr. President. If the Soviets shoot down one of our planes this weekend, then I would say that GREENHILL's interpretation is correct. The attack will be Khrushchev's sop to his hard-liners."

"And do you think he understands that I have hard-liners of my own to deal with? Hard-liners who are going to demand an attack on the SAM batteries?"

"I suspect, Mr. President, that Khrushchev is counting on you to be more firmly in control than he is."

This was too much for Bobby. "If he's not in control, why are we even negotiating with him? If he has to shoot down a plane to please the old guard, how do we know they can't force him to fire off a missile or two?"

The President looked at his watch. "It's time, gentlemen."

As they headed for the Cabinet Room, Bundy pondered Bobby's final question. He was right, of course. They couldn't make a deal through the back channel unless they had proof that they were dealing with Khrushchev himself.

The problem was how to get it.

II

"I am afraid you are correct," said Viktor Vaganian. "I received this morning a lengthy cable from my superiors in Moscow. Although Fomin remains, as a formal matter, a colonel in the First Chief Directorate, he has been secretly reassigned to the personal staff of the Comrade General Secretary. He has been given a personal cipher and cable access directly to the Comrade General Secretary's chief aide. He is not running GREENHILL as his agent. They are negotiating."

"Exactly what I told you two days ago," said Ziegler.

"That is true. But I prefer to wait for hard intelligence before acting. We are not cowboys, after all."

They were once more in Warrenton, Virginia, an hour from the city. This time, they were in a booth in the sort of rustic café that serves bad breakfasts to early-morning hunters. Nobody from official Washington ever came this far out. Here the Old South still ruled: precisely the reason Ziegler chose it.

"Well, fine," the American was saying. "Your intelligence is confirmed. So, now that we're sure they're negotiating, what are we going to do to make sure they don't reach a deal? Because the chain is pretty flimsy. Only a few people involved. And two of them would seem pretty vulnerable."

Viktor's tone was mournful. "Fomin I cannot touch. He has powerful patrons."

"You use that excuse a lot. Protectors back home."

"It is not an excuse. It is a fact. I told you. In the Soviet Union, power is divided. This is appropriate—"

"I know, I know. So the Party doesn't get out of hand. Great." He signaled for the check. "Okay. Fine. We'll try on this end, with GREENHILL." A hard look. "Nonviolently."

"Of course. But if your method does not succeed, it is possible that we shall have to try our own."

"She's an American."

"She is the only one Fomin trusts. Remove her, and the entire back channel will collapse."

III

Margo's Friday was almost normal for an intern with her job. She filed and stacked and sorted and delivered. She collected books and reports and folders and mail. She kept watching the clock, although she had no earthly idea whether the *Grozny* had turned, or what time the Soviet Union might be planning to shoot down an American aircraft. She wondered whether the story would even make the news, or whether the Administration would hush it up for a day or two. And although turning out to be wrong would shake the reputation for intelligence she had worked so hard to cultivate this past week, she hoped against hope that she was mistaken.

And knew she wasn't.

She lunched at the Museum of Natural History with another intern, and noticed a man wearing gold-rimmed glasses a few tables away, watchfully ignoring her. She had the sense that she had seen him somewhere before; perhaps even in Ithaca. But when she left he did not so much as look up from his paper, and she wondered afresh whether she was imagining.

A little past three, in the midst of her filing and ferrying, the usual afternoon summons brought her from her cubby out to the reception desk. She listened carefully to her instructions, spoke a few code words so they'd know she understood, and rang off. Only later, as she happily hummed her way toward five o'clock, did Margo realize that she had been so looking forward to the call that she'd scarcely noticed Sylvie's usual disdainful curiosity.

Her good mood continued to hold her, even after she arrived back at the apartment to find a taxi waiting and the doorman loading Hope's bags.

"She's going home," said Patsy, upstairs. "Her parents called. They want her out of the city."

"What about you?"

The Californian shrugged. "I'm staying until the end."

"The end?"

"I want to see what it's like."

"There's not going to be a war," said Margo, severely. In the shower, she went back to her singing. No plane had been shot down. Khrushchev had been bluffing; or he'd changed his mind. That was why she was so happy, Margo told herself. No other reason but that. Because the war was going to be averted.

Patsy, watching her dress, had a different theory.

"So there *is* a guy."

Margo, standing at the bathroom mirror, looked at her roommate's reflection. "What?"

The Californian slouched against the jamb. "Hope and I have been trying to figure you out. You go out every night, you're all dressed up, you come back later with your clothes all mussed. That spells guy, right? But you never seem to look forward to it. You're always down in the mouth. Hope even said maybe you were faking the whole thing for some reason. But look at you. Singing, all happy. It's a guy."

Margo had done more blushing in the past week than in the past year. "It's not a guy. I can't explain, but—it's not."

"I know that look, Margo. It's a guy all right. I can hear it in your voice and see it in your eyes."

"It's *not*," she said, too fiercely. Patsy wandered away, chuckling. Margo knew her denial would never be believed. The entire operation rested on the fiction beneath the fiction beneath the fiction: if Patsy didn't think her roommate was lying, then the cover story wasn't working.

But as she headed downstairs to catch the bus, she wasn't smiling any more.

IV

"Is your President going to stop our ship?"

"He won't let it cross the blockade line."

Fomin was shoveling food into his mouth. "Did you explain to him that the Comrade General Secretary must please his war faction?"

"I told him." She glanced around the restaurant, then leaned across the table. "What happened with the ship? You told me it would be at the quarantine line this morning. Did the Navy stop it?"

He barely glanced up. "The Comrade General Secretary has decided to give your President more time to gain control of his war faction. The ship is still proceeding, but more slowly. It may reach your country's illegal blockade tonight. I do not know the details."

"You misled me. You implied that your side was going to shoot down a plane."

"I cannot tell you what our side will do, Miss Jensen, any more than you can tell me what your side will do. I can only tell you that we have a war faction, just as you do." He signaled the waiter for more water. "I sense that your President is uneasy."

"Everybody's uneasy."

"I am referring to his role as the commander in chief. Your Constitution is a curious document. The voters select a leader, and the leader holds the highest rank in the military, whether or not he has served, and whether or not he has the confidence to perform the role. Or the confidence of his soldiers and sailors."

"President Kennedy was in the war."

"He allowed his patrol boat to be run over by an enemy destroyer. This was careless of him. In the Red Navy, a man who did this would face court-martial."

Margo knew better than to argue. Fomin might be right or he might be wrong, but it wasn't her place to debate the point. He had a goal in mind.

Fomin took another largish sip from his water glass. He wiped his mouth on his sleeve. His tone was brisk. "You may inform your President that the Comrade General Secretary will not insist on immediate removal of the Jupiter missiles. He will agree to dismantle our missiles in return for a public promise by your President never to invade Cuba." He paused as if awaiting contradiction, but Margo was waiting for the other shoe to drop. "Provided, however, that he understands the need for the Comrade General Secretary to reassure his war faction."

"Are you saying that if we let the *Grozny* through the quarantine line the General Secretary will take the missiles out of Cuba? Is that what will satisfy the—the war faction?" She could not believe that things could be so simple. "The crisis will be over? Or is there something else you want?"

But she had forgotten how the proud Russian hated to be questioned. "The response of the Comrade General Secretary is as I have stated it. I am not able to amplify the words in any way."

Again she sensed a hidden meaning. She had from here to the townhouse to work it out.

FORTY-THREE

Another Celebration

I

Tomorrow night would be given over to Ziegler's plan, but Viktor Vaganian doubted that the plan would succeed. Therefore, he had come up with an idea of his own, in keeping with both his talents and his inclinations.

Ziegler said he could not allow the killing of another American.

But not all direct action involved death.

Once more Viktor sat outside the apartment house. He did not have long to wait. GREENHILL's roommate, the tall blonde one, came out the front door. A young man in a cherry-red sports car was waiting. He kissed her on the mouth, then she kissed him on the mouth, then he kissed her again. Viktor frowned at the showiness of their affection. At last they disentangled, and the car shot down the driveway and out into traffic on Fourth Street.

At a safe distance, Viktor followed.

II

"This calls for a celebration," said the President.

Margo stood near the window, hugging her hunched shoulders as she modeled her fourth new gown of the week. "I'm not sure, Mr. President. I don't think it's necessarily over."

"Khrushchev said he doesn't need the Jupiters, right? All he needs is my public promise not to invade. Even the biggest fire-breathers around the table will agree to take that deal."

She felt hot and frightened and uncertain, and wasn't sure why. Perhaps it was the setting—a continuation, evidently, of whatever last night might have been. Once more, all the guards were outside the townhouse. Once more, Sinatra was playing on the paneled Victrola. Once more, Kennedy was in his socks with tie and collar undone.

Her lack of enthusiasm seemed to bother him. He came over and stood beside her. Together they looked down at the side street. Night mist made soft halos of the street lamps.

"You're right, of course," he said finally. "We don't know if it's really over. There's a lot to work out, and the Russians can be tricky."

"Yes, sir."

"A public promise," he said.

"Yes."

"I can do that."

Margo hesitated. She thought she had figured out the rest, but her last guess had gone terribly wrong. "Mr. President, there's more. Fomin said that the General Secretary still has to placate his war faction, and I think he might mean—"

The President waved her silent. "Please. I've got a roomful of advisers to tell me what Khrushchev *might* mean. Let's stick to what Fomin actually said."

She tried again. "Yes, sir, but Fomin also said that the General Secretary would not require the 'immediate' removal of the Jupiters. I wonder whether he was trying to say that he would expect you to move them later."

Kennedy was plainly exasperated. "We can't run this thing according to your hunches."

"Yes, sir, I—"

"And didn't he tell you not to amplify his message? Because I'd say that reading some dark meaning into his words counts as amplification. Secret messages, secret promises . . ." He was running his hand through his hair, obviously agitated. "We can only go by what he actually says. Okay?"

"Yes, Mr. President."

An awkward beat. "Long day, Miss Jensen," he said, not looking at her. She supposed this was an apology of sorts for losing his temper.

"Yes, Mr. President."

"I've got people telling me I have to invade." His suit jacket was slung over the back of a chair. The thick brown hair was mussy, and, before he departed, would be a good deal mussier.

He talked for a while, unwinding, and then, once more, they set about creating the fiction, balling up the bedsheets and wrinkling their clothes. Just like last night, Margo was unable to look at him as they worked; and, just like last night, she sensed his eyes a little too steady on her body. She went over to the sofa and, unbidden, sat. She realized that she was trembling. Without asking, he fixed her a drink.

"Nobody shot down any planes," he said, speaking slowly and softly, as we do around invalids. "All that worry about Khrushchev's hard-liners was for nothing. That's why we can celebrate. It may not be over, but it's close. The Jupiters were the only stumbling block."

Just as with Fomin, her questions were plainly beginning to annoy him. She wondered what it was about powerful men, their annoyance at women seeking entrée to their thoughts.

"It just all seems too easy," she said.

"If there's one thing I've learned being President . . ." he began, but then sensed that she was in no mood to be lectured. "Look. Take my word for it."

"Fomin says the General Secretary still has to—"

"Please his hard-liners. I know. But, believe me: In a confrontation like this? Once a guy twitches? He'll back down."

Margo thought about Niemeyer's classroom, and his theory about bluff: the key was to keep the other side guessing. Maybe this time he means it, maybe this time he doesn't. Your adversary had to be uncertain.

"The *Grozny*," she began, but again Kennedy interrupted her.

"Has slowed to half-speed. We're fine, Miss Jensen. The Cuban missile crisis is essentially over."

III

It was dinner and dancing. Viktor and one of his associates followed Patsy and her boyfriend of the moment to a fancy restaurant in Chevy

Chase and then to a dance hall a few blocks away. Inside the hall, they sat at the bar, amidst spoiled young people whirling and shimmying to decadent music that a more cultured country would ban. Viktor worried briefly that he and his associate might stand out, but then he noticed that any number of men of middle years were there without women. It took him a few minutes to work out that these men were prospecting for girls to go home with them for the night.

"Disgusting," he whispered.

"It is," said his associate, raptly watching the dancers, the women especially.

And these were the Western values that the United States wanted to teach the world.

At last their opportunity arose. Patsy excused herself and headed for the ladies' room. Viktor had already mapped the route, including the fire door with a broken lock. He sent his associate outside, then positioned himself in the dingy corridor. Viktor removed the gold-rimmed glasses and slipped them into a pocket. As Patsy approached, he nudged the door with his foot. His associate tugged it open. Viktor grabbed her around the throat and mouth and yanked her into the alley. His associate slammed the door.

Nobody noticed a thing.

Viktor continued to hold her as she struggled in panic. But the position of his hands made it impossible for her to cry out.

"Twice in the stomach," he said.

Her eyes widened.

Viktor's associate punched her, very hard. Her body tensed, she shrieked into his palm, but he didn't let go. The other man punched her a second time. Viktor released her. She fell on her hands and knees, in terrible pain but unmarked.

He crouched beside her.

"That's a warning," he said.

Patsy was coughing and choking. "What—what did I do?"

"Pull your legs up to your chest," Viktor murmured. "It will help with the pain." Groaning, she did as bidden. "The warning is not for you," he continued. "It is for your roommate. Tell her what happened here. Tell her it is time to stop."

They ran off, leaving her in the mud.

IV

Margo was seated on the sofa, knees primly together. She was having trouble taking in the President's words. "The crisis is over," she repeated. "That's it? We're done?"

"Not quite. I'm sure you'll be carrying a lot of messages the next couple of days, while we work out the details." Kennedy laughed. "Don't worry. Not every night, like this week. But intermittently. Something to write about in your memoirs."

Margo shook her head. "I could never write about this."

"National security concerns don't last forever, Miss Jensen."

"It's not that, Mr. President. It's just"—miserably—"it's too embarrassing."

"Ah. You mean our little façade."

"Yes, sir."

Again the silence, as he sat on the bed, glass in hand, watching her with those amazing eyes. He took a swallow, tilted his head to the side, seemed to consider.

"You're still nervous."

"A little."

"It's okay. Nobody's shot down any planes, and your secret is safe." She said nothing. Kennedy tilted his head the other way; grinned. "You know, Miss Jensen, it doesn't have to be like this."

"I'm sorry, sir?"

"You're so stiff. Worried sick, I know. Scared. Well, that's natural. But it's over, I promise you. Here. You should have a drink." Gesturing toward the bottle. "Not the sips you take so the Secret Service will smell alcohol on your breath. A real one. Take some of the edge off."

"No, thank you."

He downed his glass, then crossed the room in his socks and stood looking down at her. His white shirt had lost its crispness. She found the tousled hair and weatherproof smile warm and welcoming, magnetic somehow. Here he was, the most powerful man in the world, and all of his considerable charm was being focused on her.

"I'm not a bad guy," he said.

Margo dropped her eyes. Her hands were shaking. "I know that, Mr. President."

"Look at me, Miss Jensen." He put a finger beneath her chin, and the touch sizzled. He tilted her head back. "We could be friends, you know."

"Sir, I—"

"Good friends," he said, and took her hand.

He tugged slightly.

Margo allowed herself to be lifted to her feet.

"You're a very beautiful young woman," he murmured, stroking her jaw. "You're going to make some lucky man very happy one day, Margo. May I call you Margo?"

She was dizzy. Warm. Frightened. "Of course, Mr. President."

"Jack. When we're alone, you should call me Jack."

"I—I think maybe we should—"

"Try," he murmured. "Jack. Say it."

Margo swallowed. "Jack," she said, voice strangled.

"Again."

"Jack."

"Good girl." Margo went very still. She wondered whether the President was going to kiss her. In her topsy-turvy world, she knew she wouldn't stop him. But Kennedy stepped toward the sideboard. She shut her eyes, heard rather than saw the ice plopping and the Scotch pouring. "Now, how about that drink?" he said heartily.

She had thought the spell was broken, but when she looked, he was in front of her, disheveled and mesmerizing, holding out the glass.

"Thank you," she said, dropping her gaze. She gulped.

"You can relax," he said gently. Somehow she was seated again. The President crouched in front of her. He brushed a stray lock of hair from her forehead. "Now, where were we? Oh, yes. We didn't get to finish our dance last night, because you thought Khrushchev was going to shoot down a plane, so I had to go. Remember?"

"Yes, sir, I—"

"Ah-ah." Waggling a finger.

She took another swallow. "Yes, Jack."

"Right. Good. So, since you're the reason we didn't get to finish our dance last night, you owe me tonight."

"I think maybe I should—"

But he had turned the music on again, and Margo was out of arguments. The Scotch and the exhaustion and his proximity were doing their work. He lifted her to her feet, and she allowed it. He drew her into his arms, and she allowed it. More than allowed it. Participated in it.

"Relax, Margo," he whispered, very near her ear. She felt loose and boneless and warm.

"I'm trying."

"I'm trying, *Jack*."

"I'm trying, Jack."

"We're fine." He rubbed her back. "They didn't shoot down the plane."

"Right. Yes."

"They didn't shoot down the plane," he repeated, making a song of it, crooning the words. "It's all over. They didn't shoot down the plane, honey. You were wrong for once. You can relax."

Murmuring and murmuring as they danced.

FORTY-FOUR

An Unfortunate Incident

I

But Margo was right.

The news hit the ExComm on Saturday. Kennedy had just told the group that there had been a secret offer from Khrushchev, through a reliable intermediary—he avoided the term "back channel"—to remove the missiles from Cuba in return for a promise by the United States to respect the island's territorial integrity.

The room exploded—not only because the ExComm had been kept in the dark, but also because, just this morning, Khrushchev had publicly announced that he would not remove the missiles for anything less than the Jupiters.

The President suggested that they could accept the Friday offer and ignore what the Kremlin had announced today.

Hardly anybody agreed.

General Taylor reported that the Pentagon was prepared to begin a bombing campaign as early as Monday, with the invasion to follow, and did not believe it prudent to wait any longer. The B-52s were still orbiting in shifts at their "go" points, he said, and that level of alert could not be maintained indefinitely. Dean Rusk, the secretary of state, added that their European allies remained fiercely opposed to any deal involving the Jupiters. In the midst of a fierce peroration by Vice President Lyndon Johnson, who insisted that any deal would leave Kennedy's Administration "a shambles," an aide handed a note to Secretary of Defense McNamara. He called for quiet.

"One of our U-2s is overdue," he announced. "We think it's been shot down."

For a moment there was confusion. Some around the table thought he was just updating a report he had given the group a little earlier, that a U-2 based in Alaska had strayed into Soviet airspace and been fired upon. But it soon became clear that McNamara was talking about Cuba.

All at once they were in a shooting war.

The attorney general asked about the pilot.

General Taylor gave him a withering look. "The wreckage is on the ground. The pilot was in the plane." The general turned to the President. "You'll remember, sir, that we've already planned for this eventuality. The Air Force has its orders. We immediately take out the SAM site that fired the missile, and we warn the Russians that we'll treat further attacks on our surveillance aircraft the same way."

Most of the others agreed: there was no choice. Bundy was about to speak up, but the President beat him to it.

"Those SAM sites have Soviet crews, correct?" Nobody disputed this. "So, if we take them out, we'll be killing their people."

"If we don't do anything," said McCone, "we'll be sending the message that you can kill our people with impunity. No threats we make after that will have a shred of credibility."

As the argument raged on, Bundy began to form a plan. GREEN-HILL had been right all along. Fomin's warning was accurate, and they had celebrated too soon. Whether the downing of the U-2 had been ordered by higher authority or was the accident of some trigger-happy local commander, Khrushchev still needed to save face in order to make a deal. By letting the pilot go unavenged, they just might be able to give the General Secretary the leverage he would need to face down his own hard-liners.

"General LeMay has the planes at Homestead ready to go," Taylor was saying. "Just give the order, Mr. President, and the SAM site is gone in minutes."

Kennedy shook his head. "You will instruct General LeMay, in the clearest possible language, that he is not, under any circumstances, to take military action absent my direct order."

"Mr. President," McNamara began.

"You will transmit that order at once, Mr. Secretary."

But this show of resolve turned out to be a holding action, no more. With his chosen advisers almost unanimously against him, the President kept giving ground. Finally, he compromised. It was now two in the afternoon. If the crisis was not resolved by this time Monday—forty-eight hours away—the attack would begin.

Kennedy stood, and the room with him. "Bobby and Sorensen, with me." He strode out.

"Tomorrow morning, people," said Bundy. "Eleven sharp."

In the hallway, Bobby pulled him aside. "Your back channel better come up with something fast," he said.

"She warned us this would happen. We didn't pay attention."

"What are we supposed to do, Mac? Let a teenager run our foreign policy?"

"We're supposed to give the President the best advice we can."

The attorney general nodded. "Well, right now, my best advice is the same as the Joint Chiefs'. If we can't resolve this by Monday, we go in."

He rushed off to follow his brother.

II

Bundy arrived back at his basement suite to find pudgy Esman waiting in the anteroom. He sent the young man in ahead of him, then whispered with Janet, giving her instructions to convey to GREENHILL.

Inside, he shut the door and sat.

"Be quick," he said. "I can give you three minutes, no more."

"I think I've got a lead," said Esman. He noticed his superior's distracted expression. "On those leaks."

"Right. Okay. Where are we?"

"It occurs to me that we might have set our parameters wrong. We've been looking at people who knew all of the identities involved. But we should be looking at the timing, too—when SANTA GREEN was conceived, who was involved in the process."

"Makes sense," said Bundy, his mind still on the U-2.

"And there's something else. I was going over GREENHILL's debriefing. You'll remember how she said that Fomin knew about the operation in advance?"

Bundy said he remembered.

"Well, in the transcript, she says he called the operation QKPARCH-MENT." Behind the Coke-bottle glasses, Esman's eyes glowed. "Not SANTA GREEN."

"QKPARCHMENT."

"Yes, sir. You'll remember, that was the CIA's cryptonym. The Agency only used it for a couple of days, until you gave the charter to State."

"And State never used that designation."

"That's right, sir. State always called it SANTA GREEN. The White House calls it SANTA GREEN. Nowadays, even the Agency calls it SANTA GREEN." Esman closed his folder. "And that tells us two things. First, that the leak came before you decided which department would run the operation. Second, that the leak probably came from Langley, or someone in contact with Langley."

"Wait," said Bundy. He took off his glasses, pinched the bridge of his nose, and sank into thought. Esman knew his superior well enough not to interrupt.

"Very well," said Bundy after a moment. "Leave everything with me. All your notes. All the files. Everything."

"Do you want me to—"

"The investigation is concluded."

Esman could be as pedantic as his boss. "Concluded in the sense that you know who the leak is, or concluded in the sense that we're stopping?"

"Concluded," Bundy repeated. "Drop the investigation, and go back to whatever you were doing before. I have to get up to the President."

Bundy took the marble steps two at a time. He possessed certain facts that young Esman did not. And because of what he knew, he was worried. Very worried. Worried enough that he might have to warn the President.

But when he reached the Oval Office to discuss tonight's meeting with GREENHILL, he learned that his concern came too late.

III

On that same Saturday, for the first time since Borkland and Stilwell interrogated her in Niemeyer's office, Margo slept late. Or at least stayed in bed. Her limbs were leaden and restless at the same time. The events of the past month had left her without energy or affect, but the events of last night in particular. And yet she woke smiling.

She went out to the kitchen to get some breakfast, and that was when she saw Patsy.

The Californian was sitting at the table in her bathrobe. Her face was splotchy and red. She was hunched over, hands covering her stomach protectively, staring into space.

"What's wrong?" Margo asked. She supposed the date must have gone bad. Maybe Patsy had been crying all night. "Hey. What is it?"

Patsy's head swiveled slowly. Her eyes narrowed. "You selfish bitch," she hissed.

Margo blinked. "What did you call me?"

"A selfish bitch." Enunciating sharply. "I got beaten up last night. Did you know that? Do you even care?"

"Patsy, I'm so sorry. Did you call the—"

The blond woman slapped Margo's hand away. "You should be sorry. It was your fault."

"I don't understand."

"The men who beat me up. They said it was a warning to you." She turned away, shaking her head. "I don't know why they knocked me around and not you. I don't know whose husband you're sleeping with, but these guys said for you to stop." She stood up and headed for her bedroom, but paused to fire a final shot over her shoulder. "So— will you please think about somebody else for a change?"

She slammed the door.

IV

Again the President was furious. At first Bundy thought that it was the open defiance of his authority in the ExComm meeting that had him so angry. Bobby hastily explained. J. Edgar Hoover had called. His people had uncovered evidence of a cabal, he said, a group of government officials intent on wrecking the Cuba negotiations. No, no, he didn't have names yet. But he did know what they were demanding.

Here the President interceded. "They've turned your idiotic scheme on its head," he raged, waving a filmy piece of paper. "Look at this. Either I blow up the negotiations, or they'll make sure everybody knows that I'm having an extramarital affair. Not only that, but an affair with a nineteen-year-old black girl." He tossed the pages across the desk. "What am I supposed to do about this, Mr. Bundy? Tell me that."

Bobby pointed to the paper. "Hoover was kind enough to messenger that over. It's a photostat of a letter his people found somewhere. A draft, evidently."

The national security adviser was crestfallen. The point of the cover story had always been to give a benign if troubling explanation for the surreptitious meetings. It had never occurred to him that it might twist around and bite them. "Mr. President," he began, not sure where to begin. Then he stopped, and read the letter. Twice. "Mr. President, I don't believe the writer of this letter is aware of the back channel."

"He obviously is aware, Mr. Bundy. He says I'm having an affair with a black girl!"

"That's my point, sir. He seems to believe the affair is genuine. I believe that the negotiations he wants you to blow up are the embassy negotiations. Not the back channel."

The Kennedy brothers exchanged a glance. The President still looked ready to bite somebody's head off. Then, without warning, he grinned.

"Well, the embassy negotiations aren't going to amount to a hill of beans anyway. If whoever's in this cabal doesn't want them to work, they'll be happy, I expect."

Bobby was uneasy. "Maybe Hoover himself is part of the cabal. Maybe Hoover *is* the cabal. I wouldn't put it past him."

The President frowned. "What would he want?"

"A place at the table."

"Which he cannot have," said Bundy. "We have to be very clear about this, Mr. President. Bring J. Edgar Hoover into that room, and you have a very different ball game."

"You're right." The President turned to his brother. "We should thank Director Hoover for his vigilance on behalf of the nation's security at this difficult time, and assure him that there's nothing to the story of the affair, et cetera, et cetera." He laughed. "And be sure to tell him we expect him to track down this cabal as fast as he can. I want lots of arrests, tell him."

Bundy was unamused. "You know, it's possible Hoover is telling the truth. Such a cabal could exist."

"Hence my demand for arrests," said Kennedy, still smiling. "Now let's talk about this evening, shall we? Who's she seeing first, me or Fomin?"

"She's seeing you, Mr. President. We have to convey the mood in the room. We don't know exactly what's going on. Khrushchev's public statement this morning that he'll only take the missiles out if we give him the Jupiters is exactly the opposite of what Fomin told GREENHILL. She has to make clear that Khrushchev can't have the Jupiters under any circumstances, and that your decision to hold off retaliating for the U-2 shoot-down is a gesture of good faith only. It can expire at any moment."

"Do we tell him that the deadline is two p.m. on Monday?"

"No, sir. But we do tell him that Khrushchev's out of time. We can accept the Friday offer, and promise not to invade Cuba. That gives them the fig leaf that the missiles are defensive only. It's a lie, but we can live with it if they take them out. That's as far as we can go. Fomin has to be made to understand that there is nothing else to give."

"And there's one more thing," said the attorney general, all business now.

"What's that?" asked the President.

"If we're going to do a deal based on the back channel, we have to confirm, once and for all, that it's real."

"Meaning what?"

"Meaning that Fomin has to provide some kind of evidence that he really is speaking for Khrushchev."

"Bobby's right," said Bundy. "We need proof."

Kennedy shook his head. "Khrushchev is ten thousand miles away. It's not like we can pick up the phone."

"We need something."

V

As it happened, at about the same time, the Washington police responded to a report of a hit-and-run outside a posh apartment building on upper Connecticut Avenue. The victim was a man named Erroll Haar, a reporter for one of the tabloids.

He was pronounced dead at the scene.

FORTY-FIVE

Interference

I

As soon as she climbed into the car, Margo sensed that something was amiss. She was at the right corner—Wisconsin and Newark, just outside Giant Food—and she recognized the black Chevy's familiar plate. The driver, however, was not Warren. He was towheaded and charming and gave his name as Jack: "Like the boss," he said, and laughed. Jack drove with the same smooth alertness, but Margo's flight-or-fight reflex remained in overdrive. Perhaps it was the way he kept smiling and joking about where she was headed tonight: Warren had never so much as smirked.

Margo sank down into the leather seat. Patsy had been beside herself. You can't be going to see him again, she kept saying. You can't. Unable to tell her the truth, Margo had to settle for pleading with her roommate to get out of the city.

Why? Patsy demanded. Because they might beat me up again? Or will they do something worse next time?

Margo said she was sorry it had happened, she couldn't talk about it, and she would do what she could to make sure it didn't happen again.

Leaving the apartment in yet another fancy dress, she all but cringed with guilt and self-horror.

"We're here, ma'am," said the new driver. Margo looked up. They were outside the townhouse on East Capitol Street. There was no sense of excitement this time. No thrill. Only the aching guilt, and fear twisting inside like liquid heat. This time, she promised herself, she would not yield to the President's charm. Their assignations were part of a façade, nothing else.

A façade that was now threatening those around her.

She climbed from the car and crossed the street. Burning with anger and purpose, she strode past the guards without a glance.

It was well over an hour before she came back down.

II

As the car ticked through the night toward the meeting with Fomin, Margo brooded. She supposed some of Kennedy's somber mood had rubbed off. This was it, she told herself. This was the moment at which the negotiations succeeded or failed. She took out her compact and fixed her makeup. She had done it already in the bathroom but still felt dirty. She should be heading home to check on Patsy, not to another meeting. She sighed and looked at her wrinkled dress. She put her compact away and looked around. The plan was that the driver would take her up to Chevy Chase Circle, where she would catch the bus south to the Yenching Palace.

The only problem was that he wasn't heading north.

She leaned forward. "Excuse me—Jack, right?"

"Yes, ma'am."

That was it, she realized. That was the other thing that bothered her. To Warren she was always "miss."

"Jack. Where are we going?"

"Ma'am?"

"We're supposed to be heading to Chevy Chase Circle."

"Change of plans."

"Authorized by whom? I'm the only one who knows where I'm supposed to be dropped off."

"Sorry, ma'am."

He was driving faster now. They were in a neighborhood she didn't recognize, but from the sight of the Capitol dome in the misty distance, she guessed they were down in Southeast: one of the higher-crime areas of the oft-ravaged city.

"Where are we going?" she demanded. No answer. "Who are you?"

The car stopped with a jolt, and her chin struck the seat back. They were at a little park. The road was separated by a median strip, and small aging row houses stood across the way. Dark faces peered from the stoops.

"We need to talk, Miss Jensen," said the driver.

III

"Who are you?" she asked again, fingers on the door handle.

"It's locked, Miss Jensen. You can't get out until I let you. I know you have to get to another meeting, so let's not waste time. My name is Jack Ziegler. I am not, at the moment, affiliated with the government. Not officially. I represent a group of people who are aware of your meetings with Aleksandr Fomin, and very concerned about them. We have one purpose, Miss Jensen. To shut down the back channel before the President betrays his country."

A lot of things went through Margo's mind. That she herself might be in actual physical danger. That the back-channel negotiations weren't nearly as secret as McGeorge Bundy seemed to think. That her dress and face were truly a mess this time: of their five meetings, this was the one that had left her least presentable. That, although the people across the street were fellow Negroes, this was the sort of neighborhood that Claudia Jensen had raised her granddaughter to keep out of. That Jack Ziegler was somewhat shorter than average, and was the sort of small man who would always address tall girls like herself with condescension and disdain. That she now understood why Patsy was beaten last night. But most of all she was remembering the urgency of the President's message. She would have to try what Fomin called the fallback, for use if an emergency left her unable to make their scheduled meeting.

An emergency like, say, being kidnapped by some kind of rogue conspirator.

All of this actually went through her remarkable brain in about six seconds, at the end of which, remembering the lessons of Varna, she simply shook her head. "I don't know what you're talking about."

Ziegler snickered. "That's right. There aren't any negotiations, are there? You're just the President's latest girlfriend."

"That's a lie."

"Yes, Miss Jensen. It is. The point is, we know the truth."

"Who's *we*?"

"We're professionals, Miss Jensen. We know how it's done." When Jack Ziegler smiled, he looked like the playground bully after a victory. "The President isn't a bad man, but he's inexperienced. He's surrounded by amateurs. Wall Street lawyers. Academics. Limousine liberals who think they're experts on national security." Jack Ziegler pinched the bridge of his nose as if physically restraining further criticism of his titular superior. "We're the real experts, Miss Jensen. And we're being shut out. This isn't ego. It's reality. Kennedy and the intelligentsia on his ExComm are going to get the world blown to pieces."

For a mad moment she found her mind cataloguing *intelligentsia*—another double-dactyl word—before she forced herself to focus. "Why are you telling me this?"

"Because the President of the United States is being duped. Those back-channel negotiations of yours—they're dangerous, Miss Jensen. The people at the other end aren't even close to Khrushchev's inner circle. That's what our sources tell us. We've tried to tell the White House. They won't listen."

Margo covered her eyes, as much to still the trembling in her hand as to slow the whirl of her thoughts. "I still don't understand what you want."

He had the envelope ready. "Tonight, when you see Fomin, give him this. Don't tell the President. Don't tell anybody."

"I don't know who Fomin is."

A baring of teeth too large for the slender face. "Please don't play those games, Miss Jensen."

"I'm not the one playing games, Mr. Ziegler. And you can't seriously expect me to trust you."

"I'm not asking you to trust anybody. That's the point. Don't trust Fomin. Don't trust Kennedy's people. Don't trust me. You can tell Fomin exactly where the envelope came from. If you're right—if Fomin is on the up-and-up—and if he doesn't like what he reads, if he doesn't believe it, then he'll ignore it, so no harm done. But I don't think that's going to happen, Miss Jensen. I think Fomin will find the message is important. I think he'll read it and end the negotiations and probably get out of the country on the next Russian plane. You're just the messenger, Miss Jensen. It has nothing to do with you."

"Whoever Fomin is, why don't you deliver the letter yourself?"

"You know better than that, Miss Jensen. A man like me can't be seen within a mile of a man like Aleks Fomin. And he wouldn't let himself wind up in a situation—say, the back seat of a strange car—where it's possible for a man like me to hand him a note. But you he trusts. If you hand him the envelope, he'll take it." Another car was pulling up. "I'm sure Fomin has arranged a fallback. Don't worry. I'm not going to ask you where it is. This man will take you wherever you tell him to."

"I'll call a cab."

That ugly smile again. His gesture encompassed the block. "From where?"

"Just let me out. I'll think of something."

"You're resourceful, Miss Jensen. But this isn't one of those moments when you have to prove yourself." He put the envelope in her hand. At the same time, the door lock popped. The man from the other car opened the door for her. Margo already had one foot on the pavement. "A moment more," said Jack Ziegler. "Listen to me. You've done well. You're colored, but you have a grand future ahead of you. You're reliable, you're intelligent, and you're brave. You know that the people I represent wouldn't go to all this trouble unless we had good reason. We don't want to pick a fight with the President. This is for the good of the country. We don't have another motive. So, please, Miss Jensen. Deliver the envelope."

"I'll think about it."

"Think hard, Miss Jensen. And before you go running to Bundy, or call your emergency number, remember one thing." The smile was growing more confidently terrifying by the minute. "We know where your grandmother lives."

FORTY-SIX

Autobiography

I

The driver dropped her outside the Riggs National Bank on Wisconsin Avenue in Georgetown. The fallback where Margo would meet Fomin was miles away, down on the Mall, across from the Museum of Natural History, but she had no intention of helping Ziegler's associate guess where she was going.

She had been betrayed. Again. Fomin had warned that there were those in the Administration who would seek to close the back channel if they learned of it, and, oh, how right he was. But Ziegler had made an error. He had made a threat where none was necessary. He must have known that she would have no choice but to deliver the letter, and yet he had mentioned Nana anyway.

"Big mistake," Margo said aloud.

She hailed a cab.

II

"I have a letter for you," Margo said.

Fomin said nothing. On this, their fifth encounter in Washington, his reticence had expanded until it encompassed his entire being. In the darkness, his rugged face achieved, if anything, a greater immobility.

"Did you hear me?" she asked.

The Soviet was a moment answering. They were seated on a cracked wooden bench. Across the way, the floodlit marble façade of the Museum of Natural History gleamed whitely. Margo had visited the museum as a child, just after the war, when the right of colored visitors to use the bathrooms was yet an unresolved question.

"Your clothes are rumpled," Fomin finally said.

She instinctively drew her collar together. "I beg your pardon."

"This fiction you play with your President—it cannot be easy for you."

"It isn't."

"He should be ashamed of himself. In socialism, we believe in the purity of our women. We do not abuse them, as the capitalists do. To the capitalist male, you will never be other than property. You are aware of this?"

She didn't hesitate. "Mr. Fomin, I'm not here for a political debate. I told you that I have a letter."

He cocked his head as if listening to something in the middle distance. "This is why you were late?"

"Yes."

"Because you were receiving the letter, along with certain instructions?"

"Yes." She held the envelope toward him. "I didn't read it. You can inspect the seal."

"No."

"I'm sorry?"

"You may keep the letter, Miss Jensen. I would further suggest that you burn the pages as soon as practicable." He lifted his head like an animal scenting the air. "No. No. You are not followed. They would not take the chance."

"Please. Take the letter. You at least should read it."

"There is no need, Miss Jensen. I have read this letter already, many times." Fomin crossed his long legs. "I was in my early twenties when the Great Patriotic War began. Naturally, I volunteered. Everyone was expected to defend the Motherland. I was a bright lad, so they assigned me to an intelligence unit. When the Nazis invaded the Motherland, the Red Army made a temporary tactical withdrawal. I was part of a group tasked to remain behind. I was tasked with helping organize what is called a *réseau*. Do you know this word?"

"You told me in Varna. It means a spy network."

"Yes. Network. I organized a network. I pretended to be a simple farmer. I lived and worked on a farm, and meanwhile used my *réseau* to carry out sabotage operations against the fascist invader. Similar to your father's work. We put plastique in the treads of tanks by night. Once, we managed to blow up a fuel depot. And fuel, as you may know, is everything in war. Everything."

The night had acquired a campfire stillness. Margo found the story hypnotic.

"Sabotage is a nuisance," Fomin continued. "No war has ever been won or lost because of sabotage, but certainly the tactic increases the enemy's costs of doing battle. You may therefore well imagine that the fascist invader was determined to learn who was committing these acts of sabotage. They went from house to house. They smashed furniture, they stole, they raped, sometimes they murdered a son or a grandfather. They beat me twice because I was a male, and the right age. They were only making more enemies, of course, but they knew no other method than fear to achieve their ends. And at each stop they left a leaflet with instructions. To contact the local commandant if we saw anything suspicious. To cooperate with all orders of the fascist occupier. To remain indoors after curfew. And that the penalty for disobedience, however small, was death. And of course, as you know, death at the hands of the Nazis was not an honorable experience." During this last sentence, his head had turned toward her at last. The dark eyes were hard. "The letter that you wish to deliver to me is not from your President. He is too intelligent to put a proposal in writing. Therefore, it is from elsewhere in your security apparatus."

"Yes. It's from a man named—"

"His name is irrelevant. His letter will contain demands, questions, threats. It is the same as the leaflet from the fascist occupier. I refused to read the ravings of the fascists then. I refuse to read them now."

III

Margo was perplexed. Jack Ziegler's warnings bubbled through her mind. "Please, Mr. Fomin. All I'm asking is that you take the letter. Whether you read it is up to you."

"No."

"But we're not the Nazis. We're not the fascist occupier. We—"

"It makes no difference how you see yourselves. To me, to those who love Mother Russia, you are the Main Enemy, and you shall remain the Main Enemy until your ultimate defeat. For the moment we are collaborating, because the time is not right for the final battle. But make no mistake. When we are ready, at a time of our choosing, the battle will come. In the meanwhile, Miss Jensen, I have no interest in your internecine struggles." His voice softened. "Listen to me. I have no doubt that pressure was brought upon you to force you to cooperate with whoever wrote the letter. It is my advice that you ignore the pressure. Their intimidation is a tactic. If it fails, they will choose another."

She shook her head. "I wish I could believe that."

"You are a brave woman, Miss Jensen. That you would wish no harm to those you love is not what distinguishes you. What distinguishes you is the ability to soldier on despite those risks."

"But—"

"I ran the *réseau* for eight months, Miss Jensen. I courted the daughter of a local tradesman. I received the permission of her father to marry her when the war concluded. Shortly after the celebration of our engagement, I was recalled to Moscow, to be sent to a different theater to build a new *réseau*. It was difficult leaving my beloved, but I was a soldier. The Nazis were in full retreat. I went about my duties in another theater, sustained by the knowledge that the war would soon end, and I would be united once more with my beloved. After the surrender, I returned to the village to find her. But the village no longer existed. The fascist invader had taken revenge as he left, Miss Jensen. The Nazis had arrested the young woman and her father and her mother and her two older brothers and her three younger sisters. Then they burned the surrounding farms. Only one of the younger girls was left alive, and she was horribly disfigured. The rest died, Miss Jensen, none pleasantly. My fiancée was not among the survivors. Nevertheless, I performed my duty, and the war was won. My loss was not inconsiderable, but it was only a tiny piece of a catastrophe that swept the nation. I was a soldier, and, if called upon to defend the Motherland, and knowing the costs in advance, I would do the same again." His gaze was bright and intense. "Threats to your loved ones are not uncommon. Most likely they are bluffing."

Bluffing. So much of Niemeyer's course was about bluff and counter-bluff. And the purpose of bluffing, as he endlessly reminded them, was not always to fool the adversary; the true purpose was to keep the adversary uncertain. And in the case of Jack Ziegler—

"Suppose they're not bluffing," she said.

"It can make no possible difference. We are fighting one war to avoid another. It is the fate of the world we hold in our hands." He turned away, the subject of Jack Ziegler's letter closed. "Now. I assume that you have a counter-proposal for me."

Margo swallowed. She felt teary, yet another part of her mind wondered whether any part of Fomin's story was true.

"I do," she said.

"Please present it."

She did, explaining it just as Kennedy had explained it to her: that his advisers wanted him to retaliate for the downing of the U-2; that he was prepared to withhold the attack if Khrushchev would offer a gesture of good faith; that a deal was still possible if Friday's offer to remove the missiles from Cuba in return for his promise not to invade remained on the table; and that any exchange of the Jupiter missiles in Turkey and Italy was out of the question.

"I see," said Fomin when Margo was done. "Your President's proposal, then, is that we remove the missiles and get nothing in return? Does he understand that the Comrade General Secretary would fall at once from power?"

"The President said to remind you that it was Khrushchev himself who made the offer on Friday." She steeled herself. "And there's something else. Before a deal can be reached, the President wants to be sure that he is in fact dealing with Khrushchev."

"What assurances can I offer?"

"I don't know. But the President asked me to convey the importance of that condition. If you cannot persuade him by this time tomorrow that he is indeed dealing with the General Secretary, there will be no deal."

"That would mean war, Miss Jensen."

"Yes, sir," said Margo. "It would."

FORTY-SEVEN

Whom Do You Trust?

I

It was nearly eleven, but Margo's night was far from over. This time there was no Warren waiting to drive her. She wondered what had become of him: was he a conspirator, or had the conspirators gotten rid of him? But she had more immediate concerns.

She needed advice; and help.

She knew better than to call the emergency number, and she had no doubt that Dr. Harrington's house would be under surveillance. So she found a phone booth on Constitution Avenue, near the federal courthouse, and called the only other person she could think of.

Jerry Ainsley listened for thirty seconds, then told her to stop talking.

"Do you remember where I took you a week ago Friday?"

"Yes."

"Find a taxi. Go straight there. Wait for me inside, near the front, where it's bright and crowded."

"When will you be there?"

"As soon as I can. I have to check a couple of things first."

II

This time he took her from the diner to his apartment, a high-ceilinged second-floor walk-up near American University. She supposed that the building had once been a single mansion. There were three rooms, and a balcony overlooking an interior courtyard where the shrubbery had missed its autumn trimming, and probably its spring trimming, too. They sat at the kitchen table while she told him the story. He listened quietly, occasionally freshening her tea, and she could feel the tight attentiveness in his strange, orangey eyes. She had the sense that, had she asked, Jerry Ainsley could have quoted her testimony word for word.

When she was done, he stood and stretched and went over to the sink to put more water in the kettle. "Those bastards," he said. "How could they put you in this position?"

"I volunteered."

"They manipulated you." He turned on the flame. "They've been manipulating you since day one."

"This isn't about me." Margo was surprised at her own umbrage. "It's about the missiles in Cuba."

"Tell that to Jack Ziegler." A thought struck him. "How much do you know about him, anyway?"

"I know I don't like him very much."

"Well, just wait until you know him better. You won't like him at all." Jerry Ainsley's toothy grin had the same New England charm as the President's. "I've known him for a while, Margo. And what I can tell you about him is that he's a carrion eater." He saw her blank look. "You know. A beast that lives off of what more powerful carnivores leave behind. If you're encountering the Jack Zieglers of the world, that means somebody with an awful lot of influence is out to get you." Then he asked the question she least anticipated. "Have you and the President been intimate?"

Margo blinked. She could not possibly have heard him correctly. "I beg your pardon."

"You and Kennedy. The affair's a fake, right? It's not real? There's nothing to it?"

"Of course it's not real. Why would you ask that?"

"Wait here." He went into the next room and returned a moment later with the late edition of the *Evening Star*. He flipped a couple of pages. "Have you seen this?"

She looked, and looked again. There was even a photograph of poor Erroll Haar, lying bloody in the street.

"They're setting you up, Margo," he said as she continued to stare.

"Setting me up for what?" she asked, faintly. Two men who bothered her, she kept thinking. Two hit-and-run accidents.

"Lots of people know about the affair. Okay, okay." Holding up a hand. "Fine. It's not a real affair. But people think it is. It's an open secret, Margo. And the FBI knows that this guy bothered you the other day. The FBI knows, and, well, some of the people who do what I do—we also know. Are you with me?"

"Yes." Faintly.

"Now, I don't think for a moment that the Secret Service would let anybody follow Kennedy around with a camera and take pictures through the window. That means your own people leaked it. Maybe Bundy's people. Are you following me?"

"I—I had the same thought after I met him. Mr. Haar."

"Good. Now, let's work backward." Jerry leaned against the sink, folding his arms. "Think about it, Margo. Tonight is the crucial night. The key offer that you're bringing to Fomin, the key questions—that's all tonight. And today just so *happens* to be the day Haar is killed. And tonight just *happens* to be the night that Ziegler tries to wreck the negotiation. That's not coincidence. That's planning."

"You're saying they know what's going on in the White House? Not just when I'm meeting Fomin, but what messages I'm carrying? Because the President says the only people who know the details are him and his brother and Mr. Bundy."

"Are you very sure?"

"Yes."

Ainsley was seated across from her again. He took her hands. "Margo. Do you mind if I call you Margo? Listen. Carefully. I've asked you not to tell me the content of any of the messages you've carried between the President and Fomin. And I still don't want you to do that." His grip tightened. Those peculiar pupils, seen so close, were a fiery gold. She flinched away as his gaze bored into hers. "What I do want you to do is to think about tonight's conversation with Jack Ziegler. Was there anything in it—anything at all—that would suggest that he knows what's in those messages?"

"I don't think so," she said. "He said Kennedy was being duped, and he said Fomin's people weren't close to Khrushchev, but he didn't say anything about the actual content of the back-channel negotiations. I think he was fishing."

"And you didn't tell him anything?"

"Nothing. I didn't even admit knowing Fomin."

Jerry let go of her hands. "Good. Very good. Then the reason he intercepted you tonight has to do with another aspect of the crisis, external to the messages. But somebody sent him. Somebody chose tonight." Ainsley was on his feet again, the sort of active man who thought best in motion. He was very different now from the foppish diplomatic fixer she'd met in Bulgaria. "Let's go out on the balcony."

III

The balcony was cramped, aging concrete with a cast-iron rail. The furniture was modern and cheap—folding chairs, plastic straps stretched over chrome frames. Her coat was buttoned tightly against the night chill.

"Jack Ziegler used to be one of our traveling salesmen," Ainsley resumed. "Do you know what that means? No? It means he wouldn't have a permanent overseas assignment with diplomatic cover, like I did in Bulgaria. He'd go where he was needed. To fix problems that arise. I can't give you more details, but you get the picture. Men who do what Ziegler does typically are fluent in two or three languages, and understand more than a smattering of two or three more. He left the Agency a couple of years ago. I haven't kept track of him, but it sounds like he's a freelancer now. And he's very good at his work, so I'm told. Young to be so prominent—I think he's just thirty—but he has quite a reputation, let me tell you. He's not a man you want as an enemy, Margo, believe me." He glanced at her. He had poured himself a Scotch, but she was sticking with tea. "What I'm saying is, if you back out now, I don't think anybody will have cause to blame you."

"Back out?" Despite her exhaustion, she sat up straighter. "You're telling me to abandon the negotiations? What are you, the good cop?"

He laughed. "Before you start accusing me of being part of the conspiracy, let me clarify. As it happens, I don't think you should back out. I think what you're doing is heroic, and, obviously, important. But if you decide to go a different way, I would respect that decision. That's all I'm saying."

"And who'd carry the messages?"

"I'm sure they'd think of something."

"Fomin says I'm the only one he trusts."

"He might even be telling the truth." A long swallow. "But he lies for a living, Margo. Who knows what he really thinks? The point is, if Ziegler and his patron had decided to make you disappear tonight, I very much doubt that the negotiations would have ended. Slowed down, maybe, while they worked out the details. But not ended."

She remembered the desperation in Bundy's manner the night they first met, a thousand years ago. "I'm not so sure," she said. "I think if anything happened to me Fomin might run for cover."

"So—you're going on?"

She swallowed. Nodded.

"Okay. You can stay here tonight. No, no, don't argue. I need to be able to keep an eye on you. Just in case. And don't worry about your roommate. I'm sure she'll assume . . . Well, we both know what she'll assume. Sorry, Margo. That's the role you took on when you said yes."

Another nod. She couldn't meet his eyes.

"You told the President what happened to her?"

"Yes."

"Then Bundy will probably have somebody keep an eye on her. Not out of altruism—they just can't afford to have you scared off. Now. What else? I have a colleague checking, very quietly, to see if anything has befallen a Secret Service agent whose first name or last is Warren. That was one of the things I had to do before I picked you up tonight. I'll also arrange for somebody to keep an eye on your grandmother for the duration, although it's possible that Bundy has already thought of that. I wouldn't take Ziegler's threat too seriously—probably he was just trying to scare you. Still, it pays to be sure."

She sagged with relief. And dizzying gratitude at the swiftness with which he had assumed control. If he was one of the bad guys, then so be it. She was tired of fighting alone.

Meanwhile, Ainsley was still laying out the rules. "Tomorrow I'm going to drive you to meet Fomin, because, for all we know, there are Secret Service people who are part of this. And I'll also be driving you to meet the President afterward."

"Fomin won't be able to reach me with the meeting time."

"You can call your roommate and ask if there were any messages."

"I'll need clothes." She swallowed. "A—a fancy dress. To meet the President."

"We'll buy whatever you need."

"It's Sunday," she said. "What if I want to go to church?"

They both knew she was now raising objections for the sake of raising objections, but Ainsley treated it seriously.

"There's a Bible on the shelf. You can pray here if you want." He stood. "Come. Let's go inside."

The bedroom was small but pristinely kept. She was increasingly nervous, and again thought of Nana. She had never spent the night in a man's apartment.

"Thank you for helping me," she said.

"Dr. Harrington thinks the world of you," he answered. He was at the closet, pulling out towels, a bathrobe, a nightshirt. "That counts for a lot with me." He set everything on the narrow bed. "Besides, what you're doing is vital. I'm not particularly interested in seeing the world blown to bits."

She smiled.

"Well, thank you anyway," she said, and, to her surprise, got up on her toes and pecked him lightly on the cheek.

"I'll be right outside," he said, crisply. "If anything bothers you— a bad dream, some sound outside the window, anything—give a holler."

"I don't think I can sleep."

"You'll sleep fine, Margo. Don't worry."

"May I ask you one more question?"

He was like a man on a mission, forcing patience upon himself as once again departure was postponed. "Of course."

"How well do you know Dr. Harrington?"

"I'd never met her before last Friday."

"But you said you admire her."

"No. I said that her endorsement of you means a lot." He was checking that the window was locked. "Doris Harrington has quite a reputation, Margo. She's not an easy woman to impress."

"Agatha admires her a lot."

"I'm not surprised."

"Because they're both women?"

"Because they're both killers." His voice had gone cold. "I know, I know. You think everybody who works for the CIA can kill ten Commies with a swipe of a pinkie. But that's not the way it works, even in Plans Directorate. There are people who do what most of us do, and then there are people who do what Agatha does. She kills with her bare hands, Margo. She's very good at it."

"Then how—I mean, in Varna—they beat her up."

"There were eight or ten of them, according to what I heard. And if I know Agatha, she might have killed one or two before they got her down." He saw her face. "She's fine, Margo. You don't need to send a get-well card. She's like Ziegler—a traveling salesman. Saleswoman." She heard the stony disapproval in his voice, and understood that he would rather work for a Central Intelligence Agency that didn't employ such people. "I'm sure she's off on some other assignment by now."

"Well, I guess now I know," said Margo, unaware that she had spoken aloud until he answered.

"Know what?"

"Why the people we met—people who do what you do—why they all seemed to be afraid of her."

"She's said to have a temper," he conceded. "At the camp, a couple of the boys who bothered her—well, from what I understand, they were in no shape to graduate when she was through. She's made a lot of enemies, I'll put it that way." Back to the closet. This time he took down a metal box with a combination lock. He pulled out a small gun. "Do you know how to use one of these?"

"No."

He showed her. "This is the Beretta 1951. Safety on. Safety off. Work the slide like so. Eight rounds in the magazine. Just point and shoot. Don't worry about aiming. Point at your target and pull the trigger." He handed it to her. "Light and portable, but plenty of stopping power. Just in case."

Margo's lips quivered. She couldn't quite manage a third thank-you, and Ainsley's story about Agatha had rocked her, even though it was no worse than what she had suspected.

"Lock the door," he said, backing out of the room. "And keep it locked until you hear my voice telling you to open it."

"Wait."

"What's wrong?"

" 'Jerry.' What's it short for?"

That lovely smile again as his eyes softened. "Alas, my parents saddled me with 'Jericho.' Walls and all."

He was gone.

But he was right. From the moment her head hit the pillow, Margo slept soundly. So soundly that she never heard him creep from the apartment; or return.

FORTY-EIGHT

Reasonable Efforts

I

On Sunday morning, the *Grozny* stopped short of the quarantine line. Earlier, it had slowed, which was why it had reached the blockade two days later than expected. Today the ship had throttled back its engines. The President was in the residence, about to head out to 10 a.m. mass at St. Matthew the Apostle, when Bundy called upstairs with the news.

"Are they sure?" Kennedy asked.

"Yes, Mr. President. He's dead in the water."

"And it's definitely the *Grozny*? It's not—I don't know—a duplicate?"

"Sir, Navy jets have been shadowing the ship for two days. The missile components are still carried openly on the deck. It's definitely the *Grozny*."

"So Khrushchev's ready to listen to reason after all."

Relief was patent in Kennedy's voice, and his national security adviser wished he didn't have to say the rest.

"I'm afraid there's more, Mr. President. I was just on with the DDI. He says the Soviets are actually accelerating work on the missile launchers."

"The SAMs?"

"No, sir. The ballistic launchers. They're speeding things up."

A long silence. "Are we sure?"

"Yes, Mr. President."

"So, on the one hand, Khrushchev says he wants peace and he stops the *Grozny,* and on the other hand, he's getting the launchers ready for war?"

"Mr. President, you ordered GREENHILL to ask for a gesture of good faith to hold off retaliation for the U-2 shoot-down. Stopping the *Grozny* might be that gesture. As for speeding up work, well, there's no deal in place yet. Wouldn't we do the same in his position?"

"Well, that's very even-handed of you, Mac, but I'd have preferred if Khrushchev abandoned all work on the missiles. That would be a real gesture of good faith. Whereas stopping one ship while he speeds up the work is kind of . . ." He trailed off. "Anyway, it doesn't matter what I think. LeMay and that crowd will see it as a trick."

"Quite possibly, sir."

"Will they be right?"

"I'm afraid we don't have enough information. Not until Fomin gets back to GREENHILL."

"Right. And the deadline is in—let's see—twenty-eight hours. We attack Cuba tomorrow at two o'clock."

"Yes, Mr. President."

Another pause. Then, more decisively: "Get the ExComm in early. I'll be back from mass around eleven. Let's start then."

"Yes, Mr. President."

"Oh, and, Mac?"

"Yes, sir?"

"Get in touch with GREENHILL. I want to know when she's seeing Fomin."

No point in not saying the rest. "Mr. President, we may have a bit of a problem there. We've already called her apartment twice—Janet does the calling, using code words and so forth—and, well, her roommate seems to be trying to cover for her, but Janet thinks GREENHILL never came home last night."

II

Margo was still in bed. Ashamed of herself, frightened, exhilarated, confident. Despite her misgivings, she had fallen asleep the instant her head hit the pillow, and when she opened her eyes it was quarter past nine. Two mornings in a row now, sleeping late. Not like her at all.

Margo had been taught from childhood to be early to bed and early to rise.

And not to wake up in a strange man's bed—or any man's bed, for that matter, until the man was her husband.

That the man in question had slept in the other room only made the whole episode that much odder.

A bulbous stain marred the plastered ceiling, and Margo allowed her eyes to follow it. She smiled wistfully, wondering whether she and Tom were still a couple; and wondering other things besides. She yawned. She could see the other interns at the office, snickering together as they tried to figure out exactly who Margo's secret man might be. She imagined their reactions if they could see her now, in her borrowed nightshirt, hair nearly beyond repair. She rolled onto her side to look out the window, and spotted, on the bedside table, the pistol Ainsley had given her last night.

The humor went out of her face.

Everything came back to her then: not only the missiles, but Ziegler, and Patsy, and poor dead Erroll Haar, and—

A light rapping on the door.

Margo hopped from the bed. The nightshirt was really too short. She pulled on the robe, tiptoed across the plank floor, laid her cheek against the wood.

"Yes?"

"I have to go out briefly," said Ainsley from the next room. She wondered how he'd known she was awake. "There's eggs and toast for you on the table, and a bag on the sofa with a few other items you might need."

"Where are you going?"

"To check on a couple of things. Don't go out. Don't open the door for anybody. And keep the gun nearby."

A moment later, she heard his footsteps crossing the room, and she had an instinct that he was intentionally treading loud enough for her to detect him. He gave the impression that if he wanted to, he could walk across broken glass without making a sound.

She waited, then opened the door. Slowly.

Jericho Ainsley was gone.

Margo sat at the table with the gun beside her plate, wondering whether Donald Jensen ever used to eat this way. She decided arbitrarily that he had. The eggs were overdone, but she didn't care.

She felt absurdly grateful.

After breakfast, she washed the dishes in the stainless-steel sink and put them in the drainer. Then she turned to the bag on the sofa. Inside, she found slacks and underwear and a sweater, all more or less her size, along with a toothbrush and a hairbrush and deodorant. Had he gone out specially to some all-night clothing store, or did he keep a supply of such things around for his women? Embarrassed at the turn of her own thoughts, she laid out the clothes on the bed and hurried into the bathroom. In the shower, she made a mental note to call Nana later this morning, and maybe Corbin, too, just to be sure everything was as it should be. Not that Ziegler would have any reason to act on his threats. As far as he knew, she'd given the note to Fomin.

As far as he knew.

Because Ziegler's people couldn't possibly have followed her. Doing so would entail too much risk—

Wait.

Margo stood there, hot water cascading over her brown body, and frowned. An idea that had been forming in the shadows began to creep toward the front of her mind. Ziegler's people hadn't followed her, because of the risk. Bundy's people hadn't followed her, because of the risk. But in Ithaca, Fomin and his people had followed her without hesitation. She remembered Niemeyer's point in class all those days ago about the man with the grenade in the bank, and how the more the robber wants, the less certain we are that he'll carry out his threat: another of the petits paradoxes.

Fomin's people had followed her.

In Ithaca.

And Margo saw, with sudden clarity, the answer that had been staring her in the face all along.

She turned off the shower and, deep in her contemplations, dried her hair, wrapped herself in a towel, and walked out of the bathroom—

—only to find Jerry Ainsley seated at the table as he leafed through the Sunday *New York Times*.

"Good morning," he said, eyes averted.

Beet-red, Margo raced into the bedroom and slammed the door.

Another first, she told herself, as she hurriedly dressed. Kissing a President, spending the night in a strange man's apartment, then letting him see her half naked. She consoled herself with the knowledge that things couldn't get any worse.

Except, of course, they could.

III

"It's a trick," said General Curtis LeMay. "It's obviously a trick."

Around the table there were several nods. The ExComm had returned to the matter left unsettled yesterday: On Friday, via the back channel, Khrushchev had communicated an offer to remove the missiles from Cuba in return for an American promise not to invade. Then, yesterday, Saturday, he had publicly insisted anew that only a trade for the Jupiters would do. Friday's deal meant peace; Saturday's deal meant war; the question was whether the President should act as if the Friday deal was still on the table.

Kennedy glanced at his least favorite general. "Which part of it is a trick?" he asked.

"The whole thing. They're working faster on the launch sites, right?" His tone dripped disrespect. "Khrushchev says they're willing to take those missiles out, but at the same time, they're finishing them as fast as they can. Because they know, once they're finished, there's nothing we can do. At that point, the deterrent begins to deter." LeMay drew a page out of the folder in front of him. "The Friday offer obviously isn't from Khrushchev at all. Or, if it is, he's not in charge. I have here an assessment from the Agency to the effect that Khrushchev's hardliners won't let him back down." He shut the folder again. "Friday was a trick. Saturday is their real position, and it hasn't changed one iota since this blasted thing started. Add to that the fact that they've shot down one of our planes and killed one of our people. That shows real recklessness on their part. There's no longer any choice, Mr. President. We have to go in."

Again, Bundy was disturbed by the growls of enthusiasm around the table.

"Look," he tried. "Khrushchev turned the *Grozny*. That has to be a signal that he's ready to deal."

Admiral George W. Anderson, Jr., the chief of naval operations, shook his head, and unconsciously echoed the President's argument from two hours ago. "A signal would be to start dismantling the missile launchers. Speeding up the work isn't exactly an olive branch." He turned directly to Bundy. "I'm sorry, Mac. I know you think we can negotiate our way out of this. But from what I can tell, we've been had."

McCone spoke up. "And even if Khrushchev does agree to remove the missiles, there's still the matter of the IL-28 bombers he's snuck into Cuba. Lest we forget, they carry nuclear payloads, too."

"We can handle that quietly," said the attorney general. "I don't think the public's paying too much attention to the bombers. It's the missiles that have everybody spooked."

"People are terrified," said Sorensen. "They're streaming out of the cities. Buses and trains are overwhelmed. Long-distance lines are so jammed that most calls don't go through."

"That's why we should make Khrushchev's proposal public," said Bobby.

LeMay gave him a withering look. "You're talking like this thing is settled. It's a long way from settled." To the President: "Sir, I've said it before, I'll say it again. We don't even know for sure who's in charge over there in the Kremlin right now. The reason Khrushchev put missiles in Cuba in the first place was to make his hawks happy." To McCone: "That's the CIA's analysis, right?" At large: "You think he'll have the guts to take them out? Believe me, he won't. We have to take them out. We have to invade. Today!" Suddenly he was pounding the table. "Mr. President, believe me, if you make a deal with the Reds on this, it'll go down as the greatest defeat in our history."

Stunned silence greeted LeMay's challenge. Nobody could remember a general pounding the table in the face of his commander in chief.

A moment later, a babble of voices rose, but Bobby Kennedy's was loudest. "That's enough, General LeMay. There's a plan, and we're going to follow it. If we don't have a deal by tomorrow at two, we start the attack. I don't see any reason to change that."

"By tomorrow," growled Maxwell Taylor, "they could have the rest of those launchers operational."

"Not likely," said Bundy. "We can be hawks tomorrow. For today, we turned the *Grozny,* and Khrushchev says he wants to deal. It's a day for the doves."

But Bundy was arguing against his own inclination. The hawks were righter than they knew. With GREENHILL missing, there was no obvious way to verify that Fomin really did speak for Khrushchev. The war faction of the ExComm had become like a train rolling out of control, and as the argument circled the table, one adviser after another seemed stuck on the invasion express.

At last the President waved everyone silent. "We stick to the plan. We wait another day."

"Mr. President," began several members at once.

Kennedy wasn't finished. "But let's move up the operation to noon. That's twenty-four hours from now. At noon tomorrow, if we don't have a firm deal, and if we don't know for sure that it's Khrushchev over there, we go in."

IV

Bundy stood in the foyer between the Cabinet Room and the Oval Office, watching to see who left with whom, because he knew the President would ask. Gwynn, from State, walked out deep in conversation with General LeMay and Admiral Anderson: hardly the most auspicious of sights. Secretary of Defense McNamara left not with his generals but with Adlai Stevenson, the United Nations ambassador, who was one of the few strong voices for negotiation remaining: a better sight.

Unless, of course, McNamara was trying to persuade Stevenson, rather than the other way around.

By this time, Bundy was seriously worried about the fate of his agent, GREENHILL. Warren, the driver assigned her by the Secret Service, had received a priority order by telephone last night, putting him on a plane to Chicago to join the advance team for a presidential trip that turned out not to exist. Nobody knew who had made the call. Nobody knew who had driven GREENHILL to and from her rendezvous with Kennedy. According to the director of the presidential protection detail, Warren swore that he'd asked about his usual assignment, and been assured that it was being handled. The caller plainly knew the right codes. Bundy wanted to press for more but didn't dare: the director, who after all knew only the cover story, seemed to think it was a prank by fellow agents, and therefore the proper subject of a reprimand if he happened to learn who was responsible. He didn't think the episode worth a serious investigation, and might find it strange that the national security adviser was so concerned for the whereabouts of a Kennedy girlfriend.

"Mr. Bundy."

He turned. Janet, his secretary, was beside him.

"Did you try the apartment again?"

"Twice. No word. I think I'm getting on her roommate's nerves."

"Her roommate. Right. Did we assign protection for her?"

"I took care of it. Mr. Bundy, Director McCone needs to see you urgently."

He glanced around. "Where is he?"

"Downstairs, in your office." She bit her lip. "He says he didn't think you'd want your conversation to be overheard." She leaned closer. "He said to tell you it's about GREENHILL. And that he didn't want to embarrass you."

V

Doris Harrington was also beginning to worry. On Sunday mornings on P Street in Georgetown, very little ever stirred. But this morning a man she had never seen before walked his dog past her front door twice, and a van bearing the logo of a plumbing service that wasn't listed in the Yellow Pages parked at the corner for two hours. Shortly before the van left, a stretch limousine with darkened windows pulled up across the street, but nobody got in or out. Around back, a couple was arguing in the yard abutting hers. The woman was nobody she recognized, but Harrington was fairly certain that the man who was shouting, although now dressed casually, was the same one who earlier had been walking the dog.

Surveillance was nothing new to her. She had been encountering it, in one form or another, since her days in occupied Vienna. Long after she stopped running agents, she was still the subject of random checks, as was everyone with her clearance.

But this was different. This wasn't the FBI watching her briefly, to be sure she didn't have a hand in the till. This was an open, full-scale operation, the sort that was intended to deter any contact with the subject.

Harrington let the curtain fall. She rarely watched the television in the living room, but now she turned it on, in case there was news about Cuba. But the news was about America: empty store shelves, empty gas pumps, empty houses and apartment buildings in the big cities. For a decade or more, the government had been urging people to build backyard shelters or make evacuation plans. She didn't know how many had shelters, but the number of frightened evacuees was in the millions.

It occurred to her that she had never made a plan to leave the city—for example, to visit her younger sister in San Diego—in part because she had always assumed that she would be at her desk until the end, helping the President struggle to contain the crisis.

But someone else sat at her desk now, and Harrington had no idea how the negotiations were proceeding. She had become, in national security terms, an unperson.

She went to the kitchen for some apple juice. The arguing couple had vanished, but in the alley a man was down on his knees, working on his motorcycle. Back on the living-room sofa, she sipped her juice and reasoned things through. That a surveillance operation of this scale would begin so suddenly could only mean that some emergency had arisen. She wasn't sure who was responsible for the large team of watchers, but she very much doubted that they were there for Doris Harrington. They might be official; they might be the other thing. Either way, Harrington herself was a woman of late middle age; if they wanted her, they would have come through the door and taken her.

Which meant that they were there for Margo. It occurred to her that she should probably warn the girl. Unfortunately, she had no idea how GREENHILL could be reached.

So she sat, and watched television, and, like the rest of America, waited.

FORTY-NINE

Half Disclosures

I

"McCone knows," said Bundy, alone in the Oval Office with the Kennedy brothers. "He was kind enough to drop by my suite to tell me in private that the Agency has become aware, as he puts it, that I'm running an illegal intelligence operation out of the White House."

"How did he find out?" asked Bobby.

"He won't tell me that. Only that his people have worked it out. But it seems that he didn't get the key piece until this morning. A message came to him, through channels he declines to identify, that GREENHILL is safe, and under the protection of the Agency."

"She's safe," breathed the President.

"And under the protection of the Agency," Bundy said again. It was imperative that they understand the point. "McCone says that our operation—well, he thinks it's my operation—my operation went off the rails, but one of his people was able to pick up the pieces. I'm sorry, but the director has a habit of mixing his metaphors." He shrugged. "Anyway, the only good to come out of this is that I don't think McCone actually has her."

"You just said she's under his protection!" Bobby protested.

"No. I quoted him as saying that GREENHILL is under the protection of the Agency. We fenced a little—I never admitted that there was an operation, he never precisely admitted having her—but I got the idea that the message had reached McCone that one of his people had her, and he was as frustrated as I was. You'll remember that certain channels exist to get information into the right hands in the Agency without a source being identified. It seems that one of those channels was activated early this morning. The message actually sent was: 'Tell Bundy she's safe and she'll make the meetings.' McCone's people put that together with other clues they'd developed and worked out that 'she' meant GREENHILL. But he doesn't know who sent the message."

The attorney general was marching around the office. "That's ridiculous. How many people can he have in the Washington area who are unaccounted for and who'd have the skills—and the chutzpah—to do something like this? I'm sure there's some way to track him down." He pointed. "Get him on the phone, Mac. Tell him the President needs to know who has her."

"I can't do that, Bobby."

"Why not?" asked the President.

"Because McCone believes—or chooses to believe—that this is my own operation, mounted independently, and illegally. You can't be involved, sir." He closed his folder. "We can assume that McCone is doing exactly what you just described. He absolutely will figure out where she is. But there's no chance he's going to share the results with me unless I order it in your name. And then he'll know."

"Maybe it's time to cut the Agency in," said Bobby. "Maybe he's right. We're amateurs at this kind of thing."

"I don't think that's a good idea. For one thing, the Agency will want to take over the operation."

"Would that be so terrible?"

"You know how they are. They'll have half a dozen people following GREENHILL every minute. Fomin is bound to notice. He'll get spooked, believe me. He'll be on the next plane to Moscow, and five minutes later the Soviet Embassy will be burning its papers and destroying its code machines. When they burn their papers, we're at war." The Kennedys, Bundy knew, hated his didactic mode, but there were times when only instruction would do. "And there's another reason. This way, if the operation goes wrong, the blame rests on me and nobody else. If the Agency gets involved, then it's official policy. You won't be able to paint me as a rogue official conducting a bit of private enterprise."

"If it goes wrong," said Bobby, "nobody will care about who's to blame."

"I beg to differ, Mr. Attorney General. Nowadays, historians hardly care about anything else."

The President was exasperated. "Come on, Mac. You heard them in there. They want war. The whole table. Unless GREENHILL gets back to us with evidence that we're really dealing with Khrushchev, we're bombing those missile sites tomorrow noon. And we don't even know where she is."

II

They were in yet another diner, this one in Silver Spring. Jerry seemed to know them all. What he liked about diners, he said, was that nobody who was anybody ever dropped in. You could talk to anyone you liked about anything you liked, without worrying about chance encounters.

He turned out to have a friend, a mountainous blonde named Sally, who had a dress shop nearby and had opened it for him, in defiance of Maryland's Sunday-closing laws. As Margo tried on outfits, she had found herself preening for him a bit, and enjoying in return the appreciative look in his eyes. And although she knew it was all playacting, she nevertheless found—for the hour they spent in the shop, at least—that she felt almost calm, and entirely disconnected from the world that was on the verge of tearing itself to pieces.

They chose a frilly silver affair, a bit more formal than the ones Bundy had selected for her five previous rendezvous with Kennedy: closer to a ball gown than a party dress. Studying herself in the mirror, she felt more confident, more professional, more adult, more like Claudia's granddaughter and Donald's daughter.

"I'll have to let it out a little," said Sally.

"That's really not necessary," said Margo. "And I don't know if we have time."

"How long?" asked Ainsley.

"Two days. It's a busy season. Maybe two and a half." She frowned. "But I'm not really sure. I'm supposed to be going to my sister's in North Carolina. You know, just in case."

"We need it in one hour."

Sally grinned. "Ninety minutes."

As they drove away, Margo couldn't help asking him where he knew Sally from. His reply sounded as if it had been memorized for an exam; and yet she knew already that he was the sort of student who took his lessons to heart.

"It's useful to make all kinds of friends," he said. "Wherever you are, you never know what talents you'll need, what neighborhoods you'll have to hide in, what cars you'll need to borrow."

She couldn't help herself. "Did they teach you that in the CIA?"

"To tell you the truth, I learned it from my father."

"Is he still alive?"

"No, he's been dead ten years. I was a late baby. He was in his sixties when I was born."

Still Margo pressed her luck. "Was he in the same business as you?"

"My father?" He laughed. "No. All he ever did was make money and lose it again. He started out as a peddler in the street and wound up running a bank. He was a Scottish immigrant from a long line of farmers, but after he founded his bank he started telling people his Scottish accent was English, on the ground that Americans can't tell the difference. He even claimed that his ancestor was knighted by William the Conqueror. He was married three times—I'm a product of wife number two—and on his deathbed he gathered all six children and begged us to tell the world he died in a brothel. And you know what? Just last year, some book about the titans of Wall Street reported gleefully that Donnan Ainsley died in bed with a prostitute."

Jericho Ainsley seemed terrifically unimpressed by the story, but Margo secretly found it a thrilling coincidence that he, too, should have a father who managed to fool the world about both how he lived and how he died.

Five miles away, she used the pay phone at a service station to call the apartment. The woman she knew as Carol had tried her four times, Patsy said, still cross.

Margo apologized, and asked if there were any other messages.

"No. There was some guy who called twice asking for Danielle. A wrong number, I guess."

"I guess," said Margo, and thanked her. She promised to be home as soon as she could, and Patsy hung up before Margo could tell her that somebody would be watching to make sure she wasn't bothered again.

Danielle meant six-thirty tonight.

From a separate pay phone, she called the number Bundy had given her. The usual woman answered, and Margo used the code words to let her know that she was safe but refused to say where she was.

The pickup for the meeting with the President—disguised as talk about dinner the day after tomorrow—was set for seven-thirty p.m.

III

Now, as they sat in a grimy booth, Ainsley was all business again, setting out the lay of the land.

"First of all, you should be aware that I've sent a message to Bundy to tell him you've landed on your feet and you'll make your meetings tonight. Don't worry. The message isn't traceable, but I'm sure it'll get where it's supposed to go, if only because the Agency can't stand the man, and the director will enjoy throwing it in his face."

She wasn't sure what she was supposed to say, so she played with her wilted salad and just nodded.

"Second, just in case, we aren't going back to my apartment. Not until all of this is over. I'll find us a place to spend the hours until you meet Fomin." Margo felt uneasy as the coils of his concentration, competence, and ability to plan continued to draw her into greater dependency, but she saw no way out, and wasn't sure she wanted one.

"Okay," she said, studying her sandwich.

"This leads to the third point," he continued. "If Jack Ziegler knows about the negotiations, there's a good shot that he knows about the Yenching Palace. He'll be watching."

"I can skip the restaurant and just go to the fallback," she pointed out.

"Not tonight. You can't take the chance. From what you tell me, this message has to get through."

"True." She took a tiny bite of her BLT. She was less hungry than she had thought she'd be. "It has to."

"If you miss two meetings in a row, Fomin will get suspicious." His eyes kept straying to the window, and she could feel him cataloguing cars driving in and out of the parking lot. "Also, Ziegler might follow him from the Yenching Palace to the fallback. Fomin is bound to notice, and he'll run."

"I'm not so sure," said Margo, showing off for him. "If just spotting a tail would spook Fomin into abandoning the negotiations, all Ziegler would have to do is show himself, at any time, and the back channel would be closed down. I think Fomin's built of stronger stuff. Niemeyer told me he was part of what happened with the Rosenbergs and the hydrogen bomb and all that. He didn't run home after that operation fell apart. And from what Fomin says, Khrushchev is desperate. He needs this deal."

"If it is Khrushchev."

"You're like Ziegler. You don't think it's him."

"I have my doubts. Look, Margo. Anybody who does what I do would doubt it. There's always somebody who's offering to sell you the crown jewels. And they're almost always lumps of coal."

"Fomin's not selling anything. He doesn't want money."

"So it would seem." He sipped his Coke, wiped his mouth with a gentle elegance that bespoke proper breeding. "That's probably why Bundy's willing to go along. Maybe why I am, too. Because Fomin wouldn't seem to have anything to gain by making this whole thing up." He took a bite of his cheeseburger, chewed thoughtfully for a moment. "In any case, I'll be outside the whole time you're with Fomin. I'll be watching for Ziegler and his friends. The truth is, though, he's not who I'm most worried about."

Margo put her water glass down with a snap. "You mean there's somebody worse?"

Jerry nodded, leaned close. "You've met our hard-liners. Wait until you meet theirs."

"Whose?" She saw it. "Fomin's?"

"Sure. You think the hawks on our side are the only ones who want to blow up the negotiations? Khrushchev has hawks of his own. We have some reason to think they've already killed a man. Tortured him, too. His body was fished out of a swamp in Flushing a few weeks ago. Usually the KGB would cut its own throat before it would do violence inside the States. They must be pretty desperate." Another long gulp of cola. "As a matter of fact, if I were Jack Ziegler? I wouldn't go near the Yenching Palace. But I'd make sure that my opposite number in the KGB knew exactly where it was and when Fomin would be there. Let them take care of the problem."

She felt a little faint. "And when you say take care of the problem—"

"I mean, kill you both," he said, and took a big chomp on his burger.

FIFTY

Points of View

I

"I do not like doing violence in a foreign country," said Viktor Vaga-man, adjusting his gold-rimmed spectacles. "I do not like doing violence at all. But there are times when service to the Motherland demands it. Do you understand?"

"Yes," said the stocky man sitting across from him in the window of the small café across Connecticut Avenue from the Yenching Palace.

The killer sipped his coffee. "Ideally, we would do harm only to the traitor Fomin. Others are doing what for them seems normal, even loyal. Fomin is a different matter. He has betrayed our own country."

His associate had an objection. "My impression is that Colonel Fomin is acting under the orders of General Secretary Khrushchev."

"Is that your impression?"

"Yes."

"Then you are a fool." He spoke so quietly that none of the nearby diners could overhear. "The Comrade General Secretary would never be a party to this conspiracy. It was he who approved the operation to place the missiles in Cuba, for the purpose of defending the Mother-land against surprise attack by the war faction."

The stocky man was unpersuaded. "Cooperating with the capital-ists in this fashion is not like Fomin, either. He would not do this with-out authorization."

"Then the authorization does not come from the Comrade General Secretary."

"But—"

"Comrade Fomin has been misled, my friend. If he paid more attention to doctrine and less to what he calls pragmatism, he would realize that no one in the Central Committee would give these orders. His failure to appreciate the extent to which he has been misled is itself the act of a man predisposed to treason. No," he concluded, as if his associate had argued, "we cannot spare him."

"And the girl?"

"We will do what is necessary, of course, to prevent a final deal. But she is fundamentally an American problem."

Had Viktor's associate been more inquiring, he might have asked—later, in the postmortem, he himself was asked, and not gently—how it was possible that Fomin could at the same time be misled about the source of his orders and in a position to make an actual deal. But by that time the purge had become general, and the principal concern among surviving members of the intelligence directorate was saving their own skins.

II

The meeting with Fomin was set for half past six, and she was to proceed to the townhouse immediately after. At a quarter to the hour, she sat with Ainsley in the car, three blocks south of the restaurant and two blocks to the west, so that casual surveillance along Connecticut Avenue wouldn't spot them.

"Are you sure you understand the plan?"

"Yes."

"Tell me."

"I just did."

"Then tell me again."

Margo chanced a glare, but she understood the purpose of his browbeating. If they ever had a margin for error, it had vanished when a friend he called to look in on his apartment reported back that checking was impossible, so tight was the surveillance.

"I wait in the car while you study the area. At six-fifteen, I get out and start walking. If you see anything you don't like, you'll get me out. Otherwise, I meet with Fomin, I leave, I walk four blocks north, and you'll drive past me on the side street to take me to the meeting with Kennedy."

"And?"

"Don't trust anyone who says he or she has been sent for me."

"And?"

This final instruction was the only one hard for her to pronounce. "If anything happens to you, run."

III

Bundy had at last acceded to Bobby Kennedy's repeated demands. He had agreed to put one eye—one only—on Margo. A lone Secret Service agent would be dispatched to the scene. Any more would spook Fomin, but one man alone should be able to remain concealed. He was worried that McCone might have the same idea. Once the Agency had the secret of the back channel, Bundy didn't think it would take much work for their analysts to track down the location of the meetings. And if Hoover, too, were somehow to winkle out what was going on, the neighborhood around the Yenching Palace might be downright crowded tonight.

IV

Jack Ziegler was several miles away from the Yenching Palace. He hated being far from the action, but he also appreciated the wisdom of Viktor's construction. Viktor had diplomatic immunity. Should any violence transpire, Viktor could not even be questioned by the authorities; he could only be confined to his embassy and then deported. Whereas Jack Ziegler—well, he had a larger picture in mind. He had come to realize that preventing GREENHILL's message from getting through wouldn't be enough. He and his associates could not act properly unless they knew the actual content of the message.

He needed GREENHILL herself—her living, breathing body—so that they might have another talk.

Viktor would take care of that.

V

At six-sixteen, Margo stepped out of the car, locked the door, and began her walk. Jerry Ainsley had warned her not to be overcautious. Anybody watching would expect a degree of nervousness, he had explained, so she shouldn't try to hide moderate anxiety. But Fomin had to see her confident and calm, or he would start wondering whether there was something he, too, should be worried about.

A brisk northerly wind smacked her across the face as she turned up Connecticut Avenue. She leaned into it, shortening her stride. She went over both plans in her mind—Bundy's and Ainsley's—and marveled at how many heads she was wearing under her single hat.

At six-twenty-eight, she vanished into the restaurant. Three separate watchers dutifully whispered the fact of her arrival into three walkie-talkies.

Everybody settled down to wait.

FIFTY-ONE

A Question of Evidence

I

"Your President is to be commended for his restraint."

"That restraint may be coming to an end."

Fomin lifted an eyebrow. His plate as usual was heaped with egg rolls, but he barely touched them. "So the war party in your country might be gaining influence?"

She remembered one of Niemeyer's favorite mots: Ideology makes us stupid.

"You shot down a plane. I don't think somebody has to be a reactionary or a fascist to want to shoot back."

"Do you believe, then, that there is no war party in America?"

"I'm not saying that—"

"Good. Because the Comrade General Secretary does not share your somewhat sanguine view. He does not doubt for a moment that they are swiftly becoming ascendant." The dark eyes smoldered. "Nor do I."

"I understand that, but—"

"Miss Jensen. Let me be as clear as I can. If I were to be persuaded that the war party is gaining power over your President—if, for example, they were to interfere successfully with these negotiations—I would advise the Comrade General Secretary to break off the back channel and prepare for war." He made a show of eating, but without enthusiasm. "We stand at the edge of the precipice, Miss Jensen. The path back from the brink is a narrow one. You must deliver the message precisely as I shall relate it."

Margo felt terribly tired. "I always do."

Fomin's face was gray. It took her some minutes to work out that what she was reading there was defeat.

"You may tell your President that the Comrade General Secretary agrees to all of his terms." He picked at his food. "We will remove the offensive weapons from Cuba. We will accept in response his public agreement not to invade Cuba. But there is more." He frowned past her toward the door, but when she turned, she saw no reason for alarm.

"Very well," she said.

"The General Secretary will also require your President's private promise to remove the missiles from Turkey and Italy within a year."

There it was. Fomin had understood the prisoner's dilemma after all. Each side would get a part of what it wanted: Kennedy's public wouldn't know about the deal, yet Khrushchev could trumpet the result to his hard-liners. The exchange relied entirely on trust: Khrushchev would have to believe that Kennedy would keep his word.

Always assuming that Kennedy accepted the deal.

"I will convey the General Secretary's message," she said formally.

"You also asked for evidence that I do indeed speak for the General Secretary." His heavy gaze, ordinarily so intense, were focused on the middle distance. "You may inform your President that the Comrade General Secretary very much enjoyed sitting beside Mrs. Kennedy at dinner on the first night of the summit. You may further inform your President that Mrs. Kennedy on that occasion asked the Comrade General Secretary not to bore her with statistics. We presume that your President will be able to confirm this with Mrs. Kennedy. And that this evidence will be sufficient."

She saw no point in lying. "I have no way to tell, Mr. Fomin. I hope it will be enough."

"You must see to it." Flatly. "And there is something else." She waited. The eyes cut her way again, but carried little of their former fire. "We have worried up until now only about the hotheads on your side. Now, unfortunately, the hotheads on my side also know about the back channel." He managed a smile. "There is even some reason to believe that your hotheads have told my hotheads."

"I can't believe that."

"Why not? If you considered these negotiations to constitute a treacherous surrender, would you not use all measures to end them? Even trying to manipulate your enemy into doing the work for you?"

Now she understood his distraction; or thought she did. She spoke softly, even, to her own surprise, affectionately: "Are you saying you're in danger?"

"No, Miss Jensen." All at once the intensity was back. "I am not the one who is under threat."

II

She left the restaurant and turned north this time, because Ainsley would be waiting on Rodman Street. He had warned her that Bundy might consider it worth the risk to have someone watching her this time. She didn't bother to look around: She knew she'd never spot the surveillance. The night was growing colder. She walked faster than usual, knowing how urgent the message was. This was it: the end of the negotiation. True, the President had assured her on Friday that the crisis was over, and had been wrong. But this time felt different. The choice was there to be made. Either Kennedy would accept that he really was negotiating with Khrushchev, or tomorrow the world would go to war. Margo wondered whether she should have accepted Major Madison's offer to get her safely to Ohio; or if, even now, she should be searching for a way to reach Garrison. But another part of her— a secret, proud, ambitious self, so deep inside that she sometimes forgot it was there—wondered, if she succeeded, what her future might be like. The one thing she was sure of was that Donald Jensen would be proud of his daughter for trying.

Bright with this calming thought, she strode purposefully up the avenue. Had she been less distracted, she might have noticed the two men in long coats who had emerged from the bar two doors up from the restaurant and fallen into step a dozen paces behind her. But she heard the shriek—no question about that—the sudden wail of a woman who happened to be passing by and saw the men pull their guns.

Margo spun around.

And everything happened very fast.

III

There were gunshots, several of them. Later, she could not quite get the sequence right. A couple were muffled spits, two or three others were loud booms, another made a sound like a firecracker. But in her head it all registered afterward in a series of bright flashes of disordered memory:

The woman who had shrieked, lying bloody on the sidewalk.

Jericho Ainsley, looming over a car, pointing his gun directly at Margo, yelling words she couldn't make out.

Aleks Fomin, standing half a block away, just outside the restaurant, also yelling, but at something across the street.

Warren, her Secret Service driver, materializing from somewhere, gun in hand, grabbing for her arm, then stumbling, holding his chest.

The Cornell alum who'd snapped her picture, tonight sans funny hat and camera, shoving a protesting Fomin back inside the restaurant.

The man with gold-rimmed glasses beckoning from a taxi, urging her to join him.

Ainsley's gun still tracking her as she crouched and moved.

Margo herself, darting between parked cars.

Ainsley shouting: "Margo, no! It's okay!"

The man with the gold-rimmed glasses, shaking his head, shouting at her not to listen, tugging at her sleeve. "He's one of them!"

The taxi driver drawing a shotgun from somewhere, pointing it in Ainsley's direction, firing off a round as the CIA man ducked behind a car.

The other man shoving the gun down.

Then all at once her mind was working again, and she knew it was time to move.

"Bundy sent me!" Gold Rims yelled. "We have to get you out of here!" And that was almost enough to get her to join him, but Harrington had warned her a million years ago to trust nobody in an emergency, and nobody was whom she decided to trust.

Nobody except Warren, who had taken a bullet aimed her way. She longed to go to him, but couldn't. At a fitter moment, she would mourn him.

She ducked away from the man in the taxi and darted toward the shadows.

"Margo, stop!" shouted Ainsley, somewhere behind her.

Another round of gunshots.

She stayed low, moving along the line of cars. There were sirens in the distance, and she was betting that Ainsley couldn't stay long. She was right. He lifted his head at the sharp wail of approaching sirens, took a last look in the direction she had run, then melted into the darkness.

Margo waited, but he didn't reappear.

There were onlookers now, pointing and chattering and trying to decide whether to cover the body. She joined them, as wide-eyed and trembling as anyone in the group, but kept shuffling backward as the crowd grew. When the police began to move everyone away, she was already across the street, walking south. Ainsley would be waiting to the north, on Rodman Street, but just now her trust was exhausted. Though Margo needed help getting Fomin's message to the President, there was no way she was getting into a car with a man who had just pointed a gun her way. Not until she knew who was trying to kill her.

She picked up the pace.

FIFTY-TWO

The Crisis Behind the Crisis

I

"She could be dead," said Bobby Kennedy. "She could be in the wrong hands."

The President stood behind the desk, staring out into the Rose Garden. He was bent slightly at the waist, one hand pressed against the window as he fought the pain, a posture he would never have adopted in public. Not all of the pain was physical. After the shootout in front of the restaurant, Margo had disappeared. The President had waited at the townhouse for an hour, in vain.

"Let's not jump to conclusions," he said. "She was scared. She could be hiding."

The attorney general cut in eagerly, like a bully at a dance. "Hiding from whom? Who exactly do you think was out there shooting tonight? The Mafia?" He had chosen the silent Bundy as the object of his ire. "What's that look mean? You don't think the fire-breathers at the Pentagon are furious that we haven't done anything about the U-2 being shot down? You don't think a man like LeMay would do whatever he could to undermine our negotiations?" He turned to his brother. "The way he talks to you, Jack? It's inexcusable. You should cashier him. Right now. Today."

"Now, let's slow down a minute," said Bundy, careful to address himself to Bobby. "You may not like Curtis LeMay's style. He's rough and unfinished, compared to a lot of the people we deal with. But he built the Strategic Air Command pretty much single-handed. When he took over SAC in 1948, it was the poor stepchild of the Air Force. A couple of dozen obsolete, worn-out bombers, and not even a base to call its own. When he left nine years later, he'd turned it into the mightiest airborne armada on the face of the earth. Something like six hundred B-52s, along with hundreds more support aircraft. Those bombers of ours that are orbiting at their 'go' points right now, scaring the willies out of Moscow? The others that will take their places when fuel runs low? We have those planes because of General LeMay. You may not like his style, Bobby. He may have a habit of saying what he thinks when everybody else is diplomatic or even just lies about what they're thinking because your brother's the President. But don't mistake bluntness for disloyalty. And try to remember that what LeMay says, whether you like it or not, is going to represent the views of a lot of people around the table and out in the country. You may not like it, but you have to hear it."

The Kennedy brothers were staring in astonishment. "Listen, Mac," the attorney general began.

"Let me finish, please. I'm not given to a lot of long speeches, so let me be clear about this. General LeMay may not be the friendliest or most respectful man you'll meet. His politics are to the right of Genghis Khan. But we have to be realists. He possesses considerable gifts as a strategic thinker. His men revere him. He helped organize the Berlin airlift in 1948. He wanted to fight, but when Washington said no, he did as he was told. Whatever else Curtis LeMay may be, he's a good soldier and a thorough patriot. I can't imagine any circumstances in which he would turn against his commander in chief. And that matters. We're almost at war. If the balloon does go up, LeMay is the man you want running the Air Force."

The national security adviser waited, but there was no response. The Kennedys were actually chastened, which was what he wanted. Bruised egos were irrelevant. No doubt LeMay in time would be made to pay a price for his rudeness, but not now. They had to focus on the matter at hand.

"Mr. President, we face the deadline of noon tomorrow." Bundy lifted a palm like a conjurer. "You have promised the ExComm that we will begin military action at that time unless we have a deal."

The President had moved to his rocker. His face was a mask of distress, but he said nothing.

"We need Khrushchev's answer," the attorney general pointed out. "Until we have an answer, we don't know if we have a deal or not. We don't know if Fomin is really in touch with Khrushchev or not."

"Yes, sir. The trouble is, without GREENHILL, we can't get the answer."

The President brightened. "Fine. We'll just send someone else."

"No, sir. We really can't do that."

Bobby took up the refrain. "Why not? GREENHILL is just an intermediary. Fomin is just an intermediary. The messages are being carried between the President and Khrushchev. What difference does it really make who carries them?"

Bundy recognized the frustration in Bobby's voice, and knew he had to avoid sounding too professorial. The Kennedys were an impetuous clan, not thin-skinned, precisely, but quick to detect condescension. He addressed himself to the older brother.

"Mr. President, with respect, we have discussed this before. Aleksandr Fomin is a suspicious man. He went to a lot of trouble to establish that he could trust GREENHILL. If we send in someone else, we'll make things worse. Remember, he has already delivered Khrushchev's reply to our demand for clarification. Now we will be asking him to deliver it again. He'll wonder why. Remember, he was there. He knows there was shooting. If he learns that we've lost track of his chosen conduit, he will assume the worst. That assumption in turn will persuade him that we're unreliable. He will tell Khrushchev not to trust us, and Khrushchev will retreat behind the above-the-line negotiations, and we won't be able to get him back to the table by noon tomorrow. In short, if we put in a substitute, there's going to be war."

The attorney general had a suggestion. "So let's not tell him the real reason. We tell him GREENHILL is sick or had an accident or something."

"With respect, Bobby, Khrushchev survived Stalin and Beria. This was an era when getting sick or having an accident meant disgrace or arrest or worse. There is no lie we can tell that he will believe. Now, we're hiding the fact that a Secret Service agent was on the scene and got shot. Fomin will accept that sort of concealment. But the matter of the conduit stands on a different footing. Either we produce GREENHILL or we tell Taylor and LeMay to get ready."

"Then what do we do?" asked Bobby.

"We find her," said the national security adviser. "Fast."

The President's rocker had nearly stopped. "How do we do that, Mac? Without using federal agencies? What do you advise?"

"And there's another problem," said the attorney general. "The way that you describe her current state of mind, even if we can track her down, she might not trust whoever we send. She'll run a mile."

Behind the round lenses, Bundy's eyes were calm. "I believe that I may have just the individual for the job."

II

"You were on the scene," said Jack Ziegler. "How could you let this happen?"

"There were complications."

"You mean, like shooting a federal agent."

Viktor hesitated. Even the capitalists, with all of their stolen wealth, could not possibly tap every telephone in the city. He was in a booth, five blocks north of the Yenching Palace. Ziegler was in another booth, miles away.

"That was not intentional," the Russian finally said.

"How about letting GREENHILL get away? Was that intentional?"

"Perhaps she will not deliver the message. Perhaps we have frightened her off."

Ziegler did not laugh exactly. The sound he made was more like biting on tinfoil. "You've been watching her for a week. Does she strike you as the sort of girl who gets frightened off?"

"Everyone has a breaking point."

"Not this girl. She's in this for her father. Okay? This is her tribute to him. Finishing his work. She isn't going to stop."

"Then she is to be admired. But her motive makes no difference. There are not many places where she can go. We will cover the most likely."

"No." The American's voice was sharp. "We'll take it from here."

"I think not."

"What's that supposed to mean?"

"You requested our assistance. We have rendered it. But we do not take orders from you."

"Don't interfere, Viktor Borisovich. You don't want to get in my way."

"Nor you in mine."

The man in the gold-rimmed glasses hung up the phone and hurried to the waiting taxi. "Send people to site one and site two. Tell them to watch out for Americans. You and I will cover site three."

As the cab turned left and raced across Rock Creek Park, Viktor gave himself over to his thoughts. Ziegler was not merely uncultured. He was a barbarian, and, worse, drunk with power. He actually wanted to kill the young woman, when all that was necessary was to detain her long enough to prevent her from delivering her last message. But it was obvious, too, that his faction and Jack Ziegler's no longer possessed the common interest that had bound them for the past month. Viktor wanted to stop the back-channel negotiations because of the strategic importance of Operation Anadyr. If the General Secretary showed fortitude, he believed, the Americans and their weak President would back down from the final confrontation. And once the Cuban missiles were operational, able to reach Washington in mere minutes, the time when the capitalists could dictate terms would come crashing to its end, once and for all.

Whereas Ziegler, it was becoming clear, had a very different motive. He actually wanted a war, a nuclear war, preferring to fight now, when he thought his country would prevail. That such a man had been his partner in this enterprise chilled his soul.

"Drive faster," he commanded.

FIFTY-THREE

The Night Visitor

I

Later, Miles Madison would tell investigators that it was only the sheerest luck that he was home that night. Until recently, he had pulled the three-to-eleven shift in the Pod two weeks out of every three, and Sunday, October 28, fell smack in the middle of his fortnight. But with the nation's military now at DEFCON 2, the Pod personnel were doubled, and he had been moved to eleven-to-seven. So, when the doorbell rang at a quarter past nine, he was at home, dressing for his shift, rather than bunkered in a Pentagon subbasement, manning three teleprinters and six telephones. He was not expecting any visitors at this hour, but he had learned long ago not to allow his expectations to limit his perceptions. When he opened the door and found a trembling and disheveled Margo Jensen on the front step, he didn't waste time with silly questions. He swept her inside with one heavy hand, even as his gaze raked the street for danger.

Why did you let her in? asked the investigators.

"I'm a Marine. We help people."

But couldn't you see she was on the run?

"All I knew was, she was scared. She was the granddaughter of a dear friend, and I was supposed to be watching out for her, and she was frightened out of her wits."

So what did you do?

"I let her in. Sat her down. Made her a cup of coffee."

And did you call the police?

"I didn't call anybody. Not at first. I wanted to hear her story."

II

Doris Harrington was at her front window, watching the blue car across the street. It had pulled up ten minutes ago, and the driver was still behind the wheel. One of ours or one of theirs? she wondered, not at all facetiously, because the lessons of Vienna were never far away. If she had learned anything in her months behind enemy lines, it was that everybody belonged to somebody. She had just decided to open the safe and take out her gun when the telephone rang.

"Dr. Harrington?"

"Yes?"

"It's Mac Bundy. We have a small problem. I was hoping you could come down and give us a little help."

"What kind of problem, Mr. Bundy?"

"I'd rather not say over an open line."

She parted the curtain again. "Does this blue car belong to you?"

"Yes. The driver's name is Parke, with an 'e.' He'll knock in five minutes. Can you be ready?"

She looked down at her housecoat. "I'll be ready," she said.

"Thank you, Doctor. See you shortly."

In the event, he was kind enough to give her ten minutes. The knock came as she was fixing her makeup. The man at the door looked sheepish. He was tall and blond, and his nose looked as if it had once been broken, and had a bad mend. "Sorry to call you out so late, ma'am. But it's the White House."

"I understand, Mr. . . . ?"

"Parke, ma'am. With the 'e' at the end."

III

"That's quite a story, Margo."

"I'm not making it up."

The Major was trimming his cigar with a shiny gold cutter. "I didn't say you were. As a matter of fact, most of it makes sense. The factions, all that. I was on the Joint Staff. I know all about the infighting, the jealousy, the way good men chafe at taking orders from civilians who don't know the first thing about what we do."

He held the cigar in front of his nose, rolled it back and forth. Margo said nothing. She sensed that Miles Madison had a point to make.

"I'm retiring in a couple of years. I don't suppose your grandmother told you. I'll be a lieutenant colonel by then. Haven't decided if I'm going to try to make full bird. Anyway, when I've put in my twenty, a couple of partners and I are going into real-estate investing. Here and down in Florida." Still he wasn't satisfied with the cigar. He was using a slim metal tool with a perpendicular wooden handle to unplug the middle. "But the plan won't work if Washington is blown to smithereens. And Florida—well, the Reds would have pretty much the whole state on their target list. Not because of Cuba. Because we have so many bases and ports and harbors down there." His tone grew somber. "My point is, Margo, I have as much to lose as anybody. I don't want this war. Nobody I know in the military wants it. It's never the military who rattles America's sabers. It's the civilians who run the place. Have you noticed that?"

"I don't know. I guess so."

Another long draw on the cigar.

"And as for the spies—well, I'm in 7th Comm, as you know. I've been handling communications for a lot of their people for years. In Europe and Asia in the fifties. Here. A lot of the Agency people are a little crazy, and most of their schemes are half nuts. More than half. Like sending some college kid to Varna. Still. They're not bad people."

Margo wasn't sure which of them he was trying to persuade. "Somebody shot at me tonight," she said.

Still Miles Madison worked on his cigar, now brushing the leaves with some sort of steel comb. "But you don't actually know that. In combat, you can't always tell who's shooting at whom." He waved away her objection. "I know. I know. And a Secret Service agent got shot, except it's not on the news, because they're hushing it up, right?" His laugh was hearty, but, to her ear, a little forced. "Look. Let's say I believe you. My best advice is to get in touch with the people who recruited you. You must have emergency codes and so on."

"I can't use them." Margo studied the brown rug, its complex pattern marred by dozens of burnt spots from fallen ash. "There's a leak somewhere."

He hunched forward, put the unlit cigar in the obsidian tray, made a bucket of his large hands. "Then what exactly do you want me to do? Hide you? The wife and girls are in Cincinnati. My offer to send you to join them still stands, but you'll have trouble now getting a seat. All the trains and buses out of Washington are booked solid. I might be able to get you on one of the shuttles the military's running for families, but I suspect you won't want to risk official transport. Of course, you can always go back to your grandmother's house, but you'll have the same problem getting there."

"I don't want to run away, Major Madison. That's not why I'm asking for your help."

Satisfied at last, he struck a long match and lit the cigar. "Then why?"

"You used to work in the White House Signals Office."

"So?"

"So . . . I was hoping you could get me in."

"Into where?"

"The White House."

IV

Miles Madison laughed. "You don't want much, do you?"

Margo was long past embarrassment. "I have a message for the President," she said tartly. "The White House is where he lives."

The sharp eyes were still merry. He was puffing regularly on the cigar now. "You know, Margo, a few years ago, I was stationed in—it doesn't matter where I was stationed. Somewhere in Europe. I was deputy military attaché at one of our embassies. Part of my job was transmitting secure messages. We had a spy out there—an agent, a foreign national—and he had information for us. He only trusted his control. Nobody else. The trouble was, his control got captured. We traded for him later. The point is, our agent didn't dare come by the embassy. He wasn't sure which of us he could trust. So—you know how he got the message in?"

She didn't.

"He chalked it on the building across the street. Just a couple of code words. He figured that everybody would see them, so if there was a traitor in the embassy, he wouldn't be able to stop a bunch of people from sending urgent telexes to Washington to find out if any-body knew what the words meant. And that's exactly what happened. It took a little longer, but the message wound up in the right hands."

Margo was tempted. The story was warm and reassuring, and even made her feel safe. She could write the message somewhere and flee to Garrison and Nana; or Ithaca and Tom. Only—

"It wouldn't work," she said. "I can't take the chance that the message doesn't get through. I don't know how Ziegler and his friends found out about what I'm doing. That means I don't know whom I can trust. Even in the White House. I have to give the message to the President in person. That's the only way to be sure it gets where it's supposed to go." She rubbed her eyes. She had been so happy. "And it's not just that. The President told me there's a deadline."

The major's voice went dry. "I do military communications, Margo. I transmit the orders. I know about the deadline."

"Then you know I only have until two p.m. to get the message to the President."

"Actually, you only have until noon. They moved it up." Again he was examining his cigar. "Margo, look. I admire your dedication. But I can't get you into the White House. I don't have the contacts to do that. Those Signals Office rotations are very short. It's not like you meet a lot of people." He lifted a powerful finger to forestall her objection. "But I'll tell you what I can do. I have a friend in military intelligence. Name of Tillmon. I trust him, Margo. He'll have better contacts than I do, and he'll figure something out." He had pulled a small spiral notebook from his desk and was flipping pages. "He's even stationed at Langley just now."

"I don't trust the CIA."

"I'm not asking you to. Tillmon isn't Agency. He's military. He's assigned to Langley for an eighteen-month rotation. He told me about some very odd goings-on over there: a tiny group of people inside the Agency trying to run their own foreign policy. He didn't like the idea much. He didn't give me any names—he wasn't ready for that, he said—but he was planning to ask some questions." He saw her expression. "He's a good man, Margo. He might refuse to help, but once he knows who's after you, he won't turn you in. Anyway, there's no harm in getting him over here and having a talk. I'll call him."

"What if his phone's tapped?"

"Or mine. Right. It doesn't matter. Our friendship is on the record. Relax. Read a book. Watch television. I'll be back in a bit."

The Major vanished on those silent feet, heading for another part of the house.

Margo let her head sag backward until it rested atop the cushion. She studied the plaster ceiling, following a faint crack along its jagged path outward from the light fixture until it vanished beneath the dentil molding. She was deathly tired, but another part of her feared she would never sleep again. Nothing could prepare you for being shot at. Nothing. Miles Madison's self-assurance, his easy command of the situation, had calmed her, even made her believe that she might be able to deliver Khrushchev's reply after all—although, twenty-four hours ago, she had felt the same way about Jericho Ainsley. Nevertheless, she had to succeed. Had to. The fact that people were trying so hard to stop her only increased her determination not to let them win. Any more than her father would have—

Margo's eyes snapped open.

A footfall told her that the Major had returned. She looked up expectantly, then went very still.

"What is it? What's wrong? Did you reach your friend?" But the ashen face told her all she needed to know. "Something happened."

"I didn't reach him. I couldn't." The lively voice was flat. "Tillmon was shot and killed in a holdup this afternoon. He's dead."

FIFTY-FOUR

The Kitchen

I

Margo felt her already slim range of options narrowing further. While she was still trying to decide what to say, Major Madison was planning.

"I've been ordered to talk to an investigative team from the Office of Naval Intelligence before my duty shift begins at eleven. It's quarter of ten. To make the Pentagon by ten-thirty, I have to be on the road in fifteen minutes. If I'm late, they'll want to know why. I won't tell them you've been here, but if I'm late, they'll guess."

"You don't have to do that for me—"

"So this is what we're going to do." He was standing near the desk, turning a snow globe over and over in his hands. Inside, white powder flurried across a Christmas scene. "Sooner or later, whoever is looking for you will get to this point in the list. So you have to get moving. I can drop you wherever you have to go. Then we can rejoin when I get off duty at seven and figure out how to get you into the White—"

"No. That's not a good idea."

"The deadline isn't until noon. We'll have plenty of time, I promise you."

"I meant, no, I don't think you should do any more for me." She was already on her feet, reaching for her coat. "This changes everything."

"It doesn't change anything, Margo. The bastards killed my friend. All the more reason for me to help. What's that look mean? You're worried it's dangerous? I'm a Marine, honey."

"You have a family."

"Vera understands what it means to be the wife of a Marine officer. If anything ever happens to me, she'll know how to carry on."

"It's not you I was thinking of. It's them. Mrs. Madison. Kimberly. Marilyn. They're not volunteers, Major. They're bystanders. And these people—I don't think they'd hesitate."

"Even so—"

"I couldn't carry that on my conscience," she said softly. "I don't think you could, either."

Margo could almost hear his teeth grinding. His hand squeezed the snow globe so hard she feared it might shatter. For a full minute he stood there, mouth working wordlessly. Then the powerful shoulders slumped. "I see your point. Okay. Look. There are still a couple of things I can do for you. Number one, I won't tell the folks from ONI you've been here. Number two, at least let me get you safely to wherever you're going next."

Margo was touched; and, in her neediness, tempted; but she knew she had to be firm.

"I don't think that's a good idea," she said. "It's very kind of you, but I think it's best if you have no knowledge of where I'm heading." A flash of her former wit, before he could contradict her: "I think I'd be grateful, though, if you'd drive me halfway."

In the car, he had one last question for her: "I don't mean to offend you, but are you armed?"

"Of course not," Margo answered, even as her fingers touched the steel of Ainsley's gun in her purse.

II

"Any luck?" asked Bundy. He stood in the door to his office, a stack of files under his arm, on his way up to see the President.

Janet shook her head. "I'm sorry, Mr. Bundy. There's no answer at Dr. Harrington's home. Signals says Perry Parke isn't picking up the car radio, either." She hesitated. "They say he could just be in an area with bad reception, sir."

"I'm sure that's it."

Bundy took the elevator this time. Two other staffers were aboard, so he kept his face placid. But inside he was aching. Parke wasn't an agent. He was just about the junior-most of Bundy's own national security staff, and happened to be spare when somebody was needed to bring Harrington in. It had never occurred to McGeorge Bundy that the task might present the smallest danger.

III

She had Major Madison drop her on the campus of George Washington University, near Foggy Bottom, and she walked slowly south until his taillights vanished in the mist. Then she spun around and hurried up to Pennsylvania Avenue. Fortunately, the D.C. Transit bus was just trundling along. She flagged it down, paid her dime, and rode into Georgetown, where she disembarked next to the stately columns of the Riggs National Bank. She remembered Harrington telling her about the ten thousand dollars, payment for Varna, on deposit at the Riggs branch a block from the White House, to be hers upon her twenty-first birthday. She wondered whether she would ever have the chance to spend it.

Remembering the dream, Margo lifted her eyes involuntarily to the sky. There was only a gauzy moon, sallow and distant.

Harrington. She was down to Dr. Harrington. Somehow she had always known that it would come to this. Approaching the house was bound to be tricky, because the White House, as well as Ziegler's people and whoever the man in the gold-rimmed glasses might have been, would all be expecting her to turn up there.

On the other hand, she had very little time.

From Miles Madison, Margo had borrowed a hooded raincoat and a cane. The house was on the north side of P Street. She passed on the south side, leaning hard on the cane, never slowing, her head tucked so far down into the coat that in this fog nobody could notice at a glance whether she was even black or white. Lights were on in the first-floor windows. No way to tell whether she was home. Margo catalogued the blue sedan across the street, and the driver with his head cleverly down on the dashboard, as if asleep. Farther down the block, she passed a battered van that she supposed could have been stuffed full of fancy surveillance equipment. But there was nobody in the cab, and she wondered.

On her second pass, she studied the van again, how empty and silent it sat. When she drew abreast of the blue car, she noticed that the driver hadn't stirred.

The wind freshened and a tree groaned loudly, and still he made no move. Margo shivered, but not from the cold.

Caution aside.

She leaned close to the blue car, peered inside, saw the impossible angle of his neck, and had to fight not to throw up.

A second later, no longer caring if anyone saw her, she was pelting across the street, pounding on the door—

And finding it ajar.

Inside were signs of the struggle. Broken glass. A vase that must have been thrown. Blood in the foyer and in the living room.

And Harrington in the kitchen.

Hands bound.

Beside her, a small sharp knife with a wooden handle. There was a lot of blood.

This time, Margo did throw up, loud and hard, not quite making it to the sink.

When, after an eternity, she managed to straighten up, she cried out. She was not alone in the kitchen. Through her tears, she caught the unbothered stare of Agatha Milner, her minder from Bulgaria, the girl who had intimidated all the boys at training camp and scared to death all the operatives they met in Europe.

"I knew you'd come," said Agatha. She still wore the schoolmarmish bun, but without the thick glasses. She was dressed in jeans and a dark sweater and tennis shoes. Despite the cast on her right wrist, she looked every inch exactly what Jerry Ainsley had said she was.

She kills with her bare hands, Margo. She's very good at it.

Just now, thinking of the men outside and trying not to look down at the body of Doris Harrington, Margo harbored no doubts at all.

FIFTY-FIVE

Negotiations

I

They were face-to-face again at last. Margo had been begging for information about Agatha's fate since the night they were separated in Varna. Now they stood on opposite sides of the butcher-block counter, circling like wary pugilists, although Margo knew perfectly well that Agatha could kill her in half a second. That's why, even as they backed and shuffled, the counter always between them, a part of her concentration was on the gun in her purse, and the rest was on knives, frying pans, anything that could be wielded or thrown.

"Don't be afraid," said Agatha. "I'm here to bring you in."

But Margo said nothing. She was staring, fascinated, at Agatha's strong hands, the way she held those fingers half curled. She forced herself not to stare at what lay on the floor.

"This wasn't me," the older woman continued. "I got here a few minutes before you did. I found her like this." A stifled sound. Her face was very red. "I loved her more than you did, Margo."

Still Margo stayed silent. There was the door to the foyer, and there was the door to the yard, and she wondered whether she would have time to make either.

"I'm sure Jerry Ainsley told you lots of things about me," Agatha said. "And maybe some of them are even true. But believe this, Margo. I'm not your enemy. They sent me to look for you. They figured I'd know your habits best."

"How did you find me?"

"I staked out a couple of places you were likely go to. This was one of them. A lot of it was luck, Margo."

"Bring me in where?"

"My orders are to deliver you to a townhouse on East Capitol Street. I'm told you know where it is."

Margo had chosen where to make her stand. She slowed to a halt. Behind her was the arch leading to the foyer. She could make a break, pulling the Beretta on the way, and run through the front door, which was conveniently open. The cast would surely slow Agatha down.

"Suppose I don't believe you."

"I bring you in anyway." Agatha's eyes flicked to the purse, then back to Margo, as if to say she knew the plan. Agatha herself was displaying no weapon of any kind, but that meant nothing. "We don't have a lot of time. They'll be here soon."

"Who will?"

"A lot of people. The dead man in the blue car and the dead men in the back of the van played for different teams. Both teams will send people to find out why their watchers aren't reporting in."

"How do you know they're not together?"

"Because," Agatha began—

And Margo was gone, flying down the hall, gun in hand, heading for the foyer and the relative safety of the foggy street beyond.

But only in her mind.

Because no sooner did she start her turn than Agatha somehow was around the counter and sitting atop her, holding both her wrists easily with her one good hand. The gun had disappeared.

"Will you please just listen now? I said I'm here to help you, and I am." She leaned close. "Whatever you might believe about me, you know I'd never hurt Dr. Harrington."

"You would if you were ordered to!"

"Possibly. I don't know. But not like that. Not like what they did to her."

"Does it matter what I say?" Margo gasped, because the pressure of the smaller woman's knees was getting to be a problem.

"Not really. You're coming with me, one way or the other. Conscious is easier, but we can do it the hard way if you insist."

In the car, Margo had a question. "Would you really have knocked me unconscious?"

Agatha took her time answering. "Understand something. This isn't about you. And it isn't about the missiles. Not for me."

"Then what's it about?"

The onetime minder said nothing. She continued to steer smoothly along dark, empty avenues with her good hand. But Margo saw the pain in the bland schoolmarm face, and knew.

II

Jericho Ainsley was crouching in the shadows on the second-floor fire escape of a flophouse on V Street not far from Florida Avenue. The city had worse neighborhoods, but this wasn't one of the better ones. And, unlike many of the whiter parts of town, this one seemed not to have received the crisis memo, for although it was almost midnight, there was a considerable boister on the sidewalks below.

But Ainsley's focus was on the decrepit brownstone across the way.

After Margo's disappearance, he had followed the man in the gold-rimmed glasses, who had spoken to another man, who had led him here. Jerry didn't know all the players in the game, but he did know that whoever was represented by the man who'd tried to get Margo into the taxi was very well organized indeed. Though he had been at the brownstone only a few minutes, he had already counted three different men and one woman departing in two separate cars, presumably to monitor sites where GREENHILL might show up.

There couldn't be many left in the house: possibly just two or three. In any event, he needed a closer reconnaissance.

Ainsley wasn't in the hard end of the business. He'd had the courses in hand-to-hand combat and small arms, of course, but his scores had been only adequate. Still, although he might not be an Agatha Milner or a Jack Ziegler, he knew how to take care of himself.

He began the climb down.

III

Bundy stood with the attorney general on the portico outside the Oval Office. The Rose Garden greenery was dewy in the night mist.

"Nothing," Bobby said, arms folded as he stifled his anger. "We even brought in Hoover, and he's got nothing for us. No idea."

"She'll surface," said Bundy. He stifled a yawn. The President was taking a much-needed catnap, but Bundy had no time for rest. "She'll make contact."

"We don't even know if she's alive."

"Don't be melodramatic."

"I'm serious, Mac. Whoever is out there trying to stop her, they're some very serious people. Are they out of their minds?"

Bundy hid a frown. Emotion was not conducive to rational thinking. Besides, if either one of them was to be upset, it should be Bundy himself, for it was he who had persuaded the head of the presidential detail to send GREENHILL's embarrassed driver to report whether she had successfully made the rendezvous with Fomin. The idea was simply to observe; nobody had imagined that the man might be walking into a trap. But Bundy managed to put that guilt aside; now he needed Bobby Kennedy to put his own fury aside.

"Presumably, they're the same people who waylaid her last night," said Bundy. "They failed to do whatever they were trying to get her to do—to persuade her to stop, one imagines—and so they're trying again. The violence this time is a mark of their desperation. It teaches us that they think they're losing."

The attorney general was unimpressed. "That's awfully clinical of you, Mac."

"Is it? Perhaps. What I'm trying to say is, they're desperate. Desperate men make mistakes. With Hoover in the hunt now, they'll be more desperate. They're on the run, Bobby. Don't worry. Whoever they are, they're done."

"And GREENHILL?"

"She's resourceful," said Bundy. "She'll get us Fomin's message."

"I'll believe it when I see it."

An aide came along the walkway and whispered to the attorney general. When Bobby turned around, his chalky expression made Bundy's blood run cold.

"Is it GREENHILL?"

"It's Dr. Harrington. She's dead, Mac. So is the aide you sent to bring her to the White House. Now do you see what I mean?"

IV

The brownstone abutted another building on one side. On the other was an alley, and it was the alley Jerry Ainsley selected. He stumbled noisily, walking slowly and circuitously, wanting to be taken for drunk. But nobody seemed to be on guard duty.

From the alley he had his choice of three basement windows and four on the main floor. The basement was dark. The main-floor windows were curtained, but along the edges were cracks of light.

Caution to the winds.

He got up on his toes and peered through the first window. Two men were smoking and drinking and playing cards. A shotgun leaned against the wall. The next window gave on a small room with maps on the walls. A man sat wearing earphones, tuning a wireless. Last of all was the empty kitchen—

"Hey! What are you doing?"

He swung around. A heavy-fisted man was rushing toward him. Ainsley saw at once that he could never best him in a fair fight. So he allowed himself to fall to his knees, muttering nonsense syllables, and when the guard grabbed his collar to yank him to his feet, Ainsley hit him hard in the groin and, as he doubled over, harder in the chin.

The guard folded up, but his twitching fingers tried to get to his gun. Ainsley stamped hard on his hand. He grabbed the gun, then slid the guard's wallet from his pocket and raced away, leaving him for his friends to find. Let them guess whether he'd tangled with a fellow professional or just been mugged and robbed.

Several blocks away, he stopped and opened the wallet. The man was a State Department diplomatic security officer, but somehow Ainsley suspected that he wasn't guarding a consulate.

Jerry threw the gun down a sewer but kept the wallet. He was searching for a phone booth. As he had told Margo, he believed in making friends everywhere. It was time to call one in particular.

V

"Tell me what happened," said Margo. They were passing the White House, and she wondered what would happen if she hopped out and went to the front gate and asked to see the President.

"Does that mean you've decided to believe me?"

"I guess so. But I believed Jerry Ainsley, too, and he tried to kill me. What's so funny?"

"The idea that Jerry Ainsley would try to kill you."

"Why? Because he's such a nice guy?"

"Because he knows as much about killing as I know about differential calculus. Nobody who wanted you dead would go to a guy like him. He's more a thinker than a doer. That's not a bad thing," she added hastily. "It's just that he doesn't have the right set of skills."

Margo looked at her. "And you do? Is that why they sent you after me?"

"I was told that it's because I spent all that time with you. I'd know your habits, guess where you'd show up."

"Told by whom?"

"Chain of command."

That seemed wrong. Bundy had said the operation was limited to a handful of people. The chain of command sounded dangerously official.

"Who exactly—"

But Agatha was on to the next topic. "Did you see the knife?"

"I—yes." Shudder.

"It's an unusual knife. It's Finnish. Known as a puukko. It's the basic model for the fancier Soviet combat knife, the NR-40. You don't see many puukkos these days, especially not on this side of the ocean." A hard swallow. "That knife is the trademark of a Soviet assassin who uses the cover name Viktor Vaganian. We don't know his real name. The point is, nobody else in the trade uses a puukko. The Soviets killed Dr. Harrington."

Margo remembered Fomin's warning about the war party on his side. But, even granting their existence . . .

"Why?" she asked. "What would they want with Dr. Harrington?"

"I'm not sure. Bulgaria was her operation. Maybe they wanted to know who else was in on it." She made a hard turn, rocking Margo against the door. "Maybe they thought she knew who was working with Smyslov. She didn't, but that wouldn't stop them asking. And asking."

A thick unhealthy silence fell in the car.

"Dr. Harrington knew the risks of the business," Agatha finally said, but it wasn't clear which of them she was trying to persuade.

Margo's analytical half was troubled. "Does this sort of thing happen often? Soviet agents killing our people right here at home?"

"Not often." Agatha's forehead creased in thought, and for just an instant she was the librarian again. "Not ever, that I can remember, as a matter of fact. They must be desperate."

"Or you're wrong."

"I know a puukko when I see one," said the minder, her voice warm with warning.

But Margo wasn't ready to give up. "It still doesn't make any sense. If Dr. Harrington was in it from the start, then why would she——"

"Get down," said Agatha, casually, and turned the wheel sharply to the right. The car skidded, the rear end flailing wildly, and then they were headed in the other direction, the onetime minder driving hard.

"What——"

"I said stay down!"

But Margo put her head up all the same. The car jolted to a stop. She looked around. They were on the Mall, near the red towers of the Arts and Industries Building. There was a car ahead of them and another behind. Escape was blocked. Men were fanning out from the vehicles, guns trained.

"What is it?" asked Margo. "What is this?"

"I don't know," Agatha admitted. "But I think we should get out."

FIFTY-SIX

More Negotiations

I

Margo stood beside the car, still wearing the gown beneath her coat. Agatha was a few feet in front, as if she meant to place her body between her charge and the danger. There were three men, and they stood well clear of each other, so as to leave clear lines of fire. Two of the newcomers were inching forward. A tall blond man with a crooked nose seemed to be in charge.

"Stop, please," he said. His voice was a low-pitched whisper.

"We're not moving," said Agatha.

"I wasn't talking to you." To the others: "I said stop. Be careful."

One of the men had a thick black beard. "It's just a couple of girls, Kevin."

The blond man's voice was soft. "Maybe so, but one of them is Agatha Milner."

The other two men turned toward her in astonishment, and the one who was closer took a hasty step back.

"*The* Agatha Milner?" said the bearded man. "Seriously?"

"I thought she'd be taller," said his companion.

"Seriously," said the man called Kevin. "And I believe that, even with that arm, she could take both of you in about ten seconds. Keep the gun on her, but don't go near her."

"What exactly is this?" said Agatha.

Kevin had a cruel smile. "You don't remember me, do you?"

"I remember you."

"Then you remember you're the reason I was kicked out of the Agency."

"You were never in the Agency, Kevin. I'm the reason you were kicked out of training camp."

One of the other men snickered. Kevin's hand twitched, but his smile never faltered. "Well, that's water under the bridge. My understanding is that we're on the same team now." He nodded toward Margo. "We're taking GREENHILL off your hands. She's not your problem any more."

"My instructions are to deliver her—"

"To the townhouse. We know. New orders. We'll take care of all that."

"Why the change?"

"Maybe you haven't kept up with the news, Agatha. All of a sudden there are a lot of dead bodies lying around."

Margo sensed the tension but didn't understand it. She saw Kevin's companions exchange an uneasy glance.

"Would you mind taking your hand out of your pocket?" said Agatha.

"Of course." He turned up his palm to show that the hand was empty, but she plainly had noticed something she didn't like.

The minder flexed her fingers. "I'll take her to the rendezvous. You can follow us in your car."

"Don't be ridiculous." The guns were gripped firmly now, one trained on Agatha, the other on Margo. The pretense was over. "She isn't your responsibility any more."

The minder, her gaze riveted on the man with the broken nose, moved closer to her charge.

"Go ahead, Agatha. Try. My orders are to leave you alone as long as you cooperate, but I wouldn't particularly mind having another go-round."

Margo felt Agatha's bad hand on her shoulder. The fingers tapped gently. She wasn't sure what it meant, but it had to mean something.

"She's my responsibility until my superiors tell me otherwise."

"I'm not going to argue with you. Just let us have GREENHILL and you can be on your way. Mr. Ziegler will be in touch with you tomorrow."

Again the minder tapped Margo's shoulder, and this time she got it. Three taps of the fingers. Whatever Agatha was planning, it would happen on the count of three.

The blond man called Kevin took Margo by the arm. "Relax. We're taking you somewhere safe."

Agatha stepped away. "It'll be fine," she murmured.

"I know," said Margo, hoping desperately that she had understood correctly.

"You'll do fine. Just remember everything we've talked about, okay? Easy as one, two, three."

On three, everything happened very fast.

Agatha kicked out at the man beside her, striking him squarely in the groin, then pulled Ainsley's Beretta from somewhere and launched herself forward, broken arm and all, into the man by the car. At the same time, Margo grabbed Kevin's hand and, unable to come up with a better idea, bit down as hard as she could. The blond man didn't scream or let her loose, as she had hoped. He held on tight and struck the side of her head with the gun. The blow was harder than anything she had felt in her life. She was on the pavement, and he had a knee in her back and the muzzle at her neck.

II

"That's enough, Agatha," Kevin said. "You can put the gun down."

Agatha froze, then let the Beretta tumble to the grass. She raised her hands.

The man who was behind her had recovered his feet. The one by the car she had evidently pummeled unconscious.

"Search her," said the blond man. "Don't hurt her. She's on our side. We'll work this out when we get back. And now, Miss Jensen, if you please—"

He stopped, having heard something the others had missed. He spun around, leveling the gun, but was too late. Margo heard two booms, saw the red blossom over his chest, another, and he was in the dirt beside her, a look of pained astonishment on his face as he groaned and tried to speak.

Agatha, taking advantage of the distraction, had the second man on the ground again. The third had yet to wake.

"You can stop now," said Major Miles Madison, looming from behind another car. "I'd say you got him."

FIFTY-SEVEN

The Café

I

There were things that needed to be done now, and Margo stood aside to allow the professionals to discuss them. Two men were unconscious, the third dead or dying, right in the middle of the Mall, but Agatha and the major debated options and responsibilities like cautious bureaucrats. Overhearing bits and pieces, Margo sensed that she herself was the unfortunate complication they were trading back and forth. There was a lot of head shaking and pointing: *It's better if you do it. No, it's better if you do it.* It was almost two in the morning, and the deadline was in ten hours.

Finally, Agatha approached her. "Get back in the car."

"Why? What are we doing?"

"My job is to get you where you have to be, same as before. Major Madison will take care of the disposal."

Margo looked at the prone figures on the grass. *Disposal,* her mind echoed for her, and she knew better than to ask for details.

"I would usually do it, but, as he points out, this is his city, and a lot of people owe him favors. Besides, by now they probably think he's with you, since he's not at his duty post. He called to say he'd be late, and I imagine his colonel tore him a new one. Anyway, when he gets to the Pentagon, someone will be tasked with asking him where GREEN-HILL is. It's better if he doesn't have to lie when he says he doesn't know. Better for you, and better for his family."

Major Madison was kneeling in the darkness. Agatha bundled Margo into the car. "I didn't get to thank him."

"If we survive tomorrow, you can thank him at your leisure. If we don't, it won't make any difference."

A week ago, the cold rationality of the answer would have made Margo shiver. That was a week ago. Tonight, she was a jangled bundle of nerves, but managed nevertheless to focus on practicalities.

"We're going to the townhouse?"

"Not a chance," said Agatha. She was intermittently rubbing her injured wrist, and Margo suspected that, cast or no, the minder had broken it afresh in the struggle. "That's the most natural place for them to look. Also, as you yourself pointed out, we don't know whom we can trust."

They had turned south on Fourth Street. The blocky shadow of the Department of Health, Education and Welfare was on their left.

"Can I trust you?" Margo asked.

"Not entirely."

"What's that supposed to mean?"

"I never spoke to Bundy. I told you my orders were through the chain of command. The truth is, I spoke to the man who used to be deputy head of my section in Plans. He isn't connected to the Agency any longer."

Margo had her hand on the door, ready to jump out of the car. "Jack Ziegler," she breathed.

"Jack Ziegler," Agatha echoed. "He's the one who called me in and sent me to find you. First, though, he gave me this big speech about how the secret negotiations amount to surrender to the Reds, and so on—you get the idea." She lifted her bad hand, stretched the fingers. "He figured I'd have a special animus toward them, and he's right. He's right about the back channel, too. The President is making a mistake. If we make a deal, the Soviets will continue to spend and grow and build and— well, it doesn't matter. I told you he sent me. But that's all over with."

"I wish I could believe that."

"You saw what just happened. You have no idea how much trouble I'm going to be in with Jack Ziegler. And he's not a guy to be in trouble with."

Margo was watching her face. "You're saying you changed sides."

"Not exactly. I think the President is wrong, but I don't want to be a part of what Jack Ziegler is doing. Not any more." Agatha was furious now, the heat coming off her in waves. "Not after I saw the puukko knife in Kevin's pocket."

Margo's hand went to her mouth. It wasn't the Soviets who had murdered Dr. Harrington after all. It was the man Agatha had left for dead on the Mall. Murdered her after first torturing her with the knife . . .

"I assume they were questioning her about your whereabouts," Agatha said. "Jack Ziegler told me that he'd guarantee your safety if I tracked you down. He knew I'd never turn you over otherwise. I've grown fond of you, Margo." A heavy pause. "But he was lying. Maybe I knew all along. There's a reason Kevin had another puukko on the Mall."

Margo watched the older woman flexing the broken wrist, and, for a moment, ached with empathetic gratitude. A puukko knife. For questioning her. To be left beside her body so that the authorities would think the Soviets had done it, just as they'd left the other puukko beside Dr. Harrington, to make the crisis worse.

Margo shut her eyes, trying not to imagine the unimaginable fate from which Agatha Milner and Miles Madison had rescued her. The madness simply spiraled. The murder of Doris Harrington hadn't even been for the purpose of interrogation. It was meant to point Washington in the wrong direction.

Those in the Ziegler faction, she realized, weren't just trying to forestall the back-channel negotiations. They actually wanted war.

Meaning that the safety of nineteen-year-old Margo Jensen was suddenly, and literally, the most important thing in the world.

The dream had come true.

"So—what's the plan exactly?" she finally asked.

With the crisis upon them, Agatha's tone turned brisk. Margo had noticed this in Varna, too, how her minder, so mousy and quiet, would suddenly take control when the time arrived for decisions and plans. "Fomin's message has to get to the President before the deadline. We can't chance the townhouse. We can't call anybody. We don't know whom in the security apparatus we can trust. You have to speak to Kennedy directly. Nobody else."

"And how do I do that?"

"First, we find you a place to sleep for a couple of hours. In the morning I'll bring you a change of clothes. Office attire. After that, you go to the White House."

Margo's turn to laugh. "And walk up to the gate and announce myself?"

"Hardly. Aside from the fact that the guards wouldn't know you from Adam, I'm sure the ring around the place will be very tight—Ziegler's people, the Russians, who knows?—and someone will be planted inside to stop you as well."

"Then what are we going to do?"

"You go in as somebody else." They passed Margo's building and headed toward the waterfront. "Look. It's not that hard to get into the White House. Maybe one day it will be, but right now it isn't. An ID from a federal department, showing that you're a senior official, will get you into the West Wing lobby. After that, you'll have to figure out the rest."

"I'm not a senior official. I'm nineteen."

"Making a woman look older is a lot easier than making her look younger." Agatha was tapping at her chin. "Getting you an ID will be trickier."

"That's right," said Margo, mystified.

"Still. All we need is a black woman of roughly your build who has a senior executive-branch ID. A hat, a little makeup—the guards at the White House will never know the difference."

"Even if you're right, where are we going to find an ID like that?"

"We're going to steal it."

II

"That was very sloppy of you," said the man in the gold-rimmed glasses, satisfaction patent in his voice. "First you let your little command post be overrun. Then three of your men, all armed, can't stop two little girls."

"They're not little girls, and one of them is a trained killer."

"And they had help."

Ziegler looked up sharply. They were on the overgrown towpath along the old canal. The brown, fetid water might have been trapped there since the Civil War.

"Oh, yes," Viktor continued. "My people observed. There was a Negro with a gun."

"Your people were there and you didn't do anything?"

"As you may recall, you instructed me in the clearest terms to commit no further acts of violence on your soil." Viktor bared his teeth. "What I would really like to know, however, is why one of your people was carrying a puukko knife. No, don't tell me. I can guess. You really are a fool, aren't you?"

Jack Ziegler was bland. "I don't know what you're talking about."

"This," said Viktor, drawing a puukko of his own, and making as if to lunge. There was macho comedy as they struggled. The Russian stepped away, laughing. "You really do believe it is possible to emerge victorious," he said. "Remarkable."

"You think I can't take you?"

"I am talking about the war you are trying to start."

"We didn't start it. You know when it started? April of 1945."

"When we defeated the fascists, and your country deemed it expedient to end our alliance?"

"When your country, contrary to your promises, occupied Czechoslovakia and Poland and installed puppet regimes." They were walking again, back toward their vehicles. Ziegler was keeping his distance. "You tried to snap up Denmark, too, but the British were too fast for you."

"You do not regard the dictators you support in Latin America as puppets?"

"I'm only saying your side started it."

Viktor stifled a groan. Such splendid circularity. A Trotskyite could not have done better, the way those wreckers used to answer every question with *Because only the proletariat can do that!* There was no way to get through to such a man. Nevertheless, the Russian tried. "If you bomb Cuba, we shall be forced to retaliate. Then you will retaliate. And so on. You know that, of course. And perhaps you are right. You could do far more damage to us than we could do to you. But you would suffer casualties in the millions. Your way of life might never recover. Is that what you want?"

"The time for that debate was before your people put the missiles into Cuba."

"Perhaps. But to practicalities." All professional again. "Last night we had a good sense where GREENHILL would be hiding. We could have acted then. We didn't. Now we don't know. I thought this Milner was part of your group."

"So did I." Ziegler frowned. They were standing still now, the odoriferous wind whipping their coats. "She may still be. She was a little upset tonight, but she knows we're right. She might yet decide to take care of the problem for us."

"Or she might decide to assist GREENHILL instead."

"It's possible."

"What do we do to prevent that? You don't know where she is. You don't know how to reach her. Has it occurred to you that she might simply deliver GREENHILL to a public phone booth, from which she might call the White House?"

"Then you won't have your purge and I won't have my war." He puffed out a lot of air at the awful prospect. "But think about it. Whom can she call? Bundy? For all GREENHILL knows, he's the reason she's compromised." An angry shake of the head. "So—what's left for her to do? Call the President's office? Assuming she can get through to his secretary, what exactly is she supposed to say? 'Hi, this is Margo Jensen, I'm the one everybody thinks is having an affair with your boss, can I get in to see him, please?' No. She won't call. She'll show up in person and insist on giving the message to the President herself. We'll be watching. We'll spot her."

"You won't." The wind was howling now, but no rain was forecast. "Time and again, this girl has made fools of you. She is not even trained, but she has escaped you. She will be in disguise. I do not know how she will get into the White House, but she will get in."

"Do you have a better idea?"

Viktor adjusted the gold-rimmed glasses. "I do."

III

Every weekday morning, on her way to work, Victoria Elden stopped for coffee. A woman of some sophistication, Torie disdained both the foul brew from the cafeteria downstairs and the fouler brew from the percolator in the corridor. Her chosen source was a noisy café a block north of the Labor Department, along Twelfth Street. Later, Torie was not able to pinpoint precisely what happened. She remembered nobody bumping into her or brushing her or shoving her. She didn't even need her identification when she returned to the office with her tall, steaming cup, because she was friendly and warm and all the guards flirted with her; and besides, she brought them coffee, too. Only later that morning, when she happened to open her pocketbook to take out her compact, did she notice that her wallet was missing.

IV

"Do you have the files?" asked Bernard Stilwell.

Jack Ziegler sat across from him in the FBI safe house. Of course their every word would be recorded, but it made no difference: no one but J. Edgar Hoover and his most trusted minions would ever hear the tapes.

Trusted minions like Agent Stilwell, who was tasked, Ziegler knew, with collecting embarrassing information about political leaders, to provide Hoover with ammunition for—well, for whatever his mad little mind might hatch.

Ziegler passed a folder across the table.

"This is one file," Stilwell objected. "The deal was for three. Two from your clients, with information on the men most likely to be elected President in 1968 after JFK's second term. One from the KGB archives that will help us make some arrests."

"You get the other two when we get what we want."

Ziegler could see the calculation in Stilwell's eyes. The agent was said to be an excellent judge of what Hoover would approve or disapprove. Rarely did he use as his excuse the need to check with his boss.

"Very well," said the FBI agent. "You get GREENHILL, we get the files. But do understand one thing, Mr. Ziegler." A warning finger. "If this scheme goes south on you, we never met. Mention us to anybody, even in secret, and we'll know within the hour. We'll hunt you to the ends of the earth and shoot you down on sight."

"Blah-blah-blah," said Ziegler, unimpressed.

"And we'll want those files available at the handover."

"That won't be a problem."

V

The D.C. Transit bus crawled through the Monday-morning traffic on Pennsylvania Avenue. It was rush hour, and the bus was packed. The white people who thought they ran Washington were leaving the city in droves, but the Negroes who kept things running were on their way to work. Margo felt restless, hemmed in, needing to move. The effort of standing still—there were no seats—was making her half crazy. But even in her impatience and frustration, she saw the genius of Agatha's idea. Ziegler's people, the Russians—whoever was trying to stop her would be counting on her to rush to the White House as swiftly as she could. They would be watching cars, taxis, pedestrians. The notion that she would take her chances with the capital's aging and unreliable buses might never occur to them.

Nevertheless, she kept leaning down to look out the windows for anyone taking too great an interest in this particular bus, and whenever she was jostled, she spun around, half expecting to find a puukko waving at her.

It had been a long and painful journey from New Rochelle to Garrison to Ithaca to Varna to Washington to this moment, and when she thought of Dr. Harrington, her knees felt like jelly and she wanted to run home. But Agatha, who had known Harrington a good deal longer, was able to remain tough and focused; Margo was determined to do no less.

They had met an hour ago in one of the city's grimier neighborhoods, on the wrong side of the Anacostia River, where Margo had spent the night at what amounted to a flophouse. Agatha had handed over the promised business clothes, along with the purloined identification, made her up to look ten years older, then schooled her one last time in the details of what she called the operation.

"And where do we meet up afterward?" asked Margo when the minder was done.

"If all goes according to plan, the President's people will take charge of your welfare."

Margo had suffered too much recent loss not to recognize the implicit farewell. "When will I see you again?"

"If all goes according to plan, you won't." Agatha touched her cheek. "You'll do fine."

Now, standing amidst a crowd of pedestrians in Lafayette Park, waiting to cross the street to the White House, Margo wondered why her minder was so certain that they wouldn't meet again.

The light changed. She lifted her head, patted the handbag that contained Torie Elden's identification.

The wind was back, swirling Margo's coat around her long legs. She composed herself. *You aren't nineteen. You aren't an intern. You aren't a college student who's been secretly meeting the President at a fancy townhouse. You're thirty, you work in the Labor Department, and you have the right to be here.*

Ready. Go.

She began her final march.

FIFTY-EIGHT

Morning Rush

I

On that same Monday morning, Bundy reported to the President and the attorney general that no one had been able to locate GREENHILL. Bundy himself had scrutinized the logs of crank calls from people demanding to speak to the President, and the Secret Service records of people who had been refused entrance at the gates.

Nothing.

"If we don't have GREENHILL," said the President, glumly, "we don't have Fomin's reply."

"Without his reply," added Bobby, "we have no proof that we're actually dealing with Khrushchev." His tone was bleak. "We still don't know who's in charge over there. This whole back channel could be a deception to get us to lower our guard."

Bundy cleared his throat. "The Bureau reports that the Soviet Embassy is burning its papers and has instructed the other Warsaw Pact countries to do the same."

"Like the Japanese just before Pearl Harbor." The President rubbed the small of his back. "All right, gentlemen. We've done what we could. Let's go give the ExComm their war."

II

In Ithaca, too, it was the Monday. The great Lorenz Niemeyer had his bad right hand on the lectern while his left swept derisively through the air.

"Now, let's think, children," he intoned. "As we watch the Cuba crisis advance, let us think about what it means to have an adversary. Plutarch says that Julius Caesar wept when he heard about the death of Pompey, his sworn enemy. Ha. If the story is true, then Caesar was a sentimental fool." His swiftly surveying glance lingered briefly on the empty seat that should have been Margo Jensen's. "Here's the truth about war, gentlemen. *And* ladies. Ponder it as the crisis of the moment wends its way toward one conclusion or the other. Winners do what they have to do. That's the only secret to war. You do what you have to do, no matter how grubby."

Somebody raised a nervous hand to ask whether Niemeyer thought there would be a war.

"The war began long ago, Mr. Jimenez. The question you should be asking is what we're willing to sacrifice for the sake of victory. And whom. Ultimate success often demands the lives of those we love best." A shadow danced across the pudgy face and was gone. "If you can't face that truth, I suggest that you return to the nursery and ask Mommy to read you a bedtime story."

FIFTY-NINE

Infiltrator

I

Margo was surprised by her own calm. At the Northwest Gatehouse, she showed her pass to the uniformed guard, who checked it against her face and asked whom she was there to see.

"Victoria Elden for Christopher Gallegos," she said.

The guard had her sign the book while he called. Gallegos was on the domestic-policy staff, and she had selected him in accordance with Agatha's coaching: because Torie, according to what the other girls said, dropped by at least once every other week or so. Margo couldn't hear the conversation, but things evidently went fine, because the guard passed her through and pointed her up the sloping driveway to the West Wing entrance.

Just like that, she was through. Climbing the asphalt, her goal so near after the terror of the night, she felt the dream slip away, replaced at last by the euphoria that came with knowing that she had carried out her mission after all. No burnt, desperate fingers clutched at her legs. No secret police, ours or theirs, materialized from the bushes to snatch her away. The nightmare that had plagued her since Varna was fading at last.

At the top of the driveway, a Marine in dress blues opened the door. Inside, Margo presented the stolen identification card for a second time. At the desk, a second uniformed guard wrote down Torie's name.

"And whom are you here to see?"

"Mr. Gallegos."

The guard looked at her card again. "Victoria Elden? From Labor?"

"Yes."

"One moment," he said. He indicated a long sofa. "Please have a seat."

She sat as bidden. A moment later a plainclothes Secret Service agent was in front of her. "Would you come with me, please." No question mark in his intonation.

He led her into a hallway, where two more agents stood, neither looking friendly.

"What's this about?" she asked. "What's going on?"

"May I see your identification card?" said the oldest of the trio, with chilly politeness.

No choice. She was caught, and she knew it. She gave him the card.

"This card is stolen," he said, handing it to another agent. "It was reported half an hour ago." To Margo: "Give me your hands, please."

She did; and was duly cuffed; and duly led away.

Failure after all.

II

She told them more than once that they were making a mistake, but they seemed uninterested in anything she had to say.

One of the agents opened a hidden door in the smooth white wall. They descended a narrow stair, an agent in front and an agent behind, and emerged in a basement corridor. Black and yellow pointed the way to the fallout shelter, but the agents led Margo the other way. They took her into a small office, sat her down, then undid the cuff from her right wrist and attached it to the chair. Full circle, she thought, remembering Varna.

Two agents left. The third stayed behind.

"Did you really think you'd get away with this?"

"Just call Mr. Bundy," she said.

"Who?"

"McGeorge Bundy. The national security adviser." Margo lifted her free hand beseechingly. "Please. Just call him. Tell him I'm down here."

The agent shook his head. "Out of the question."

"He'll want to talk to me."

"I doubt that. You've broken a number of laws this morning." Ticking them off on long white fingers. "Theft of government property. Impersonating a federal employee. You enter the White House with a false identification card, and you think we'll make a call on your behalf?" He stood. "Our orders in any case are to hold you incommunicado."

"Whose orders?"

"Orders," he repeated. "The FBI will be here soon. You'll go into their custody, and I'm sure they'll be happy to let you call whomever you like."

"You don't understand. You don't know what's going on. I have a vital message for the President and—"

"I've heard about that, too." The Secret Service man was on his feet. "We have to accept the peccadilloes of the people we protect, but we don't have to like them." His face was grim. "Really, Miss Jensen. Did you think you were Jack Kennedy's only little chippy? How stupid are you?"

He locked the door behind him, and this time there was no window.

III

The ExComm was in an uproar.

The President was trying one last time to persuade the ExComm that the informal message from Khrushchev on Friday trumped the formal proposal of Saturday. Nobody bought it. Even Bundy thought Kennedy was reaching. At this point, they could only accept or reject what was actually on the table. Bundy had warned the President that nobody would believe Khrushchev could be trusted, and Bundy had turned out to be exactly right.

Without the back channel, the Saturday letter was all they had; and the Saturday letter, in the ExComm's eyes, was cause for war.

"We're out of options," said McNamara. "Whatever Khrushchev might have offered informally, he's obviously changed his mind. Or has there been additional word?"

The question was rhetorical: had there been further communication, Kennedy would have told them as soon as the meeting began.

"There's no choice any more, Mr. President," said LeMay. "It's time to give the order."

"That was our agreement on Saturday," said Gwynn, from State: clearly feeling his oats. "Either we have a deal by noon or we go in."

"And it's almost ten-thirty," added Taylor.

The President glanced at Bundy. "Perhaps we could go over the military options," the national security adviser said, playing for time.

McNamara was exasperated. "We've gone over them already."

"Then please be kind enough to go over them for us again."

There was grumbling around the table, but the Joint Chiefs duly opened their folders.

"Excuse me," said Bundy as soon as Taylor got two sentences out. "I noticed some visual aids in the foyer."

"We decided we don't need them," the general snapped.

Bundy's tone became if anything meeker. "I would consider it a great favor if, this once, you would use the easel and the charts. For clarity's sake."

An aide was dispatched to bring in the materials. Another aide appeared an instant later and handed Curtis LeMay a message slip.

The Air Force chief of staff jumped to his feet. "Mr. President, with your permission, I apparently have an urgent call with some bearing on the matter before us."

Kennedy nodded. LeMay left. The aides needed three minutes to set up the easel for Taylor, who picked up a pointer and launched at once into a lecture about the types of planes and ordnance that would be involved in the attacks. The first wave would disable the surface-to-air batteries, the second and third would both target the missile launch sites . . .

Five minutes into the presentation, LeMay returned to the Cabinet Room. Rather than going back to his seat, he walked around the table to where Bundy was sitting. Taylor was still at the easel, where the map was now covered by a different transparency, marked "DAY 3," showing what seemed to the national security adviser an overly optimistic vision of the progress that the invading troops could be expected to make.

LeMay leaned close. "Mac, may I have a word?"

"This really isn't a good time," Bundy whispered back.

"It's urgent. As a matter of fact, it might be the key to this whole blasted thing."

Bundy didn't hesitate. LeMay was gruff, but he was nobody's fool, and he wasn't given to exaggeration. The national security adviser hopped to his feet, excused himself, and followed the general from the room, watched closely by the President both men served.

"Make it fast, please, General," said Bundy as soon as they were in the anteroom.

LeMay was quite unfazed by the little man's brusqueness. "I just had the darnedest phone call from General Hellman. He's a two-star, and a good man. I've known Hack Hellman for twenty years. Hack tells me that he's been approached to set up a telephone call between the President's national security adviser and one Major Miles Madison, who evidently served under Hack in Korea until they rotated back Stateside eighteen months ago."

"I don't really have the time—"

"Make time, son. Because, from what I understand from Hack, Major Madison purports to have information vital to the resolution of this crisis. And if Hack Hellman vouches for him, then he's on the up-and-up."

A small light went on. "Wait. Madison, you said?"

"That's right."

"How soon can you set it up?"

"Hack is on hold right now. Say the word, and I'll have you on the secure line with Major Madison in five minutes."

"Make that three. Because, if he's calling for the reason I think he's calling, I imagine we'll be calling him 'Colonel' soon."

IV

At the safe house, Ziegler took the call. He listened, acknowledged, hung up. Then he turned to Viktor Vaganian.

"That was one of Agent Stilwell's minions. She's in the White House, but she's been arrested. She's under guard, being held incommunicado, as arranged. The Bureau will have her shortly."

"And then?"

"And then we trade. Do you have that file for me?"

With a small pang, Viktor slid a few pages across the table, details of the KGB's penetration of civilians employed in certain defense plants. The FBI would get some nice arrests, and a diplomat or two would be expelled. A small price to pay in order to keep the missiles in Cuba.

Jack Ziegler smiled savagely. "You know they'll hang you for this, right?"

"We are a civilized people. They will shoot me in the back of the neck."

V

"This is Bundy."

"Mr. Bundy, my name is Miles Madison. I'm a major in—"

"I know who you are, Major Madison. I understand that you have some information for me."

A pause. "I take it you haven't spoken to her, then."

"To whom, Major?"

"A certain young woman you've been searching for. She should have arrived by now."

"Arrived? Are you saying she's here?"

"My understanding as of an hour ago is that she was on the way to the White House."

"Then where is she?"

"I'm sorry, sir. I don't have any further information."

SIXTY

The Lineup

I

"You're sure she's not here?" said a bewildered McGeorge Bundy.

"Absolutely," said the chief usher.

"There's no way she could have snuck in?"

"The Secret Service are very good at their jobs, Mr. Bundy. That's why they've never lost a President."

The two men were standing in the hallway outside the Cabinet Room. Inside, the ExComm was marching toward war. The usher was impatient. He was an Irishman of some years, and Kennedy was his fifth President. He had a great deal of work to do, coordinating with the Secret Service to arrange the movement of the President and his family should the attack on Cuba go bad. Bundy couldn't figure out what he had missed. Major Madison had been adamant in his assurances that GREENHILL was in the building. Was Madison wrong? Had the Russians managed to stop her? It would seem so, because the head of presidential protection was right: it was unlikely in the extreme that his detail would miss a black woman entering—

Wait.

"Can you tell me how many Negro women are in the building at this moment?"

The usher was surprised. "We don't keep track of their race, Mr. Bundy. I'd guess, secretaries and maids and cooks included, thirty. Perhaps a handful more."

"Visitors?"

"I'd have to check."

"Okay. On my authority, I want every black woman who works in the White House assembled in the East Room inside of ten minutes. And track down every one who's here on a visit."

"Uh, Mr. Bundy, that smacks of—"

"I know what it smacks of. Just do it, please. On my authority."

"Of course. But I shall need the assistance of the Secret Service."

"Get whoever's help you need. If they have problems, have them give my office a call."

The usher hurried away. Bundy wished he could handle this, but he had to get back inside the Cabinet Room, to do what he could to stave off war. He glanced at Nate Esman, who was sitting in an armchair nearby in case he was summoned to the meeting. Esman knew nothing about the current operation, but . . .

"Nate."

Instantly the pudgy young man was on his feet. "I'll take care of it, boss."

"Let me explain what you're looking for."

"Margo Jensen, alias GREENHILL." A proud grin. "Don't give me that look, boss. Come on. You had me skulking around looking for the leak, you had me delve into her background, and it's pretty obvious that there's been a back-channel negotiation and . . . never mind. I know you have to get back in there. If she's in the building, I'll find her."

II

Margo had given up trying to escape the cuffs. She slumped in the chair, trying and failing to invent a strategy. She told herself that Donald Jensen wouldn't have found it any sort of problem. And she had to get out. She had to get the message to Kennedy. But all she could do was bang her wrist against the table in frustration.

The door opened. The same Secret Service agent stepped in, followed by two other men in suits.

"Miss Jensen, these gentlemen are from the FBI. They're here to take you into custody."

One of them was already releasing her from the chair and cuffing her wrists afresh behind her back.

Margo looked around at the hard faces. Then she turned back to the Secret Service man. "Please. Even if they have to take me, you have to let Mr. Bundy know where I am. He's going to be looking for me."

"Somehow I doubt that."

"Will you just try? It's vital to—to the nation's security."

"Miss Jensen, believe it or not, with the missiles in Cuba, the President's special assistant for national security affairs has bigger things on his mind than your fate. Now, please don't make any trouble."

III

It took longer than the chief usher estimated to gather all the Negro women who worked at the White House to the East Room. Esman, whose parents had marched for civil rights in the 1950s, and whose sister had been beaten during last year's Freedom Rides, was offended. The young man admired everything about his boss except a single-mindedness of purpose that distracted him from ordinary moral concerns.

"Let them leave," he told the agent on duty, a pleasant Georgian in his late thirties called Youngblood.

As the women filed out, some bemused and some angry, he kept a lookout for anyone who matched the photograph he held in his hand, but nobody did.

The chief usher was beside him. "That's everybody," he said.

Esman frowned. "These were all staff?"

"Yes."

"No visitors?"

"Not officially," said Youngblood.

Esman rounded on him. "What's that supposed to mean?"

"There's one girl who snuck in with a false ID."

"Why didn't you say so? Where is she?"

"Last I heard, she was locked up in the basement."

IV

At ten minutes past eleven, Bundy slipped out of the Cabinet Room into the foyer. Janet was waiting.

"Any word?"

"I'm sorry, Mr. Bundy. Nate Esman went off with the chief usher half an hour ago, and I haven't seen him since."

The national security adviser looked around. The foyer was unusually crowded. Most of those waiting were military aides. A direct line had been set up to the Signals Office, so that the President's attack order might be transmitted precisely at noon.

In the Cabinet Room, a couple of members of the ExComm were continuing to fight a holding action, but support for any option except bombing and invasion was crumbling. Even Bobby Kennedy was finally running with the hounds—and not just as devil's advocate.

Bundy slipped back into his chair. It was time to put aside childish hopes and begin planning for the war.

"We have to discuss evacuation," he said.

Several heads turned. "Of what? Essential personnel?"

"Of our cities," said Bundy.

V

Infected by Esman's energy, Youngblood led him in a charge down the winding staircase. They burst into the room, only to find it empty.

"I guess the FBI already came for her," said the agent.

VI

Jack Ziegler and Viktor Vaganian were sitting in a car three blocks north of the White House, along Sixteenth Street.

"You should have arranged to take her yourself," said Viktor.

"Too complicated once she's inside the gates."

"But surely your President can order her release!"

"The idea is to get her out of the building before that happens. Sure, eventually they'll find out that Margo Jensen has been arrested. But look at the clock. Almost eleven. The planes will be in the air soon. The FBI only needs to hold her until noon. Then the attack begins."

Viktor watched the thin stream of pedestrians. He had never known Washington to be so empty.

"Has it occurred to you, my friend, that, in our efforts to prevent our governments from appearing weak, we are bringing down horror upon all of these innocent people?"

"Are you turning sentimental on me, Viktor Borisovich?"

"To be a true socialist is also to be a realist. It is you capitalists who cannot live with the consequences of your actions and therefore constantly deny them or blame them on others. I refuse to hide my eyes from that which I have caused."

"You're not going to cause anything, because there isn't going to be a war." Ziegler checked his watch again. "We're going into Cuba, and your man isn't going to do a thing about it."

"You are wrong, my friend."

"You can stop all that 'my friend' stuff, too. I'm not your friend. This is a business collaboration. We've always been enemies. We'll always be enemies."

Nyekulturny, Viktor reminded himself. Not the man's fault.

"I must return to my embassy now," he said.

This got Ziegler's attention. "Why?" he asked, suspiciously.

"I have an appointment with the traitor you call Aleksandr Fomin. He has betrayed the Motherland and must be placed under arrest."

"He was acting under Khrushchev's orders."

"Once the bombing begins, the Comrade General Secretary will either deny that order or no longer be giving any."

VII

The FBI agents led her politely to a dark sedan parked at the crest of the driveway on the Pennsylvania Avenue side. One of them joined her in the back seat while the other slid in beside the driver. Up to this point, they had been deaf to both her entreaties and her arguments. The car headed down the drive, and Margo, turning her head, watched disbelieving as the White House into which she had so easily gained entry receded—

The driver slammed on the brakes.

A pudgy young man was standing in the road. A dark-haired Secret Service agent looked on curiously from the grass.

One of the FBI men stepped out.

"What's going on?" she heard through the open door.

"I'm afraid you can't take Miss Jensen," said the pudgy man.

"And who are you exactly?"

"Nathaniel Esman, chief deputy to the President's special assistant for national security affairs."

The FBI man folded his arms. "Well, Mr. Esman, I don't work for your boss, and I certainly don't work for you. Now, get out of the way, or I'll place you under arrest for obstruction."

Esman turned to the man on the lawn. "Agent Youngblood. Do not let this car leave the grounds. I'll be right back."

SIXTY-ONE

Payback

I

It was another room, much like the first, although this time there was a window giving on an air shaft. A guard removed the cuffs and left her alone. A moment later, McGeorge Bundy stepped inside.

"Thank God," he said, and the Catholic in him seemed to mean it. "We've been looking all over for you."

He ordered the agent to wait outside.

Margo rubbed her wrists. "How did you even know I was here?" she asked, a bit stupidly.

"I got a call from your friend Major Madison. He seems like a good man, Miss Jensen. Never mind. Now, please. Tell me the message from Fomin, so that I can convey it to the President."

"No."

Bundy was startled. "What did you say?"

"I said, no. I'm sorry. The message is for the President's ears only."

He took his time. "You know who I am, Miss Jensen. I recruited you. I briefed you. I have the President's ear, at this moment, more than anyone else, with the possible exception of his brother. You can tell me."

"I don't think so."

"If you tell the President, I'm the first one he'll consult in any case."

"That's up to him, Mr. Bundy. But after last night, I'm afraid I don't trust anybody." She lifted her chin, every inch a Jensen. "I have to see the President myself."

Bundy shook his head. "I'm sorry, Miss Jensen. I don't see how that's going to be possible. We're just about out of time. The President is in an emergency meeting. He can't duck out to come down to visit you in the basement."

"Then take me upstairs."

"If you go upstairs, Miss Jensen, everyone will see you."

"So what? All that will do is confirm what they already believe. That I'm having an affair with the President." She almost smiled. "The fact that I'm being escorted by the national security adviser will simply add a certain spice to the tale."

"I'll seem to be a procurer. And what people will think of the President—"

"Mr. Bundy, you and the President have asked me to risk my reputation for the good of the country. I've been arrested twice, I've been kidnapped, and I've been shot at. It seems to me entirely reasonable that you and the President should also pay a small reputational price. If my presence in the White House embarrasses you, I apologize. But remember. History will record me as just another presidential mistress. If you take me upstairs, maybe you're right, and history will record you as a procurer. But I'm ready to convey Fomin's message only to the President. The question, then, is whether you and he are prepared to pay the same price you've demanded of me."

Bundy pondered. He took off his glasses and polished them. Margo didn't know what had gotten into her, speaking that way to a man of his eminence. And Bundy evidently wondered the same thing, or so she judged from his moue of disapproval. She wondered whether she had pressed too far. But then, to her surprise and immense relief, Bundy almost smiled—not quite, but it was a near thing. He slipped his horn-rimmed glasses back on. "And he that rolleth a stone, it will return upon him. Well, well." He stood. "You make a reasonable point, Miss Jensen. I can certainly see why Fomin trusts you." He walked over to the door and knocked. A guard opened it at once. "Come with me, then."

II

"It's good to see you again, Margo. I hear you've had a time of it."

"Yes, Mr. President." She had met the President on five occasions now, had allowed him certain liberties, but she was awed nevertheless to be in his presence in the fabled Oval Office. She wondered whether people were whispering already about why Kennedy had left his meeting.

"Would you like a drink?"

"No, thank you, sir."

"Mind if I have one?" He was already pouring. He poured a second, held the glass toward her. She shook her head. He smiled ruefully, set it down on the coffee table, and seated himself in the rocker. "So. I understand you have a message for me."

"Yes, sir." Margo had spent every calm moment rehearsing the words, so as to leave nothing out. "I am told that the General Secretary agrees to the entire arrangement, with one amendment. Whatever you decide to say publicly, you must agree privately to remove the Jupiters within a year. Khrushchev will trust your word on this."

Kennedy took a moment to ponder. "You know, I just might be able to sell that to the ExComm. It won't make everybody happy, but . . ." He trailed off, and his eyes found her again. "What about the other matter? Making sure of who we're dealing with?"

"I am also told that, on the first night of the summit, the General Secretary sat beside the First Lady. The First Lady asked him not to bore her with statistics."

Kennedy was perplexed. "That's it?"

"Yes, sir."

"That's the entire message?"

"Yes, Mr. President."

"I asked you to call me Jack when we're alone." But the teasing was distracted, automatic. He put down his glass too hard. He seemed angry, and his next words told her why. "That might not be enough. Anybody could have overheard Khrushchev saying that. An aide. A translator. For all I know, it was in *The Washington Post*." He smacked his fist into his open palm. "I'm sorry, Margo. I can't go to Taylor and LeMay with 'I know it's Khrushchev because he flirted with my wife.' They'll laugh me out of the room."

"You don't have to," she said softly.

"What was that?"

"I said, you don't have to, sir. You don't have to justify your decision to them. You're the President of the United States. It doesn't matter if they believe you're really dealing with the General Secretary. It only matters if you believe it."

The gray-green eyes widened, and it was as if he was seeing her for the first time not as a messenger or potential conquest but as a mind.

An instant later, everything was motion. Kennedy was striding toward the door. His secretary had stepped in and was inviting Margo to follow her. She showed her into what was obviously somebody's office, with files and papers and a half-covered typewriter.

"You're to wait here," the secretary said. "Can I bring you any-thing?"

Margo blinked. It had been days or more since what she had wanted had mattered. She needed a moment to readjust. Perhaps the nightmare was over after all.

"I'd like to call my grandmother," she said.

"Of course. I'll get you an outside line."

III

"So we have failed," said Viktor Vaganian. They were in the safe house, sitting in the kitchen while their fellow conspirators cleansed the place of evidence. The Russian was spreading thick butter on black bread. "I am relieved, in a way. I would not want my country to be humiliated in this fashion, but I also would not want a war."

Ziegler was pacing. "There wouldn't have been a war. Maybe your guys would have tried a little something in Berlin, but that would have been it." His fists were clenched. "We were so close. So close."

"It makes no difference." He finished the bread, began carving another heavy slice. "I shall be summoned home. Perhaps they will shoot me. Perhaps Comrade Khrushchev will fall and I will be among the victors. There is no way to tell." He was drinking beer rather than vodka, and wiping his mouth with his sleeve. "Perhaps you should come with me."

"Why would I do that?"

"Your government will likely try you for treason."

Ziegler laughed. "Won't happen. I have powerful friends, believe me. And the Kennedys, well, they're pragmatists. They won't want to take on—"

The doorbell rang. One of the others went to answer, and returned a moment later with Jerry Ainsley.

"What do you want?" asked Ziegler, nastily.

"I'm here to arrest you," he said. "I assume you won't be resisting."

"You can't arrest me. You're unarmed, number one, and, number two, you're Agency. You have no domestic jurisdiction."

"But I do," said Agent Stilwell, stepping into the room. "Mr. Ziegler, you are under arrest. Captain Vaganian is to return to his embassy at once."

Ziegler went purple with fury. For a bad moment, Viktor thought he might actually draw a weapon—or, far worse, blurt out the truth, that he and Stilwell had made a deal. Whereas, as even the Russians knew, with Hoover there was never a deal, there was simply the director himself, skulking in the shadows, using to his advantage whatever information he gleaned.

But Ziegler controlled himself. His anger softened into a smirk. He used two fingers to remove his weapon, and put out his hands for the cuffs.

The house was full of agents now. Viktor gathered his associates and headed for the door. Half the neighborhood lined the street. The Russians were walking along the sidewalk, under the wary escort of a pair of FBI agents, when Vaganian felt a sudden terrible pain in both legs.

He cried out and collapsed.

One of the agents knelt beside him. The other was chasing a woman into the crowd.

Viktor lay on the pavement, sweating in sharp red pain. They would never catch her, of course, and he would never know whether the attack had been staged. He did know that both of his kneecaps had been crushed, and that in all likelihood he would never walk again. He even found a grim admiration for the swiftness and skill with which Agatha Milner had taken out both knees with one roundhouse kick.

SIXTY-TWO

Additional Terms

I

In later years, the events of the next couple of hours remained hazy in Margo's memory. She sat in the office, eating the sandwich the secretary had brought her from the mess and washing it down with milk. Possibly she dozed a bit. She had a sense of frenetic activity just beyond the range of her perceptions, as if people were running here and there, but offstage. At one point, two men she didn't know peered through the doorway, one wearing Air Force blue festooned with ribbons, the other in glasses and an expensive suit.

"Is that her?" said the military man.

"That's her."

"A coed?"

"That's right, General. Nineteen years old."

"Brave kid. She should get some kind of medal."

"Maybe so."

"Not that I trust the Commies further than I can throw them," said the general, the two of them chatting as if she weren't even in the room. She might even have dreamed them, because, when she looked again, the pair was gone and the secretary was back. Margo's lunch dishes had magically disappeared.

"Are you up for some company, honey?"

She sat up straighter. "Of course. Thanks."

McGeorge Bundy stepped into the room, shutting the door behind him. "Your nation owes you a great debt, Miss Jensen," he began. "Even though the world will never know of your contribution—"

"It's over?"

"Not quite. There's still a chance that they might renege. But, for the moment, war seems to have been averted." Behind the glasses, his eyes were exhausted. "Unfortunately, we shall have to call upon your assistance one final time."

"You mean, I have to see Fomin again."

"That's exactly what I mean, Miss Jensen. I apologize. But there are some final details to be worked out, and, at the moment, I believe you are the only one he will trust. Remember, they shot at him last night, too."

A beat.

"Who's 'they'?" she asked. "You must know by now."

"I can't tell you everything. Some of their people are being deported. Some of our people are under arrest."

"And Ainsley?"

"What about him?"

"Is he under arrest?"

"Jericho Ainsley? Goodness, no. Why would we arrest him? He saved your life last night, Miss Jensen. And he also tipped off the Bureau to where the conspirators had their safe house."

"If he knew about the safe house, it's because he was one of them! He tried to kill me last night!"

She was on her feet now, and every bit as tall as the diminutive Bundy. But he responded to her anger only with amusement.

"No, Miss Jensen. He didn't. Evidently, you ran away before he could explain that he was pointing his gun not at you but at the man standing behind you. Look. You can talk to him yourself."

"He's here in the building?"

"We thought it unlikely that you would trust anyone else to take you to the rendezvous with Colonel Fomin."

II

They met on the park bench across from the National Gallery of Art. The late-afternoon sun was low and listless. There was no wind, but the chill was rising all the same.

"You have done well," said Fomin. "Will they be arranging a suitable reward for you?"

"I just want to go back to what I was doing before."

"Your life will never be the same. You understand this. I refer not only to the memories that will plague you—some wonderful, some horrible, all of them impossible to escape—no, I refer to you. The changes in you. You are not the person that you were a month ago, or even a week ago. You belong to them now."

"I don't belong to anybody but myself."

"*Chush*. Nonsense. The fact that you are here tells me that you are no longer your own woman." He nodded toward the street, where a pair of quite obvious watchers kept vigil. "Have they sent you to tell me we have an agreement? Or does your war party wish to change the deal?"

"The President agrees to your terms."

She expected him to exhibit some sign of relief, or joy, or satisfaction. Again his calm surprised her. "And is that all?"

"No. In exchange for your additional conditions, the—the White House also has additional conditions."

Fomin detected the hesitation. "The White House. Not the President."

Margo chose not to answer. Her hands were on the bench, fingers pressed into the cold wood. "I also have reasons of my own for wanting to see you."

"First tell me the conditions. Then we will discuss your reasons."

She tilted her head back, remembering Bundy's words. "Violence has been done on our soil, to our people. There has to be a reckoning. That's the first condition."

"What you are telling me is that they believe Captain Vaganian was responsible for what happened to Dr. Harrington."

"Was he?"

"Such a thing is possible. But it is also possible that it was your own war party. You should look to punish your own traitors. We know perfectly well how to deal with ours. Vaganian will return to Moscow under arrest and stand trial. Will that satisfy them?"

"I believe so."

"Then what is the second condition?"

"In addition, the General Secretary must agree, privately, that, within a year after the removal of the Jupiter missiles, he will resign his office and retire." When he said nothing, she added, "I am told that unless he agrees to this condition, the quarantine will remain in effect, the bombers will stay at their 'go' points, and the promise not to invade Cuba will be void."

She felt embarrassed even saying the words. Fomin was silent for a bit, but when she chanced a look at him, he seemed to be smiling.

"Already there are plots against the Comrade General Secretary. There are many in the Party who would prefer new leadership. Under Comrade Stalin, nobody would have dared suggest such a thing. In this sense, Comrade Khrushchev has advanced the concrete conditions for socialism in our country. It is not right for a socialist people to be afraid of their own government." He shut his eyes. "That your war party feels the need to threaten and bluster when they already hold the advantage is evidence of the utter corruption of the capitalist system. You would prevail against us, today, in a war. This is not a tribute to the superiority of your system. It is an outgrowth of the fact that we, not you, bore the brunt of the struggle against the fascists in the Great Patriotic War."

"Colonel—"

He rode right over her. "But the struggle of the next decades will be ideological, not technological, and in that struggle we shall defeat you."

"I think—"

"I find the additional term proposed by your war party offensive. However, I believe that the Comrade General Secretary has already considered the possibility of retirement. It is possible that he has already done his greatest service to the Motherland. I believe it is likely that he will agree."

Margo let out a long breath. She actually sagged against the bench. Over. It was finally over.

"You said that you had a question of your own," he reminded her.

"I do," Margo said. She steeled herself. With the Cuban crisis resolved, it was time to deal with a crisis of her own. "You chose me for this role as your back channel."

"You were the obvious choice."

"I'm not so sure about that. In any case, it was you—you personally—who selected me. Is that fair?"

"I approved you." His voice was flat. Again she sensed his dislike of being cross-examined by a woman.

"That implies that I was chosen by someone else."

"Do you expect me to break operational security?"

She had rehearsed the next part since her epiphany at Ainsley's apartment. "I think it's more a matter of tying up a loose end."

Margo talked for several minutes. According to the surveillance detail, Fomin shook his head several times, nodded once, then leaned over to whisper something. Finally, he stood and walked away, not looking back.

III

"She did well," said the President. They were meeting in the residence this time, standing together on the balcony above the South Portico. "GREENHILL. An impressive young lady."

"Yes, Mr. President."

Kennedy caught something in his national security adviser's voice. "Come on, Mac. Out with it."

"It's not really over."

"Why not?"

"For one thing, we won't have forces on the ground to be sure they crate those missiles. We'll have to do visual inspection of the cargo ships as they leave Cuban waters."

"That doesn't strike me as a big problem."

"No, sir. But there's more. The negotiations included only the strategic warheads and the missiles. The Soviets still have the IL-28 bombers on the ground in Cuba, and they can reach our territory in minutes. It's possible that they might be leaving behind tactical nuclear weapons, too. Short-range. Useless for attacking our territory, but useful in self-defense."

Kennedy's eyes narrowed. "Why didn't you mention this, say, two days ago?"

"I decided that these were side issues, sir. Once the IRBMs and MRBMs were dealt with, we would be able to negotiate these out."

"Is that really it, Mac?" That famous grin, this time ironic. "I was thinking maybe you didn't mention it because you thought it would derail the deal. You sat there and kept your mouth shut and hoped to hell General Taylor didn't bring it up. Actually, I'm a little surprised that he didn't. It had to be on his mind. Maybe you squared him earlier." The President brushed a bit of lint from his sleeve. "Are you really that clever, Mac? Putting one over on me? On the entire national security apparatus of the United States?"

"Sir, my only cause is the security of the nation."

"Well, I'm just glad you're on our side." Kennedy leaned on the balustrade, gazing out over the city that was now safe from nuclear destruction. "I assume you have a plan?"

"Yes, Mr. President. Now that we've persuaded Khrushchev we're willing to act, I don't think we'll have trouble negotiating the removal of the bombers. As for the tactical warheads, Castro will do his best to get the Soviets to leave them in place, because he's terrified now that we might invade. But, under the circumstances, I would think that Khrushchev won't listen to him. The tactical warheads will be gone before the end of the year, and we won't have to give anything up to get them."

"Unless you're wrong."

"Yes, sir. If the bombers or the tactical warheads are still in Cuba two months from now, you'll have my resignation."

"Oh, I think if those bombers stay in Cuba, the United States might have slightly bigger problems than the fate of one McGeorge Bundy." Then he laughed. "You and Niemeyer. They say you don't get along, but you're just like him. Sitting there, thinking you're smarter than everybody else, manipulating everybody to build the world you want." The President was leafing through a folder. He pulled out a memorandum, waved it toward his national security adviser. "So tell me, then. Off the record. As long as you're busy rearranging the world, what do you think we should do about Vietnam?"

"Sir?"

"I followed your advice on Cuba and we didn't do too badly. So give me advice about Asia. The Joint Chiefs want to send more troops. My political people think we're in too deep already. They think it could kill the party in '64. Now I want your view. And remember"— waggling a finger—"the future of America is at stake. Again."

SIXTY-THREE

Powerful Friends

I

Jericho Ainsley had driven her to the meeting with Fomin. She would ride with no one else. Their reunion had taken place in a crowded White House anteroom. Now they were once more alone together—for the last time, she suspected—as he drove her back to the apartment. Margo still was not sure precisely who had conspired against her, but she accepted Agatha's word that Jerry was one of the good guys. And she doubted entirely that all of the bad guys were in custody.

As it turned out, she was righter than she could have imagined.

"That man Ziegler," she asked sleepily, "the one who tried to push things off the rails. What's going to happen to him?"

Ainsley was a moment answering. "Nothing, I suspect."

This jolted her wide awake. "I thought he'd been arrested!"

"They'll have to let him go."

"Why? I don't understand. He tried to stop the negotiations. There could have been a war. Isn't that treason, or disobedience of orders, or something? He can't just get off!"

"Grow up, Margo," said Ainsley. She had never heard his voice so harsh, but understood instinctively that his anger was not directed at her. "Washington has factions, just like the Kremlin. Part of the job of any successful President is to balance them one against another. Jack Ziegler and his coterie represent a faction, and a powerful one, within the government. Oh, there might be some resignations and early retirements, people forced to move to the private sector, that kind of thing. But that's all."

His fingers tightened on the steering wheel.

"And I'll tell you something else that you don't want to hear. After the President made his deal with Khrushchev, General LeMay, the chief of staff of the Air Force, sent a confidential memorandum to the White House. Believe it or not, he wanted to bomb Cuba anyway. He called the decision not to do so the greatest defeat in the history of the nation. And do you know what the President is going to do to General LeMay as a result? Nothing. Not a thing. The good general will continue in his post, because the faction of which he is a part is a faction without which it is not possible to govern. Not now. Maybe not ever. That's the brutal truth, Margo. I'm sorry."

"But people are dead. My roommate was beaten up. Those aren't factional squabbles. Those are crimes."

"Oh, they're going to say the Russians did it."

"Even Dr. Harrington?"

"Especially Dr. Harrington. Because the alternative is to admit the truth."

"What truth?"

"That, contrary to what you may have heard, the President doesn't run the government."

Margo wasn't sure what to say to this, and so said nothing. She watched the grand federal buildings pass, and probably she fell asleep, because when she looked out again they were in the turnaround beside her apartment building. Jericho Ainsley courteously got out first and opened her door.

"Do you need me to come upstairs?"

She shook her head. "At this point, the only person I'll need protection from is Patsy." She hesitated. "But, Jerry, I—if you're ever in Ithaca—not that anybody ever is . . ."

She dropped her eyes, unable to believe she was being so forward. He held on to her hand, touched her chin, made her look. That strange orange gaze was warmly assuring. "I'll bear that in mind," he said softly.

They hugged, awkwardly. But by now her analytical self was back, and before they parted she had another question.

"What you said before—if the government really is that divided— well, their side lost, right? They won't take that lying down."

The CIA man was gazing at the elementary school across the street. "You may have a point," he finally said.

"Well, shouldn't somebody do something?"

"There's nothing to do, Miss Jensen. There's nobody to do it to. This is just the way it is." He gave a little bow and shut the car door behind her. "Still, if I were the President, I suppose I'd watch my back."

PART IV

Credible Commitment

October 1962–March 1963

SIXTY-FOUR

Pilgrim's Progress

I

And so the two Great Powers stepped back from the nuclear brink. The world sighed with relief. For a little while, anyway, people even remembered to give thanks, because every day was a blessing. Then the news moved on—the Sino-Indian War, Richard Nixon's campaign for governor of California, Cassius Clay calling his fourth-round knock-out of Archie Moore all had their innings—and, as goods returned to grocery shelves and residents to the cities, the world moved on, too.

That's what they told Margo to do: Move on. Forget. Discover your life once more.

She tried.

II

Nana's house was like a foreign country. Margo wandered the many rooms, the furnishings scarcely changed since her childhood, and felt as if she was seeing it all for the first time. Had the living-room sofa always been quite this chintzy? Had the seascapes that lined the hallways always been so dismally rendered? Had the gravel driveway always been so pitted and warped? She pressed her anxious mind against these meaningless questions in order to drive away the meaningful ones.

For the first week, at least, Margo was convalescing royalty. It was plain to Claudia Jensen that her grandchild had been to terrible places and seen terrible things, and if she wanted to eat dinner on a metal folding table in front of the television in the study—previously a breach of etiquette so severe that Nana would practically faint on the spot, but only after the bawling out—well, if that was what Margo wanted, that was what Margo got. And if she preferred to spend hours sitting in the rotting wooden playhouse down the slope from the mansion, Nana left her alone to do exactly that, never troubling herself, as only months ago she would have, over what venomous memories were whirling through her granddaughter's head.

In the second week, Margo's brother, Corbin, arrived from Ohio, wife Holly and two children in tow—but his physical presence only confirmed what both siblings already knew: they had little in common these days. Each found the other a constant reminder of a painful childhood both would rather forget. So Corbin spent his hours with Nana at the house, while Margo played with his children out in the yard, and Holly, who earned a nice living photographing families, shuttled back and forth.

One afternoon, Tom Jellinek came to visit, and Nana could not have been more pleased to meet him. They lunched in the sunroom, Tom and Margo and her brother and his brood, the moment immortalized by Holly, the professional, with her clunky camera. In the photograph, which today is owned by a collector of Kennedy memorabilia in Colorado, Claudia Jensen is beaming as though she could not have been happier. Her gaze seems directed at Tom, whose arm is shyly around Margo's shoulder as they sit very close. Nana's bright smile at first glance might be taken as a sort of delighted approval of her granddaughter's choice—although, in fairness, it must be said that her wise old eyes no doubt sensed what the young lovers, with the tendency of all those of a certain age to confuse tenderness with devotion, did not: that the relationship had not long to run. Margo had in some indefinable way moved beyond him, and their lack of comfort with each other was slowly outgrowing their affection.

Corbin left the next day. Tom came twice more, but never stayed long.

With Annalise and Jerri, who dropped in on a Saturday, Margo was scarcely more animated, although she did allow them to coax her into driving into New York City to see *Who's Afraid of Virginia Woolf?* But they left the theater early, because Margo experienced an unexpected fit of tears during the second act, when the actors played their game of "Get the Guests." On the way back to Garrison, they apologized, and said they should have taken her to see a comedy instead. They stayed the night, sitting up with her and playing cards to all hours, because she couldn't sleep. On Sunday afternoon they left, but assured her they could hardly wait until January, when Margo was scheduled to return to school.

Miles and Vera Madison also dropped in one day for tea, along with Kimberly and Marilyn, the toddlers. Miles had been bumped all the way to a full colonelcy, and also granted early retirement. He shared with Nana his plans to go into real estate, all the same details he had shared with Margo on that night neither one of them would ever mention again, especially to each other.

Patsy had returned to California. Margo wrote, but never heard back.

Jericho Ainsley visited twice, and on those occasions Margo seemed to brighten. Mainly they walked together on the property, scarcely saying a word, evidently quite content to be in each other's company. To Claudia Jensen, this represented courting behavior. After the first visit, she asked around and learned of the Ainsley father, and the Ainsley money. Moreover, she found the young man's manner impeccable, even suitably diffident in her presence. It occurred to her that she should encourage his suit, notwithstanding his race. But after the second visit, Margo explained that Jerry had been promoted and reassigned and was moving abroad for an extended period. Other than that, she refused to speak of him. At first, Nana supposed that Ainsley had wounded her. But as time passed, Claudia Jensen sensed in her granddaughter not a broken heart but a kind of fatalistic optimism that reminded her of Donald.

Margo spent time with a psychiatrist, too, a certain Dr. Aprahamian, who worried about how much she refused to tell him, and was skeptical of those bits she deigned to share. After a few visits, Margo stopped going. Aprahamian was undeterred. He had a theory that her imagined experiences were cloaking a deeper trauma, and worked out an approach to her cleverly invented tale in which the various characters stood in for family members—the unnamed powerful politician for her absent father, for instance, and thus her insistence that he was attracted to her—and the psychiatrist decided to write it up for one of the journals. A week after he submitted his paper, he received a quiet visit from the Federal Bureau of Investigation. The journal, he was told, would not be publishing his piece, and if he ever breathed to anyone the smallest, most carefully camouflaged and hypothetical word of what Margo Jensen had related in their sessions, he would find himself behind bars. The agents confiscated his notes, and even the daybook that listed her appointments. Shortly thereafter, a grand dinner was held in Manhattan in honor of Dr. Aprahamian on the occasion of his retirement from active psychoanalytic practice.

III

Just before Thanksgiving, a lawyer arrived, representing not the government but the Kennedy family. His name was Chancellor. He was about seventy, and skinny as a rail, with a shock of startlingly white hair. And he had plainly done this before, for he was donnish and reassuring yet cautious and firm, everybody's favorite grandfather, dignified to the point of funereal in his smoothly understated black suit.

"You look well, Miss Jensen," he announced as if he hadn't seen her in a long time. They were in the study, facing each other across the desk. Nana had offered to sit in, but Margo had assured her that she would be fine.

"Thank you," she said, and waited.

"I know you've been through a terrible ordeal. I want you to know that my clients are terribly sorry for everything that's happened. They very much want to make it up to you."

To prove it, the lawyer had brought along an impressive sheaf of papers for Margo to sign and a handsome check for Margo to accept in return for her perpetual relinquishment of the right to discuss publicly any part of what may or may not have occurred in Washington over the period from twenty-third October through first November last, et cetera, et cetera. And the part that amused her most, even as she shoved both back at him and gently shook her head, was that he plainly believed that he was trying to purchase her silence about a presidential dalliance. She could read in his clever eyes the thinly veiled judgment of his class, contempt for a woman skilled enough to snare her prey but sufficiently amateurish not to keep her hooks in him. He despised her, and perhaps the man he was protecting as well: and his scorn was the surest sign that the deception was holding.

"This isn't a negotiation," he explained as he packed everything away. "There won't be a second offer."

"I understand."

"I hope you understand as well that the family takes its reputation seriously. Part of my responsibility is to see to it that no defamation should occur."

"Of course."

"Thank you for taking the time to see me, Miss Jensen."

"Thank you, Mr. Chancellor," she said, and shook his hand mannishly.

In the grand foyer, the lawyer took a last look around, as if satisfying his curiosity: yes, there were Negroes who were neither singers nor boxers yet lived this way. Or perhaps he was totting up the family assets, in case, despite his warning, defamation should occur after all. Then he was gone, never turning. He'd kept a chauffeur waiting. Margo stood in the window, watching them descend the gravel drive, pass the stone lion, and disappear.

"Are you okay, Miss Margo?" murmured Muriel, materializing beside her.

"Never better."

"You look peaked."

"I feel wonderful."

This was a lie. She felt somewhere well to the south of criminal. But her crime had no remedy just yet.

IV

On the Monday after Thanksgiving, McGeorge Bundy came. He didn't call first, and he arrived without ceremony: no driver, no aides, just the President's national security adviser, all five foot seven of him, standing on the front step in the whirling autumn wind, and inviting her for a walk. Like Harrington and Agatha and Ainsley, he plainly mistrusted walls.

They strolled along the river above the possibly poisonous rushes, hands thrust in the pockets of heavy jackets: the same route, as it happened, that she had walked twice with Ainsley.

"The crisis is officially over," Bundy said. "I'm sure you saw the news reports when the cargo ships left Cuba with the disassembled missiles aboard. The bombers, too, are being withdrawn. And that will be that. We won, Miss Jensen. And without you I'm not sure we could have done it."

She mumbled something about being glad to do her small part.

"I'm serious. I want you to remember that, always. What you did for your country, and at enormous risk."

Margo allowed herself a small chuckle. "I'm not likely to forget."

They were on the promontory now, the wrecked dock down below. The same smashed red boat from her childhood, now just rotted timbers, faintly crimson, mostly mud. A week and a half ago, she had stood at this very spot with Jerry Ainsley. She was about to mention the fact, but had a shrewd suspicion that Bundy already knew.

"Let me tell you why I'm here," he said, facing not Margo but the water. "I would like you to consider coming to work for me."

She shook her head, trying to loosen the cobwebs. She could not possibly have heard him right.

"You're smart, you're brave, and you say what you think. You don't let rank intimidate you. We need people like you in Washington, and in national security particularly. And of course Niemeyer thinks the world of you." Her continued silence seemed to irritate him. "We'd be happy to have you next summer, but I was also thinking of something long-term. When you've finished your education, say."

"I don't know if I'm going back to school," she said after a moment's thought.

"Of course you are. You have academia written all over you. I see you as a professor one day."

"Ha" was all she said, turning away so that he wouldn't notice the color in her cheeks.

"You did wonderfully well, Miss Jensen. I told you before that the nation owes you a debt, and it's true. We can never repay you. If at any time there is anything I can do for you, you need only call."

"Thank you," she managed, but the excessive tone of his remarks had become a warning gong. There was something else, something she wasn't going to like hearing.

"So now we have a problem, Miss Jensen." Bundy turned his face deliberately into the wind, and she had to lean close to hear him. Again she was impressed by his instinctive avoidance of prying ears. "Your mission was successful, the country owes you, but we need to find a way to guarantee your silence."

"You mean, other than sending Mr. Chancellor to bribe me."

"That wasn't me, and it wasn't the President, either. It was done, let us say, automatically. Once the rumors started flying—well, there's a way the family deals with such matters. It isn't pretty, but it's the way it's done."

"If there's a way of handling it automatically, it must happen quite often."

Margo was secretly proud of the clever sauciness of her reply, but Bundy remained unimpressed. "I took you as above that sort of comment," he said, and for a moment his voice was Nana and her mother rolled into one. "Never mind. It can't have been easy. And no doubt there will come a time—perhaps in the President's memoirs, perhaps later—when the truth can be told. I hope so. You deserve the accolades of history." He pursed his lips, as if in disapproval of the next words he would speak. "Nevertheless, Miss Jensen, now is now, and I still have to ask. What is it you want? What's the price for your silence?"

"I don't have a price."

"The point is—"

"I'm not going to talk about it, Mr. Bundy. I promised I won't, so I won't. I know Washington doesn't work that way, but in my family, a promise is a promise. You don't have to buy me off or threaten me. You don't have to persuade me of the vital importance of keeping the secret. I'll keep it."

"Of course," he said, and for a moment Margo thought she was being mocked, and squared for another battle. Then she realized that he accepted her vow, that he perhaps had even counted on it. "Nevertheless, you should be aware that you now officially have a very wealthy distant relation who's recently died and who has left you a significant amount of money, currently on deposit in your name—"

"I don't want it."

"I know. But you have to take it."

"Why?"

"Because the kind of people we have in Washington only trust what they think they own." He raised both hands to forestall her objection. "I know you'll never be owned, Miss Jensen. I know it and *you* know it. But there's no reason they have to know it. You can give the money to charity if you like. You can convert it to cash and burn it in the fire. The one thing you mustn't do is turn it down."

"Give it to Agatha," she said tartly. "She's sacrificed a lot more than I have."

"I'm afraid we can't do that, Miss Jensen. We don't know where she is."

Margo drew a long breath. "You're saying Jack Ziegler got her."

"No," said Bundy, with fierce confidence. "He didn't."

"How can you be sure?"

"We're sure." He glanced around: finally, the true point of the visit. "And you haven't heard from her? She hasn't visited, called, sent you a note?"

Margo walked him to his rented car.

"I'm serious about the job offer, Miss Jensen. I like people who are smart, reliable, combative, and discreet. You'd be perfect for my staff."

"I'll think about it," she said, turning her face away to hide her excitement.

"Do, please." All at once he sounded diffident and uneasy, the Boston Brahmin after all. "The President joins in the offer. He says he likes the idea of having you closer."

Suddenly they were both embarrassed, and in a great hurry to say their goodbyes. Watching the President's special assistant for national security affairs back into the turnaround and make his way down the gravel drive, she reminded herself that he was just the messenger.

V

And where was Agatha Milner?

For a while longer, the mystery occupied Bundy's time. After meeting Margo on the morning of October 29, she had vanished—except, of course, for her brief reappearance that same afternoon to cave in Viktor Vaganian's knees. Both FBI and CIA were searching for her, but neither had turned up a trace. Probably the Russians were looking, too.

"I suppose that just breaking Vaganian's knees was a way of respecting his diplomatic immunity," said Bundy to his wife, one of his few confidants.

"That isn't terribly amusing, dear."

"She could very easily have killed him. She wanted us to know that."

Following his release from custody, Jack Ziegler, too, had disappeared, presumably to avoid Agatha's wrath. He had friends everywhere who would protect him, and doubtless was mounting his defenses. But passive waiting was not natural to the traveling salesmen of the clandestine world, and it was assumed that at some point he would commence his own private hunt for Agatha.

"They deserve each other," said a Langley deputy director during a meeting to announce no progress in the search. "She may have switched sides at the end, but remember that she was part of his cabal."

Gradually, this came to be the accepted wisdom. The search for Agatha Milner was moved to a back burner, and then to one even farther to the rear. There were too many immediate crises demanding the attention of those tasked with protecting the nation. Tracking two ex-spies who were fighting a private war against each other was a waste of resources. As long as they weren't killing bystanders, they weren't the government's problem.

Bundy reluctantly acceded to this view. But, as he told his wife, he continued to worry. Suppose Agatha Milner's list of enemies wasn't limited to those who worked directly with Jack Ziegler. The chain of events that had led to the death of Doris Harrington comprised many links. From Agatha's point of view, there was plenty of blame to go around. Sooner or later, she was bound to aim higher.

VI

On the afternoon of New Year's Eve, Bundy was in his office, trying to catch up on paperwork while tamping down several freshly brewing crises. He and his wife were supposed to go out later. He had warned her that he might have to work late, and she had been married to him long enough to understand that "might" often cloaked an imperative. Nevertheless, he was determined, for once, to make it home on time.

There was more information to be entered into the Cuba file, including the confirmation that the last bombers were gone. There were the continuing protests from the Commonwealth nations over Dean Acheson's speech suggesting that Great Britain was no longer a world power. And then there was the matter of recommending that the resignation of one William Borkland, formerly Dr. Harrington's chief aide, not be accepted, and that Borkland instead be promoted to serve as acting deputy assistant secretary of state for intelligence and analysis.

A very peculiar case.

The incumbent, the ambitious Alfred Gwynn, had surprised everyone three days ago by requesting reassignment, effective immediately. From the stories Bundy had managed to put together, Gwynn had received a strange envelope at the office just before Christmas. When he opened it, he went pale, grabbed his hat and coat, and fled the building. He hadn't been back since.

Esman, as usual, had a theory:

"Look at it this way. We were searching for the leak that told Fomin that GREENHILL was our asset. You took that one away from me, and at the time I was puzzled, but eventually I saw what you'd worked out: we had things backward. There never was any leak to Fomin. The whole operation was Fomin's from the start. Getting Vasily Smyslov to drop his hints to Bobby Fischer, then somehow pressuring Fischer to demand that GREENHILL accompany him to Varna—the whole plan was intended, even before we knew the missiles existed, to set up the back channel. Khrushchev yielded to his hard-liners by putting the missiles in, but he's a wise old dog. So, at the same time that he approved Anadyr, he also instructed Fomin to find a way to let him negotiate in secret to get the missiles out again."

"Then why not turn down the hard-liners in the first place? Why all of this rigamarole?"

"Because the hard-liners had to see how we'd respond: the planes in the air, missiles on alert, forces ready to invade. Khrushchev could never have gotten them to stand down unless they saw what we were willing to do." Esman adjusted the thick glasses. "Anyway, you figured that the operation was Fomin's. At that point, you immediately decided to stop my leak investigation. You didn't want the identity of

Fomin's collaborator disclosed. We both know why. I don't think we need to go into details."

Bundy didn't smile exactly, but he did give a curt nod of approval. Once more, Esman proved himself the smartest of the bunch.

"No," said Bundy, "we don't need to go into details."

"But there was another leak, later. Somebody was giving information to the Ziegler faction, too—information that wound up in the hands of Colonel Vaganian. Maybe I should say the late Colonel Vaganian, seeing that we heard the Soviets shot him last month, broken knees and all. Anyway, the Ziegler faction had information from Langley, obviously, but they also had details from inside Dr. Harrington's shop. And we know that Gwynn had a habit of referring to the operation as QKPARCHMENT rather than SANTA GREEN. So maybe there was a trade involved—you give us information, we'll support your climb up the ladder—follow me?"

Bundy said he believed he could stretch his mind around it, yes.

"So Agatha figures it out, and she tells Gwynn she's coming after him next—and, well, by now I bet he's moved his family to Vancouver."

"I believe he's requested a consular vacancy in Tierra del Fuego."

That conversation had taken place this morning. Secretary Rusk had already recommended that Gwynn's transfer request be granted. A part of Bundy wanted to turn it down, just to let the wretched man sweat and suffer. Leave him to Agatha Milner's vengeance. But there was no actual evidence to support Esman's theory. If there had been, Gwynn could have been arrested and tried. Without it—well, there were times when McGeorge Bundy stifled his conscience for the sake of the nation, but in truth the Catholic moralist who lived deep inside him detested the loss of life, even when it was deserved.

His hand hovered above the paper. Approve? Disapprove?

He chose, and signed, and dropped the stack of papers on Janet's desk. "Heading home," he said.

"Happy New Year, Mr. Bundy."

"What? Oh. Happy New Year to you, too." He found a smile somewhere. "Anyway, this Administration can't possibly have a worse 1963 than 1962, right?"

SIXTY-FIVE

Back in the Pool

I

In January, Margo returned to Ithaca, and school. Once more the dean had been spoken to. Margo's fall semester had been canceled. She would in effect start over. This would leave her a term behind her classmates, but she could make it up next summer. That is, unless she chose to accept Bundy's invitation to spend more time in Washington; or perhaps Bill Borkland's offer of an internship in a European capital of her choice.

"It's on the merits," Borkland assured her. "The interest in you is genuine."

"You don't understand," Margo said kindly. "I don't want anything from you."

Actually, her return to school could not have come at a better time. Relations with Nana had deteriorated swiftly after Jericho Ainsley arrived the day after Christmas and swept Margo away for two days and two nights. Nana was appalled; she had never heard of such a thing. A well-bred young lady would never go off with a man not her husband. And of course Margo's poor parents must be rolling in their graves.

"It isn't that kind of trip," Margo protested—an objection that met the sneering disdain Claudia Jensen reserved for those who tried to bury their sin beneath layers of lie. So her granddaughter gave up on that argument and simply announced that the world had changed.

"Not for the better," snapped Nana.

Margo left anyway. Forty-eight hours later, she was back, but Nana scarcely stirred from her room for a day or so, even to take her meals.

"She's fine, Miss Margo," said Muriel. "She just wants you to know she's still mad."

"I think I know."

"Maybe if you apologize."

But Margo could neither apologize nor explain. She had gone away with Jerry Ainsley for reasons she considered good and sufficient. Of course, they could have avoided upsetting her grandmother by postponing the journey, but he would be off to his new posting on the first of the year, so now was the only time. He had organized the expedition with enormous caution, and although in truth she held but a single meeting, the extra day was necessary so that they might take a circuitous route, with Ainsley watching for surveillance the entire way. And while it is true that they shared a motel room for a night, the only purpose of the arrangement—so Margo would have insisted, had she admitted this fact to her grandmother, which she did not—was security. The security, too, was necessary, even though she could never tell Nana the truth:

The crisis wasn't over.

II

The campus had changed little since her departure, except that she felt as if every step bogged down in the beautiful but endless Ithaca snow. She enrolled in no courses in the government department: she was giving serious consideration, she told her adviser, to changing her major to French.

"But why?" he asked, very surprised. "You're a B student in French. You have straight A's in government and, well, everything else."

"Government is too stressful," she answered, knowing and not caring that he would misunderstand.

Margo went out with Tom Jellinek twice, but by the second time, it was plain that he was ready to move on, and probably already had. She was kind and even warm in releasing him, though later she felt more lonely than she could have imagined. Annalise and Jerri both insisted that Margo was better off, and she supposed that listening to their fluttery reassurances was the price of friendship. Meanwhile, her grades slipped a bit. She was having difficulty with her concentration, and one afternoon her French professor even taunted her: *"Avons-nous votre attention, mademoiselle? Vous vous ennuyez?"* She resolved to work harder. But when, in mid-February, a cheery Nate Esman from Bundy's office telephoned to remind her that they were still waiting to hear back about the offer of an internship this summer, all she could think about was how he stood in front of the FBI car in the White House driveway.

She noticed that nobody talked about Cuba. Everyone seemed to have forgotten, in days or weeks, how close the world came to annihilation. But of course great disasters are also great abstractions, easily buried beneath layers of the practical triviality we call everyday life. And Margo's inability to accept that truth pushed her away from her friends, thus increasing the isolation that she had in any case come to prefer. On the long nights when she found herself unable to sleep, she scribbled cautiously affectionate letters to Jericho Ainsley in Paris, none of which she posted.

In February, Bobby Fischer showed up in Ithaca without warning, and spent three nights in Tom's dorm room before moving on. Bobby at first refused to see Margo at all, but she prevailed upon Tom, who finally talked him into it. Over coffee at the student union, Bobby announced his decision to forgive her for leaving Varna without warning. It was not Margo's disappearance that had ruined his game against Botvinnik, he'd realized. It was the Russian cheaters. He was thinking he might retire, except that he didn't know how to do anything else. Margo reminded him that he was the best player in the world, and kept stroking his ego until he was calm enough to answer a couple of pertinent questions.

And all the while, she avoided Lorenz Niemeyer like the pest. Once or twice, when she noticed him crossing the Quad, she made an ostentatious point of turning around and heading the other way. When she read in the campus paper that he had been appointed to the legendary Forty Committee, which evaluated intelligence operations for the White House, she raced to the bathroom and threw up.

Finally, in early March, her nerves stretched near breaking, Margo received the telephone call she had been awaiting and dreading. Her role in the Cuban crisis would at last have its final act.

III

She made the appointment through the great man's secretary. Usually Mrs. Khorozian protected his time with a fearsome dedication, but when she learned that it was Margo Jensen on the line, she was able to clear half an hour that very afternoon.

"An hour would be better," said Margo.

"I'll see what I can do," Mrs. Khorozian promised.

The meeting was set for half past four, right after the end of Niemeyer's graduate seminar on nuclear strategy, and when Margo arrived ten minutes early, she was at once shown into his grand office to wait.

She didn't sit. She wandered along the walls, peering at the photographs of Niemeyer with the leaders of the world, Niemeyer receiving awards and medals, Niemeyer in major's uniform during the war. There were no photographs of Niemeyer with Donald Jensen; or Niemeyer with his wife. Her reconnaissance over, Margo stood in the bay window that gave on the courtyard where Niemeyer had first told her that he knew her father, and so ensured that she would accept the assignment to accompany Bobby Fischer to Varna and set in motion the chain of events that had nearly taken her life.

"Miss Jensen," said the great man, stepping inside. "How wonderful to see you again."

Margo turned in time to see Mrs. Khorozian sweeping the heavy door shut. Niemeyer crossed straight to the trolley and poured himself a rye, neat. He didn't offer her anything, and it occurred to her that he was terribly nervous.

"Professor," she acknowledged.

For as long as it takes to stare your adversary down, they stood at opposite ends of the room, not speaking. Niemeyer finished his drink in two gulps.

"To what do I owe the pleasure?" he asked, with a hint of his old bonhomie.

"I wanted to thank you," she said pleasantly. She even smiled. "And to talk about what happened."

He studied her a moment longer, then motioned her to the sofa. He seated himself in an Eames chair that groaned beneath his bulk.

"There's nothing to thank me for," he said. "I'm delighted at your success, but not surprised." He crossed his plump legs. "Mac Bundy tells me they've offered you a position. Will you take it?"

"I haven't made up my mind."

"Take it, Miss Jensen. Or perhaps you might rather join the spies. I'm sure Langley would be happy to have you." His confidence was back. "You won't be surprised to learn that Dr. Harrington sent them a memorandum strongly urging your recruitment."

Margo hunched forward. "She was a wonderful woman. You must miss her terribly."

"Indeed. The last time we spoke, you accused her of being a Soviet spy. Working with Aleksandr Fomin. I assume you realize by now that such a notion is absurd. She'd never have given secrets to the Communists. She dedicated her life to protecting this country. She would no more commit treason than I would."

"But would it be treason if it was intended to protect the country?"

"Sophistry, Miss Jensen. That's the excuse every double agent gives."

She nodded. The ticking of the grandfather clock was suddenly very loud, the way it had been on the day when Stilwell and Borkland recruited her. "That's what leads to the part that bothers me."

"Which part is that?"

"The part about who killed Phil Littlejohn."

IV

The great man's eyes widened. "I beg your pardon."

"He was run down by a car right after he turned out to know what had happened in Varna. That's one heck of a coincidence."

Niemeyer leaned back in his chair. His bewilderment seemed so genuine that she knew it had to be feigned. "Then most likely it was the Soviets. Fomin, or the other fellow. Vaganian."

"And how exactly did the Soviets know that Phil Littlejohn was pestering me? Who would have told them?"

"Come, Miss Jensen. You were Fomin's chosen conduit. Surely after Varna he had agents in Ithaca, watching you. Vaganian, too."

"Yes, but an endless supply? Somebody ready to step in and pretend to fit on the campus? All of them with perfect English?" Not long ago, it had been Niemeyer who peppered her with questions, not the other way around: back in the days when he intimidated her. "On the other hand, you were there that day when Phil wouldn't leave me alone, when he brought up Bulgaria, when he hinted at special knowledge. You rescued me, as you put it, from his clutches. But now, looking back, I wonder how long you were standing there. I wonder what else you heard."

"You're stretching, Miss Jensen."

"Am I? I'm not so sure. That fake alum who took my photo on the first day you asked me to meet after class. He wasn't waiting at the front door of the building where all the students leave. We went out the side, and there he was. How would he have known I'd be using that exit unless he knew you'd be inviting me to walk you to your office?"

Niemeyer said nothing, but the look of faint amusement never faded from the pudgy face. In the light of his glowing confidence she faltered briefly, but forced herself to press on.

"And there's more. Fomin knew Ithaca awfully well. Almost as if he'd been here before. For instance, he knew Stewart Park would be accessible at night, and also that we'd be undisturbed if we met there. Then in Varna, Fomin knew that I'd been inquiring about my father's fate. But at that point the only person I'd discussed my father with was you. Most important, when he asked me in Washington if I'd told anyone else, I mentioned two people—one here and one there—it was the one in Washington that upset him. He had to know that you were the one in Ithaca. He didn't seem to care."

"He presumably accepted that you needed my help."

"'Presumably.' That doesn't sound like the Professor Niemeyer I know." She almost smiled. "It seems to me that the other possibility is that the two of you know each other. Maybe pretty well."

Niemeyer stood up. He rumbled over to the other bay window and folded his arms as he gazed upon the Quad.

"The way your mind works is fascinating," he said, not turning. "When you put the facts together that way, yes, you can reach the conclusion you suggest. But in the analysis of intelligence information, we have a word for people who make up their minds too quickly and then try to make the evidence fit. We call them amateurs." His laugh was ugly; she didn't know why she'd never noticed before. His laugh was a mirror of his brilliant, precise, very ugly mind. "The trouble with your theory, Miss Jensen, is that there's another explanation. If Fomin knew Ithaca well, that might mean only that he and his people are good at their jobs. We can't infer anything from his having a photographer in the proper position to cover your exit from the back of the building unless we know whether he had other people covering the other exits. And as to how many English-speaking operatives the KGB employs in this country, I haven't any idea, and neither has the CIA or the FBI. Probably there are hundreds. Why couldn't two or three of them spend a few weeks in Ithaca, looking you over?"

"That still doesn't explain why he was looking me over at all before I'd even been invited to Washington."

That awful laugh again as he turned to look at her. "The fact that you hadn't been invited doesn't mean the decision hadn't been made. The leak most likely came from State or the Agency. After all, several dozen people knew about SANTA GREEN. Is it too much to assume that one of them might have spoken out of turn?"

"You're making assumptions again."

"As are you, Miss Jensen. The difference is, I'm making an educated guess that some unknown individual out of thirty or forty might have been indiscreet. You're focused on one individual you believe to be the guilty party."

"Which makes me an amateur."

"Precisely."

Margo stood. "I'll always wonder, you know: How much of the planning was yours. How much was Fomin's. And whether you'd worked together before."

"Miss Jensen, I really think—"

"You must have already known each other, I guess. Otherwise, there would have been no reason for him to approach you. Fomin knew how to reach you, didn't he? And he came to you on Khrushchev's orders and said there were missiles in Cuba and he needed a go-between to serve as a back channel, somebody trustworthy and ambitious but utterly unobtrusive. Maybe you asked him if it would be safe, and he lied and said yes, and so, since you knew my father, and maybe felt a little guilty about letting him get blown to bits, you thought this would be good for my career. So you gave him my name. Then you sent somebody—maybe Vale, maybe Mr. Khorozian—to see Bobby Fischer to make sure he'd demand the company of his good-luck charm in Varna. All Bobby remembers is that the man came in a shiny old green car, and offered him a lot of money."

"There are a lot of green cars, Miss Jensen."

She refused to let him deflect her. "And after that you took yourself out of the loop—probably by design—and events took on a momentum of their own. But the part I'll really wonder about is whether you'd have gone down this road if you'd known what it would cost. Your ex-wife died because of this plan. Doesn't that bother you a little?"

He was shaking his head. His expression was troubled but unreadable. "You have a magnificent imagination, Miss Jensen."

"Does Fomin?" He looked startled, and she rushed right on. "Do you know what he told me the last time we met? That the Gestapo had a report of another man fleeing the farmhouse just before they found my father. A short, heavyset man, they said. And the interesting part is that he fled after the explosion, not before. Almost as if he'd waited to make sure Donald Jensen was blown to bits." She was on her feet. "Goodbye, Professor Niemeyer."

V

Margo didn't close the door behind her. She didn't smile at Mrs. Khorozian. Her heels clocked along the hall. She shoved open the doors and burst into the sunshine. She felt unstoppable. Descending the very steps where the fake alum had snapped her photo a million years ago, she felt the future stretching endlessly ahead of her.

Until a sudden prickly shiver brought her to a halt.

Margo stood on the walkway, glancing around. She felt watched. But around the Quad she saw only students, all ignoring her as they hurried along their various ways.

She turned and looked at Niemeyer's corner office.

He stood in the window, watching her without expression.

For a moment she felt she should march back in and apologize, or in some other way make peace. But she shook off the conciliatory mood. She was done with him. She was free. It was all over.

That is, unless, of course . . .

VI

Margo crossed the Quad, not looking back. At the northern edge of campus, she walked along the gorge where Fall Creek cut through the middle of Ithaca. She descended the muddy wooden steps to the pedestrian bridge.

Agatha Milner was waiting at the near end. She had cut her hair short and wore jeans and a thick sweater to go with her hooded parka, adding plenty of bulk and obscuring her face. No surveillance team would have recognized her.

"What did he say?" she asked.

"He denied it."

"Do you believe him?"

Hesitation. "I don't know. I can't be sure."

Agatha's smile was flinty. "You do know, Margo. You just don't want it to be true." She counted on her fingers. "He killed Littlejohn, or he had Vale do it, or he told Fomin, which amounts to the same thing. That poor man who was tortured in the swamp. That would never have happened except for his grand scheme. He would willingly have sacrificed your life for the sake of his operation. The way he sacrificed Dr. Harrington's."

"He couldn't have known they would go that far!"

"Couldn't he? Aren't you the one who told me that the first rule of conflict theory is to keep your adversary guessing? To strike out in ways that look like the acts of madmen? Do you really imagine that Niemeyer is so simple that he thinks nobody else knows the winning strategy?"

Margo was near panic. "But that's all assuming that he's guilty. That he and Fomin are"—even now she could scarcely pronounce the words—"agent and handler. And we can't know that for sure. Don't you think we should gather more evidence?"

"I'm willing to wait, Margo. But not long. I'm good, but I'm not perfect. Sooner or later, they will track me down and they will kill me. And I want to finish my work first." The minder fixed her with that disapproving librarian's stare. "And stop telling me we're not sure. There are plenty of people in my business who can't make up their minds whether some guy is the enemy or not. Know what we call them?"

"No."

"Dead."

Agatha slipped away along the sodden path, descending toward the gorge, and disappeared into the twilight.

Epilogue

That was all more than half a century ago. Margo Jensen, later Margo Waterman, has recently retired from her faculty position at Cornell. She's been in and out of government over the years, and has taught at three or four different institutions, but Cornell, where she also received her doctorate, is the place she considers home. The national security bug bit her after all, just as Lorenz Niemeyer predicted that it would. He survived for some years, by the way, and when he died during the Clinton Administration, his obituary made the front page of the *Times,* above the fold. Margo professes to have no idea what became of Agatha Milner.

What about the other players in the tale? Jericho Ainsley, as you probably remember, rose through the ranks to become director of central intelligence, although a scandal would later force him from office. Jack Ziegler survived and even thrived. In the 1980s, he was indicted for arms trafficking—charges subsequently dropped, after two witnesses vanished and the rest decided to lose their memories.

President Kennedy kept his side of the bargain, withdrawing the Jupiter missiles from Italy and Turkey within a year. Khrushchev kept his less known side, too. Faced with growing opposition after the Cuba humiliation, in 1964 he agreed, with remarkably little resistance, to retire as General Secretary.

Margo's friend Annalise Seaver, as you probably know, became a power in the Republican Party. Her friend Jerri dropped out of Cornell the following year and found her way to Hollywood, where she worked for many years as a publicist. Margo never heard again from her Washington roommate Patsy, but when Hope married a young man from her church the following year, Margo was in the wedding. Nate Esman left government shortly after these events to pursue graduate work in computer science. He rose to become chief technologist at Hewlett-Packard, back in the days when Silicon Valley was young, and later cofounded a venture-capital firm.

As to how I got wind of this story, it began at my father's memorial service a few years ago, when I overheard an African-American woman of some years, a member of what Claudia Jensen would have called one of the old families, asking another woman, someone she hadn't seen in decades, if she knew what had become of little Margo.

"Who?"

"The one who had the affair with JFK. You remember."

This line naturally intrigued me, but when I approached them, both women clammed up. After that I returned to my other work, but the notion that some black woman had been involved with the thirty-fifth President of the United States continued to tantalize. I pored over a couple of Kennedy biographies but found no mention. One was written by an acquaintance of mine, but when I asked him, he only laughed. "That rumor's been around forever. Nobody believes it."

Acting on the assumption that Margo, whoever she was, would also have been a member of one of those old families, I studied genealogy tables until I narrowed the possibilities to three. When I learned that Margo Jensen had actually worked in Washington briefly during the Kennedy Administration, I went back to my friend the biographer, who in turn directed me to a Kennedy retainer who'd been one of his sources. This man, now over ninety but with a mind clear as a bell, remembered that Margo had once been arrested at the White House. Nobody knew why, he said. But the national security adviser, McGeorge Bundy, was the one who got her out.

Armed with this skimpy information, I still wasn't sure what I had. Certainly there wasn't enough here to justify a direct approach. Once more I put the research aside. And once more it wouldn't leave me alone.

Finally, I gave in. I had to have the details. Before I made my approach, I visited Vera Madison, an old friend of my parents, who has a lovely condominium in a retirement community on Hilton Head. After a bit of prodding, she was kind enough to share her late husband's diaries. After that, I was home free.

I tracked Margo to Garrison, where she still summers at her late grandmother's house. She was surprised that anyone had worked it all out, and even helped me frame my central question in a way that was relatively inoffensive. Only later did it occur to me that she had been eager to talk to someone about what had happened, if only to set the record straight. She had heard, she said, that I was sniffing around. Sooner or later, the tale might come out, and she wanted her version on the record.

Margo wasted no time in denial. We sat in her grandmother's old study, surrounded by silver-framed photographs of her late husband, her three children, and her four grandchildren. A big nervous sheepdog kept padding in and out, perhaps to make sure that his mistress was being well treated. Margo gave me tea, along with cookies from the same bakery Priscilla Littlejohn had frequented, in Poughkeepsie—now run by the niece of the original owner—and as we sat in the corner, with a view down to the river and the same ruined dock, she told me her story, much as I have told it to you.

I returned the following morning, and the morning after that, until I had it all.

Or almost all.

"You haven't told me what you thought of Kennedy," I said toward the end.

"He was a great man," she said, with a winning smile. "He would have done great things if he'd survived." The smile vanished. "And you know, Mr. Carter, in the missile crisis, I don't think there was anyone else who could have held the middle ground so well."

"That's not exactly what I meant." I pondered the safest way to put the question. "I couldn't help noticing how, toward the end, you got sort of vague about the details of your meetings with Kennedy. Particularly on that last Friday and Saturday. Those accounts sounded a little, um, truncated."

"I told you everything I remember," she said slyly. "Everything relevant."

"So there might be things that happened that were irrelevant?"

"Most of life is irrelevant, Mr. Carter." A lovely wink. "Although I must say those often tend to be the more wonderful parts."

She had been working for decades on a double dactyl about the Kennedy years, she said, but somehow couldn't get it done.

The last question I asked was why she had decided to accept the offer to spend the summer of 1963 working for Bundy.

Margo smiled.

"Was it just the experience you wanted?" No reply. "Did you maybe miss the excitement of being on the inside?" Still she had nothing to say, but her smile never wavered. "Or was it maybe because Kennedy wanted you nearby?"

At the door, she made me take a bag of those marvelous cookies.

"When you write your book," she said, "do me one favor." The hazel eyes grew solemn. "A way to make my life a little easier."

"What's that?"

"Make it a novel. Change all the locations. Which university I'm at. Which towns and cities. Where I'm from. All that. Most important, change the names. Mine especially."

So I did.

Author's Note

Readers of my other fiction will remember Jack Ziegler as the villain of *The Emperor of Ocean Park*. His backstory is slightly different there than it is here, but Ziegler was always skilled at inventing a cover. Of course the heroic Major Madison of the instant novel is the Colonel Madison of *Emperor*, Misha Garland's father-in-law: his daughter Kimberly, a toddler here, grows up to be Misha's ambitious wife. Vera Madison is also in both novels, as is little Marilyn, who by the time of *Emperor* is known as Lindy. Agent Stilwell, the conduit to J. Edgar Hoover, plays a similar role in *Palace Council*. Eddie Wesley, mentioned briefly here as Claudia Jensen's godson, features prominently in that book. There, as here, he works briefly in the Kennedy White House, exiting well before the events in the present story. Torie Elden, who oversees Margo's work at the Labor Department, is present in several of *Palace*'s scenes. And poor Tristan Hadley, dismissed as an idiot by Lorenz Niemeyer in chapter 3 of the instant tale, is in *Palace Council* the spurned suitor of Aurelia Treene. Finally, readers of my novel *Jericho's Fall* will of course know what fate awaited Jericho Ainsley later in life.

Historical Note and Acknowledgments

This is a work of fiction, not a work of history, so there would be little point in listing all of the changes I have made to the chronology of the Cuban Missile Crisis. I have shoved around the dates and times of the meetings of the ExComm to suit my narrative, I have moved the Soviet responses to places where they better fit the story, and I have rewritten the remarks of the participants—and occasionally their identities. I have tried to remain true nevertheless to the thrust of the roles of particular historical figures in resolving the crisis itself. Some events—such as the evacuation of the White House on October 24, 1962—never occurred. On the other hand, the premise of my fictional evacuation—the false report of the launch of a Soviet intercontinental ballistic missile—did indeed happen, and on that very day. (The other two false reports that I mention were also delivered during the crisis, but not on that Wednesday; my point was to imagine the panic had all three reports come in at once.)

The conversation about the Bay of Pigs between President Kennedy and former President Eisenhower really did take place at Camp David, largely along the lines that I describe in chapter 29. Kennedy actually received the intelligence report that the Soviet Union was burning its papers—considered a prelude to war—on Saturday, October 27, not Monday, October 29, as in my novel. The report turned out to be false. The comments that I attribute to Curtis LeMay after the end of the crisis actually combine two separate communications. The subsequent deal to remove the IL-28 bombers from Cuba was reached much as I describe it.

The quotations from documents are all accurate. In a debriefing from before the missile crisis, Oleg Penkovsky, known as YOGA, really did try to persuade his handlers to attack the Soviet Union. The last National Intelligence Estimate before the missiles were discovered really did go disastrously wrong—not the last time that has happened! The letter from Khrushchev really did call Kennedy a degenerate. And so forth.

And there really was a back channel, with several of the meetings held at the Yenching Palace restaurant, which closed its doors in 2007. The real back channel involved John Scali of ABC News, rather than a nineteen-year-old college student. But the Soviet end was indeed Aleksandr Fomin (whose real name was Alexander Feksilov), the KGB *rezident* in Washington, who had been involved in recruiting the Rosenbergs. The details of his life that Fomin vouchsafes to Margo, both in Varna and on the Mall, are uniformly and without exception false: wisps, as Doris Harrington might have called them, spun perhaps to make GREENHILL more comfortable following his lead.

How important the back channel really was in resolving the crisis has been debated by historians. Certainly there is no evidence that the Soviets ever tried to persuade Kennedy to mothball the TX-61 "gravity bomb." The United States in fact completed development of the weapon, which evolved into the B61, a variable-yield thermonuclear warhead that remains part of what is known as the "enduring stockpile"—nuclear weapons that the nation chose to retain following the end of the Cold War. (By the way, Fomin's English was quite good, but not nearly as perfect as in my tale. His NPR interview and his autobiography are both fascinating.)

The military activities that I mention, from the Neptune P-2H that buzzed and photographed the *Poltava* during its September journey, to the U-2 overflights of Cuba, to the movement of troops and planes to Florida, all took place largely as and when I describe them. Lorenz Niemeyer's tales about both sides shooting down the other's surveillance planes are all matters of public record. According to declassified CIA documents, it is a fact that the eleven survivors of the C-130 downed over Soviet territory were never heard from again. A 1993 report suggested that as of that date, some might still have been alive in Soviet custody. On the other hand, the story of the Soviet aircraft that overflew Kuskokwim Bay, although accurately reported by Niemeyer, actually took place in March of 1963, not March of 1962, and did not remain secret. I chose to advance the start date of Operation Jedburgh by a year or so, to allow Niemeyer and Donald Jensen to be part of it. Civil-rights leaders, by the way, really did complain about the refusal of OSS to send black operatives into the field. One source does mention an unnamed black truck driver who was recruited in a manner that provides the inspiration for Donald's story here. (Several OSS headquarters employees were black, among them Ralph Bunche.)

Jack Ziegler's discussion of CIA digraphs in chapter 5 is accurate. The digraph for the Soviet Union was indeed AE; JM was the digraph for Cuba. The significance of QK is not publicly known, but I decided to appropriate it for Bulgaria because the Agency's operation in the 1950s aimed at psychological warfare against the Bulgarian regime was known, at least initially, as QKSTAIR. (The code name of this operation was later changed to BGCONVOY, but BG is a very unlikely digraph for Bulgaria: the Agency never chose letters suggestive of the name of the target.)

In the same chapter, my reference to the chain of command in the KGB reflects the teaching of declassified CIA documents. A major really would give commands to a full colonel in appropriate circumstances. The reference in chapter 9 to Department T of the First Chief Director-ate may not be accurate, as some sources suggest that responsibility for "direct action" was not handed over to T until 1963. The reassignment of direct action to the infamous Department V came shortly afterward.

The mention of secure telephone lines at several points in the nar-rative is anachronistic, if the term is understood in its contemporary sense. The first telephone capable of scrambling and unscrambling voice communications, the STU-1, was not developed until the late 1960s, and did not go into widespread use until several years thereafter.

Niemeyer's classroom lectures are largely based on historical fact and the early writing of conflict theory. His hypothetical about the bank robber with the hand grenade is borrowed without attribution from an important early paper by Daniel Ellsberg. In his meeting with McGeorge Bundy in the White House basement, Niemeyer is relying upon the work of Nobel Laureate Thomas Schelling, among others. The story in chapter 3 about the Civil Defense planners failing to tell Ohioans that a mock evacuation was to be staged there is true. Niemey-er's account in chapter 18 of the weakness in fallout shelters is drawn from the proceedings of a National Research Council symposium on the topic that was not actually held until 1965.

The rumor that Bundy hired a Kennedy girlfriend for the National Security Council staff is repeated in at least two sources, but neither gives any detail. Esman's story of the refusal of the Pentagon to let the White House see a copy of the Joint Strategic Capabilities Plan is true. Oleg Penkovsky really was arrested in the middle of the Cuban Missile Crisis. Note that some historians do not believe that Bundy was aware of YOGA's true identity.

As to Bundy's defense of Curtis LeMay, as far as I know nothing like it ever took place. LeMay was a narrow-minded man, of hateful politics, and his fury at the resolution of the Cuban Missile Crisis is a matter of record. On the other hand, although he is routinely cast as the villain in both fiction and nonfiction about the crisis, I found nothing on the record to suggest that he was ever anything but a thorough patriot who followed the President's orders to the letter—whatever he may have said about Kennedy behind his back. The story about his successful single-handed efforts to build the Strategic Air Command from scratch is true.

Where I could, I have tried to get minor details right. But some I intentionally changed. For example, the Trimline phone was not available to the public until 1965, and therefore the Madisons could not have had one for Margo to talk on. On the other hand, the term "limousine liberals" seems to have first appeared in a novel published in 1919, and was popularized by conservatives during the 1950s, so could certainly have come from the lips of Jack Ziegler, as it does in chapter 45.

As in *Palace Council,* my previous novel set partly in Ithaca, I have tried to be true to the geography of both the town and Cornell University, but here I have also tried to be sensitive to the history. The football game between Cornell and Colgate that features in chapter 1 was actually played on September 29, 1962. Cornell lost, 23–12. Cornell abolished parietal rules for female students in 1962. For the sake of my fiction I kept them in place for another year.

The facts that Margo reviews about the survival of the Bulgarian Jews during World War II are essentially true, but were not fully known until the opening of the Soviet archives after 1989. Also, there was no United States consulate in Varna at the time of the events of the novel. Jerry Ainsley's recital of the result of the fifth game of the 1962 World Series is accurate, but the game was actually played on October 10.

What about the chess? At the 1962 Olympiad, Yefim Geller really did replace Vasily Smyslov on the Soviet team without explanation, and, unlike Smyslov, Geller really did not speak any English. As far as I can tell, Smyslov never visited either Cuba or Curaçao in 1962. The notion that he might have run errands for Soviet intelligence is entirely invented. The gorillas aren't.

Bobby Fischer's brilliant game against Robert Byrne was actually played in December 1963. I moved it two years earlier for the convenience of the story. (Bobby played the so-called Game of the Century, mentioned by Doris Harrington, in 1956, against Robert Byrne's brother Donald.) My descriptions of Fischer's games at the Chess Olympiad are accurate, although I moved the relevant dates on which the games were played, and also shortened the Olympiad itself.

As to the other side of Fischer, I will freely confess to having exaggerated for the sake of the story what some call his quirks and others call early evidence of the mental illness that would later consume that remarkable brain. According to his biographer, Frank Brady, Fischer really did sail for Europe on the *New Amsterdam* for fear that his plane might be sabotaged. Most of the more bizarre comments I attribute to Fischer come from reliable sources, even though he certainly did not make all of them in 1962. Thus, for example, Fischer's dithering over whether he should buy a car or get a wife from Asia came to light in the recollections of former world chess champion Mikhail Tal. Fischer's fascination with *Mein Kampf* was noticed by the immortal Samuel Reshevsky, but not until 1970. Fischer repeated his disdain for women in several published interviews, although several sources mention the rumor that his friends snuck a woman into his room at a chess tournament in Argentina. Nevertheless, on the chessboard Fischer was always his own sternest critic, and there is no suggestion in any of the sources that he blamed any woman—or anyone but himself—for spoiling the winning endgame against Botvinnik.

Finally, what about the novel's central conceit—that the President could have hidden the back-channel negotiations behind a faux affair with a nineteen-year-old college student? We have it on the authority of biographer Robert Dallek that Kennedy, while President, did indeed have an affair with a nineteen-year-old collegian—even though she was a white intern in the White House, not a black intern at the Department of Labor. Press accounts, including interviews with the woman in question, have subsequently confirmed Dallek's account.

As so often, the list of those I would like to thank could go on for some while. I will endeavor to be brief. Let me begin by acknowledging my loyal fans, many of whom have begged for years to learn more about the lives of Misha Garland and Kimmer Madison when they were younger. Many of the questions about Misha I tried to answer in my 2008 novel *Palace Council*, where we meet a good chunk of his family in the 1950s, 1960s, and 1970s. (We meet a much younger Misha, too.) Although Kimmer was a minor character in *New England White*, the instant novel is my first attempt at fleshing out her childhood.

As always, I am grateful to my deft and wonderful editor, Phyllis Grann, and to Lynn Nesbit, my literary agent of more than twenty years, and a very fine and supportive friend. I have had the benefit, as usual, of thoughtful readings of an earlier version of the manuscript by my dear friends George W. Jones, Jr., and Loretta Pleasant-Jones. I have also had the particular benefit of a quite detailed critique from my son, Andrew, whose comments caused me to rewrite significantly several chapters.

Andrew and my daughter, Leah, mentioned in all of my author's notes over the decades, are grown now, but when I write, I still think of them and my wife Enola as my principal audience. My family has been God's gift to me in this life, and for their love, and the opportunity to love them in return, I will be forever grateful.

—*Cheshire, Connecticut*
March 2014

JERICHO'S FALL

A riveting spy thriller, *Jericho's Fall* is the spellbinding story of a young woman running for her life from shadowy government forces. In a secluded mountain retreat, Jericho Ainsley, former CIA director and former secretary of defense, is dying of cancer. To his bedside he has called Rebecca DeForde, a young single mother, who was once his lover. Instead of simply bidding farewell, however, Ainsley imparts an explosive secret and DeForde finds herself thrown into a world of international intrigue, involving ex-CIA executives, local police, private investigators, and a US senator. With no one to trust, DeForde is suddenly on the run, relying on her own wits and the lessons she learned from Ainsley to stay alive.

Thriller

ALSO AVAILABLE

The Emperor of Ocean Park
The Impeachment of Abraham Lincoln
New England White
Palace Council
The Culture of Disbelief

VINTAGE BOOKS & ANCHOR BOOKS
Available wherever books are sold.
www.vintagebooks.com
www.anchorbooks.com